BLANKET

of

VIOLETS

Elyn Eden

National Library of Australia Cataloguing-in-Publication Data available.

ISBN 978-0-9953938-2-0 (Paperback)
ISBN 978-0-9953938-3-7 (eBook)

Cover: Blue Wren Books
Image: draganab, iStock
Formatting: Integrity Formatting

elyn.eden@gmail.com
elyneden.wordpress.com

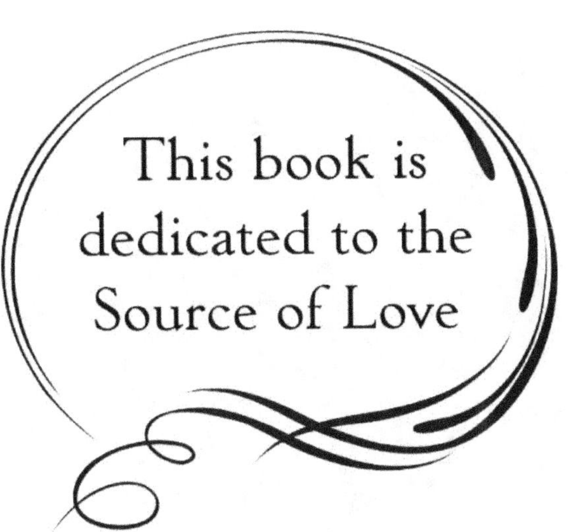
This book is
dedicated to the
Source of Love

*Grateful thanks to my wonderful family and friends
who have supported and encouraged me*

Prologue

2010

A YOUNG MAN, HIS GAUNT face etched with pain and grief, hesitated by the entrance to an ancient graveyard, a strange place to come to for he was in search of life not death. His heart twisted with bitterness for he could not help but wonder if he would soon be joining those whose bones lay deep beneath. What if the reason he had travelled so far turned out to be nothing but illusion?

Above him, an eagle, its wings outstretched, circled high upon the updrafts in a sky of infinite blue. In the distance, a lake gleamed with reflected sunlight, surrounded by windswept peaks.

Despite the weakness in his limbs, the young man made his way along a path between the grassed over graves. The longer he walked with no sign of what he sought, the heavier his illness lay upon him until a flash of colour led him over to an old yew tree, its gnarled branches bent and twisted under the weight of years.

The young man stopped and gazed down at a grave covered with purple flowers. It was said the violets had bloomed this way every spring for many generations and that healing could be found here. Exhausted, he sank down onto a nearby wooden seat.

He looked at the simple granite headstone and saw someone had gouged away the inscription. Such a mean-spirited act saddened him and the self-pity he fought so hard to keep at bay surged up from deep inside. He could no longer hold it back for this place held his last hope.

The young man stared at the grave. Well, here he was, what now?

Nothing happened at first but, as he waited in silence, everything stilled. He held his breath and the colour of the violets blurred to become a purple haze, which drifted up from the ground to enfold him. He felt a gentle touch upon his head and his eyes closed. A sublime sense of comfort spread throughout his body and all the fear that had so marred the last year melted into an infinite peace in which his illness no longer mattered.

Sometime later, his eyes flew open and he became conscious again of sitting on the seat. He had fallen asleep! Everything remained the same: the flower covered grave, the dark tree above his head, the sunlit hillside beyond. And yet, he felt different: brighter, more alive than he had for a long time! He stood and took a few steps. A new strength filled his limbs and his whole body vibrated with vitality. He knew then he had been healed. It was a miracle, a second chance at life!

"Thank you," he whispered, tears in his eyes.

The young man stared down at the grave for a long time, aware he stood in the presence of something way beyond his ability to comprehend. As he did so, the tiny flowers trembled in the breeze and he found himself wondering, like all those others who had received healing before him, who is it that lies sleeping beneath the blanket of violets?

heavily on a wooden stick and stared at Claire with dark eyes set in a face carved by pain. "Can I help you?" she asked, staring at the fragile girl before her. Bedraggled shoulder length blonde hair, wet from the heavy shower, framed a pretty face with delicate features. Anxious eyes returned her gaze. A lost waif, the shopkeeper thought.

"I, I, er, wonder if I could look at something in your window?" Claire stammered.

"And what would that be?"

Claire pointed. "The amethyst necklace."

The woman's eyes widened as if in shock and a look of sorrow passed across her face. She scrutinised Claire for some moments with an odd expression but then sighed and her shoulders sagged, "I knew this time would come." With these words, she turned and, in obvious discomfort, shuffled into the shop. "Come inside."

Claire followed her into a world of stillness and gloom. The traffic sounds from the street faded into silence as the door shut behind her. A scent of roses drifted in the musty air and the only light came from a few small lamps positioned here and there throughout the shop. Old furniture filled the place, every surface crowded. Her gaze took in sparkling cut glass bowls, silver candlesticks and painted figurines in all manner of poses. Glass cabinets held jewellery, oriental carvings and delicate bone china tea services decorated with flowers. Dark brooding landscape paintings hung on the walls and an old grandfather clock ticked in a corner.

Usually, Claire loved wandering in old antique shops, making up stories about the objects from bygone eras, but this time the shopkeeper's strange reaction unsettled her. She watched her reach into the window display to pick out the necklace. "It's Art Nouveau," the woman said and held it out. The moment Claire touched it, a strange sensation shot up her arm but she soon forgot it in her excitement. The necklace was even more beautiful up close. The jewel flickered and glowed and she stared at it, transfixed, oblivious of the speculative gaze of the shopkeeper upon her.

Patterns shifted in the facets as Claire moved the stone to better see inside it. Light and dark vied for ascendancy. They pulled her in, deeper and deeper, until her whole existence became the jewel. Nothing else mattered. She felt dizzy and would have fallen had the shopkeeper's voice not cut through Claire's absorption. "Do you want to try it on?"

She nodded and allowed the shopkeeper to place the necklace around her neck. A shiver ran throughout her body at the touch of the ice-cold metal. As it did so, she imagined she heard an orchestra playing a gentle melody in the distance and smelt a subtle floral perfume. These faded away but left her with a sense something important had been lost. The woman pointed to a large gilt framed mirror pitted with age and Claire moved over to view herself.

Nothing prepared her for what she saw. In the mirror, she wore a mauve dress. It hung low on her shoulders then cinched in tight around her waist before flowing down in soft folds to the floor. Made of a shiny material, the sheen caught the glow of the candle she saw in the background. The necklace nestled at her throat, framed by her long blonde hair. "The dress matches your necklace perfectly," the voice of a man whispered. Claire spun round but saw only the shopkeeper who watched her with an indefinable expression.

The man spoke again. "The necklace becomes you." His words caressed her with their intimate tone. "You have never looked more beautiful."

Claire swayed, as if about to faint and turned back to the mirror. The necklace still hung around her throat but now surrounded by the green collar of her supermarket uniform. No candle burned behind her. "Did someone come in?" she asked.

The woman stared at her with curiosity. "No. There's no one else here. Why do you ask?"

"Oh, no reason, I just thought, no, it... it's nothing." Claire looked back at herself. Light flickered in the amethyst. "How much?" she asked.

The woman reached out and removed the necklace. "Four hundred pounds," she said and took the wonderful thing away. Claire felt naked without it and touched the skin where the necklace had lain. "I, I don't have that much," she stammered. Her heart ached. How could she walk away from something so special? The woman gazed at the necklace for a few moments before laying it back on the black velvet pillow. She looked pleased, as if glad the piece of jewellery had not sold.

Claire could not bear the necklace being taken by anyone else, it would be wrong. She had to prevent it happening. "Wait! Could you put it aside for me? I can get the money." She hoped she sounded convincing.

The shopkeeper scowled, "I'll keep it for a week but no longer." She removed the necklace from the window, took it over to a desk at the side of the shop and placed it in a white envelope. "What's your name?" she asked.

"Claire Robinson."

The woman wrote it on the envelope and locked it in a drawer. "Remember, one week."

"Thank you. I'll be back," Claire said and left the shop.

The spring downpour over, the clouds parted to flood the London street with sunlight, bathing Claire in radiance, but she did not notice. Unsettled and confused, the image in the mirror of her wearing a mauve dress played through her mind. How had it happened? It was as if reality had somehow shifted in that moment and she wondered if life was more than it seemed, that perhaps it had layers and depths she had never before imagined.

The man's voice had been weird, too. It echoed again in her mind, "You have never looked more beautiful." No one had ever spoken to her like that. No man had touched her nor looked at her with love. Invisible, she lived her life alone, isolated, in a world that did not care.

The man had spoken with such tenderness, as if embracing her with his words. The insane thought came that perhaps the shopkeeper had lied, someone *had* come in, but why would he speak with such tenderness to her, Claire, a stranger to him? It was ridiculous, her loneliness had become so intense she was now imagining things that did not exist, *could* not exist.

As she manoeuvred her way through the crowds on the busy London street, the experience in the shop took on a dreamlike quality. She didn't have time to think about the necklace during her shift at the supermarket as she dealt with a flood of shoppers but her thoughts returned to it on the walk home. It had felt so right around her neck.

The necklace was meant for her, she knew it!

Claire walked through the gate of the house where she lived and up the garden path. The dirt and peeling paint on the front door oppressed her. She hoped Mrs Andrews, her landlady, wouldn't be lurking, ready to pin Claire to the wall with more stories of the inadequacies of various members of the annoying woman's family, but, in particular, her vile husband. Claire hated the way he stared at her. She peered round the door. Grateful to see an empty hallway, she sprinted along it and up two flights of stairs to the top floor.

She slipped through the door of her tiny flat and walked into a small, shabby lounge. Claire flung her heavy bag down on the worn brown carpet that at least did not show the dirt, then moved over to the small kitchen area crammed in along one side of the room.

Claire made herself a mug of tea and rummaged in her bag to find the pasty she had bought on the way home. Squashed and cold, it lacked any appeal. Nevertheless, she sat down and ate it followed by an apple as a concession to healthy eating. To combat the growing darkness of evening, she switched on a lamp and thought about anaesthetising herself with the TV as she often did but the necklace came into her mind again. On a tight budget, to find four *pounds* would be a struggle let alone four *hundred* pounds. How could she even think of owning such an expensive thing?

But she longed for it. The piece of jewellery spoke to her of another era, of a life lived in decadence and elegance, a time of beautiful evening gowns (that might explain her vision of the mauve dress), of going to parties and being courted with deference and politeness by men who treated their women with respect and chivalry. But more important than all of these, she had the strangest feeling that, if she owned the necklace, her life would never be the same again.

Claire sighed and peeled off her clothes in preparation for bed. She caught a glimpse of herself in the bathroom mirror. No one could love someone so ugly. She liked her green eyes but loathed her face, her nose too thin, her mouth a tight line of disapproval and pale cheeks. Around it, her straw-coloured hair hung limp and lifeless. Claire hated her boyish, skinny body too, longing for more voluptuous curves. *Then* she might get someone to love her. Now twenty-nine, she despaired of ever finding anyone.

She left the bathroom and walked through into her bedroom, irritated by the garish orange wallpaper and shabby furniture of the room, so in contrast to the opulent mansion she was reading about in her latest romantic novel. She settled down in bed and turned out the light. The ancient springs creaked but, once she found a position of comfort, the night became still, at least in her room. The muted sound of traffic on the nearby main road permeated through the window. People would wander along there, often late into the night. A club would open about nine where they would dance, drink and laugh like she never did but tonight it didn't matter for all she wanted to do was sleep.

Claire dreamt she wore the necklace with the mauve dress. The fabric, soft and cool, swirled around her as she danced across a lawn, spinning and whirling, moving with the silent music that played in her mind. She came to a lake and stopped to gaze up at a brilliant moon. Mist swirled across the water and a quiet breeze caressed her skin. Although unable to see him, she knew he watched her so she began dancing again, this time in slow motion, with grace and sensuality, allowing the powerful life energy flowing through her body full expression.

The shrill tones of her alarm clock jarred her awake. Morning light flooded in through the yellow curtains onto the water stains on the ceiling. The irregular brown marks created by successive leaks intrigued her. Like blots in a Rorschach test, they became an open invitation for her mind to construct images depending on her mood. Today the shapes looked like clouds floating over hills and perhaps a lake. This brought the dream back into Claire's mind. She remembered dancing for a lover who wanted her. She shut her eyes and allowed the scene to develop. The man approached and brought her into his arms. What would happen next? Should they make love there on the grass? No, it would be too soon. She imagined him kissing her. Their passion built then he drew back, stared into her eyes and whispered, "I love you."

"Oh, shit! I'm late," Claire threw back the bedcovers. She had to be at work at six this morning. How could she have forgotten?

The bloody child wouldn't stop screaming. Why didn't parents stop their children acting up? Claire massaged her temples to relieve the headache brought on by the rush to get to work. She hadn't even had a coffee break yet, despite being on the supermarket checkout for over four hours. Seeing the child and his mother approach, she sighed.

How much more could she tolerate? She needed to look for another job or she would go insane. Claire had often thought this over the past few years but here she still stood, a prisoner of her circumstances. As if to rub it in, an old man shuffled up and laid his few small purchases on the conveyer. "How do you stand it here, love?" he asked. Claire gave him a weak smile as she looked into his pale, watery eyes sunk into a face blotched with the broken veins and sunspots of advanced age. How *did* she stand it? The answer came: fear. She didn't know how to do anything else. She had started at the supermarket after leaving school. It wasn't that she was stupid but no subjects had ever interested her, although she did love history, but what career could you make out of that except, perhaps, teaching? The thought repelled her.

School had been an ordeal. Isolated from the cliques of "cool" kids, she spent most of her childhood and teenage years alone. Depressed by the continual bickering of her parents, she often went to the local park or stayed in her bedroom with a succession of romance novels, life-lines to another world, one where heroines lived fascinating lives and attracted handsome lovers. When her father left and her mother moved Gerald in, a brute of a man prone to heavy drinking (Claire could never understand what her mother saw in him) she found the flat where she now lived. Nothing had changed since. She lacked the confidence to try anything new, hadn't even tried for promotions at work. No one liked her. Misinterpreting her shyness, they thought she was stuck up.

The old man moved on and a hard-faced young woman replaced him. No warmth here. Then the mother with the child came. He still screamed and struggled to escape the shopping trolley. And so, the day passed, in the same way it always did with an endless line of unhappy people and the monotony of packing shelves until her shift ended.

When Claire reached the antique shop on her way home, she remembered the necklace. She should go in and tell the shopkeeper she had no way of finding the money but couldn't bear the thought of someone else buying it. She'd tell her tomorrow. It looked shut anyway.

But when she went past the next day, even though the door stood open, she carried on walking. This went on every time she passed until the time came to pay for the necklace.

It was her day off and she woke late. The pattern on the ceiling now looked like smoke. It shifted in her imagination to become a curving road that led over to the door. Why hadn't she noticed that shape before?

Her thoughts turned to the necklace. She decided not to go back to the shop, unable to reject something she longed for with all of her being but could not afford. It wouldn't matter that much, surely? She decided to go to the library and find another good romance to read. It would take her mind off the necklace.

At four o'clock she sat overwhelmed by hopelessness on a torn plastic settee in the library. Nothing would ever change. This was how it would be for the rest of her life. She felt guilty for not being honest with the shopkeeper, too. Claire rose, checked out her books and found herself walking in the direction of the shop. The door stood open. She hesitated for a few moments then passed into the dim interior.

The shop absorbed her into itself and the outside world receded, as if she had stepped through a portal into a different time. The place was deserted so Claire roamed around the room. She stopped to admire a graceful porcelain statue of a woman in a long yellow dress, her glazed face shining with painted happiness.

"You're here for the necklace?"

"I, no, that is. I..." Claire spun around and stared in shock at the shopkeeper. The woman had a tormented expression on her face, as if some sort of internal struggle between anger and sadness raged within her. She walked over to the desk, removed the white envelope and slipped the necklace out. As she dangled it from her fingers, the amethyst crystal glinted in the light. Claire tried not to cry for she wanted it more than anything in her life before. The shopkeeper noticed and her expression softened. "You love it, don't you?"

"Yes, I do," Claire whispered. This was awful but she had to get it over with. "I, I..."

"What is it?"

The woman waited for an answer. When it didn't come, realisation dawned. "You don't have the money for it, do you?"

Claire hesitated, reluctant to admit it, but had no choice except to shake her head.

The woman looked down at the necklace then back at Claire. "Just what would you be prepared to do to have this?"

"What do you mean?"

"Would you do *anything?* It's very valuable, after all."

All kinds of lurid possibilities rushed through Claire's mind as to what she might be asked to do but the woman smiled. "Don't look so worried. I'm only thinking that, well, it looked so good on you it's a shame for you not to have it. As it happens, I'm looking for someone to help me with my mail order business. I have a great deal of packing to do at the moment and so, if you're interested, you could perhaps earn the money."

"Yes!" Claire did not hesitate, amazed by this miraculous turn of events. She couldn't believe it. The necklace would be hers!

"Good." The woman smiled again. "I'm glad. I wouldn't like the necklace to go to just anybody. It's special."

"I know," Claire said.

"My name is Laura Harcourt but you can call me Laura, if you like, and you are..." she looked down at the white envelope she still held, "Claire." Laura replaced the necklace in the desk drawer then said, "Come with me."

Laura shuffled through the shop. Claire, jubilant, followed behind. They came to a large workroom at the back filled with cardboard boxes and several trestle tables. "We sell a lot of reproduction antiques," Laura explained. "My son will print out the address labels and invoices. You will do the packing." All around were shelves laden with plates, figurines, clocks and boxes of jewellery. "Do you think you could come tomorrow?"

"My shift at work finishes at one so would two-thirty be okay? I can work until quite late, if you like."

"That'll be fine."

Laura showed Claire out of the shop. "Until tomorrow," she said and shut the door. Going over to the desk, she took out the white envelope. Her arthritic fingers shook but she managed to put the necklace on. She relaxed back into a nearby armchair and shut her eyes. "Oh, my darling," she whispered, "it has been so very, very long." After a while, sleep claimed her tired mind and her breath grew slow and even.

She slipped into a dream, of a time long ago when she had been happy, before the necklace came into her life.

Before the nightmare began.

Chapter 2

C LAIRE PICKED UP THE NEXT invoice then searched through the boxes until she found the appropriate item, a figurine of a shepherdess with a tiny lamb nestling in the folds of her long blue dress. Picking it up, she walked back to the table. These were easy. Already packed in a polystyrene filled box direct from the manufacturer, all she had to do was check they weren't damaged, put them in a padded envelope and stick on the appropriate label. Her stomach rumbled and she glanced at the clock on the wall: 9 pm. She had been at the shop for over six hours and the work had grown tedious. Laura had shown her what to do then disappeared. Claire had not yet met the son who also ran the business.

She finished packing the figurine and placed it in the container for items to be taken to the post office. Tired, she left the workroom in search of Laura, hoping to finish for the day. Only one small light glowed near the entrance and, as she wandered through the shadowed shop, a prickle of apprehension ran up her spine. "Laura?" Claire called but no reply came. Hands outstretched, she felt through the antiques. Grateful to reach the lit area, she turned to look back and screamed!

A hideous face with bared teeth leered out of the shadows! Claire leapt back but realised she had been frightened by the standing figure of a bear, its face frozen in a snarl. She hated taxidermied animals; they never looked nice (they were corpses after all). Why people wanted them was beyond her. Someone had probably shot this one for a trophy, she thought, and shuddered.

A clock chimed, sounding like the one in the front room of her grandparents' house where she remembered seeing her grandfather, his lifeless face shrunken and pale, laid out in his coffin. Not an image she wanted to see right now. Something banged and Claire whirled around. "Laura? Is that you? I was just wondering if I could go now?"

Claire waited but no one answered. She went to the front door but found it locked. Now on the edge of panic, she stared out of the window at the street, longing to be a part of the normal world once again. Had she been forgotten? What if Laura had gone home? Claire did not know how to contact her. She felt sick. Would she be trapped all night? Stay calm, she told herself. There had to be something she could do, perhaps ring the police? How awkward that would be, though.

She decided to explore the area behind the room where she worked. Perhaps Laura had gone out the back. Hopeful, Claire returned through the shop and located a door at the end of the passageway near her workroom. Finding it unlocked, she walked through, stopping in amazement.

A short distance away, in the middle of a small garden, she saw the glowing figure of a semi-naked woman. She stood holding an urn in her hands from which water poured into a circular pond illuminated by small lights. The statue had a rapturous expression on its face. Claire stepped out into a beautiful cultivated area of various shrubs and small trees. More lamps positioned here and there gave the place an ethereal quality.

For a moment, she thought she had stepped into another dimension, a hidden world full of magic and mystery, innocence and peace—so unexpected in the heart of one of London's shabbier neighbourhoods where the tourists did not go and people feared to walk at night. Her worry forgotten for the time being, she moved closer to the pool.

"I love it here. My son built this garden. He has such a way with plants."

Claire swung round and saw Laura standing by a flowering bush, her face full of anguish. Around her neck, hung the amethyst necklace. Noticing her staring, she put a hand up to protect it. "It's mine!" she shouted and glared at Claire who stepped back, scared by this unexpected hostility. "It's mine," Laura repeated but with less conviction. "You can't have it." She clenched her fists as a last bolt of tension shot through her body and then it was over. The dark force that possessed her disappeared and she slumped over like a rag doll. Shocked, Claire moved forward to guide her onto an ornate garden seat positioned near the pond. Laura sank onto it and remained there, motionless, her gaze fixed on the water. Unnerved, Claire sat down next to her.

The sound of the fountain washed over them and they sat in silence for several minutes until Laura whispered, "I'm so sorry, my dear. I didn't mean to frighten you."

"If the necklace is yours and you still want it, Laura, why did you put it in the window to sell? I can't take it if you love it."

"I *have* to give it to you."

"What do you mean?"

"I knew as soon as I saw you that you were the One. I didn't want to accept it but I knew."

"The One?"

"The one I had to give the necklace to. Take it off me," Laura instructed, turning around to allow Claire to undo the clasp. "Now."

"But I don't want to take it from you."

"Take it off me NOW," Laura commanded.

"Okay, okay. Could you come under the light more?" Laura complied and Claire removed the necklace. Her fingers tingled the moment she held the beautiful piece of jewellery in her hand and she longed to place it on her own body but, instead, held it out. "There you are," she said.

Laura pushed Claire's hand away. "No, you must take it. Put it away. Don't ever let me see it again." Tears ran down her cheeks and she pulled a tissue from her sleeve to blow her nose.

Claire stared down at the necklace in her hand. None of this made any sense.

"Please put it away," Laura pleaded. "I want you to take it now and go. You don't need to work for it anymore, have it as a gift."

"But I couldn't, it's not fair."

"You must. Honestly, it'll be better for me if you do."

Claire slipped the necklace into the pocket of the jacket she wore. "I don't understand."

Laura recovered her composure. The tears stopped and, after mopping her face, she replaced the tissue in her sleeve. "I had a dream," she explained. "It was last week, the night before you came into the shop. In it, I saw you wearing my necklace." Her voice softened. "You looked beautiful. You were dressed in a full-length mauve silk dress and dancing by a lake under the bright light of a full moon."

Claire gasped in shock. She had dreamed the same thing! How could this be?

Laura carried on. "Someone watched you from the shadows but I couldn't make them out. Then I heard a voice that said, 'You must give it to her, your time for it has passed.'

"I wanted to make you work for it because I felt angry that you were supposed to take it from me, also I thought you would think it odd if I just handed it to you. But it's true, my time for it *has* passed. I know that now. You are young and so, so... I don't know, like an unopened flower. You haven't allowed life to touch you yet but it will, my dear, it will, have no fear of that. You've been waiting in the wings but now it's *your* turn on stage and the spotlight will shine on you. Don't waste any more time. Get out there and find out what it's all about. You only have one chance at this life and, let me tell you, it doesn't last long." Laura's voice took on a tone of wistfulness. "Before you know it, it's over."

"Is that how you really feel?" Claire asked with compassion.

Laura took a long, deep breath and shut her eyes. When she opened them again, she looked brighter. "I'm sorry. Don't take any notice of me. I'm not like this all the time." She managed a slight smile.

"Talking to you now, I know I'm doing the right thing. My life is almost at an end." She reached out and put her hand on Claire's and continued, "Don't worry. I'm ready now. I was reluctant to give the necklace to you because I loved it so much and I got it when I was young.

"You always remember the time when you first fell in love. I was given the necklace by someone I cared for very much so it's hard to relinquish something he gave me but I know he would want me to. In truth, I don't need the necklace any longer, so take it with my complete blessing.

"There is something else you must have, too. I don't want any reminders of the necklace now." Laura winced as she stood and leaned on her walking stick. "Follow me." They returned to the shop and to a door in the side wall. "Wait here," Laura said, and unlocked it. It led into a dark hallway with a staircase leading up to another level. Beside it, a chair lift had been installed. Laura positioned herself on it and ascended.

Claire now left alone, realised she stood next to the snarling bear. She shuddered and moved away. After a while, Laura descended again holding an embossed silver box. She held it out. "I want you to take this, too."

"Oh, I couldn't, you've given me so much already."

"No, you must have it. This is the box the necklace came in. You should keep it in it. When you've not got it on, of course," she added. "Wear the necklace often. It was made to be worn—to bring out the beauty of the wearer." Laura paused then whispered, "But, most important, to link her to the Source of Love." Her eyes took on a faraway look and she fell silent.

The atmosphere in the room grew still, as if something of great significance had been spoken. "The Source of Love? Whatever do you mean?"

"You'll find out, my dear. Oh, yes, you'll find out," Laura said, her tone conspiratorial. "Surrender to it is my advice and you'll discover more than you ever knew possible."

She placed the silver box in Claire's hands, limped over to the door of the shop and unlocked it. "You must excuse me now. I am very tired."

"I'll come back tomorrow and do some more packing."

"No, I told you, that won't be necessary. I don't want to be reminded anymore."

Claire passed through the shop entrance but felt something more needed to be said or done. Laura, however, shut the door with a curt, "Goodbye and good luck," leaving Claire with a hundred unanswered questions.

"The Source of Love," she whispered, staring at the beautiful box. The words carried a strange resonance, as if she knew what Laura meant but had just forgotten. The shop lights went out, throwing her into darkness and she became aware of how late it had become. Being out alone at night in her neighbourhood was something to be avoided. She felt conspicuous, as if everyone would know she had the necklace. Wasting no more time, she put the box in her bag and hurried off down the street.

Fifteen minutes later, Claire shut the front door behind her and climbed up to her flat. Excited, she sank onto a chair and took out the silver box. She hadn't had time to examine it in the shop. A rectangle, about twelve by eighteen centimetres long, its silver surface had been decorated with the same interweaving forms as the necklace. Thinking of that, Claire removed it from her jacket pocket and held it up. It was even more beautiful than she remembered and she couldn't believe she now owned such an incredible thing.

The jewel shone, its facets glittering in shifting tones of light and dark. As if in a hypnotic trance, she became absorbed in its beauty. Her body relaxed and she had a sensation of opening out. As she focussed on it, the room disappeared and she felt herself to be enveloped in purple light. In the distance, she fancied she heard the same faint music that played in the antique shop but it soon faded away.

Claire put the box down and placed the necklace around her neck. When she walked into her bathroom to look at her reflection in the cracked mirror above the sink, she could not recognise the woman who stared back at her. The necklace hung perfectly at her throat and she looked almost beautiful with a soft smile on her lips and a gleam in her eyes. She combed her bedraggled blonde hair back with her fingers and tied it behind her head in a bun. Now she felt elegant and looked as if she belonged in the nineteenth century.

She stood up straighter then picked up a sheet left on a nearby chair. She draped it around her like a ball gown and paraded around the flat. She twirled and laughed out loud. Look at me, prancing around like a fool, she thought. Claire laughed again and something inside her shifted. She felt different, no longer a dowdy shop girl but someone who could move with dignity and grace, who could look beautiful, maybe even attract someone to love her.

And it was in that moment, Claire's desire to change her life was born. The long-held belief of hopelessness, which had chained her for so long, loosened its grip. The necklace had given her a different image of herself. She continued to glide around the room for a few more minutes until she noticed the silver box on the table. Letting the sheet fall to the floor, she sat down and opened it.

As she did so, Claire realised it contained a folded piece of cloth. A delicate floral perfume wafted up. Intrigued, she removed the fabric and discovered it to be a fine silk scarf dyed in swirling hues of purple and blue. She shook it out and watched as, light as air, it drifted down.

Claire put aside the scarf and turned her attention back to the box, noticing paper inside. Lifting it out, she found it enfolded several photographs. The first was a head and shoulders shot of a man with a pleasant smiling face. He had shoulder length brown hair and looked to be in his mid-to-late thirties but she was drawn to his dark eyes. They gazed right into hers and she had the distinct sense he could *see* her but, not only that, *loved* her. His passion emanated from the photo as if he wanted the person he looked at to know what lay in his heart. She felt touched by it but also knew the look of love was not for her. It had been meant for the lady whose box this was: Laura Harcourt.

Claire shifted her attention to the next photo. It showed a wide lake surrounded by woodland in front of a vista of distant peaks. Above, clouds billowed across a grey sky heavy with the threat of rain yet the overall effect of the image was gentle and appealing. For a moment, Claire felt as if she were walking through long grass. She even smelt the odour of vegetation! Weird, she thought, but the impressions soon faded. The next picture showed a small stone cottage set in trees in front of which stood the man in the first photograph. He looked happy.

The one after that showed a woman in a long floral print dress standing in front of the same building, a much younger Laura. She too looked happy and in love as she gazed at the person holding the camera. Claire sensed it was the man featured in the other photos. She felt absorbed into their passion for each other, so obvious in the pictures. She longed to feel like that herself, to love and be loved by another. It was the stuff of her fantasies, the dreams that kept her sane in the bleakness of a life lived alone. For some reason, the words of Laura came into her mind. What had she said? Something about getting out there, stop waiting in the wings, it's time to take centre stage. The words resonated and sank deep into Claire's subconscious and she knew she could no longer bear it if her life continued along the same path it had. Her daydreams had kept her chained.

Claire continued looking through the photos. All the pictures showed what looked to be the same area. Most had views of hills and lakes or grey stone buildings until she came to the last photo.

The moment she saw it, the room around her darkened and a strange vibration shot up her arm causing her to flinch. Shaken, she stared at the image, a circle of large upright stones on a desolate hillside with a vast sweep of craggy peaks behind. Some kind of a bird flew in the sky. She had a strong sense of the antiquity of the monument and, as she took this in, the flat around her disappeared. It was as if she were sucked right into that very place and stood by the stones herself. Something made her look up and she saw what looked like an eagle circling overhead. Knowing it must be able to see her, she felt exposed and vulnerable. She stared up at the eagle for a long time until it flew away to become a tiny dot in the distance. As it vanished, the vision faded.

Claire's heart pounded and her stomach churned. What the hell happened? She had felt herself to be present where the photograph had been taken. But that was insane. Her brain couldn't cope and sought to reduce the experience to something understandable like a waking dream but it didn't quite work. It had been like no other dream she had ever had.

She placed the photo on the table and paced around in a futile attempt to draw comfort from the simple familiarity of her possessions. It worked to some degree so she returned her attention to the picture. This time nothing happened. Relieved, she gazed at the stones, somehow knowing they had been important to a lot of people.

Claire had always been fascinated by the past and the way things evolved over time. Her whole life had been spent in the city but now an arrow of desire shot into her consciousness, a determination to one day travel and see some of the historical sites that so captured her imagination. The idea took root in her mind and grew. She did not realise it yet but the structure of her entire life had begun to crumble. The seeds of inner change had been sown.

At the bottom of the box, Claire saw another piece of paper. With great care, she drew it out and unfolded it. As she did so, several small pressed flowers fell onto the table. Violets. Her attention returned to the paper for she saw it to be a letter. It was written in a neat cursive handwriting and dated 22nd July, 1971.

Darling Laura,

I am so very sorry about what happened yesterday. I cannot put into words how much I love you. Thank you so much for still being with me. I know that sometimes it is challenging for you and my heart breaks when I hurt you. Please forgive me and know that, through it all, no matter what happens, I love you and please, please, never lose faith in me.

All my love,
Philip.

Claire put down the letter. What had he done? She felt guilty for reading something meant for Laura. Had she forgotten about the things in the box? She had been so upset when she gave it to her. Feeling uncomfortable keeping such personal things, Claire decided to return them.

She spread all the pictures out on the table and admired the beautiful views of lakes and hills. A little wary, she picked up the one with the stone circle again. As she did so, she felt a strong connection to the stones, as if they held some secret she needed to understand. As her attention moved to the eagle, she became captivated by its flight, feeling as if she were the bird itself as it circled and soared, floating on the wind high above and watching those below. The chills came again but this time with a sense of foreboding. Claire dropped the picture and the experience faded, although it left her shaken and in no doubt something bizarre was going on. Nothing like this had ever happened to her before. Could she be going mad?

Claire gathered all the photos together and wrapped them in the scarf then realised she had forgotten about the letter and flowers. She picked up one of the violets and held it. So flat and lifeless, yet it still contained an echo of the vibrant life it once held. As she stared at the flower, the room darkened again. She tensed but this time felt herself to be in a wood. Golden sunlight shafted down through the trees and onto the carpet of violets at her feet. The sound of birdsong filled the air and, as it did so, she sensed a subtle melancholy entwined with love and longing.

Minutes passed, then the wood faded away. Claire replaced the flowers in the letter and sat still, overwhelmed by the intensity of what she had experienced. All her senses had heightened and she felt uplifted. The room around her appeared more vivid, more *real* in some bizarre way.

Tired now, she decided to remove the necklace. As she did so, the intensity of light in the room faded. How curious. Had what happened been something to do with the necklace? Claire dismissed the idea but could not help but stare spellbound at the amethyst on the necklace. It flickered and shone in the light, drawing her attention into its infinite depths. Mesmerised, she could not look away and felt as if she stood poised on the edge of some important discovery, that the amethyst did indeed have some mysterious power. Could it be true? It would explain what just happened. But, if it *were* true, it would throw everything she believed about life into question. The world would become a place of unknown rules. Anything might happen. Could she handle it if it did? As she sat there, Claire realised there was only one way to find out.

She would have to wear the necklace again!

But not now. Claire slumped, overwhelmed by strangeness, unable to cope with any more. She placed the necklace inside the box and put the letter with the photos in the silk scarf. It had been such a long day; all she wanted to do was sleep. If she could.

Chapter 3

CLAIRE OPENED THE DOOR OF the antique shop and waited by the front desk. She had not worn the necklace knowing Laura might be upset to see it again. When no one came, she walked further in. "Hello?" she called. A few minutes passed before Claire heard the sound of footsteps and Laura appeared, a mixture of surprise and concern on her face. "What are you doing here?"

Delving into her shoulder bag, Claire pulled out the scarf containing the letter and photos. "I'm sorry, I know you didn't want to be reminded of the necklace, but I found these in the box you gave me. I thought you might like to have them back."

Laura gasped, "Oh my God, I..." Her voice trailed off but she reached out and took the scarf. She placed it on a nearby table and, with great deliberation, unfolded the material and stared at what lay inside. "Yes, oh, yes. I forgot I put these in the box. Thank you." She sorted through the photos and drew out the one with the man. As she held it in trembling fingers, yearning and sorrow played across her face.

"You loved him very much," Claire said, her heart filled with pity.

"Yes, I did. We had been married for only a few weeks when he vanished. He never came back, disappeared completely without a single word." Laura caressed the scarf with her fingers. "I don't know what happened to him. It has haunted me all these years."

"You've no idea where he went?"

"No."

"Is he the man who gave you the necklace?" Claire understood Laura's bitterness of the day before.

"Yes." Laura stared for a long while at the photo then continued. "His name was Philip. These were taken in the Lake District. We loved it there." Her face took on a wistful look and Claire sensed Laura's mind had travelled back into the past.

"Tell me about him," Claire said. "If you want to, that is." She did not want to intensify the older woman's pain.

"Maybe it would help to talk about it. I've held it all in for so long." Laura sighed and lowered herself into a nearby chair. "Ow!" she exclaimed.

"Are you all right?"

"Yes, it's my arthritis. I'm waiting for a hip replacement but my turn never seems to come."

"I'm sorry to hear that." Claire perched on a wooden stool nearby and silence fell. A clock chimed followed by a different one a second later. "I met him back in the spring of 1971," Laura murmured. "I'd led a very sheltered, uneventful life, so was completely unprepared for someone like him." She stared at Philip's picture. She had replayed her relationship with him in her mind many, many times and so, as she told her story, the past flared into life as if it were all happening again.

Couples moved slowly around the hall to the music but no one asked Laura Harcourt to dance. They never did. And who could blame them? No man would ever want to know a girl with an ugly nose like hers. The bump on it disfigured her as far as she was concerned. At thirty-three, she had given up hope of ever finding a boyfriend resigning herself to focussing on her career as a librarian and being alone. She looked at her cousin with envy; she looked so gorgeous in her satin wedding dress, her new husband at her side.

Laura sighed. Why had she allowed her mother to persuade her to come to the reception? She turned away from the dance floor to examine a landscape painting on the wall for the twentieth time that night. A solitary boat sailed across a blue sky reflected in the calm waters of a wide lake. Trees gathered along the stony shore and, behind them, craggy peaks in soft tones of grey and purple rose up into the distance. The scene looked so realistic she could be looking through a window.

Someone touched her on the shoulder and she turned to find herself looking into smiling brown eyes. "It's a wonderful painting, isn't it? It's the Lake District. I'm going to take you there when we're married. You <u>will</u> marry me, won't you?"

Shock and embarrassment coursed through her body as she stared at the man standing next to her. His wavy brown hair touched his shoulders and framed an oval face with even features. He wore a grey suit with the bell-bottom trousers that were all the rage. He looked to be a bit older than her, mid-thirties perhaps.

Laura smiled in remembrance. She had worn a new purple maxi dress that day with matching platform shoes.

"I'll take you in that boat and we shall sail all day, then come back to our house by the lake where we'll spend the whole night making love."

Laura blushed. He must be drunk to say such things, she thought, but, as she stared at him, she became mesmerised by the expression in his eyes and could not look away.

"I didn't take him seriously when he asked me to marry him, of course," Laura said to Claire, "but there was something about the way he looked at me. I felt," her voice caught, "I felt a connection between us, right from that very first moment. For some unbelievable reason, he saw some quality in me he loved at first sight for he told me so later. I couldn't understand it. But I loved him too. How could I not when he looked at me as if he actually cared about me? *Me!* No one had ever looked at me like that before so I couldn't resist him. I craved love, had always craved it, but men had never seemed interested in me."

Claire knew the feeling all too well. Laura continued her story.

A folk ballad began to play. "Dance with me," Philip whispered. He took Laura's hand and led her out onto the dance floor. He positioned his hands around her waist. The touch of him burned like fire through the soft fabric of her dress and the spicy scent of his aftershave made her dizzy. They began slowly then warmed to the music, their bodies swaying. Halfway through, he pulled her closer and she leaned against him, intoxicated with the excitement of having a man touching her body.

They danced together the rest of the evening then he took her outside and stared into her eyes. Amazingly, he brought his lips down on hers and she found herself responding to him even though she had no experience with men whatsoever.

"It all happened so fast," Laura continued. "Philip insisted on introducing himself to my parents at the reception, and he came around to see me the next day. We went for a walk by the Thames. The sun was shining and we found a children's playground."

The swing lifted her right up into the sky then fell back. Laura shrieked with joy as Philip's hands pushed and sent her sailing upwards again. Her self-consciousness forgotten, she cared only about the wind in her face and the sensation of moving through the air. He stopped pushing and grabbed her so he could spin her around and around until the swing wound up tight. He let go and she spun out of control but he caught hold of her again, this time stopping the swing so he could kiss her. Already dizzy, she found herself responding to him in ways she had never imagined. Her head swam and her heart beat fast. She had never known anything like it and could not believe she was with him in complete contrast to her loneliness of just the day before.

"I love you," Philip said.

"But how can you? We only met yesterday."

"I knew then. I meant it when I said I wanted to marry you. You <u>will</u> marry me, won't you?"

"You're insane."

"Yes, you have that effect on me."

Laura stared at Philip, unable to believe it. "You <u>are</u> joking, aren't you? Don't do that. Please don't do that."

"Look at me. Do you really think I'm joking?" Philip stared into her eyes and Laura's heart turned over.

"But I'm so ugly."

"Don't say such things about the girl I love," he said with mock anger. "To me you are beautiful. I love all of you." He moved forward and kissed the tip of her nose.

Laura gasped. He had guessed her deepest pain and it broke through the barrier she had erected around herself to shield her from the taunts of others. She stared at him in amazement. He had that look again and so she believed him. "Yes," she whispered. "I <u>will</u> marry you."

"He swept like a hurricane into my life until I didn't know which way to turn." Laura's face glowed as she remembered. "It was crazy, *he* was crazy, but he had such a way with him I could not help but love him. He always knew the right things to say.

"On the third day he told me he had to leave. He lived in the Lake District and had only come to London for a few days to attend the wedding. He was a friend of the groom, they met at university."

"Come back with me, Laura. In fact, I shan't leave without you." They sat in a café with a cup of tea. Philip leaned across the table and touched her cheek.

A look of anguish passed across Laura's face. "I can't do that."

"Why not?"

"I have my job."

"You don't need to work. I'll support us."

"But..."

Philip put his fingers on Laura's lips. "Do you love me?"

"Yes."

"What is more important than that?"

"Nothing."

"My parents didn't want me to go but by that time I was crazy for him. I couldn't imagine being without Philip and so, only five days after we met, I went away with him. I left my home, my job, friends, everything, but I didn't care."

Laura stared out of the train window at the passing countryside overwhelmed by the unreality of it all. Her life had been turned upside down in a matter of days. She glanced at the man at her side. He hadn't told her that much about himself yet she was about to head off into the unknown with him. It seemed insane but then he turned and gazed at her with that now familiar look in his eyes and it all made perfect sense.

"Are you all right?" Philip asked. "You look worried. It'll be fine. You'll love the Lake District, I promise."

He took Laura to a grey stone-built Victorian house on the top of a hill in a place called Bowness, a small town by Lake Windermere. He unlocked a front door that had two stained glass panels decorated with entwining flowers and showed her into the long hallway. "I was born here." A shadow passed across his face. "My parents died in a car accident three years ago so I live here alone."

"I'm so sorry."

"It's okay." The joy swept back into Philip's face. "Let me show you around." He grabbed her by the hand and led her through the lovely old house with its stripped pine panelled doors and elaborate plasterwork on the ceilings until they ended up at the top of the building. They entered a boyish room, full of comics and hundreds of books. Laura smiled when she saw the worn teddy bear sat on a chair. "He's cute." She picked it up. "Oh, one of his arms is loose."

Philip laughed. "He's been through a lot that bear. I used to take him everywhere."

The window drew Laura's attention. It looked out over the nearby lake and wooded hills. Heavy clouds covered the sky but they parted for a moment and a sunbeam shot through to light the lake beneath with gold. "Oh my God," she whispered. "It's so beautiful here."

"I told you, you would love it." Philip came to look out too. "I've always felt a strong connection to this place." He turned and put his arms around Laura. "I can't believe I've found you. I thought I'd have to spend my life alone but, when I saw you at the reception, I knew you would be the one to share this with me. We must be married soon." His lips came down on hers and Laura responded to his kiss in a way she had never imagined ever doing and longed to be closer to him, to

feel his naked body next to hers. She coloured at the thought but a thrill of excitement ran through her and knew she would not resist if he wanted to take things further. Somehow, she trusted he wouldn't hurt her and felt disappointed when he drew back to gaze into her eyes. "I want you so much," he said "but we must wait."

They didn't wait long. She slept on her own in a room one floor down from his for the first few days but then came the night of the thunderstorm.

Laura's eyes flew open as a terrible crash shook the house. Soon another came, louder this time. A violent wind howled outside and the room lit up as a flash of lightening arced across the sky. More thunder followed. Laura hated storms. Another flash followed by a mighty crash sent her rushing, terrified, for the door. The storm must be right overhead. Afraid the house could be struck at any moment, she dashed up the stairs and hammered on Philip's door. He opened it and drew her into his arms. "It's okay," he soothed. "Don't be afraid." Laura shivered. "You're cold. Come." He drew her into his bed, still warm from his body.

"God knows I shouldn't do this," he murmured but he put his arms around her and held her close. Then, as the thunder rolled overhead, he held her tighter.

Laura loved his warmth and solidity and the strength of his arms. She relaxed against him. He wore pyjamas and she only a thin nightdress. The close proximity of their bodies aroused her in a manner she had not experienced in her life before. Philip felt it too. "Oh," he moaned, "you shouldn't be here. Not in your nightgown."

She looked at him. A flash of lightening lit up the room and, in that moment, their eyes locked and neither could prevent their lips drawing together. Once initiated, the kiss intensified as passion for each other coursed through their bodies. Philip moved to lie half over her and Laura loved the feel of him: the weight of his body, the beat of his heart. The fabric between them felt like a barrier and she allowed him to undo the buttons of her nightgown and pull it away from her body. He moaned when he saw her and moved his head down to kiss her breasts. He lifted himself up and pulled off his pyjama top then the trousers. Once naked, their passion took them over, a powerful magnetism urging their bodies into an ever-closer union until, with a pain she felt would pierce her to the core, he entered her.

He took it very slow and gentle at first, mindful of her obvious discomfort, and she loved him all the more for it. She opened her legs wider to allow him to go deeper and the rhythm of their lovemaking and the depth of her feelings for him took her away from the pain to a place of joy where nothing mattered in that moment except the union of their two bodies.

"We became ... close." Laura's cheeks reddened and she reached for the tissue in her sleeve.

The next day they went for a walk into the nearby countryside. They stopped to rest at the top of a hill to look out over Lake Windermere in the distance. Bluebells spread a carpet of blue through the wood around them and white blossoms shone from nearby rhododendron trees. A more perfect day Laura had never experienced. She thought she simply couldn't contain it all, that her mind would burst with the wonder of it. She closed her eyes and surrendered to the trickling sound of the nearby stream. Philip's arms came around her shoulders and he placed his lips on hers. When he pulled away from the kiss, he whispered, "I will never leave you, or this place. It is in my blood and so are you."

"Nothing bothered us. All we cared about was each other and exploring his beloved Lake District. I really loved the place too. It was so beautiful. I miss it so much but I can't bear to be there without him. Philip had some sort of a private income and so, although he didn't have a lot of money, we had enough. We married in a registry office, neither of us wanted to have a big wedding. It was just us; my parents didn't approve and refused to come. Philip had a sister but she'd gone on a trip abroad. We had to have witnesses from the office.

"The days passed, then weeks, and we were happy, at least most of the time."

"Most of the time?" Claire asked.

They had spent the morning toiling up a hillside to look at the loveliest waterfall Laura had ever seen. Philip laughed and pulled her closer to it. The spray sprinkled their faces with cool water as they kissed. "Hey, I'm getting wet!" she exclaimed and moved away. At that moment, the sky darkened as clouds passed over the sun. Laura knew from experience a shower of rain would follow. She looked at Philip. He stared up at the sky at what looked like an eagle as it slowly circled. As he watched it, the joy in his face drained away and his whole demeanour changed. He looked sad and afraid.

"What's the matter, Philip?" Laura laid a hand on his arm.

"It was the first time I realised he had another side, that he fell into dark depressions. He would go from a fun loving, happy person to someone trapped by a dark brooding despair or else he'd be angry, often over nothing. He took it out on me sometimes. He didn't hit me or anything like that but he could be unkind, bitter, almost as if he hated life. It was so strange. I could do little to snap him out of those moods. Sometimes he clung to me and said, 'You keep me safe, Laura. You're my anchor in this world.' I asked him what he meant but he would never say. It used to scare me but I learned to let him be by himself at those times." Laura still held the photos. She picked out the letter from among them and touched it gently. "He was always so sorry afterwards. It upset him that he behaved in such a way but he did have an inner strength so would always bounce back and be his happy self again a little while later.

"One of those times he told me he wanted to go to a very special place. He'd lost his temper with me in the morning but later in the afternoon he became sad. He said he needed to go somewhere and took me to visit this cemetery."

"That's an odd place to go if you feel down," Claire said.

"Yes, I know, that's what I thought, too. Anyway, it was at an old church built next to a stream in a small valley near a village called Oakdale."

Laura followed Philip up the path through the graves to a group of yew trees. "Look at this," he said. "All the other graves are grassed over but this one is covered with violets."

"How beautiful, I wonder why."

"It's been this way every spring ever since I can remember. I used to come as a boy and they were always here. I still visit from time to time just to see and I'm never disappointed. I think the person buried here must be special in some way. There's no name on the headstone but I met a man here once who told me it was a woman. She had obviously been very important to him but he didn't tell me her name." Philip looked around him. "I know this sounds odd but, when I come here, I feel peaceful, uplifted, as if there is more to life than what we see. I don't know, I can't really explain it. Can you feel it?"

Laura stood still and, as she looked around, a quietness settled around her and she felt somehow comforted, a strange feeling to have in a graveyard. The breeze rustled the leaves of the nearby trees and, for no apparent reason, a subtle joy bubbled up within her. "Yes, I think I know what you mean," she murmured. "It <u>is</u> a lovely place." She gazed at the grave covered by the dense mass of tiny purple flowers. They grew in a perfect rectangle although no walls contained them. Strangely, not a single violet bloomed on any other grave. "A blanket of violets for the one who sleeps below," she murmured.

"A blanket of violets, I like that. You sound like a poet." Philip laughed and, to her relief, the dark mood that had possessed him for most of the day lifted.

Laura moved over to look at the headstone but someone had obliterated all trace of the inscription. Who lay buried here? Had the person in the grave loved violets in life so their relatives planted them here as a living memorial? How touching, she thought.

"He gave me the necklace there that day," Laura said.

Claire felt a prickle on the back of her neck at these words.

Philip came over. "I have something for you, Laura," he said and rummaged in his backpack. "I've carried it around with me for a while now, just waiting to find the right moment. I know it's odd, but here, now, in this cemetery, I feel it's the right time." He drew out a package wrapped in tissue paper.

"What is it?"

"Open it and see."

Laura took it from him and unwrapped the parcel to reveal a silver box engraved with entwined plant forms. "Oh, this is lovely!" she exclaimed.

"Look inside."

She opened the box and saw an interior lined with purple velvet. Nestled in the centre lay the loveliest necklace she had ever seen. "Oh, my goodness!" she exclaimed. "It's so beautiful." She picked it up and stared at the amethyst heart-shaped crystal sparkling with reflected sunlight.

"Let me put it on you." Philip took it from her. As he placed it around her neck, Laura shivered at its coolness on her skin and swayed as a sudden wave of dizziness overcame her.

"Hey, are you all right?"

"Yes, I'm fine." Laura turned to kiss him. "It's wonderful. Thank you so much."

"An odd thing happened when he gave me the necklace," Laura continued. "Everything looked different, brighter, more vivid somehow, as if all my senses had been heightened, almost to an unbearable degree. I was intensely aware of the sound of the trees rustling, the smell of grass, the gentle touch of the breeze on my skin. Philip wanted to leave then so we walked away but something made me turn and look back at the grave with the violets."

A young woman stood by the headstone staring at her. She was dressed in a long white lace dress with three quarter length sleeves. Laura's heart skipped a beat as her eyes locked with those of the woman and she stopped, moved by the pleading look on her face. She sensed the woman wanted to speak and yet no sound came.

"Laura, what is it?" Philip asked. She looked over at him then turned back to the grave to find the woman had vanished. Laura ran forward and checked behind the gravestone and through all the trees. She stopped and scanned the whole area but saw no sign of her. How could the woman have disappeared? It wasn't possible.

"Did you see her?" she asked Philip.

He looked confused. "See who?"

"The woman by the headstone there wearing a white dress. She had long dark hair. You <u>must</u> have seen her."

"I'm sorry, no, I didn't." Philip looked concerned. "Are you all right?"

"Yes, I feel a bit dizzy, that's all." Laura reached up to touch the jewel hanging at her throat and, as she did so, felt better.

"Let's go, then."

They didn't have to wait long for a bus. On the way back, Philip dozed while Laura stared out of the window entranced by the emerald hills and craggy peaks they passed. Everything still looked more vibrant, the scenery so breathtaking she felt blessed to be alive in such an amazing world. It had never seemed quite that way before.

When they arrived home, Philip looked at the necklace around Laura's throat. "Do you like it?" he asked, touching the crystal with the tip of his fingers.

"I love it," she replied and kissed him. "Thank you so much. Where did you get it?"

Claire tensed, curious to know the history of her new possession. Laura stared unseeing, her focus back in the past as she described what happened.

"A friend gave it to me," Philip said, "well, one of my mother's friends, actually."

"Oh?"

"She gave it to me when I was a child. I was ten, that would make it 1946, about twenty-five years ago. Anyway, I thought it odd at the time that this woman would give me, a young boy, a necklace but she insisted I take it, so I did."

"What was this woman like?" Laura asked, intrigued.

"Oh, old, very old, to me, anyway. Her name was Elizabeth. She was the one who first took me to the cemetery where we've just been. She came one day, a few weeks before she gave me the necklace, and told my mother she wanted to show us a miracle. We went and stood by the grave, the violets were so dense, hundreds of blossoms, I would say.

"'Be quiet and listen,'" Elizabeth told us.

"I wanted to go and explore but my mother made me stand there. That's when I knew it was a special place. I felt this wonderful peace flow over me. It happened every time I went to the grave so I returned on my own many times over the years.

"Elizabeth used to come and talk to my mother all the time. I don't know why she didn't give the necklace to her, now I think about it.

They got on very well. They used to talk for hours. Sometimes Elizabeth brought these interesting cards. She spread them out on the kitchen table and they discussed them. I loved those cards and would sneak a peek at them but they would shoo me away. They had all kinds of pictures on them. One had the figure of the grim reaper on it. I knew about him. He used to appear in one of my comics. Those cards scared and excited me but Elizabeth and my mother wouldn't let me listen. They also held what I found out later were séances. People would come to the house some evenings and they would all go into the front room. Sometimes I heard a scream from inside or the sound of things dropping on the floor. It scared me. I wasn't allowed in but Bella, my sister, went in sometimes and said they communicated with the spirits of dead people. My mother was interested in the psychic world and Elizabeth was a medium."

"So, this woman gave you the necklace?"

"Yes. One day she came round, a few weeks after she took us to the cemetery for the first time. I answered the door. 'My mother is out,' I told her.

"'No matter,'" she said, 'it was you I wanted to see,' and sailed into the lounge. She sat down and asked me lots of questions about my life: how I found school, what did I like to do, that sort of thing. Then she got a bit weird. She leant forward and put her hand on my shoulder. I don't remember what happened after that. I fell asleep."

"That's a bit odd."

"Yes, I woke up and saw her staring at me with a worried look on her face. She tried to hide it, acting all happy as if nothing had happened. She fished about in the large bag she always carried and came out with the silver box. 'You need to have this,' she said.

"I was surprised to see a necklace inside. 'It is not for you,' she said, 'but you must keep it near you and one day give it to someone you deem worthy.' I asked her what she meant and she told me, 'You will know when the time is right.'

"I laughed, not sure what to make of this, then she went on, saying, 'Don't tell your mother, she might not like it.' I had to promise her. She stared at me as if to assess me in some way. 'You will need to be strong,' she said 'but look for what is true, what feels right in your heart, and you will prevail. The necklace will help you.' I thought this very peculiar but, do you know, I've never forgotten those words.

"Anyway, she gathered up her bag and walked to the front door. As she left, she said, 'Don't look so sad. You will find the strength when you need it.' We never spoke of the necklace again. I just put it in my cupboard and forgot about it.

"Until now. I think that <u>you</u> should have the necklace. Elizabeth said

I should give it to someone I deem worthy and you're definitely that. Very worthy," he said, lifting Laura's chin with his forefinger and kissing her gently on the lips. She responded and they forgot the necklace as the power of their passion for each other took them over, leaving them no other option but to retire to bed early.

"I asked Philip if we could visit Elizabeth," Laura went on, "to ask her about where she got the necklace and why she said what she did, but he told me she had died several years before."

"An intriguing story," Claire said.

"Yes. I didn't wear the necklace that often. I thought it too dressy for just slouching around at Philip's home or hiking, which is how we spent most of our time, but I did love it. It also made me feel a bit odd when I wore it. Strange things happened. A voice whispered things I could not understand and I saw these funny, hazy colours around people. It frightened me, to tell you the truth.

"I did start to wear it more when Philip disappeared, though. It helped me then. I thought I would lose my mind when he left. I wanted something to connect me to him so when I missed him or felt upset, I would put the necklace on and it calmed me down. I found that if I thought of the stone, or looked into it, I had the feeling of a purple blanket wrapping itself around me and I felt loved and safe."

"How did Philip disappear?" Claire asked.

Laura slumped as if collapsing in upon herself, a look of profound sadness on her face.

"I'm sorry, if you don't want to talk about it, that's fine. I don't want you to be upset."

"No, that's all right, dear." Laura rallied and straightened. "I *want* to talk about it. I've held all this inside for nearly forty years. I think I need to let it out. Maybe then I'll finally be able to find some sort of peace."

Chapter 4

"MY WORLD ENDED THE DAY he left," Laura said, her fingers twisting the tissue she held into a snake.

"I had been in the Lake District with Philip for about two months when he said he wanted to get a bus to Keswick, stay in a guesthouse there and do some hiking.

"We explored the town on our first day but on the second we decided to walk to Castlerigg, an ancient monument out in the countryside near Keswick. Philip was so happy that day, no trace of any dark mood, not until, that is, we reached the stones."

They had the place to themselves, with the exception of a few scattered sheep. Philip and Laura walked across a grassy field toward a circle of rough, irregular shaped stones. Some were quite small but others were almost the height of a person. Laura paused at the edge to admire the wonderful view of peaks in the distance. The sun shone and the blue sky stretched all around, clear except for a few thin clouds. A perfect day, she thought, until she glanced at Philip.

He stood motionless in the centre of the circle staring up. All colour had drained from his face and he looked afraid. Laura followed his gaze and saw an eagle. It flew in a wide circle above him. Aware of how distressed Philip had been the last time they saw one, she hurried over and laid a hand on his arm. "What's the matter?"

Philip remained silent, his attention riveted on the eagle. All of a sudden, the bird plunged and flew right over their heads, so close Laura heard the flap of its wings. She ducked and put her hands up to her face, convinced the eagle would attack but Philip remained immobile as if in a trance.

"Let's go back to the guesthouse." Laura shook Philip's arm but he appeared not to hear.

Clearly agitated, he said, "Can you hear the voices?"

Laura listened. "I can only hear the wind. What are they saying?"

"I can't make it out. They're whispering."

Had Philip lost his mind? Laura pulled at his arm to make him move away but he shrugged her off. "Don't. You must leave. Go!" he shouted. When Laura stayed, he shouted louder. "Go, I said! You must."

"But this is crazy, Philip. I don't like you this way. Stop it now."

He turned to look at her and appeared more reasonable. "I'm sorry. I'm really sorry. You must go back to the guesthouse. I'll see you there later. I, I just need to spend some time on my own." A semblance of his old self came back at that moment for he wrapped his arms around her and held her close. He said, "I love you. Never forget I love you. Now go," and pushed her away.

Laura had no idea what to do. She didn't want to leave him when something was so evidently wrong but Philip turned away and returned his gaze to the sky. The eagle had resumed circling above. Despite repeated entreaties to come with her, Philip remained impassive and, in despair, Laura had no choice but to walk away. She looked back once and saw he had not moved.

"That was the last time I ever saw him." Laura's voice cracked.

"Oh my God!" Claire could imagine how awful it would have been.

"I told myself he'd be all right and returned to the guesthouse. He often wanted to be alone when he felt depressed and the mood *did* always pass."

"What happened?"

"I waited all morning, then into the afternoon but by the time it got to about four o'clock I was beside myself. I didn't know what to do so I walked back up there."

The moment she saw the stones in the distance Laura saw Philip had gone. She hurried on into the circle and scanned the whole area but knew it was pointless. He had vanished. She looked up, fearful of the eagle, but the sky remained clear. "Oh, Philip," she whispered, "where are you? Please, please come back." Her feeling of unease became true fear. Had someone attacked Philip? Could she be a target too? Feeling vulnerable and exposed in the open field, she hurried back down the track as even more lurid possibilities ran through her mind.

When Philip did not return by eight o'clock that evening, Laura phoned the police but the grim sounding man on the other end of the line told her he couldn't do anything about it as he hadn't been gone long enough. "Contact us again in the morning if he still hasn't returned."

Laura tossed and turned all night, tormented as to what could have happened. She prayed the door would open and Philip would creep in and tell her it was all right. But he didn't. Mrs Pearson, the landlady, made her a cup of tea when she found her pacing the lounge at six in the morning. "He'll be okay, dear, you'll see."

"I hope you're right," Laura said, her face a mask of anguish. She called the police again at seven thirty and they agreed to do a search of the area. Two policemen came. She told the older of the two, a burly, dour faced man with frizzy grey hair, what had happened while the younger one, tall and lanky, in a uniform slightly too big for him, took notes. He looked ill at ease which increased Laura's anxiety.

"It's still too early to get concerned," the burly one tried to reassure her. "Are you sure you hadn't had an argument or anything like that?"

"No, no, we were fine."

"Mmm," he murmured knowingly.

"Please can you help me find him," she pleaded. "I know something terrible has happened." Tears ran down her face.

The policeman's expression softened. "We'll do what we can, love."

They drove her up to the stone circle. She watched as the policemen walked around. They searched the area for some minutes before the older one came over to Laura. "We haven't found anything, no evidence of any struggle, blood or other sign that someone attacked your husband. You said he was distressed when you last saw him. Has he had any mental problems in the past?"

Laura had to tell them he got depressed sometimes and they wrote it down.

"What about drugs, did he take any?"

"No, he didn't."

"It sounds as if he might have had some sort of breakdown, then. We'll keep a look out for him," the policeman said. "I'm sure he'll turn up," he added.

"But he didn't. I stayed at the guesthouse all through that day," Laura said. "The police went to Philip's home but he hadn't gone there. I returned to Bowness the next morning hoping he had returned overnight but, of course, he hadn't.

"I never want to experience anything like that again. I don't know how I got through the next few weeks. I rang the police all the time but they never found any trace of him. They checked all the hospitals, especially the mental hospitals, and circulated a description but nothing turned up.

"Luckily, Philip's sister, Bella, returned from her trip overseas two weeks after he disappeared. She came round to visit him and I told her what had happened. From then on it got easier because she took over dealing with the police. She was able to contact Philip's friends and other relatives but none of them had seen him.

"Eventually, I came back to live in London with my parents again, in the apartment over this shop, actually." Laura looked around her. "My father owned it. I inherited the place when he died. Anyway, Bella kept me informed as to what was happening in the Lake District. They never found a body. Policemen came to interview me a few times but could do no more. After about six months, I lost all hope. I tried to get on with my life but it hasn't been easy."

"I'm sure it hasn't," Claire said, moved by Laura's story.

At that moment, a tall, clean-shaven man in his mid to late thirties walked in. Claire couldn't help but notice how his well-cut business suit fitted his slim body and his short, dark wavy hair framed his pleasant features. He exuded an aura of power and control. As he approached them, something about the man's face looked familiar but she couldn't place him.

"Hello, I wasn't expecting you back until tonight," Laura said, smiling.

"No. I finished earlier than I thought," the man said and bent down to kiss her on the cheek. As he straightened, he looked at Claire, his brown eyes lingering on her with curiosity. She coloured, uncomfortable under his scrutiny.

"This is Claire," Laura said. "She's been helping me do the packing." To Claire she explained, "This is my son, Jared."

Jared extended a long fingered, well-manicured hand towards Claire which she shook. "It's nice to meet you, but you must excuse me as I have some urgent paperwork to attend to." With that he disappeared into the back of the shop.

"I love him so much, but he's a constant reminder," Laura said with a wistful smile.

"Ah, now I know why he looked familiar," Claire exclaimed. "He's Philip's son, isn't he?"

"Yes. I feel so lucky to have him now but I fell to pieces when I first found out I was pregnant. I just couldn't cope with the idea of a baby. With Philip gone, I felt as if the very heart of me had been ripped out. I thought for a while he might have changed his mind about wanting to be with me but it just didn't feel right, not the way he was so loving towards me so I knew something truly awful had happened. He promised he would never leave me. My parents were wonderful, I don't know what I would have done without them, but I couldn't stop thinking about it all.

"It was then the necklace helped me the most." Laura touched her neck but her hand fell back with the realisation she did not wear it.

Laura lay in bed, her stomach churning with nausea as she stared up at the ceiling.

Her mother, Julie, peered around the door. "Do you want some lunch?"

"No, no, I couldn't."

"You must eat something, Laura. You have the baby to think of now. I hate to see you like this. You just lie there and you haven't had any decent food in days."

When her daughter didn't reply, Julie sighed and left. As the bedroom door closed, tears flowed down Laura's cheeks. She felt so empty. She didn't want to live anymore, not with this terrible sense of unknowing and loss within her. It was too much to bear. The image of Philip came into her mind yet again and she reached for the photo that lay on the bedside table. "Why?" she moaned and touched his face with her fingers. "I loved you so much." A wave of rage boiled up: at the universe which had taken her husband away, then at Philip for somehow being stupid and putting himself at risk. The feeling burned like fire and she feared it would consume her.

After a while, the anger diminished. Laura put the photo back on the bedside table, noticing the box with the necklace inside. She took it out and stared at the jewel, captivated by its flickering facets. The colour of the amethyst grew in her consciousness seeming to enfold her in purple. As the sense of this wrapped itself around her like a blanket, she felt warmed and protected.

Laura placed the necklace around her neck and lay back. With the purple came a wonderful feeling of peace and Laura's mind drifted back to when she had been with Philip: the happy times making love in their bed at home, taking bus rides around the countryside and wandering through the bluebell woods by the lake. The memories filled her with a joy that spread throughout her body releasing all the pent-up tension of the weeks since Philip disappeared.

A vision arose in her mind and she found herself back at the stone church with the grave of violets but not with Philip. The woman in the white dress stood behind the headstone.

"Things are not as they appear," the woman said. "Feel for the strength within you, you are stronger than you know. Let love guide you and you will find peace. Look for the blessing."

Laura's eyes flew open. The image had been so real and the voice... so gentle and loving. She felt calm. "The blessing," she murmured and touched the swelling mound of her abdomen. For the first time, she felt the flutter of the baby and acknowledged she carried another living being, someone who had sprung from the love between her and Philip. More tears flowed down her cheeks but this time tears of joy for she realised that all had not been lost that day at the ring of stones because she now had something precious beyond measure.

Another human life had been created and with it she would find purpose, something to focus on. After a while she rose and went downstairs. "I'll try and eat something," she told her much relieved mother.

"I wore the necklace all the time after that. It gave me great comfort. I felt connected to Philip but also to a well of strength within me I didn't know I had before. We don't until we're tested. We go along, living at a very superficial level, but when someone dies or there's a tragedy we have to dig deep." Laura paused, a wistful look on her face then continued. "It's a very special necklace. You know how you keep seeing the same thing sometimes, as if life is trying to tell you something?"

Claire nodded.

"Well, after that experience of the woman in my vision, I saw violets everywhere: embroidered on napkins my grandmother gave us when we went for tea, passing a shop I saw a book about wild flowers and violets were on the cover, then my mother bought me toiletries with them on the packing. Violets always reminded me of the grave and of the woman in the white dress. I felt lighter and more at peace when I thought of them."

"It's strange you felt like that, a grave is such a morbid place," Claire said.

"I know, you'd think so, wouldn't you, but this one wasn't. It had a special atmosphere. The place helped Philip when his dark moods lay heavy upon him. And the woman I saw there, she had something special about her: an aura of calmness and the look on her face was full of love and compassion."

"Who do you think she was?"

"I don't know, Claire. I've gone over and over it in my mind. I'm certain I saw her when I went to the graveyard with Philip, she was so real, but she didn't have time to leave the graveyard before she vanished. So, if she wasn't my imagination, that means she ..."

"... was not of this world," Claire finished and shivered.

"Yes." Laura rubbed her arms. "Gosh," she said, "can you feel that? I've gone as cold as anything."

"Me too, how weird." The two women fell silent but a sudden crash came from the back of the shop and they both jumped. Claire leapt to her feet, afraid, but then came, "Damn it to hell!"

"Jared?" Laura called. "Are you all right?"

"They just bloody fell," he replied, angry. "I wasn't anywhere near them. I swear they moved on their own."

Laura and Claire glanced at each other and walked through the shop to find Jared standing by a number of china figurines lying on the floor. "They're all bloody broken," he shouted, making no attempt to hide his anger. "This is going to cost us."

Claire moved forward. "Here, let me help you." She bent down and picked up the pieces of broken pottery. Some of the figures looked intact at first but then she noticed a hand lost here or a skirt cracked there.

Together they cleared the floor. "Thanks," Jared said in a gruff voice when they finished. "Oh, look, you've cut yourself."

Claire glanced down and saw several drops of bright red blood on the side of her thumb.

"I'll get the first aid things." Jared disappeared for a moment then came back with a box from which he removed a small bottle of antiseptic and some cotton wool. "Let me see it," he asked, his tone brusque.

Claire felt uncomfortable being so close to this unpleasant man but held out her thumb and watched as he cleaned the wound and placed a dressing on it. She noticed he had flecks of grey in his hair. He would be good-looking if his face weren't creased with irritation. He also had a gentle touch. It belied the harshness of his manner, but she couldn't warm to the man.

Jared straightened up. "Sorry about that," he said, this time with more kindness. Their eyes met and held for a moment before he turned his attention to the box of broken figurines. "What a bloody waste," he growled.

He picked up the box, stalked to the rear entrance of the shop and slammed the door behind him.

"Don't mind him," Laura sighed. "He's under a great deal of stress."

As the two women walked back to the front of the shop, Laura continued her story. "It hasn't been easy over the years but, as I said before, I found the necklace helped. It always made me feel connected to Philip and, not only that, it always had the power to make me feel better. When things became too much, I would take it out and hold it. I used to stare into the jewel, like in a meditation, and my sorrow and fear would ease. I loved it very much."

"You should keep it, Laura. I don't want to take away anything that connects you to Philip."

"No dear, it's all right. I told you before, I had a dream where a voice told me to give the necklace to you. It was the same person I always heard when I wore the necklace, the woman from the grave of violets. I know it sounds bizarre, but over the years I've often heard her in my dreams and when I wore the necklace and her words always eased my spirit. She told me to put the necklace in the window many times but it never drew any buyers, even though it is so very beautiful. I was always glad for I wanted to keep it for myself. But now you have come.

"I don't have an explanation for you. I must sound like a crazy old woman but what the voice told me has always felt true in my heart. You know the feeling you get when something just seems right?"

"Yes, yes, I know what you mean."

"I've got that feeling right now. It's telling me you must have the necklace. It's up to you if you wear it or not but, if you do, be prepared for anything. I have a sense when you put it on, things will happen to you, like they did to me."

Jared came back through the rear entrance of the shop. "Mum," he called out. "You've got your doctor's appointment. We need to leave soon. Get ready as soon as you can."

"All right, all right," Laura sighed. "He's always in a hurry. Thank you for returning my things. I am glad to have them back."

"Did Philip give you the scarf?" Claire asked.

"Yes. I admired it in a shop window one day. Philip went back without me knowing and bought it. He was always doing things like that. I..."

"MUM!" Jared shouted. Laura looked over to where they could hear him clattering about then back at Claire with a rueful smile. "Don't judge him too harshly. Life hasn't been kind to him but he *does* have another side."

Claire left the shop, her mind whirling with all she'd been told. Her suspicion the necklace had a strange effect when she wore it seemed to be valid for Laura had also had unusual experiences with it. Then there was the fact that Laura had been given the necklace because Philip's mother's friend, someone who held séances, told him as a young boy to give it to someone he deemed worthy. And now, it had been passed on to *her,* a person with no special attributes, all because a spirit had apparently said that she, Claire, was now meant to have it.

Laura's story seemed too fantastic yet why would she make it up? Claire felt sorry for her. How hard it must have been to lose the person she loved and never know what became of them.

Had Philip been murdered and his body hidden where no one had been able to find it? If not, why would he just disappear, leaving his whole life and the woman he loved behind? Claire remembered holding the photo of the stone circle and feeling herself to actually *be* there. The place Philip was last seen! She had somehow known the place held a secret. What on earth did it all mean?

Chapter 5

THE MOMENT SHE ARRIVED BACK at her flat, Claire went over to the silver box on the table. Opening the lid, she removed the necklace and stared at it. Now she knew it had some sort of power and a connection to a spirit, she felt afraid. The amethyst glinted and sparkled. It was *so* beautiful; she *had* to put it on. Claire went into the bathroom, her hands shaking as she placed the piece of jewellery around her neck and looked at herself in the mirror.

She needn't have worried. Nothing happened. Why would it? Claire thought bitterly after about five minutes. She was just a person who spent her days in a supermarket and nights buried in a romantic novel or watching TV. She imagined wearing the amethyst necklace with her pale green work shirt as she worked on the checkout. It wouldn't look right. The necklace didn't belong on someone like her. No, she didn't deserve the necklace. Elizabeth had told Philip it should go to someone worthy of it. She, Claire, was hardly that. The necklace belonged on a woman who would do important things in her life and wear glamorous clothes. She would be on the arm of a handsome man, someone powerful in the world, a banker or stockbroker, a doctor or lawyer.

What sort of life did she want if she could have it? Claire asked herself, definitely not living in a crappy flat in a depressing city street. An image flicked into her mind of herself walking through a magnificent landscape of mountains and green valleys with a wide expanse of dramatic sky above.

She imagined exploring wonderful old buildings like castles or stately homes and saw herself travelling abroad, seeing other cultures, meeting interesting people, maybe even helping them. Life could be so much more, she knew it, but how could someone like her move into that? She had no money, no powerful friends, no intelligence or proper education. She had nothing that mattered when it came to it.

Claire reached up to take off the necklace, annoyed and depressed by a vision she could never attain, but some force stayed her hand and she remembered what Laura said: "I knew as soon as I saw you that you were the One."

And, in that moment, as Claire's hand hovered ready to remove the necklace, she realised she stood at a fork in the road. If she took off the necklace and never wore it again nothing would ever change. She would remain a shop assistant and live where she was for the rest of her life. Oh, in time she might marry and have children but life would be determined by her surroundings, limited by her fear of stepping out of her comfort zone.

Or she could leave the necklace on and be more of the sort of person who would deserve to wear it, the person she dreamed of being, no longer trapped but open to a wider world. Which path should she take: the known or the unknown?

Claire's hands fell back to her side.

She would wear it, at least for a while, and see what happened. Why not?

Having made this decision, she surveyed herself in the mirror again. The necklace didn't match the red T-shirt and jeans she wore. Claire went to her wardrobe and rifled through the clothes but couldn't find anything that suited the necklace. I need something with a lower neckline, she thought, and decided to go shopping the next day. She had to admit her clothes were terrible, no wonder men didn't notice her.

Claire made herself a meal and watched a crime show on TV but couldn't get into it. A comedy on another channel seemed pointless, the audience's laughter irritating. She decided to go to bed but noticed one of the pressed violets from the silver box lying on the floor. As she picked it up, a draft of cold air moved across her face. She shivered and her mind filled with the image of a grey stone church in a grass-covered graveyard. The faint sound of singing came from within the building. The branches of a nearby group of yew trees writhed as a strong wind whipped across the countryside.

The scene intensified, growing more vivid, so much so, Claire felt as if she were there. The church bell tolled eleven times. She walked over to the trees and came to a stop by a rectangle of tiny purple blooms, the grave of violets. A figure appeared off to one side, a slim young woman with curly short brown hair wearing jeans and a blue shirt. She looked familiar: Laura as a young woman.

Claire became aware of a man in the scene. Philip. He stared down at the grave, then bent down and picked some of the violets. He gave them to Laura who smiled and lifted them to her nose to smell their fragrance.

The vision lasted less than a minute and then it faded, leaving Claire standing bewildered in her flat holding the dried violet. Where had all that come from? It had all seemed so *real*.

She stared down at the violet. It had been taken from a grave. Claire shuddered. The flower looked so dead, an empty shell, like the body of the person out of whom it must have grown. Her first thought was, ugh, that's disgusting, but for some reason, she remained staring at the flower. It had been so beautiful when alive. It reminded her of the two people she saw by the grave, unaware they were destined to be parted, and she felt like weeping.

Feeling off centre and dizzy, Claire decided to go to bed. She lay down, too tired to get changed into a nightdress or remove the necklace. Her eyes closed and her attention drifted, but not into the oblivion of sleep, for another vision came. A single star sparkled in a sky darkening towards night and she heard the sound of rushing water. As her eyes became accustomed to the dim light, Claire realised she stood in a forest. The call of a bird she had never heard before echoed through the trees and she noticed a man standing on a large rock next to a turbulent river. Before she could make him out fully, his image vanished as if he had never been, leaving her alone.

She opened her eyes and stared around her, the roar of the river still reverberating through her brain. The apartment appeared insubstantial and, to her astonishment, she saw a luminescent glow around a plant on a nearby chest of drawers. Claire blinked and sat up. The strange effect vanished but, as she stared at the green foliage, the glow returned. She must be dreaming, she thought, but felt wide awake. Confused, she lay down again. Nothing more happened but she tossed and turned until dawn.

After only a few hours of sleep, Claire woke and sat up to find the plant still glowed. She blinked but it did not diminish. She had always loved that plant. As she thought this, the luminescence increased. How odd. Looking down, she noticed her own hand had a radiance around it, too.

Needing to get to work, she removed the necklace and glanced at the plant. It appeared normal, so did her hand. Had wearing the necklace caused the strange effect? Claire put it back on and the plant glowed once again.

Could the glow be an aura? She had never taken the existence of energy fields around things seriously, nor all the rest of the psychic stuff, ghosts, premonitions and the like. They had seemed unrelated to real life but now the necklace was showing her a different world. Perhaps all the weird and wonderful things people said about the paranormal *were* true. Claire felt dislocated all of a sudden. Nothing in her life up until now had prepared her for the fact reality may not be as predictable as she thought.

Her speculations would have to wait. The supermarket supervisor, a cold and sarcastic woman who needed little excuse to come down scathingly on her workforce, would give her a hard time if she was late.

Should she wear the necklace to work? Claire wondered. She remembered her decision of the night before to wear it and see what happened. Well, she was finding out that things certainly *did* happen. It scared her and yet, deep within, a courageous and adventurous spirit she had not known existed, flared into life. Yes, she thought, let's see what the outside world looks like wearing the necklace. She could always take it off. Claire grabbed her bag and rushed out the door focussing now on getting to work as soon as possible.

Nothing untoward happened on the walk to the supermarket. The world looked the same way it always had. By the time Claire arrived at the shop, she had convinced herself seeing the visions and the glow had just been the work of an overactive imagination.

She started work on the checkout and concentrated on dealing with a long line of customers. The morning progressed without incident for about an hour but then she encountered a short elderly man with a haunted expression on his face. His hands shook as he laid his purchases on the counter. As she looked at him, her heart filled with grief and the image of a woman lying in a hospital bed came into her mind with the thought, "She's dead!" Claire also saw roses, pink roses. At that moment, a middle-aged woman came up. "How are you, John? I was so sorry to hear about your wife."

"Thank you."

"How are you managing?"

"My daughter is helping me. I don't know what I would have done without her. She arranged everything for the funeral. She even managed to get the pink roses Janice always loved for her wreath."

Stunned, Claire stared at the old man. How could she have known about the roses? She touched the necklace at her throat.

"Are you all right, dear?" the middle-aged woman asked.

"Oh, yes, I'm fine," she replied but felt off balance. She forced her attention back to the purchases and, for a while, nothing unusual happened but then, out of the corner of her eye, she noticed a dark shadow off to her left. It vanished as she turned but appeared again a moment later. This time, just for a second, it took the form of a man staring at her! In shock, she dropped the bag of flour she had been holding onto the floor. It split open and white powder spilled everywhere. "Sorry, sorry," she mumbled to her customer. "I'll get someone to bring you another."

Claire called for assistance and a new bag of flour was brought. She refocussed on her work but, not long after, saw another shadow, this time to her right. It vanished when she looked directly at it but not before she saw it was a woman. She froze in shock. It couldn't have been, she told herself, but without conviction. She knew what she had seen. Was the necklace doing something to her mind, Claire wondered, or was she seeing a reality normally invisible to the human eye?

She took off the necklace and put it in her pocket. No more shadows or visions appeared during the day so it had to have been something to do with the necklace. At four o'clock, the end of her shift, she plucked up her courage and put the necklace on again before she left the shop. To her relief, all she saw were coloured auras around a few people but then, halfway home, she stopped at a pedestrian crossing. Claire felt the presence of people standing behind her. She turned and, for a moment, saw several shadows. They disappeared but the experience scared her. If *this* was going to happen when she wore the necklace, she didn't want it.

What should she do? She loved the necklace, how the amethyst sparkled and drew her attention, but she didn't want to see scary stuff. It freaked her out.

The idea came to ask Laura about what was happening for she had experienced odd things wearing the necklace herself but she didn't want to remind her of the past again. However, the appearance of yet another shadow sent Claire hurrying towards the antique shop.

She pushed through the door. The noise of the busy street faded and the now familiar stillness of the shop's interior enfolded her. The place was deserted. Claire waited a few moments but, when no one came, walked through the shop. "Laura?" she called but received no reply. "Laura?" Claire repeated, louder this time, but still no one appeared.

Disappointed, she turned to make her way back to the front of the shop but a hand grabbed Claire's arm and swung her around. "What are you doing with that?" Jared demanded.

"Hey, let me go!"

"Not until you tell me why you're wearing my mother's necklace. She treasures that. You took it, didn't you?"

"No, no, I, she..." scared, Claire couldn't get the words out. "She..."

"I gave it to her, Jared. Let the poor girl go and apologise." Jared released Claire and swung around to glare at his mother.

"Why did you do that? It's a valuable necklace."

"I gave it to Claire because I wanted her to have it."

"But you hardly know her."

"I know her enough to believe she should have it." Laura's eyes sparkled with amusement as she looked at Claire. "I'm glad to see you're wearing it. Come up to my apartment and have a cup of tea with me. I want to find out how you're going." Laura turned and glared at her son. "I didn't hear you apologise, Jared."

He managed a clipped, "I'm sorry," before he strode off, annoyance all over his face.

Laura positioned herself on her chairlift and ascended. Claire followed.

"I'm so glad you came back." Laura said when they reached the upper floor.

"Are you really? I thought you might be upset. I know you don't want to be reminded of things."

"Well, I know I said that, but I've been wondering how you were getting on."

"You were right. Things *did* happen when I wore the necklace," Claire explained.

"I rather thought they would."

While Laura made some tea, Claire told her about her experiences with the auras and shadows.

"Come in the sitting room," Laura said. "You bring the tea."

They settled in two armchairs and Claire also described her visions with the photographs and the violet.

"Oh my God!" Laura exclaimed. "You saw us together? Philip and I?"

"Yes, I believe I did."

"You and I are linked in all this. I don't know how but I have a strong feeling we are. I saw auras around things when I wore the necklace too, such amazing colours."

"But how is it happening?" Claire asked.

"I don't know," Laura replied.

"Did Philip ever tell you anything more about the necklace or the woman who gave it to him?"

"No, I only know that she was a medium and held séances at Philip's house with his mother. And the fact Elizabeth told him to give it to someone worthy. He didn't like to talk about himself and his life much. He went quiet if I asked him and sometimes it triggered one of his dark moods. I think maybe something happened to him in the past but I don't know. We focussed on the present."

Laura's eyes glazed over as a memory filled her mind.

She and Philip stood on a sunlit hillside. On a wild impulse, inspired by the bubbling happiness in her chest, Laura ran off down the grassy slope. "You can't catch me!" she called. "You can't catch me!"

She heard Philip laughing behind her. "Just you wait!" he replied. "You won't escape me, you know!"

Laura sped up, her skirt flying in the wind. She startled several sheep standing near a tree. Reaching the lake, she ran along the edge.

"We were like children, only interested in having fun," Laura whispered.

She ran on through the woods, skirting the water's edge, until she tired. Breathing hard, she stopped and turned but saw no sign of Philip. She stood alone surrounded by bluebells, their graceful heads shifting in the wind. The leaves rustled above and birds sang an exquisite accompaniment to the moment. She stared out at the lake, captivated by the sight of a boat gliding over the sunlit surface. All of a sudden, she was grabbed by the waist and spun around. "Caught you, my little butterfly!" Philip exclaimed and pulled her into his arms. "Did you really think you could fly away from me?"

"Where did you come from? I didn't see you."

"I know these woods like the back of my hand." Philip laughed. "I told you, you wouldn't escape me. I'm never going to let you go. We're destined to be together forever, you know." With that he kissed her and they lost consciousness of their surroundings as the passion that so readily surged up between them pulled them into its powerful embrace.

Laura's eyes brimmed with tears. "We were only together a few months. It was no time, no time at all." She sniffed. "We were so much in love. I don't believe he wanted to leave me. He told me over and over how happy I made him and that we'd always be together. It makes no sense. Something terrible *must* have happened to him." Laura brushed away a tear and straightened up. "Anyway, I'm afraid I don't know much more about the necklace than what I've already told you. All I *do* know is that it has some sort of power and that it heightened my senses when I wore it. I didn't see any visions or shadow people like you have except for the time I saw the woman near the grave of violets. I believe she might have been the spirit of the person buried there but I don't know for sure.

"I never saw anything scary, thank God. As I told you before, the necklace gave me a great deal of comfort, especially while I carried Jared. It was a painful and frightening time but I always felt peaceful and connected to Philip when I put the necklace on. It has given me hope over the years that there's more to life, a reason for it all, that maybe Philip and I will be reunited when I pass over. Sometimes I don't think that'll be long now and, in all honesty, I'm ready. I get so tired."

Claire felt tears welling up in her own eyes. Even though she had only known Laura for a short while, she felt close to her in that moment. They shared a connection with the necklace but maybe also with something else she could not yet define. She reached out and took Laura's hand. They sat together like this for a while then the door opened and Jared came in. The feeling in the room changed and Claire removed her hand. Jared stood there and glowered at them, his bad mood visible as a grey shadow around his head. "I think I'd better go," she said and rose. "Thank you so much for the tea, Laura."

"Come and see me again, won't you?"

"Of course, I will," Claire replied and walked to the door.

"I'll show you out," Jared said. Halfway through the shop, he said, "You can't have anything else from my mother."

Claire stopped in shock. "Do you think that's why I've been seeing her?"

Jared looked uncomfortable. "Well, isn't it?" he demanded.

"No," Claire said firmly then had a sudden thought. "You *really* don't want me to have the necklace, do you?"

"I don't want to see my mother taken advantage of, that's all. She's very gullible. People only have to spin some sort of a sob story and she's putty in their hands." He glared at Claire and his tone hardened. "I'm wondering what you've been telling her."

"You'll just have to ask your mother, won't you," she snapped, irritated by this horrible man. At that moment, she caught sight of a shadow off to one side of Jared, then another. A draught of cold air wafted across her face and more shadows came, closer this time. She forced herself to look at them but, unlike before, they did not vanish and she saw their faces. They were definitely people.

Staring at her!

She couldn't handle it and the room went dark as Claire dropped, senseless, to the floor.

Chapter 6

S HE BECAME AWARE OF A wet cloth on her forehead and the feel of hard floorboards beneath her back. Claire opened her eyes and stared up at the concerned face of Jared.

"Thank God!" he exclaimed. "Are you all right?"

Claire took a deep breath. "Yes, I think so."

Jared sighed in relief. He'd been scared by the way she had fallen like that. "Here, let me help you up." He took hold of one of Claire's arms and assisted her onto a chair. "I'll get you some water," he said and disappeared. He returned a few moments later with a glass and Claire took a few sips.

"What happened?" he asked. "I've never seen anyone go so white."

"I, I don't know. I...saw...saw people."

Jared looked around. "There's no one here."

"I know, I, I think they were..." She couldn't say it.

"You're surely not suggesting you saw ghosts, are you?" Jared's expression changed to mocking amusement.

Claire glanced around the room. No shadows hovered. Thank God! Whatever they were, they scared her and she didn't need such things in her life. Her fingers trembled as she reached up, undid the necklace and held it out to Jared. "Here take it. You don't want me to have it, then fine. I don't want it anymore."

Jared stared at the young woman in front of him, at the fear in her eyes, and wondered what the hell was going on. He reached out and took the necklace. "My father gave this to my mother. It should stay in the family. She shouldn't have given it to you."

"I think that is for me to decide and no one else, don't you?" an angry voice said from behind Claire. "What's going on here?"

Jared looked at his mother who had entered the room. "My father gave it to you. How could you give it to *her?*" He scowled at Claire.

Laura sighed. "There are things you don't understand."

"What things?" he snapped.

"It's all right. I gave it back to him," Claire interrupted. "I don't want to cause any trouble between you. Anyway, I, I'm not sure I want it anymore."

Laura noticed the fear in Claire's eyes. "Has something happened?" she asked.

"Yes, I..." Claire faltered, not wanting to speak about it in front of Jared.

Laura understood. "Claire and I need to talk. If you don't mind, Jared, I'm sure you've got work to do. I will discuss it with you later. I'll have this," she said, taking the necklace from him.

"Very well." Jared strode out of the shop, slamming the door shut behind him.

Claire looked at Laura in anguish, "I'm so sorry. I don't want to come between you two."

"You're not," Laura said. "He just doesn't understand. I'll try and explain it to him but he'll find it all a bit hard to accept." She lowered herself onto a nearby red velvet settee. "Now tell me, dear, what happened to make you look like a frightened rabbit?"

Claire explained what happened. "I've seen quite a few now and they give me a horrible feeling. They only appear when I wear the necklace. I don't think I can handle it."

Laura stared at the necklace in her hand. "I never saw anything like that. It only ever made me feel good, I think maybe it's working in a different way with you."

"What are the shadows?" Claire asked.

"I don't know for sure, but I think they may be spirits."

"Oh my God, that's what I thought." Claire felt sick. Hearing Laura say it made it seem real. "I haven't had a clear view of them until now but this time I saw their faces. How is it possible? What do they want, Laura?"

"As I understand it, sometimes people aren't able to pass over into the next realm and instead remain in this world in spirit form. I think it happens when people are lost or confused, if they're not fully aware they have died, or because something still ties them here. I don't know much about it but I *do* believe there's more to life than we can see and touch, the necklace taught me that. I don't think it's bad, Claire. I think maybe it's opening up your perception in some way."

"I don't want to have it opened anymore."

"Tell me what you feel when you hold it." Laura held out the necklace. Claire took it and stared into the jewel for a few moments. It was so beautiful. Her gaze was drawn down into the flickering depths and she began to feel calmer.

"Just try to stay still." Laura advised. "That's what I used to do when I had it on and felt upset. Are you okay?"

"Yes, fine."

"Let me put it on you again."

Laura took it and placed it around Claire's neck. It felt cool against her skin.

"It may have responded to your state of mind. Were you angry, upset?"

"I was a little, yes, well, quite a lot."

"Anyway, try and relax. Maybe lie back in your chair."

Claire allowed her body to become limp. She took some slow, full breaths, which calmed her more until only a faint nervousness remained but, reassured by Laura's presence, it soon left.

"Just be aware of what you're experiencing and wait." Laura said. "Allow whatever happens to happen if it's going to. It's best, I think, to have no expectations."

The sound of the clocks ticking in the shop grew louder then faded into the background and Claire became aware of a purple haze at the edge of her consciousness. It grew to feel like a blanket of peace wrapping itself around her, bringing with it a sense of comfort and protection beyond words.

"Do you feel all right?" Laura asked. Claire nodded.

"Now open your eyes and tell me what you see."

Claire did so and gasped. The room glowed with coloured lights but, as she focussed on them, the effect vanished. "Oh, they're gone!" she exclaimed.

"What's gone?"

"The lights, everything was shining," Claire whispered.

"Don't worry, they will come again. Trust the necklace and yourself."

Claire stared at the room again, this time with a soft focus and the effect returned. She glanced at Laura and saw she had a wonderful golden light around her head.

"I can see the auras again. You look radiant." She continued to gaze at her in amazement but then remembered the ghosts and the light vanished. "What if the shadows return?"

"I have a feeling the necklace will protect you if you have faith in it."

"You really think so?"

"Yes, I'm certain of it," Laura said firmly. "How do you feel now?"

"Light and peaceful."

"I felt like that, too. I believe the necklace is opening up your awareness. We are all more than we think, Claire. We're connected to something greater and more powerful than our ordinary selves. I've come to realise this since I received the necklace and it's always given me great comfort."

"Is that what you meant when you said to me before it would connect me to the Source of Love?"

"Yes. I believe if you start to pay attention to how you feel when you wear the necklace and trust it, the experience of support will increase and it will guide you."

Claire did feel loved and protected in that moment so perhaps Laura could be right.

"Knowing this has helped me when things got tough and I think you must remember it if what you experience is frightening."

"What *is* this necklace, Laura? How can it have the power to do this to me?"

"That I don't know."

The grave covered with violets flashed into Claire's awareness. "I think it must have something to do with the grave in the Lake District where Philip gave you the necklace," she mused. "It's just come into my mind, I can see it as clear as anything."

"Has it? Oh, how interesting! Try not to force it, just let whatever occurs to you come. Surrender to the process, perhaps you'll see something more."

Claire watched the image in her mind. As she did so, it became more defined and people appeared. They stood around the grave and she noticed a hole in the ground where the violets had been.

"I can see the grave open," she said, "and a lot of people around it. Their clothes look different to now. The women are wearing long coats and hats. It must be winter. An older lady has one of those horrible fox stoles around her shoulders. The men, they're wearing coats too and old-fashioned hats. There's a road near the graveyard... with several vintage style cars parked. It has to be in the past, maybe in the Twenties, I would say."

Now she was fully in the scene. "I can see a coffin in the grave. It's wood and, oh, now everyone is moving away. I guess the funeral is over." Everything faded.

"I think you saw back into the past!" Laura exclaimed, excited, but then her expression changed to anguish. "Oh, how I wish I'd known the necklace had this power. I would have worn it and gone back to the hill with the ring of stones. Perhaps the necklace would have shown me what happened to Philip. Oh, if only I had known. Maybe I could have helped him or... if that wasn't possible, then at least I would have had closure."

Laura looked at Claire in despair. "It's the not knowing that's so hard. We had no funeral. No body to grieve over, nothing. I didn't know if he was dead or alive. I *still* don't know." She began to cry. "If only I had known."

"Please don't torment yourself." Claire hated to see Laura so distressed. "You said yourself you didn't see that much with the necklace. You don't know you would have seen anything to help."

"That's true," Laura sighed.

"As you said, the necklace seems to be working in a different way with me."

Laura crumpled. "Yes, you're right." She leaned back in her chair with her eyes closed as if exhausted but a moment later sat up with a new animation in her expression. "*I* couldn't see back into the past with the necklace but maybe *you* could!" She gave Claire a penetrating look. "If you went to Castlerigg and wore the necklace perhaps you could see what happened?"

"Oh... oh, I, I don't know," Claire stammered, taken aback. "There's no guarantee I'd see anything. I can't control the effect of the necklace."

"No, but there's a chance, even if it's only small, isn't there? What about the man in the supermarket? You told me you sensed his wife had died, then you found out it was true. You said you experienced visions when you held the photographs. You've just seen back in time to the funeral of the person in the grave of violets. You *obviously* have the power to see things when you wear the necklace. Would you consider doing it for me? I'll pay your expenses, of course."

Claire stared at Laura in amazement. "Go to the Lake District?"

Laura's body sagged in defeat. "Oh, I know. It's crazy, isn't it? It's only the ramblings of a sad old woman. You don't have to go. Don't worry. It's too much to ask for you to go off on some bizarre trip to the back of beyond. You're right, there's no guarantee you'd sense anything."

"I'll go!" The words sprang out of Claire's mouth with no warning. She couldn't believe what she just said. To her amazement, although the thought of going terrified her on one level, on another, she was curious about what happened to Philip and wanted to know more about the necklace itself, something that had come to her by a bizarre series of events she still couldn't get her head around. She wanted to help Laura, too.

It would be stepping out into the unknown. *Could* she do it? Claire remembered her decision to wear the necklace even though she felt unworthy of it. She didn't want to stay at the supermarket forever. If she didn't take this opportunity to step out of her comfort zone, she might regret it for the rest of her life.

Laura put her hands up to her mouth. "You will? Oh, my goodness!"

"I'll do it but only if you accept that I may not be able to pick anything up. We don't know for sure I saw the actual past. It could have been my imagination."

Laura's face fell. "You're right. I won't have any expectations. I promise."

Claire's voice softened. "There's something else, too. I could find out something distressing. I know it's been hard, but it might be better to leave things alone. It was so long ago."

"No!" Laura broke in. "I'll never be able to do that. It's haunted me for forty years and it'll continue to do so for the rest of my life. I know he's probably dead but I just want to know what happened. He said he would never leave me."

"You could come with me," Claire said. "I'll look after you."

Laura considered Claire's proposition, sadness and confusion on her face. "No," she decided. "I can't go back there. It would be too painful to see it all again. I also have trouble walking now. Wait a moment; I'll get my cheque book. You'll need enough money to get you there, find accommodation, all that sort of thing. I don't want you to go short. And then I'll tell you everything I can about all the places you could go." Laura went over to the shop counter and took out her handbag from underneath it.

As she wrote the cheque, the door opened and Jared entered. He stopped and stared at them in shock. Claire's heart sank. What would he think?

"Now what's going on? You're giving her money?" His voice rose in anger and he glared at Claire who cringed. She felt a growing heaviness in the room as he spoke. It became almost palpable, a force field of rejection emanating from Jared. It knocked her off centre. She sensed bitterness but also, beneath it, deep sadness. What had happened to make this man so angry at the world? He had grown up never knowing his father but she sensed it was something more.

"Look, I think I'd better go," she said.

"Yes, perhaps that would be best," Laura agreed, shutting her cheque book. "You and I need to have a talk," she said to Jared. "There are some things you need to know." Looking at Claire, she continued, "Come back tomorrow afternoon about four. I'll give you what you need and tell you everything I can that might help you."

"Like hell you will," Jared stormed. Glaring at Claire, he said, "Look, I don't know what kind of hold you have over my mother but I'm not going to let it continue, do you hear?"

Claire's cheeks flamed red and she fled the shop.

Thoughts whirled in her head as she walked home. What had she done, promising to go to the Lake District? Oh well, she decided, Jared would put his foot down and stop the whole thing anyway so why worry? She turned her attention to her surroundings. She still wore the necklace. At first, the world looked normal but then she noticed a small group of young men gathered on a street corner who wore jackets with hoods up over their heads. She sensed darkness around them and knew they were out to make trouble so she ducked down a side street to avoid them.

The world became stranger as she continued along the road. Vague colours flickered around people and sometimes a sort of swirling energy. She tried to stay as calm as possible and observe it all with detachment as Laura had suggested. As she did so, her nervousness faded to some extent and she became interested in what she saw. To her relief, that did not include any shadow people.

But then she went into a shop to get some milk. The woman behind the counter glanced at her, and, in that split second of contact, Claire experienced an overwhelming feeling of grief as if it were her own and her mind filled with an image of a motionless baby in a cot. She saw the woman lift the child and hold his limp body to her chest, terrible anguish in her eyes, and knew she still carried the loss within her, although many years had passed. I don't think I can take too much of this, Claire thought, shaken. Maybe she *would* be able to sense something at Castlerigg. But if she did, could she handle it?

"You would," a voice whispered. Claire whirled around but no one stood behind her.

She paid for her milk and hurried out of the shop. Who whispered? This is getting too crazy. The moment she reached home, she removed the necklace and placed it in the silver box. Needing to zone out, she made a meal and spent the rest of the evening watching television. Just before bed, the announcer on the late-night news described how a gang of youths had mugged an old man on the street where she saw the group earlier. Claire felt sick.

After her shift at the supermarket, Claire pushed through the antique shop door, disappointed to find Jared sitting behind the counter. She looked at him with apprehension as she approached, waiting for his attack. He looked up. "My mother is upstairs but I'd like to speak to you first." He seemed calm but the coldness in his eyes increased her discomfort. She fingered the necklace at her throat but this time saw no dark shadows around him or anything else untoward. She hadn't seen anything more than a few auras so far that day.

Jared continued. "My mother is insisting on paying for you to go to the Lake District to find out about my father. She has told me about the necklace, what she thinks it can do and what you claim you've seen. Personally, I think the whole thing is a complete pile of crap. I'm worried she may get hurt if you go and she has suffered enough. God knows, I understand what it feels like to wonder about something your whole life. I, too, want to know what happened to my father, why I had to grow up without his support."

He gave Claire a penetrating look. She cringed but held her ground and met his eyes.

"I love my mother and she has convinced me it's very important to her that you go," Jared continued. "I, however, don't believe you would go to the Lake District if she gave you the money. My mother and I have no guarantee you won't just disappear."

"Thank you," Claire retorted.

"You have to admit we don't really know you at all. You could be a convicted criminal."

"Yes, I suppose so," she conceded.

"But my mother is insistent and I have decided there might be something to be gained by looking into what happened. By that I mean asking around, looking up records and talking to my father's sister. Maybe this will help my mother find closure, peace of some sort. Me too, I suppose, if I'm honest. Anyway, for this reason, I have decided to come with you and my mother has agreed."

Claire gasped.

"Don't look so pleased about it," he said with a sardonic smile.

"I, I, it's not what I was expecting."

"Oh, I'm sure it's not, but I'm afraid it's a condition to you going. You can, of course, decide not to now."

Claire considered it. She despised Jared but didn't want to let Laura down. After her experiences with the necklace yesterday, she now felt she had a good chance of picking something up. The thought intrigued her. How great it would be if she *could* shed some light on Philip's disappearance. She might also find out more about the necklace. She longed to know where it came from and why it had the power to open up her perception.

She wanted to visit the violet covered grave. She had seen it in her visions and felt it might hold an important clue to the necklace. Perhaps she could find out who was buried there. Last night, before going to bed, she had looked violets up on the Internet and found out they flowered in the spring. Now mid-April, if they went quite soon, the flowers might well be there. Although the whole thing freaked her out, she had the strong feeling all the strangeness with the necklace was happening for a reason and so couldn't turn her back on it all now.

"No, I'm not going to change my mind. I believe I may be able to find something out." A look of surprise passed across Jared's face and she smiled to herself, he thought she'd back out.

Jared soon recovered his composure. "All right, then. When would you be able to go?"

"I checked with my work this morning and organised some time off in three weeks."

"Fine." He kept his tone even but his pursed lips spoke with eloquence of his annoyance. Ever since the discussion with his mother yesterday, his interest in finding something out about his father had grown and he had decided to go to the Lake District himself anyway. He hadn't envisaged going with this exasperating young woman, though. He sighed. It looked like he had no choice.

"I'll go and talk to your mother now," Claire said. Jared nodded.

Laura sat dozing on the settee but her eyes flicked open when Claire came through the sitting room door. "You haven't changed your mind about going?" Laura asked, her expression concerned.

Whatever her feelings about Jared, Claire knew she couldn't let Laura down. "No."

Laura smiled. "Come and sit down next to me."

As Claire did so, Laura grasped both of her hands. "I can't thank you enough. I hope you don't mind going with Jared but he made such a fuss. I think it's the money more than anything. He's very sensitive about it. Don't judge him too harshly, though. He's got a bit of a temper but he's a good boy underneath. There's a lot of Philip in him." She paused, sadness in her eyes. "Anyhow, enough of that, when can you go?"

"I just told Jared in three weeks."

"Oh, yes, yes... It'll be gorgeous at that time, you know. It's when Philip and I went there. The bluebells will be out everywhere and the lambs. You'll love it."

"I think I shall," Claire agreed. "It sounds wonderful."

"Jared can drive you both up there and I'll get him to arrange for accommodation so you don't need to worry about anything. He can take you to visit Philip's family home. Philip's sister, Bella, a lovely, lovely person, lives there now. I think she still has all his things. You can hold some of them. I know that helps with sensing information. I'll ring her. We've stayed in contact over the years although we don't meet up often.

"You must visit the church where the grave of violets is and, of course," Laura hesitated, "Castlerigg, the stone circle in Keswick where I last saw Philip. Bella will have the information from the police findings."

"May I perhaps have another look at the photo of Philip, the one that was in the box?" Claire asked.

"It's with the others over there on the dresser."

Claire went over and picked up the photos and found the one of Philip looking directly at the camera. She stared at him whilst touching the amethyst crystal. Like the last time she looked at the photo, she felt intense love emanating from Philip. Knowing now that the necklace could help her tune into information, she sat motionless and allowed whatever she sensed to come up. Aware of Claire's intention, Laura also remained quiet. A profound stillness fell, holding them both within its thrall as Claire looked at Philip's face, and felt her attention drawn into the dark depths of his eyes.

He loved her. It poured from him. He loved life and he loved *her*. Claire experienced his passion for Laura as if it were directed at herself. It moved her so much a tear trickled down her cheek. As she continued to stare at the picture, however, it blurred and she caught a sense of something hidden behind his eyes.

A shadow, a secret, a dark fear!

Deep down, despite his happy expression, something haunted this man when the photo was taken. Without warning, Claire saw a dark shape, wings outstretched, wheel across a leaden sky. An eagle. She continued to sit but nothing more came.

"Do you know why he didn't like eagles?" she asked Laura.

"No, I don't. He hated them, though, always looking up when we were out as if he expected one to be up in the sky." Laura looked stricken. "We saw one that day... at Castlerigg."

"Yes, you told me it swooped down."

"It did. I was quite afraid and Philip became upset. He talked about whispering voices and insisted I leave him."

"Let me look at the photo of the stone circle you have." Claire held it for some moments but no impressions came. She felt a wall, a barrier of some kind. It made her nervous and unsure. She glanced at Laura who watched her, desperate for something that threw light on Philip's disappearance. Claire knew she had to try and stay calm about it all or she wouldn't be able to help Laura.

"I can't get anymore," she said. "You're right, I'll have to go there."

Chapter 7

CLAIRE OPENED HER EYES. LOOKING at the clock in the car, she realised she had slept for over an hour. She glanced at the man in the driver's seat next to her. Jared stared straight ahead, a grim expression on his face. He hadn't spoken much on the long drive up from London and neither had she. He made it quite obvious every chance he got he didn't like or approve of her.

The trip had fallen into place. Jared arranged everything so Claire hadn't had to do anything except pack and worry. She had wondered over and over what she was getting into, going away with Jared was the last thing she wanted to do.

He had picked her up at eight that morning. They hadn't spoken much even when they stopped at a café on the way. Jared had spent most of the time on the phone while they ate. He had been polite but cold and distant.

Claire turned to look out of the window and gasped. They had driven through heavy rain for much of the day but now brilliant sunshine shone over a landscape so beautiful it took her breath away. It could not be more in contrast to the grey of the London she knew. The road wound through tree clad hills and fields divided by walls of rough stones. In the distance, mysterious shadowed peaks reached up to intersect with a blue sky dusted with clouds. Here and there small waterfalls gushed over jagged rocks and every so often they passed a quaint stone cottage nestled in the landscape.

Captivated, Claire wound down the window and breathed in the fresh air. Her spirits lifted as she noticed a mother sheep with two small lambs on the side of the road. "Oh, look at those!" she cried out in joy before she could stop herself. "There's one black and one white." She turned and smiled at Jared, the tension between them forgotten for a moment in her childish excitement. Brought up in the city, such things were a novelty to her.

Jared looked at Claire's obvious delight and, in that moment, could not help but smile back. Their eyes held for a moment before he had to turn his attention back to the road. He stole a few discrete looks at her and for the first time realised how pretty she was with her blonde hair blowing over her shoulders. He noticed her fine evenly placed features, small straight nose and smooth skin. She was tiny and fragile with her long delicate fingers and narrow wrists. It gave her an elven quality and he could imagine her as a water nymph in a diaphanous robe stepping lightly over rocks and around trees, moonlight outlining her taut body. Wow! Where had that image come from? Damn, he didn't want to be attracted to her, Jared thought, irritated. He reminded himself she was just out to exploit the situation; he mustn't forget that.

Claire, in turn, realised she had never seen Jared smile. It made an enormous difference to his face, making him seem almost human. Just for a second, the hardness in his expression had relaxed showing another side of him and she sensed that, perhaps, in other circumstances, he might be very different. But now he looked angry again. She couldn't make the man out at all.

She sighed and turned her attention back onto the magical scenery around her. "How much longer until we get there?" she asked.

"Only about half an hour, I reckon," Jared said. "We're well into the Lake District now."

Forty minutes later they wound through a small town nestled on a hillside beside a wide lake. "We're here," Jared said.

Claire's heart lifted with joy at the sight of the vast expanse of blue grey water surrounded by tree-covered hills. She loved Bowness instantly with its picturesque old buildings, gift shops and cafes clustered along the narrow streets. They located their hotel, a rambling Victorian house halfway up a hill on a tree-lined street and pulled up in the car park. Stiff, Claire eased herself out of the car and walked over into a small garden. "I'll go and get us checked in," Jared said, leaving her alone. Now early evening, although the sun still shone, a chill wind blew and Claire shivered. It seemed inconceivable that she should be standing in such a place. The thought of returning to London filled her with depression. This was the kind of area she wanted to live in, a small town like Bowness right next to the countryside where the wind blew clean and you could hear the sound of birds and sheep instead of traffic. And, in that moment, Claire decided that, when she finished what she had come to the Lake District to do, she would move to this wonderful place. She smiled, marvelling at the change in her attitude. She felt the lure of a wider world now and had the feeling that, just maybe, there were things she could do with her life. The necklace had given her more confidence.

It waited in her bag, safe in its silver box. She hadn't put it on that morning, unwilling to suffer the heaviness Jared emanated. As if in response to her thought, he reappeared scowling. "Idiots! They stuffed up the booking. They thought I wanted one double room although I quite clearly stated two separate ones."

"Oh no, what are we going to do?"

"Don't worry. Luckily, they have a single room they can put you in. They're preparing it now. It's right at the top of the house, though, and very small, they said. You don't mind that, do you?"

"No, that's fine," Claire said, mourning the end of the era of chivalry.

Jared's phone rang and he wandered away to answer it. She heard him arguing with someone on the other end. She wondered why he had to be so unpleasant. All he did was complain, first the traffic, the rain, the food in the service station café on the motorway and now the hotel. God, she could do without it!

Claire loved her room anyway. Although right up in the attic and reached by several twisting staircases, it had its own small bathroom but, best of all, a window overlooking the lake and tree-covered hills beyond. Her bed felt divine, soft and welcoming, and the room, although cold at first, soon warmed up when she turned the radiator on. Paradise, she thought, relaxing on the bed.

Her mobile rang. Jared.

"They only offer breakfast here so do you want to go out and see if we can find some dinner?"

"Yes. I'll be right down."

A few minutes later, they both stood by the dark expanse of Lake Windermere. A small group of majestic white swans floated by and Claire noticed a sign on a large boathouse advertising short cruises. "Oh, you can go on the lake!" she exclaimed, excited. "That would be great."

"This isn't a holiday, you know," Jared snapped. "We're here to do a job, not enjoy ourselves. I've booked the hotel for a week but I'm hoping we can do what we came to do sooner than that. I should be in London at the moment. And my mother mustn't be left alone for too long."

"Oh, no, no, of course not," she said but couldn't stop rolling her eyes at him when he turned his back. Stupid bastard! Why did he have to be so bloody unpleasant?

"Let's go to the restaurant on the corner over there," Jared suggested.

While they waited for the pizza they ordered to arrive, he said, "I spoke with Bella on the phone yesterday and arranged for us to visit her tomorrow. I want to talk to her in detail about what happened. I've only ever heard my mother's side of things and she can be a bit emotional. I think she gets it all a bit muddled at times. Bella may know more."

"That sounds good," Claire said. "Maybe I can pick something up by holding some of Philip's possessions."

"Humph, well, of course, you can try. You're not wearing the necklace at the moment, why?"

"I haven't been wearing it that much," Claire said. "I find it hard to take for long periods. The longer I wear it, the more aware I am. It's as if veils are being pulled aside, and I can sense so much more than normal. I see auras around people and often feel what they are feeling, which is pain of some sort.

"Most people are unhappy. I have enough trouble with my own feelings let alone those of others." She thought of Jared himself. She sensed how much he disliked her and found it hard to take.

"Sometimes I see things that frighten me as well." The shadows freaked her out even more now she knew they were spirits. "I'll wear it tomorrow."

"Hmm, we'll see then, I suppose. My mother is very gullible but I'm not. It's going to take a lot to convince me that what you say about the necklace is true. It's so unlikely."

"Do you absolutely know for sure it couldn't be true?" Claire asked. "Really?"

"Well, I suppose not," he conceded, "not absolutely, but you have to admit it's far-fetched."

"Yes, I guess so."

A silence fell as neither knew what else to say. They stared at each other for an awkward moment but then the pizza arrived so they focussed on the food. Claire stole a few glances at Jared every now and again. He looked tense. She didn't need the necklace to sense his discomfort. She could see subtle echoes of his father in his face, they had the same shape of nose and similar wavy hair but Jared had a furrowed brow giving his face a seriousness absent in the photos of his father. Laura had told her that when Philip wasn't in one of his moods he was always laughing and teasing. Claire couldn't imagine Jared ever being like that.

Claire wished she had the necklace on in that moment. Jared appeared closed off, walled up behind barriers she doubted anyone ever penetrated and she wondered if he had a woman in his life.

Jared also thought about the person who sat before him. The candle on their table cast a glow on her face. She had beautiful skin, he thought, and eyes. He remembered her simple joy over the two lambs earlier, so childlike, and a brief flicker of amusement passed across his face. It didn't fit with the image he had of her as a user.

Claire watching Jared in that moment sensed a softening about him, something about the way he looked at her, but then it vanished and the barrier went up again.

"The pizza's nice, isn't it?" she commented after a while and smiled at him, hoping somehow to bring that flicker of softness back, perhaps even get him to accept her to some degree but he glared at her.

What was she up to? Jared wondered. She must be playing a subtle game of trying to win *him* over now, knowing she'd be shown up when she wore the necklace and failed to produce information. He needed to be very careful and not lower his guard. "I've had a lot better," he grumbled.

"Of course, you have," she said, unable to hide the sarcasm in her voice but, before he could react, she continued more sweetly, "*I'm* enjoying it, though, so thank you."

The meal continued in a painful silence and Claire was glad when they rose to leave. Jared's obvious tension relaxed a fraction when she offered to pay and he opened the restaurant door for her but otherwise the atmosphere between them remained strained.

They made their way through Bowness back to their hotel. After a terse goodnight, Jared went into his room leaving Claire to climb up the staircases that led to her attic room.

Claire woke the next morning, nerves twisting in her stomach and with a slight headache. What would happen today? Even the amazing view of the lake and hills from her window did nothing to relieve her growing concern. Jared expected her to fail and she herself worried that, when it came to it, she wouldn't sense anything. The necklace didn't always work.

Going to her bag, she drew out the silver box and lifted out the necklace. She caressed it with her fingers then placed it around her neck and looked at herself in the dressing table mirror. The amethyst gleamed in the light. She admired it for a few moments but something caused her to look at the reflection of the room behind her. A woman dressed in white stood by the window! Their eyes met and held for a few seconds before Claire swirled around to find herself alone.

Shaking, she sank down on the bed. Jesus, the woman had been in the room with her! Who *was* she? Claire tried to calm herself by taking several deep breaths and, as she did so, became aware of a subtle purple haze around her. A sense of comfort arose and the grave of violets came into her mind. Was the woman she just saw the same one Laura had encountered at the grave? If so, it was obvious she needed to go there as soon as possible. The grave felt important. Philip had always liked it so that had to mean something. Claire waited. Nothing else came but she continued to sense the colour purple and a feeling of ease pervaded her whole body. She marvelled at the necklace's ability to freak her out, yet also at the same time relax her. Claire rose feeling more confident for she now knew what she had to do: go to the grave of violets.

Jared was already eating his breakfast in the small dining room of the hotel when Claire came in. His eyes flicked to her throat as she sat down opposite. She glanced at him, then around the room. She saw coloured glows around the other people present, all different. Looking back at Jared, she noticed his aura looked muddy grey and pitied him. It flashed into her mind he had been hurt by someone so much he'd built thick walls to stop anyone ever getting close again but, in so doing, had stopped the flow of his life force.

"What are you looking at me like that for?" Jared barked and Claire realised she had been staring at him. "Oh, I... I'm sorry."

"Don't tell me you can see something about me." Claire flinched at the sarcasm in his tone. "As a matter of fact, I can," she said then wished she hadn't.

"What? Come on; spit it out. You can't say that and expect to get away with it."

Claire took a deep breath. "I can sense you're very closed off, that maybe something or someone has hurt you a great deal and so you've decided to never let it happen again."

The shock in his eyes confirmed what Claire sensed but he quickly recovered himself. "I think you could say that about anyone in this room. It's just life, isn't it? Everyone gets hurt."

"Her name was Andrea." Claire said it without thinking. The name just popped into her mind.

Jared's eyes widened than narrowed again in suspicion. "Who told you about her? I bet it was my mother. You questioned her about me so you could convince me you *know* things, didn't you?"

Claire sighed, realising it would do no good to continue the conversation. He wouldn't accept anything she said. To her relief, the waitress came so she ordered her meal.

Ignoring the annoyed look on Jared's face, she asked, "Did you sleep well?" When he didn't reply, she carried on. "I did. My bed is so soft and I love my room. It has a wonderful view." Claire became aware of the weight of the necklace around her neck and it gave her a sudden confidence. She sat up straighter. It didn't matter what Jared thought, she knew she spoke the truth, that the necklace was something special. The name Andrea had appeared out of nowhere. Laura had never mentioned her. Claire knew nothing about his life.

She gave Jared a dazzling smile. "This is going to be exciting. I can't wait to meet Bella. What do you know about her?"

"Not very much at all. I did meet her once when she came to visit my mother about five years ago but I had a business meeting and couldn't stay to talk. She seemed like a nice woman, older than my mother. She must be in her early eighties now. She was a teacher, never married."

Bella lived not far from the hotel so, after breakfast, Claire and Jared walked the short distance up a hill through the narrow streets to her house, an attractive Victorian terraced house built in grey stone, still with original wrought iron railings at the front.

The creaking front gate opened to a short path passing through a small lawn bordered by bluebells and bushes covered with tiny white flowers.

Claire loved the place. It had a charm and character not often found in the houses in her London suburb. Jared rang the bell and, a few minutes later, the door opened to reveal a short, plump elderly woman with cropped hair. She was dressed in a large white T-shirt and orange trousers. Two small crescent moon shaped silver earrings glittered on her ears and a necklace of small amber stones hung around her neck.

"Jared! How wonderful to see you." She beamed and clasped him in a bear hug. Claire smiled at the pained look on his face. Bella hung onto him until he managed to extract himself then she turned her attention to Claire. For a moment, her eyes flicked to the necklace and a look of curiosity passed across her face. "And you must be Claire."

"Yes," Claire said, then also found herself crushed against the woman's large chest and overwhelmed by the scent of lavender.

Releasing her, Bella said, "You make such a cute couple."

"Oh no, no!" Claire exclaimed, aghast, but Bella turned and walked away down a narrow corridor.

"Come on in," she called back to them and led the way to a large and pleasant conservatory at the rear of the house. It looked out over another lawn bordered by small trees, many flowering shrubs and yet more bluebells. "What a lovely garden," Claire said.

"Thank you. I love gardening. It's my passion. I spend hours and hours out there just pottering. I had this room built on when I came back here to live so I could enjoy looking at the plants even in bad weather. After Philip disappeared, I let the place out because I had my own house and job in Kendal but then, when I retired, I felt a strong compulsion to return to Bowness. I sold my house and used the money to renovate this place. I love it here." Bella looked first at Jared and then at Claire. "Well, this is wonderful. When are you two getting married, then? I hope you invite me."

Jared scowled. "No, Aunt, we're not," he said, his voice ice cold. Claire had to suppress a smile.

"Oh, you mean you haven't asked her yet?" Bella winked at Jared. "I'm sorry, I've put my foot in it, then. I'm always doing that."

Jared looked pained. Claire thought she'd help him out. "No, we're not getting married. We're..."

"Tea!" Bella broke in. "Do you want some? Or coffee, if you prefer?"

Jared sighed, "Coffee, please."

"Me too, thanks," Claire replied.

"I'll be right back. Sit down and make yourselves at home." Bella hummed to herself as she left the room,

"Sorry about that," Jared said. "I just told her I was bringing someone with me. She's made two and two equal five."

"It doesn't matter," Claire said. "I like her. She's a real character. Bella's aura glows with bright rainbow colours. It's nice to meet a happy person for a change," she added, giving him a meaningful look. He glowered and turned away to stare out at the garden.

"I love this place," Claire continued with enthusiasm, determined not to let him get her down.

"Yes, she's done a good job of it."

Claire walked over to a sideboard to look at several photos in silver frames. She picked one up, recognising Philip even though he looked to be only about eight. He had a cheeky expression on his face. No shadows lurked behind his eyes. Whatever haunted him later had not yet made its appearance.

Bella returned with a plate of cupcakes. A beautiful pink and purple glow surrounded her head. She exuded an aura of fun, as if she didn't take anything very seriously. "We had such a happy childhood, Philip and I," she said when she noticed Claire had the picture. For an instant, sadness tinged her features but then she brightened again. "The drinks are just coming, help yourselves to cakes." Bella bustled off and they heard her singing in the kitchen.

"I'll see if she needs a hand,' Claire said, following the sound down a corridor to a room at the end. "Can I help you?"

Bella jumped. "Oh, my Lord, you scared the life out of me."

"I'm so sorry."

"No, I should be used to it."

"What do you mean?"

"Oh, well, I don't know if I should say." Bella scrutinised Claire for a moment. "Are you a timid person?"

"I... don't think so," she replied, wondering what she was about to be told.

"There are things that go on here," Bella whispered.

"What kind of things?"

"This isn't a quiet house."

Claire looked confused.

"I don't live alone, if you know what I mean."

"Oh," Claire said, still not understanding.

"There's a man standing right behind you, dear."

Claire turned and saw a tall, elderly man in a long black jacket standing looking at her. He bowed then turned, walked down the hall and vanished. Claire gasped. It was the first time she had seen one of the shadows with such clarity.

"Oh, my goodness! You saw him, didn't you?" Bella said. "You have the Sight."

"Yes, I did," Claire said. "You saw him, too?"

"I see him all the time. He throws things around sometimes, so disconcerting." She grinned.

"Who is he?"

"I think his name was Edward. I found some old photos in the loft some time ago. I believe he lived here before my parents took it on. Died in this house, I would imagine, which is why he still walks around here. My mother saw him, too."

"Oh, yes, she had séances here, didn't she?"

"That's right. How did you know that?"

"I've been talking to Laura. Philip told her. Actually, that's why Jared and I are here. We're not... *together,* by the way. I'm only a friend of Laura's. Jared and I have no relationship."

"Oh, I think you do, dear." Bella smiled knowingly. "You just haven't realised it yet."

"But he's insufferable," Claire retorted. "Sorry, I know he's your nephew."

"That's all right, dear." Bella paused. "Tell me, you're here because of Philip?"

"Yes. I've got to know Laura quite well recently and when she realised I had psychic abilities she asked me to come up here and see if I could sense anything about Philip. She never got over his disappearance. It still haunts her."

"It haunts us all," Bella said, the joy falling from her face.

"Do you have any idea what happened to him?"

"Don't you think you should have waited until *I* was with you to ask her?" came a disdainful voice from behind them. Jared stood stiffly in the doorway. "I came to see what was taking so long." He scowled at Claire. "Why are you trying to exclude me?"

She sighed. "I'm not."

"Sure."

"Okay, okay, Jared, it's my fault, I think," Bella soothed. "We just sort of started talking after we had the visitor."

"Visitor?"

"A ghost," Claire said.

"Oh my God, not another one," Jared sighed, looking at Claire then Bella.

Bella laughed. "Oh, we'll soon make a believer out of you, won't we, Claire? Anyway, what am I thinking, leaving you two without your drinks? They won't take a moment." She made the coffee and put the steaming mugs on a tray. "Right. Let's go back to the conservatory."

"What are you up to?" Jared whispered to Claire on the way back.

"Nothing," she said, "honestly, nothing." God, she detested him. Why did he suspect everything she did? A relationship with him? Bella couldn't be more wrong.

They settled themselves in chairs overlooking the garden. Jared helped himself to a cupcake. "Don't let me stop you," he sneered. "You two carry on your conversation."

Bella smiled at Claire. "Don't take any notice of him, love."

"Don't worry, I won't." Claire replied. Jared glared at her.

"Anyway," the older woman became serious. "Claire has told me why she's here. Poor Laura. She took it very hard when Philip disappeared. I did my best to help her but they were so close and she was pregnant with you, Jared. It was a terrible time."

Jared bit his lip. "Can you tell us what happened from your perspective?"

"The first I heard of Philip's disappearance was when I called round to visit him. I didn't live here then, had my own place in Kendal, as I told you. I hadn't met Laura before. I didn't even know Philip had a girlfriend, let alone a wife! I'd only just got back from a long trip around Europe. Anyway, Laura explained who she was and what had happened.

"She was so lost and frightened. I rang the police but they hadn't found any trace of Philip. They never found *anything*." Bella sighed. "It was as if he vanished into a void. All we had to go on was his strange behaviour before he disappeared."

"What strange behaviour?" Jared asked.

Bella told him what she knew, how the eagle had swooped down and Philip became very agitated, saying he heard voices whispering. "He told Laura to go, which she did."

"Oh, yes," Jared said, "my mother did tell me that. I think it's evidence of mental instability."

"Was he... you know, psychic at all?" Claire asked. "I mean you are, perhaps he heard spirits." She couldn't believe she was talking like this. A few weeks ago, she, like Jared, would have thought the whole idea ridiculous but not now she had the necklace. She touched it. A cloud of vibrant colours shone around Bella and Claire felt a sense of kinship with her.

"I don't know for sure. He never talked about it. I myself am but only in a very minor way. I see spirits sometimes but they don't talk to me. I can't pick much up from them. It's very frustrating. I used to go to the séances my mother held here but while others were seeing all kinds of things, I just sat there. I wanted to be like my mother. She communicated to the dead all the time."

"You must have known Elizabeth?"

"Did Laura tell you about her as well?"

"Yes. She told me all she could remember of what Philip said and did, hoping it would maybe help me pick something up. You've never sensed anything? Did *you* go to Castlerigg?"

"I did, about a week after I first heard all about it but, as I told you, I was never that psychic. I walked up and spent a whole hour in the stone circle but nothing happened. I didn't pick up a thing. I felt blocked, as if perhaps something was preventing me. I felt uncomfortable and couldn't stay long."

"You know what I think about spirits," Jared interrupted. "It sounds to me like my father had some sort of nervous breakdown and wandered off."

"That's what the police thought," Bella said. "They checked all the hospitals at the time, especially the mental hospitals, to see if anyone matching his description had been admitted but nothing turned up."

"Do you think Philip's still alive?" Claire looked at Bella. "Perhaps in some mental hospital somewhere. What if he forgot his name? No one would be able to trace him."

"It's been nearly forty years but I suppose it's possible," Bella replied.

"They never found a body," Jared said.

"That doesn't mean anything." Bella looked at him sadly. "Maybe they didn't look in the right place. There are some desolate areas in the Lake District where you could do anything and not be seen. Do you do psychometry, Claire?"

"What's that?"

"It's holding an object belonging to a person and seeing if you can pick up any psychic impressions about them from it. I can't do it myself although I'd love to be able to."

"I don't know but I was going to ask if I could have a look through Philip's things. I thought I might be able to sense something. Laura told me you still have some."

"His room is just as it was. I didn't have the heart to put the stuff away. I just locked it up when I rented the house out. I'll take you up to his room now, if you like."

Claire and Jared followed Bella up several flights of stairs. Halfway up, Bella stopped, overcome by wheezing. "Sorry, need to take a breather. My asthma, it's such a damned nuisance. I don't come up here much. I have a bedroom on the ground floor." They waited for about a minute then Bella carried on and showed them to a white painted door. The moment she entered the room, Claire felt the echo of Philip's presence, Laura's too. Sunlight streamed through a window illuminating the bed and Claire sensed the power of their love and passion for each other.

Back in London, Laura came awake. She glanced at her bedside clock. Claire and Jared would be at Bella's now going through Philip's things. Laura desperately hoped they would find something. She wouldn't open the shop this morning, she decided. Her back aching, she shifted position, enabling her to relax into the bed. As she drifted back into sleep, the image of Philip came into her mind, the way he looked the day they made love in the woods beside Lake Windermere.

They stood together looking out over the lake. The wind blew Philip's brown hair over his face. Laura reached up and pushed it aside then stared into his eyes. Their gazes held and it was as if each melted into the other. He brushed her cheek with his fingers then laid his lips on hers with a kiss so light as to be barely discernible. Slowly, he ran his fingers through her hair then reached for her hand, lifting it to his lips and kissing her palm. A tingling ran through the length of her body and she felt a yearning to lie naked again with this man in his bed back at the house. It had always been this way between them ever since she looked into his eyes on that dance floor. An invisible force bound them, always drawing them together.

"I love you," he whispered. "I love you," he said again. "Love you, love you, love you." Each time he repeated the words, he kissed another part of her body then moved to undo the buttons on her blouse.

Laura stopped him. "No. Let's go home."

Philip reached for her hand and began walking, pulling her behind him. "Come, there's a place we can go to near here."

"Philip, I know what you're thinking. We can't."

He continued to pull her, laughing, and guided her along a small track into a wood. The sun flickered through the trees as they walked and Laura loved the pressure of his hand in hers. The sound of their feet echoed in her ears and she became acutely aware of her body and his. Right in the middle of the wood they came upon a house. Philip took her through a gate in a high stone wall into the back garden. They made their way along a path to a small clearing surrounded by trees. "This place belongs to a friend of mine. He's not here at the moment. We will not be disturbed."

"Oh, Philip, no, we can't."

"Shh," he whispered, putting his finger on her lips.

"I want you to feel the breeze on your skin. I want to stand naked with you here in this place. Let the sun shine on us in our simplicity. Trust me. You are safe. You will always be safe with me. I love you. Take off your shoes," he said.

Laura looked at him, still unsure, but did as he requested, discovering it felt quite pleasant to feel the cool grass under her feet. When she straightened up again, Philip undid the buttons on her blouse one by one and slipped it from her shoulders. Then he undid her skirt and she let it fall. With infinite gentleness, he removed her undergarments. Even though her face flamed red, Laura allowed him to do it.

"Close your eyes," he said. "Feel the breeze on you."

"It's cold," she said, as her skin tightened.

Philip guided her to an area where the sun shone through the trees and Laura felt the warmth fall on her face and shoulders. "You're so beautiful," he said with great tenderness. "Relax and let go. No one will come, I promise." She felt him moving away. "Keep your eyes shut," he said, "and just feel." Laura took a slow breath in and out then stood still.

The cool breeze caressed her gently and she felt a sudden arousal in her body as she stood, naked, knowing Philip watched her. Nothing awful happened, so she relaxed. What did it matter? He had seen her naked before. She allowed herself to embrace the experience and found it curiously pleasant. Freeing.

As she continued to stand, she became aware of a sudden motion nearby. She felt his lips kiss her breast. "Keep your eyes closed and don't move," he whispered and planted kisses all over the upper half of her body then pulled her into his arms. She felt the cool softness of his naked body and her eyes flew open with surprise. He smiled and kissed her lips. Aroused, she kissed him back with an abandon she had not thought herself capable of and he, in turn, pulled her down to where he had placed their clothes. Laura didn't care where they were after that; all embarrassment melted away as their passion intensified. They remained in the wood for several hours making love and enjoying the feel of the sun and air on their bodies.

Half asleep, Laura moved through the memory several times, savouring it, allowing it to awaken her body again. She wasn't dead yet, she reflected, although now long past the freshness of youth. Oh, how she missed him, even now so many, many years later. Where had he gone? The next day they left for their trip to Keswick and their ill-fated walk to Castlerigg, which had left her bereft with only memories for comfort.

But what memories they were.

As Claire stared at the bed in the Lake District many miles away, she caught a sense of Philip and Laura making love in a sunlit wood and felt the strength of the passion between them, their powerful bond. Tears came into her eyes at the thought of their relationship being severed. She felt glad she had come and hoped she could find something to put Laura's mind at rest. She had suffered enough and needed to find peace.

"What are you picking up?" Bella asked.

"They loved each other very much, Laura and Philip."

"Yes, they did. She was desolate when he disappeared. She spent days lying in this bed crying. I feared for her sanity. Can you feel if he's still alive? I tried myself so many times to try and sense him but, as I told you, my power is too weak. I always felt blocked."

Claire saw a teddy bear sitting in an old cane chair and picked it up. Breathing in deep, she stayed as still as possible and became aware. Running her fingers lightly over the bear, she opened up to see what could be sensed from the toy. She felt its worn fur and the embroidered tip of his nose, slightly soiled and with a thread hanging off. One of the bear's arms hung at a strange angle. It needed repairing.

She heard laughing and, in her mind, saw Philip as a young boy rolling over and over down a hillside. Then she saw him hiding in a hayloft and knew he should be at school. A montage of other childhood images came, of running free through the countryside, climbing trees, wading through streams. He had been happy then.

Swept up in childish joy, the sudden vision of the bear lying crumpled on the floor came as a shock. Philip, still a child, although older, maybe nine or ten, lay on the bed staring at the ceiling, his eyes glazed, his mind distant. She could no longer sense him; an invisible barrier had sprung into existence, as if she was looking at him through glass. It didn't make any sense.

"Something happened to him as a child, didn't it?" Claire asked Bella.

"I think so but my parents and I never knew what it was. One day this terrible mood came upon him. He seemed angry and upset but wouldn't explain it to anyone. Then he disappeared."

"He disappeared? How long for?"

"Only a night, but my parents were beside themselves."

"How old was he?"

"About nine. He turned up the next morning and he seemed okay, as if nothing had happened. That was the way it was with him. He'd be fine then all of a sudden something changed and he'd become depressed and angry, even frightened. Sometimes he'd get up to mischief, steal things, stay out late, pick fights with other boys, be rude to teachers, that sort of thing, so unlike him the rest of the time when you wouldn't find a more loving person.

"My parents took him to various doctors, even a psychiatrist once, but no one ever got to the bottom of it."

Claire held the teddy to her chest and focussed on the image of Philip lying on the bed. She tried to connect with him, but, without warning, a powerful, almost physical, force pushed her backwards. She staggered and fell to the floor.

Chapter 8

"ARE YOU ALL RIGHT?" BELLA'S voice sounded far away. "What in God's name happened? You've gone as white as a sheet."

Feeling dizzy, Claire struggled to rise. "I, I don't know. I felt the presence of something... I don't understand it. I saw Philip lying on the bed. I felt, I felt..." Breathe, breathe, she told herself. An instinct told her to touch the necklace and she sensed the purple haze enfolding her. The words, "Do not be afraid, I am with you," came into her mind. She had heard that voice before, in the shop with the woman whose baby had died. "He cannot touch you now."

He? Claire wondered, clutched by a sudden dread.

"The Lost One," the voice said. A chasm opened up beneath Claire at these words but the purple blanket intensified, wrapping her in peace and a sense of protection.

"I felt a force that pushed me back," she told the others.

"What kind of a force?" Jared demanded.

"I don't know but I heard a voice saying something about a Lost One."

Bella frowned. "That doesn't sound good."

"This is ridiculous," Jared said, irritated.

Tears pricked Claire's eyes at the harshness of his tone. "You think I'm making it up, don't you?"

"Well, it does sound a bit dramatic."

"I'm just telling you what happened. I don't understand it. This kind of stuff is new to me too."

Jared glared at her and sat down on the bed.

"How come?" Bella asked. "Haven't you always been psychic?"

"No, no, I haven't. It's the necklace I'm wearing. I'm only psychic when I put it on but, when I do, the world looks different... I can see and hear things... not normally there. Don't ask me to explain it because I can't. Laura gave it to me."

"I thought I recognised it. I saw her wearing it once."

"She got it from Philip."

"Philip?"

"Elizabeth gave it to him as a boy and she told him to give it to someone he deemed worthy."

"How strange." Bella gazed at the necklace and an odd expression came into her eyes. Instinctively, Claire's hand came up as if to protect it.

"It's exquisite," Bella said. "I never knew Philip had such a thing. He kept it to himself."

"Do you remember much about Elizabeth?"

"Yes, I do. She was a close friend of my mother's. Elizabeth was a medium."

"Tell me about the séances."

"We children were never allowed in but, when I was about fifteen, I begged my mother to let me watch. They held the meetings once a month. Elizabeth would come and run the sessions. She and my mother would go into the front room and draw the curtains then, at about seven in the evening, others would arrive. Two or three would come on a regular basis but different people came as well, sometimes up to ten or twelve."

Claire had a sudden vision of a group of men and women sitting talking around a large round table covered with a red velvet cloth.

A woman, aged in her late sixties or early seventies, sat with her eyes shut while the others chatted. She was dressed in a purple skirt with a black blouse. A large amethyst crystal hung from her neck and her hair had been tied back in a bun from which several strands had come loose. "It is time," she announced. A young woman rose, turned off the lights and returned to the table. Everyone shut their eyes and sat still, the glow of the coal fire playing across their faces.

"Elizabeth would say a short prayer asking for protection from her guides," Bella continued.

"Guides?"

"Spirit people. We all have them with us, you too. They can help us sometimes, under certain conditions. Anyway, Elizabeth could talk to hers and they assisted her on the other side, on the astral plane. It's where you go when you die."

Could the voice she heard, Claire thought, be a guide speaking to her? After what she had already experienced with the necklace, it was entirely possible. "Go on. What happened?"

"Elizabeth would ask if there were any spirits present. She would communicate with them and tell the others what she picked up. Sometimes she went into a trance and her voice would change as the spirits spoke through her. Anyway, the point of it all was to give messages from the spirit world to the living. Often people came to the sessions because they'd lost someone and wanted to contact them again. We heard some sad stories, I can tell you.

"I learned to open up at those séances. I began to see spirits sometimes but I never could get messages. It was so frustrating. I wanted to be like Elizabeth." Bella's eyes again flicked to the necklace.

A phone rang down below. "Excuse me, I have to answer that," Bella said. "You stay here if you want."

"I have a call to make myself," Jared huffed and followed her out. Claire felt uneasy. She liked Bella a great deal but sensed she wanted the necklace, then there was what just happened. A distinct force had pushed her back. She shivered, picking up echoes of sorrow and fear in the room.

She looked out of the window, drawing comfort from the sight of the lake and trees in the distance and her heart lifted. She thought of the love Philip and Laura shared. They had such a strong connection. Laura had never found anyone to replace him and lived her whole life for her son. The sound of birdsong filtered into Claire's consciousness and she became quiet. She touched the necklace and, strangely, felt like crying.

Claire sat down on the bed and her mind filled with an image of the grave covered with violets. A young boy sat nearby on the grass writing in a sketchpad. Behind him she could see the woman with long dark hair who wore a white dress, the one Claire had seen in the mirror earlier. The woman reached out and touched the boy on the head. He looked up but appeared unaware of the figure standing behind him. She smiled gently and withdrew her hand. She looked up at the sky and Claire saw the shape of a bird circling high up above the hillside.

The eagle again, Claire thought, coming back to the room. What did it mean? "Who are you?" she whispered, thinking about the woman. "Who *are* you?" She waited, alert for any sign, but nothing happened. Why weren't the visions consistent? To her annoyance, her psychic power only came in its own timing.

She thought about what she had seen. Philip had been writing by the grave of violets. Claire stood up and searched the room. She looked in various drawers, touching things to see what she could sense. Nothing came but then she opened a wardrobe and saw what she hoped she would find at the bottom: a sketchpad. Lifting it out and opening up the cover, she saw lines of neat handwriting in blue ink.

She had the strongest feeling it was important. Too much to read through all at once, she took it down to the lounge where Bella and Jared sat talking.

"Any luck?" Jared asked, the mocking expression on his face showing he had no expectation of her discovering anything.

"I think what happened to Philip as a child is very important, that it might be linked to his disappearance later."

"How?"

"I don't know."

"Well, that's not a lot of good. I thought you were going to *see* what happened when you came here."

Already sensitised by the frightening experience in Philip's bedroom, Claire couldn't take the disparagement in his tone. She sank, exhausted, into one of the armchairs. "I can but there's too much that doesn't make sense. I don't always understand what I see. I have to put it all together. I only said I would try."

"Leave her alone, Jared," Bella scolded. "What do you have there, Claire? Oh, his writing. Yes, he often wrote. He threw a lot of it away, though. I guess he was his own worst critic."

Claire focussed on the book, scanning each page. "They're stories he must have written as a child. This one is about a super hero called *Dogman*. That's so cute." She laughed and showed the others a picture of what looked like a brown and white spaniel wearing a blue and yellow cape zooming through the sky. "There are more drawings." She held up pictures of cars and rockets and some landscapes. "They're so well drawn."

"He was a good artist," Bella said.

Claire turned over another page and saw a dark scribble done with such force it had gouged into the paper, even tearing it in one place. "Oh my God. Look at this. Wait, there's something underneath this mess. It's a drawing of a church on a hillside. There's also something written. I think it's the start of another story. She read it out.

> *The old, old church stood on a hillside by a tumbling stream.*
> *Little did people know that the place held a secret no one knew.*

"It's odd, the style of writing changes here. It's like a poem:

Beneath the violets I lie,
under the yew tree,
dark and spreading.
Let me speak to you for,
although my voice has stilled,
I cannot be silenced.
My heart is full of love for you,
so young and innocent, but vulnerable.
Take heed of my words for they will
fortify you against the darkness.
Remember who you are
in your deepest soul.
Keep its light burning bright.
Know it is your strength
and, if you let me, I will be with you.
Do not shut me out.

"That's not something a young boy would write. How odd." Claire laid her hand on the writing and the words became purple in her mind, then she smelt a sweet perfume and heard the rustling of clothing. The image of the woman in the white dress filled her mind and she felt caressed by loving gentleness. The words, "He did not listen," came in a now familiar voice. "I tried to help him but it was too late." A feeling of grief flooded through Claire.

The scene from the churchyard returned. This time, Philip flung the sketchbook down and began to cry. Claire's heart broke at the sight of the child knowing somehow that at this point in his life the darkness she sensed in him had come into being.

"I tried to help him," the voice repeated, this time with infinite sadness.

Claire heard the rustling of satin clothing next to her and felt the gentle touch of a hand on her hair. "Tell me what happened," she whispered, unaware she had spoken aloud.

Jared and Bella waited to see what she would say next but Claire remained silent and just sat staring off into space.

"Claire? What's the matter?" Jared demanded after a while. "Claire?" When she didn't respond, he reached out a hand towards her.

"No," Bella said. "Don't touch her. She's in trance. It might harm her. We must wait and listen."

"Trance? What are you talking about?"

Claire heard their voices but as if from far away and she found herself surrounded by a purple haze.

"Who are you?" she whispered. No answer came but her hand traced the lines of writing. "You wrote this?" she asked.

"I tried to help him," came the voice again. "But I could not."

"Help Philip? I don't understand."

"It was too late."

Claire waited, knowing she needed to sit and allow the impressions to come in their own time so the tenuous link with this person who had, by some incredible manner, connected with her, could strengthen. Nothing happened for a while, though, but then the sadness lifted and out of the silence came a feeling of peace. Claire felt herself floating within it and sensed a loving energy surrounding her.

The voice came again. "He had a darkness around his heart so I could not help him. You, you are different. You are open but you must connect to the love inside you. Hold to that strength and it will guide you, protect you. He could not."

"This is ridiculous," Jared said. "I won't sit here and be a party to this. She's putting it on, can't you see that?"

The words cut through the peace like a knife and the presence of the woman vanished. Claire came out of the trance and glared at Jared. "Thanks to you she's gone. That was the best connection I've ever had with her."

"Her?" Bella asked.

Claire turned her back on Jared. "I've been hearing a woman's voice when I wear the necklace, just in my mind, but it's different from my own. All I get are a few words here and there but she had some connection to Philip and might know what happened to him. Claire pointed to the drawing in her lap. "He often went to a church, didn't he? I think Laura said it was in Oakdale."

"He was always wandering around the countryside. He could very well have gone there."

Claire turned back to Jared. "I want to go to the church, now if possible."

"It's not far, only a few miles away from here." Bella said. "Do you mind if I come along?"

"No, I guess not." Claire didn't feel comfortable with Bella coming but did not want to offend her. Something in the older woman's attitude had shifted and it worried her a little.

Bella found her coat and they walked down the hill to the hotel where they'd left the car. Jared remained silent, his expression strained. Claire looked at him. He didn't know how to deal with this, she thought. Beyond his experience, he rejected it. If it wasn't for the necklace, she too would have found it all too much to believe. Still, he needn't be so rude.

They reached the car and drove off through Bowness. "Take that turn," Bella indicated. Jared drove along a winding lane between dry stone walls covered with moss and out into a verdant countryside sprinkled with grazing sheep. Claire forgot the reason they were driving as she gazed at the sunlit fields, loving all of it. They passed some hikers. Many people came to the Lake District to trek and she understood why. She would love to walk through the hills but knew Jared would never consider it. She would do it when she came back in the future, though. She felt at home in this landscape in a way she had never done in London.

"Here, turn off the road by this bridge and park," Bella directed. Jared pulled over by a rocky stream pouring down a nearby hillside. As Claire got out, the sound of the water filled her ears and she felt a deep connection to the surrounding hills and fields. The shadows she felt earlier dissipated and she felt uplifted. This was her land. Her home. Nearby, a mother sheep called to her lamb. Claire went over to admire the tiny creature. "Isn't it gorgeous?" she said to Bella who came up behind her.

"Yes, it is."

"Come on, you two," Jared snapped. "Let's get on with it. Look there's the church." Beyond the field, Claire saw a square tower surrounded by dark trees.

"Who shoved the stick up his arse?" Bella whispered and Claire burst out laughing at the incongruity of the remark coming from the elderly woman beside her.

"I don't know," she replied, "but they made a good job of it." Still laughing, they started walking along the road to the church. Jared, sensing he was the subject of the women's private joke, glared at them and strode on ahead.

He stopped and waited for them at a wooden gate leading through the low stone wall surrounding the churchyard. Looking around her, Claire saw a low hill of grass with many headstones leading up to a simple church with grey stone walls. Her attention soon focussed on a group of yew trees she remembered from her visions as being near the grave of violets so headed in that direction. As she drew closer, she felt a prickle of apprehension. What would she sense? Would the grave be covered with violets? She hoped so otherwise they might be unable to find it. They had come in the right season but it had been forty years since Philip had been there so a lot could have happened. Jared followed Claire. Bella took it more slowly, the exertion of walking making her wheeze.

Reaching the trees, Claire moved into the shadows beneath their dark hanging boughs. It took her only a moment to find the grave. "Oh my God," she whispered. "Here it is." She stopped by an old worn gravestone, a perfect rectangle of purple violets at its base. Bending down, Claire gently touched one of the delicate flowers, in awe at their fragile beauty.

A sudden weakness overcame her as the realisation of where she stood sank in, the place she had seen in her visions. She touched the necklace at her throat and sank onto her knees, heedless of the dampness of the ground but taking care not to crush any of the flowers.

"What's she doing?" Jared asked Bella.

"Shh! I think we should leave her alone for a while." The two of them moved back. Bella waited and watched Claire from a short distance away in case she needed help of any kind while Jared wandered away into the church, his mind full of thoughts about how they might find something out about his father. He intended to talk to the Keswick police as soon as possible to see if they would tell him anything. As he wandered into the cool, calm interior of the church, a sudden tiredness overcame him. He sat down on a pew and put his head in his hands. He found it all too hard sometimes.

The pain of never knowing his father surged up from deep inside and he felt empty, as if a part of him were missing. It had always been that way. His mother had done her best, been a wonderful parent, but the mystery of what happened had always been present in Jared's consciousness. He hated not having a father. All the other children at school had one: someone who played with them, a male figure who understood what young boys needed. He had suppressed the feeling of loss, ignored it, focussed on other things, but it had always been in the background undermining the security of his childhood view of the world. How could people just disappear? In his imagination he worried that one day someone or something would take *him* away, or his mother, and it had made him fiercely protective of her.

Jared thought of the young woman out in the graveyard doing God knows what and for a purpose he couldn't understand. Why was she doing it? On one hand he cursed her for upsetting his mother and himself by dredging up the whole issue with his father but on the other, he hoped she would find something out. But then, he realised, if she did, he would have to accept that forces existed in the world he could never understand and he didn't want to have to do that. He liked the concrete and measurable, the world of money and objects, buying and selling, having a nice house. His mind shied away from the one thing he didn't have: someone to share it with. The wound within him from Andrea's betrayal still hurt like hell.

Back at the grave, Claire closed her eyes. Breathe, breathe, she told herself, relax. The thought, this is madness, no good will come of it, flicked into her mind but she ignored it and remained still. Fear came up, fear of the unknown, but then a warm, comforting sensation eased itself into her consciousness and the now familiar haze of purple settled itself around her.

"You have come. Long have I waited for someone to help me put right the wrong that has been done." The words sounded in her mind but Claire knew they had not come from her. She recognised the voice, the same one she heard when wearing the necklace before, but this time it sounded louder and more certain.

"Who are you?" Claire asked, also in her mind, not expecting an answer. The wind blew across the graveyard and ruffled through the violets. No reply came but the faint figure of the woman she saw earlier in her hotel room appeared. Long, wavy brown hair fell around her shoulders to the waist of the white dress she wore. Claire had an impression of the exquisite lacework of the fabric then the image faded although she still sensed her presence and felt embraced by love and peace so profound tears fell from her eyes onto the flowers below.

The voice spoke again, "Your tears are blessings, my dearest one. They bring such hope. You have to help him."

"Who?"

"He took him beyond my reach."

"Who took who? Do you mean Philip?"

"Yes."

"Someone took Philip?"

"He used to come here. He sensed the power of this place, that I was here, that maybe I could help him but, in the end, I could not. His was a sensitive spirit and he could not ward off the darkness."

"What," Claire hesitated, not sure she really wanted to know, "is the darkness?"

"The shadow cast by the Lost One."

A feeling of dread gripped Claire as she heard these words. "You talked of him before."

"No, no, do not be afraid. Stay connected to me, to the love I hold for you and you have nothing to fear. Philip could not do it, he doubted too much. I could not help him, but you, you are different. You are strong and will become stronger as you perceive the Truth inside you, the Light that illuminates all shadows."

Strong? Claire felt anything but strong. She knew, however, that somehow she had to stay focussed, keep the connection to this voice, "What happened to Philip? Can you tell me? Is he dead?"

"He lives."

"Oh my God!" Claire cried out loud, covering her mouth with her hands.

Bella, watching, wondered if she should do something but Claire relaxed and placed her hands back in her lap.

"He's alive?" Claire asked mentally, still bewildered by this strange way of communication.

"Yes."

"Can you tell me where he is?"

"No. He is very distant, far beyond my reach, and I am blocked from helping him. His energy is too weak for me to link to. I have very little power in the physical world. If you are willing, though, I can help him through you."

"I *am* willing. I promised his wife, Laura, I would try and discover what happened to him. If he's alive then I have to find him. But how can I do that?"

"You must go to the ring of stones and follow the signs."

"What signs? How will I know what to look for?"

"You will know when you see them."

"But how?"

"Do not worry, have you not been seeing visions and the shadows of those who have passed into death?"

"Yes."

"More of that will come if you are willing to open up."

"What do you mean, *open up?*"

"To be quiet and aware, to bring your attention into the present moment and use all your senses to explore your surroundings, to see what you notice and how it makes you feel, so that you may be guided to find what you seek. Centre in your heart, in your living inner essence, and ask for what you need to know and it will reveal itself."

The feeling of the purple blanket intensified and the words came, "Try now, my dear one."

Claire continued to kneel by the grave of violets and, despite feeling awkward, became aware of the earth beneath her knees. She stared at the tiny violets for a moment then swept her awareness over the surrounding graveyard and hills beyond. Returning her attention to the grave, she sensed the presence of the woman's spirit nearby, insubstantial and yet *there,* and Claire's fear intensified again.

"Do not worry, dear one. I would never harm you. If you wish, I will leave. You are free to walk away, to never think of this again. I would not blame you for what I ask is great indeed."

The presence diminished but Claire knew she couldn't let her go. "No. No. It's fine. It's just so strange." Yes, she thought, so out of her comfort zone as to be ridiculous.

"Stay quiet, my dearest. Let go of your fearful thinking or you'll become lost in the labyrinth of the mind and that will never do. Come back to the present, to feeling the living essence in your heart."

"But I can't help feeling afraid."

"Allow your fear to be but know it is not you, the real you, which is so much more than you know. You are that which is aware of what you are feeling. The real you is always safe and can never be destroyed and, if you connect to it, you will find your courage. Never forget this. Cast your attention within. See if you can find the one who looks."

Claire let go of the nervousness vibrating through her chest, and allowed it to be. It seemed to intensify its grip but, all of a sudden, she realised, there was indeed a part of her watching it. For a moment, she sensed stillness and peace and the anxiety eased a little.

"Good, *good*. Now look beneath your fear. What else do you feel?"

"Confused. Oh God, very confused."

"That's all right. Let that be. Is there anything behind this?"

Claire became aware of sadness in her chest, which, as she paid attention, grew bigger. It swelled up and became an intense outpouring of grief as if a lid had been removed from the dark recesses of her heart, liberating all the pain and suffering she had felt through life but sought to push away.

"Let it flow from you, my dear one. We carry far too many sorrows, but you are not your feelings, or the thoughts that seek to take you prisoner. You are so much more. This knowledge will give you the strength you need to heal your pain. Tell me, what is beneath your grief?"

Claire sank into herself, down and down, until a feeling of utter emptiness made her falter. She felt as if life had no meaning at all. "There's just nothing," she murmured.

"Drop below this, too," came the gentle command.

"I can't."

"You can." It seemed so pointless but Claire delved into the feeling and, just when she thought she couldn't bear the emptiness any longer, felt the presence of something else, the sense of being there, but clear and free, not lost in meaninglessness. A deep peace arose in which there was nothing to do, nowhere to go, everything was perfect. Love arose in her heart, faint at first but it grew to fill her body and flowed out to become a sea of love expanding in all directions.

The words came, "Now you are in your true conscious being. In this there is power, peace and wisdom for it is one with the infinite intelligence behind all of life. Trust it. Allow it to guide your actions.

"Remember this, feel it, know it, be it whenever you can and you will find the strength you need. Your inner perception will open up more and more. Then, when you go to Castlerigg, you will be able to sense the memory of the place. The stones will tell you where Philip went next. His trail can be followed in this way."

It sounded insane and yet, on another level, it made a certain sort of sense.

"You need only take one step at a time and, as long as you have the necklace, I will be able to help you. The necklace was mine in life and it is my link to you now. Wear it always."

With this, the wonderful clarity and peace faded leaving Claire back in normal consciousness with a crowd of questions and other feelings clamouring for attention. And yet a resonance of it remained. She knew what had happened was very important, as if her whole life had been leading up to this one moment. Claire sat staring at the small flowers on the ground, coming to terms with what she had experienced.

After a while, she became aware of Bella nearby. Claire turned and looked at her. "He's alive!" she whispered. "Philip's alive!"

Chapter 9

CLAIRE SCRAMBLED TO HER FEET. Dizzy, she reached out to the moss-covered headstone for support. Bella moved closer. "Are you all right?"

"Yes, yes. I'm fine."

"How do you know Philip's alive?"

Claire told her what had happened.

"Jesus, Mary, Holy Mother of God! I can't believe this. Are you sure?"

Claire sighed. "No, I can't be sure of anything. This is all so strange but I think I trust this spirit. Anyway, she said to go to Castlerigg and I'd be able to find out more. Maybe from there we can find some concrete evidence." Claire ran her fingers over the top of the headstone. "This is the grave of the woman I connect with through the necklace. I wish I knew her name but someone has chipped away the information. Now why would they do that?" Claire looked down at the violets below. "I want to know more about her. She alluded to some wrong which has to be made right. I wonder what she meant. I came here looking for answers but I just have more questions."

"I'm sure we can find out who she is," Bella said. "The church will have a record of burials, but we need to go to Castlerigg. If there's a chance Philip could be alive we must follow it up as soon as possible."

"Yes, you're right, of course, we will." Claire fell silent for a moment. "Where's Jared?"

"He went into the church."

They left the graveside and entered the nearby building. Claire felt uplifted and somehow more alive, as if a veil had been lifted. Her awareness had intensified and life felt more meaningful. She noticed Jared sitting in one of the pews looking up at the vivid stained-glass windows shining against the shadowed interior, "Jared?" she said but he ignored her, as if oblivious to her presence. She stared at him in shock. He looked like a different man. Gone was the arrogance, the irritation, and instead she saw a lost boy. He looked tired and she realised it took an enormous amount of energy to maintain the cynical facade he presented to the world. Her heart went out to him and she longed to help him.

She touched Jared on the shoulder. He jumped and looked up. As she stared into his eyes, she felt his pain and sensed the presence of the woman she picked up on before in his mind, Andrea. With her, came a sense of betrayal.

As he became aware of Claire, Jared straightened and his mask slid back in place.

"Sorry, I didn't mean to startle you," Claire said softly.

"You didn't," Jared snapped as he fought for control of his emotions. The last thing he wanted was to look weak in front of this woman. "So, I suppose you've spoken with the dead," he bit out sarcastically. "What did you find out?"

All Claire's compassion for him evaporated. What an insufferable man. If she never saw him again it would be too damned soon. She felt like turning on her heel and walking out. She no longer wanted to tell him what she had learned. The dark force of his negativity penetrated her and gave voice to the doubt in her abilities she still felt. What if she *were* wrong and Castlerigg held no clues? Jared would never forgive her for telling him his father was alive, she felt sure.

Bella resolved the dilemma. "Claire says Philip's alive."

Jared's eyebrows raised in surprise. Claire groaned, sensing his doubt and knowing he would find some hidden motive in her.

"And how can you possibly know that, Claire?"

His barbed words sliced through her with no mercy but she forged on.

"You know the voice of the woman I've heard?"

"Yes."

"Well, she came through just now by the grave outside and told me that Philip is still alive."

"So where is he?"

Claire cringed, knowing what he would think. "I don't know."

"You don't know?" Jared repeated with disdain.

"She says Philip is far away," she stammered, "but she said if I went to Castlerigg I may be able to find out where he went."

"Isn't this exciting?" Bella said, her eyes alight with enthusiasm.

"I think I'm going to reserve my judgement," Jared said, "unless, of course, we *do* find my father. What are you going to do when we don't, Claire?"

"Oh, shut up, Jared, of *course,* we're going to find him," Bella said.

Claire felt sick. She hated Jared. Unable to stand his resentment of her any longer, she walked away down the church and out of the door. Jared and Bella remained in the building so Claire wandered alone over the grass of the churchyard back to the grave of violets. The wind stirred the yew trees and she stopped by the headstone. As she did so, Claire felt a sudden shift in her consciousness and a lightening of her mood. A flood of reassurance and love enveloped her. A silence fell and she relaxed in the peacefulness of the place. The slight headache she woke up with evaporated as if it had never been.

"Are you there?" she whispered, wondering if the voice would speak again but the presence did not come. How did these things work? Where did the spirit go? Why did she only speak at certain times? Claire remained standing. For a long time nothing happened, but then, on the edge of her consciousness, an insane idea grew, one she rejected at first but it refused to go away. She had a powerful impulse to dig down through the soil by the headstone.

God, no, she thought, repelled by the idea and yet watched herself kneel down and search through the violets until she found a spot that called to her hands. She scraped at the soft earth with her fingers. Once she had the momentum going, she gouged with more determination. She sensed Jared and Bella come up behind her but did not stop, the urge to dig now in full possession of her will.

"What are you doing? For Christ's sake, woman, have you gone mad?" Jared's voice sounded far away.

"What is it?" Bella asked. "What do you think is there?"

Claire, intent upon her work, did not answer. She lifted several of the violet plants to one side and continued to dig. Jared and Bella stood watching, wondering if they should stop her.

They decided to wait and see what happened. After a while, Claire's fingers, stained brown with soil and her nails chipped, reached a hard surface. They both craned forward to get a look. "What is it?" Bella asked.

"I'm not sure," Claire said, continuing to work until they saw what looked like an old metal biscuit tin, the remnants of some floral design still evident on its corroded surface. She lifted it free of the ground and placed it to one side of the grave. Jared and Bella both moved closer so they could see better as Claire tried to open it. The lid wouldn't budge at first but using one of her remaining nails, she managed to prise it open.

Inside was a package wrapped in brown paper, which contained some stained white cloth. The moment she touched it, the image of a young child came into her mind. Claire unfolded the cloth and held it up.

"It's a baby's christening robe," Bella said. "It would have been beautiful once. Look at all that lovely embroidery."

"But why on earth is it buried in this grave?" Jared said. "You'd think it would be in the coffin not on the surface like this. It seems like someone added it later but why would they do that?"

"I've no idea," Bella said. "Do you think we should put it back? Claire?"

Claire, however, ignored her. She sat looking straight ahead for she could hear a child laughing. Something told her to walk towards the church so she rose and entered the building through the old wooden door. As she did so, she saw a little boy about eight or nine years old with blonde hair standing near the altar staring up at the window. He turned and looked back then simply vanished.

She stopped in shock for a moment then made her way forward into the church. The laughing came again but from behind her now and she turned to see the child by the door. The boy smiled and Claire felt a wave of happiness flood through her at the sight of the beauty of his face and the innocence in his expression. Jared and Bella entered the church and he disappeared again.

"Are you okay?" Bella asked, worried.

"Yes, yes, I'm fine, but, to be honest, I feel a bit out of my depth here." Claire told them what she had seen. "Such a beautiful child," she said. "I wonder who he was and what connection he has with the woman in the grave. Was he *her* child? None of this makes any sense. I wish I could see more but it all comes veiled in images I don't understand. I'm sorry, Jared, I know what you're going to say but I'm doing my best here. I'm not out to trick you, I'm just trying to understand all this for myself now."

For once Jared said nothing, the expression in Claire's eyes stayed his tongue. He didn't know what to make of it all. What happened a moment ago at the grave turned his stomach. He thought she had gone way too far in her psychic playacting but, as he looked at her now, she seemed genuinely confused, not the behaviour of someone out to deceive. For the first time he wondered if maybe he had misjudged her intentions, although he still thought the psychic stuff far-fetched.

"Let's go and find something to eat now, shall we?" Claire asked. "I'm hungry and tired. Then perhaps we can go to Castlerigg."

"What are you going to do with the robe?" Jared asked.

Claire studied the cloth in her hands. "I'm going to keep it." She looked at Bella. "I know keeping something from a grave is a bit gross but I have a strong feeling I've seen the boy for a reason. Maybe this will connect me to him. Can we ask someone about burials here? I'd like to find out what I can about the woman in the grave."

"Already on to it," Jared waved a piece of paper. There was no one here to ask but I found this Parish newsletter. It has the vicar's contact details in it. We can ring him."

"Let's go back to my place and I can make us lunch," Bella offered. "I'm starving, too."

Claire insisted on going back to the grave to repair the damage she had created as best she could. She filled in the hole and carefully replaced the violet plants she had removed so her violation of the grave wouldn't be noticeable. Her task complete, she stood up. "Let's go."

Back at the house, Claire helped Bella prepare sandwiches while Jared rang the vicar. It didn't take him long. He came into the kitchen. "We can meet him at the church at four this afternoon. It means we can't go to Castlerigg today, though. Is that okay, Claire?"

"Yes, I could probably do with a break before I go there, today's been full on."

"It would be good to have the whole day to go to Keswick, anyway," Bella said. "You need to be able to take your time."

Claire excused herself to go to the bathroom before eating. When she returned, Bella looked at her in surprise. "You've taken the necklace off?"

"Having it on all the time is taking it out of me, I think." She looked at her with a rueful smile. "I need to have a dose of normality."

"Yes, good idea. Come on, let's eat."

After lunch, Jared excused himself to make some business calls in the car where he had his briefcase. Claire started to help Bella clear away. "No, you go and sit down, dear. You look washed out."

Claire sank into one of the soft armchairs in the conservatory, grateful for the time alone. She had a lot to take in.

Her eyes flew open. She had drifted off to sleep and dreamt of someone crying out. When another cry came she realised it hadn't been a dream. Claire got up and rushed through the house searching for the source. She found Bella in Philip's room hunched up on the floor. She looked up with anguished eyes. "I'm so sorry," she said. "I know I shouldn't have."

"What?" Claire asked then noticed the amethyst necklace around Bella's neck.

"I took it from your bag but I only meant to try it on for a moment, see if I could sense anything in here. I thought maybe because I was his sister the connection would be better. I meant no harm."

"It's all right." Claire helped Bella to her feet and onto the bed then she undid the necklace.

Bella relaxed. "Thank you. I'm so sorry. I just couldn't help myself. I've always wanted to have the Sight like my mother; to help people like she did, but all I ever get is a few vague images and perhaps a wisp of information, nothing reliable.

"Oh, Claire, it was awful. I came in here and put the necklace on. The moment I did, I felt this terrible darkness in here. I, I felt so alone; as if everything I cared about was an illusion. Such a sense of hopelessness, I, I couldn't take it." Bella began to cry. "I never want to feel like that again."

Disturbed to see Bella so distraught, Claire laid a hand on her shoulder until she calmed enough to continue. "It was awful but then, the moment before you came in, a woman's voice said to me, 'Take it off. The necklace is not yours to wear.' It wasn't an unkind voice just firm."

"I wonder if that was the person who speaks to me," Claire said.

"What *was* that feeling?" Bella asked. "It was so horrible. It had something to do with Philip, I know it. I'm so afraid for him. Where is he, Claire? What happened to him all those years ago and who is the Lost One your woman spoke of? She said someone had Philip. Do you think a spirit has possessed him, taken him over?"

Claire shuddered at the thought. "Is such a thing possible?"

"I think it can happen sometimes, if the conditions are right. My mother and Elizabeth sometimes helped people who had a spirit attached to them. They guided the spirit on into the afterlife. People can remain on the earth if they die very suddenly and don't realise it, or else they have some unfinished business here. Oh God, I'm so scared."

"Don't worry, it'll be all right," Claire soothed, trying to reassure herself as much as Bella. This whole thing had gone way beyond her ability to comprehend. She put her arms around the elderly woman and the two of them held each other, seeking strength in the contact. They broke apart when they heard Jared calling out below in his usual irritated manner. "Hello? Where *is* everybody? We should be leaving."

They found Reverend Mountjoy in the church, a jovial looking man of around sixty dressed in rather shabby jeans and a blue jumper. "Forgive my appearance but I've been doing some clearing out." After introductions, they all went outside and Jared showed him the grave with the violets.

"Oh, this one. I've had a few queries about this grave. It's the violets, you see. Year after year they bloom here, never any weeds. It's quite lovely. I like to sit here myself and look at it sometimes. Someone paid for the seat over there so they could spend time here. She used to say she found peace in this place. I know what she meant, there's something about this spot, maybe it's the location: the trees, the view, I don't know, but I always find myself cheering up if the day hasn't gone well. I can tell you whose grave it is without looking it up, Eleanora Waterford, died in 1923, I think. We'll go and check in a moment."

Eleanora? Now I have a name for you, Claire thought, touching the necklace. Eleanora. "Who is the woman who put the seat there?" she asked the vicar.

"Joanna Langley. She's quite elderly now. In Woodland Court, poor old dear."

"Woodland Court?"

"An aged care facility near Ambleside. I must go and visit her again soon. Anyway, let's go inside."

They watched as the vicar unlocked a cupboard in the vestry and laid several large worn volumes on a table. "Here we are. It should be in one of these," he said, opening one of the books and leafing through the pages with great care. "This goes back many generations. Now let me see." The vicar ran his finger down the entries. "There are quite a few Waterfords listed here before Eleanora. Yes, here we are, Eleanora Waterford of Bluebell Cottage, Honeysuckle Lane, Bowness, born 1887, died 1923. Didn't live that long. She was only thirty-six. Occupation: seamstress."

Claire thought of the christening gown and the child spirit she saw earlier. "Is there a child with the name Waterford buried here around Eleanora's time?"

The vicar scanned the burial listings. "No."

How odd there should be no mention of a child. Claire felt sure the boy she saw must be connected to Eleanora, that the christening gown had been his. She felt sad he had died so young. "Can you look up births, say around 1910?"

"I can look up baptisms," the vicar said, reaching for another book and looking through. "Yes, here. Charles Waterford, baptised the 16th of July, 1914, address Waterford Hall, Cranleigh Road, Oakdale, parents Eleanora and William Waterford."

Eleanora hadn't been living at Waterford Hall when she died. Claire wondered what had happened. "Are you sure there's no mention of Charles dying?"

The vicar checked the burials again. "No, definitely not."

Claire looked down at the register, at the tide of humans passing on through the years as people were born and died. Page after page of names yet they had been real people living real lives. What had Eleanora's life been like? Claire wondered, and why could she not rest? Bella had mentioned spirits having unfinished business earlier. That made sense. Eleanora had referred to a wrong that needed to be made right.

"Do you know if there are any other Waterfords living in the area?" Claire asked.

"I'm not aware of any myself, I'm afraid, but you could always look in the phone book or online if you're interested."

"Okay, thank you so much," Claire said.

They said goodbye to the vicar and walked outside. Claire stood for a moment looking over at the grave. Everything remained normal even though she now wore the necklace again. "Can we find this Woodland Court?" she asked. "I want to speak to Joanna Langley."

"Do you think that will help us locate my father?" Jared asked.

"I have no idea. I just have a feeling about her. I want to follow up anything I can. It intrigues me why she would put a seat here."

"I know the place," Bella said. "I'll guide you there. It's not far."

"It's just a nice view; I wouldn't go reading anything into it," Jared said.

"I know, but it's worth a try."

Twenty minutes later, they drove along a winding drive and through some elaborate wrought iron gates. Jared pulled up on one side of a large gravel area in front of an imposing building built with two square castellated towers on either side giving it a style reminiscent of an old castle. The three of them got out and went over to the entrance, a large wooden door decorated with an intricate pattern of interweaving ironwork. Next to an intercom on one side, a sign read: Woodland Court Aged Care Centre. Please ring bell.

Jared did so and they heard it echoing inside. A moment later, a voice asked, "Yes, can I help you?"

"We're here to visit one of your residents," Jared said.

"Okay." They heard a loud click as a catch released. They opened the door and went in.

"Locked away," Bella said.

"For their own safety, I expect," Claire replied, "or they'd wander over the countryside. My grandmother was like that at the end, didn't know where she was half the time."

They found themselves walking through a hallway lined with dark wood at the end of which they saw a reception area. A young woman looked up from her computer as they approached. "Hello, may I help you?"

"We're here to see Joanna Langley," Jared said. "Is that possible?"

"I'll ring through to her area and see." The woman spoke on the phone for a few minutes then turned back to them. "Mrs Langley is a bit agitated, I'm afraid."

What if they wouldn't let them in? Claire worried, feeling now she *had* to see Joanna somehow. It was important. Her hands began to tingle, as if full of energy.

"I haven't seen you here before. Are you family?" the receptionist asked.

"Yes, *I* am," Claire said.

Chapter 10

JARED AND BELLA LOOKED AT Claire in surprise but said nothing.

"Well, perhaps if you went in first, then we'll see how it goes," the receptionist said. "Sign in there, please"

Claire smiled and signed her name in the visitor book. "Thank you so much." She wrote her name, then turned to the others, "You wait here."

The woman walked over to a lift, keyed in a combination and the doors opened. Claire grew more and more nervous as they rose two floors and then walked along a wood panelled corridor. They passed a large sitting room with various armchairs, several of which held elderly people. A television in one corner played to a disinterested audience. Everyone looked to be asleep, except for one old man who glanced up for a second. They met two old ladies walking arm in arm along the corridor.

"We don't know where we're going," one of them said, beaming at Claire with such an angelic smile she couldn't help smiling too. The old ladies looked at each other and giggled.

"To the dining room, Nora," the receptionist told them, pointing behind her, "that way."

Her guide showed Claire into a bright room with three beds. "I'll leave you here. Ask one of the staff to show you out when you're ready."

Two old women sat in armchairs by a large window. One of them, a tiny frail lady with short ruffled curly white hair emitted a low repetitive moaning sound. It wrenched Claire's heart. Why was she so distressed? A male care worker stood beside her. For a sickening moment, Claire worried he would think it odd she wouldn't know which woman to go to but, to her relief, the worker said, "Joanna, you've got a visitor." The elderly lady making the sound turned and looked at Claire but did not stop moaning.

"She's been like this all morning," the man said. "Maybe you can cheer her up." Claire, her heart beating fast, approached the fragile-looking woman. The care worker helped the other resident out of her armchair. "Time for dinner, Betty." He guided her from the room, leaving Claire alone with Joanna. Feeling bad for intruding like this, Claire hesitated but then felt the presence of Eleanora. "Touch her and she will know me," the spirit said.

Claire laid her hand on the elderly lady's shoulder. The low keening noise ceased and she looked up, her face full of fear. A strong current of energy ran down Claire's arm and the lady's eyes widened in surprise. To her amazement, Claire found herself saying, "Joanna, dearest one. It has been such a long time."

Joanna's eyes lit up with joy. "Eleanora, it's you. Where have you been? I have waited so long. Have you come for me?"

"Not yet but it won't be long."

"I'm afraid, Eleanora."

"You have no need to fear death, Joanna. It is but a transition. Those who you love await you there."

Despite feeling self-conscious, Claire found herself laying her hand upon the woman's head and, to her astonishment, Joanna closed her eyes, relaxed and smiled. "Thank you," she murmured. When she opened them again, she looked more alert and at ease. Claire removed her hand and the strong sensation passed as she felt Eleanora fade into the background.

"Oh, who are you? Do I know you?" Joanna asked, as if all that went on before had not happened. Claire swallowed, unsure of what was going on but knew she had no choice but to go with it. "Hello, I'm Claire. I'm... a friend of Eleanora's."

"Eleanora? Oh yes, she was just here." The old lady looked around the room. "Where did she go?"

"She..." Claire decided to tell the truth, hoping Joanna would be receptive. "In a way she's still here."

Joanna stared at her in confusion. "I don't understand. I..."

"Eleanora is with me. She speaks to me."

"But I saw her." Claire saw comprehension dawn in Joanna's expression. "But I couldn't have, could I? She's dead, of course. I'm sorry. I get so confused nowadays."

"She was here, with me. I see and hear her."

"You have the Sight?"

"I guess I do, at the moment, at least."

Joanna's gaze lowered to Claire's neck. "That's such a beautiful necklace."

"It belonged to Eleanora. Did you ever see her wearing it?"

"No, I didn't. But how did you get it?" Joanna looked confused. "Eleanora would have died many years before you were born."

"It was given to me by a friend but I think someone called Elizabeth had it at one time. Did you know her?"

"No."

"Never mind. Eleanora is helping me find someone who has been lost for a long time. I'm trying to find out what happened to him."

"Who is that?"

"Philip Harcourt."

"I'm sorry, I don't know that name."

"No, that's all right. Anyhow, Eleanora is involved but I don't know how yet. Could you tell me about her, please, if you can? What was she like? My connection with her is often unclear. I find it all so confusing."

"I'll try."

"First, I'm intrigued, why did you place a seat near her grave?"

"It was so beautiful there. The violets, did you see the violets? Are they still there?"

"Yes, they are. Did *you* plant them?"

"No, they just came, all by themselves. A miracle! I used to sit by the grave hoping she might speak to me but she never did, although I felt a great peace there, a stillness I could never find in my life. I had six children, you know."

"Who was she?"

"A great healer. People used to come from miles around. She never turned anyone away. She would touch their head and miracles would happen. I know, I saw some of them. One day my mother asked her to come to our house and she healed my little brother, David. He almost died from whooping cough. So bad he was. I thought each cough would be the one to take him but she touched him and he fell silent, just went to sleep. He was fine when he woke.

"People continued to visit her even when she died. They would sit by her grave or touch it. Some claimed they were healed. When the violets came, people used to take the flowers. Keep them for good luck. She had such a powerful soul."

"How did she die?"

"A tragedy it was. She died from a blow to the head. I heard of it from my friend. She told me it was Eleanora's husband."

"Oh, my goodness. Do you know why he attacked her?"

"No, I don't. No one knew much about the husband; he didn't live with her."

"What happened to him?"

"He hung for it."

What a sad story, Claire thought. Eleanora had been murdered. Was that why she could not rest?

"Did she have any children at all?" Claire asked, thinking of the child she saw in the church.

"She had a child living with her for a while, a boy, but one day her husband took him away." Joanna's eyes closed for a moment then opened again. "I don't know what happened to him. I'm sorry, I can't think of anything more to tell you. I was very young at the time, only about twelve. It was a long time ago. I'm ninety-nine, you know."

"Goodness, you don't look it. I think you're a bit of a miracle yourself."

Joanna smiled but her eyes closed again.

"I've tired you. I'll leave you in peace now. Thank you so much for talking to me." Claire stood up.

"I hope you find who you're looking for, dear."

"Yes, so do I."

Claire found her way back to the lift. Not knowing the code to operate it, she went in search of someone to help her. The two old ladies she saw before sat together at a table in the dining room. Claire waved to them. They waved back and laughed. How lovely they had each other, she thought. She hoped she could be cheerful when she got to be that old.

A few minutes later, she came out of the lift. After thanking the care worker who had accompanied her, she rejoined Jared and Bella. As they drove away from the aged care home, Claire filled them in on what she had learned from Joanna.

"Well, that's all very interesting but I don't see how that helps us find my father," Jared said. Bella rolled her eyes at Claire.

"I don't know yet either," she replied, "but I feel it's important somehow. With luck we'll learn more tomorrow at Castlerigg."

When they arrived back at Bella's house a short while later, Bella asked, "Do you think I could come with you tomorrow?"

"Of course." Claire smiled. "We'll pick you up about ten."

Claire lay on her bed. On their return to the hotel, Jared said he needed to make some phone calls so she had left him to it and come to her room to rest. She relaxed and allowed all that had happened in the day to settle inside her. Drifting off to sleep, she dreamt of the child she saw in the church. He ran through the graveyard to the grave of violets where he picked one of the delicate flowers and held it out to her.

She woke to the sound of her phone. "Oh, Laura, how are you?"

"I just had to ring and find out how you're going."

"Jared didn't call you, then?" Claire asked.

"No."

"Oh, I'm so sorry. I would have rung you earlier but Jared said *he* would." Poor Laura, Claire thought. How hard it must be for her waiting back in London. Jared was such an idiot.

"That's all right, dear."

"Well…" Claire outlined what had happened during the day although she left out Eleanora's assertion Philip still lived. She didn't want to raise Laura's hopes only to dash them if nothing came of it. "Do you think he could have had a spirit attached to him, affecting him in some way?" Claire asked.

"I don't like to think of it but it would fit with his behaviour," Laura replied. "He was so loving and caring. Everyone liked him. He always had time to stop and chat to people. He truly cared about others and they responded to him. But not when he had one of his moods.

"I couldn't get through to him when he had the darkness upon him. To be honest, he frightened me a little then. It felt to me like he struggled with something in himself. It *was* like he was a different person. Maybe the spirit won that day at Castlerigg, took him over."

Her words gave voice to Claire's own line of thought.

Laura continued, "It would explain how he could leave me and his life, everything. But where would he go and why?"

"I just don't know, I'm afraid," Claire answered, "but I'll do my best to find out. None of it makes much sense at the moment."

"No, but you've learned so much in one day. That's wonderful. As your connection to Eleanora strengthens, maybe she'll be able to help you more. One day it'll all become clear, I'm sure of it."

"Yes, I hope you're right. We're going to Castlerigg tomorrow. That's where I'm thinking I might be able to pick up what happened the day Philip disappeared."

"Thank you so much for doing this for me. I know it's a lot to ask."

"It's my journey too, now," Claire said. "It wasn't an accident I walked into your shop that day. I believe I'm meant to be involved somehow and so it's important to me to find out what happened to your husband as well. I'm coming to realise life isn't as simple as I thought, that there is a deeper purpose behind it we can't see and I want to find out what that is. Anyway, I'd better go. You take care. I'll talk to you again tomorrow."

The moment Claire stopped talking to Laura, Jared rang. "Let's go and eat now," he said. She met him in the hotel foyer and they walked down to the town. They found a restaurant that Jared liked the look of near the waterfront, a white-painted building with a dark wood panelled interior. They sat down at a table covered with a crisp linen tablecloth and ordered a meal. Jared's phone rang and he left the restaurant to talk in private. He had his bloody mobile almost permanently glued to his ear, Claire thought, irritated. She watched him walking up and down in the street and wondered if it was a business or personal issue. He seemed upset.

A few moments later, the restaurant door banged and Jared strode back to the table. Claire recoiled at the negativity emanating from him. It intensified when he sighed.

"Problems?" Claire asked.

He looked at her, his brows furrowed with an expression taut with tension, but she felt the shutter go down. "No, no, it's fine, just a few issues with a business associate."

Claire still wore the necklace so knew he was lying. She wondered why.

"I hope this place serves decent food," he snapped.

Claire hated his prickliness. "I'm sure it will but if it doesn't, it's not the end of the world."

"Nothing matters to you much, does it," he sneered. "You're one of those people who float through life, not worrying, uncaring about the effect they have. Not everyone can do that, you know." Bitterness barbed his words.

"You can't possibly make a judgement about me like that," Claire returned, hurt. "It's not true. Why do you hate everyone, Jared?"

He looked surprised but ignored her question and focussed on fiddling with his knife and fork instead. Claire said nothing and waited. When he next met her gaze, she noticed some kind of a veil lift from his eyes and the face of a woman came into her mind. She saw her talking to Jared and walking away. Other images flickered in and out and Claire understood. "I'm so sorry," she said.

"About what?" Jared asked, surprised again.

"You trusted her, wanted to give her everything but she betrayed you."

"Who?"

"Andrea."

"What are you talking about?" he demanded. "What has my mother been saying?"

"Nothing. You loved Andrea a great deal, didn't you? She was the One, you thought."

"Stop it!" Jared said, his voice rising in anger. "You've no right to talk about these things."

Claire went on anyway. "You gave her money." Another image came. "And she gave it to someone else."

Shock and hurt flared in Jared's expression. "How could you know? I never told anyone about that."

"She told you she loved you but all the time she was with someone else. They planned it together and tricked you." More images flashed into her mind. "She took jewellery." Claire's eyes narrowed as she focussed on what she saw. "But she stole much more. Money, a lot of money... and she cheated you out of some property."

"Stop it!"

But Claire couldn't. "She kept the ring, didn't she, the white gold emerald engagement ring. You engraved it with the words "Forever Together." She had green eyes and red hair; you loved her hair."

"Stop it, I tell you," he shouted, leaping to his feet, making no attempt to hide his anger now. People turned to look.

"I'm sorry." Claire apologised, aware she had gone too far. "I shouldn't have said all that." She looked at Jared with compassion and reached out to touch his hand. "I'm *really* sorry."

"How could you know all that?" Jared demanded, sitting back down.

"You know how," she replied.

His gaze went to the necklace.

"I didn't know any of that stuff before I sat here with you," Claire continued. "I just saw it in my mind. Forgive me for distressing you."

Jared looked lost and confused now and her heart went out to him. His exterior shell had crumbled. "I'm sorry, I know my seeing things is hard for you to take but I *am* trying to help. I can see now why you would be suspicious of me when your mother gave me the necklace."

"They did plan it together," Jared said in a voice edged with bitterness. "Andrea never loved me, just saw a good opportunity. And I fell for it. That's what hurt the most. I thought we could have a life together but it was all just a lie."

Claire sensed how vulnerable he felt, despite the capable business image he presented to the world. He had reached out to another and been used. This had affected him deeply, along with never having had a father and witnessing his mother struggle to manage alone over the years. "You blame him."

Jared looked at her.

"You blame your father for not being there, don't you? And you blame yourself for letting your mother down, for losing so many of the business assets. But Andrea wasn't your fault. None of it was your fault."

"Please don't do this," he moaned. "It's like you're inside my head. I don't like it."

"Okay. I'll stop now," Claire said, feeling guilty. "Let's talk about something else. Bella's lovely, isn't she?"

Jared took his time before replying, focussing instead on folding his napkin into a precise concertina shape. "You're right. I *do* blame my father. I always suspected he hadn't died. I believed he didn't care about me or my mother, that he just left."

"You now know that's not true. Philip loved your mother very much. No, he *really* did. Not everyone is like Andrea. And your father didn't know about you. Laura only found out she was pregnant after he left so he didn't leave you or not care. Philip had no control over what happened to him, I'm certain of that."

"If what you sense is to be believed."

"I think it is."

"I have to admit you've read me very well," Jared said. "Maybe there *is* something in all the psychic stuff after all."

"I'm not lying." Claire looked him in the eye. "And I'm *not* trying to get anything from you. I didn't ask for any of this to happen to me."

Jared looked so tired and defeated Claire had the sudden impulse to put her arms around him and allow the warmth of her concern to heal his pain. At that moment, she became aware of the presence of Eleanora.

"Touch his hand," the spirit commanded and so Claire, cringing with embarrassment, laid her hand on his.

He looked at her in surprise but also with suspicion as his distrust of others surged to the fore.

"It's not me that wants to do it," Claire whispered. "It's Eleanora. She is with me. Just let me hold your hand."

Jared looked uncomfortable but allowed Claire to do so. Eleanora was supposed to be a great healer. He decided it would be interesting to see what happened.

Right away an outpouring of a loving energy flowed through Claire's hand and into his. She knew he felt it too for when he glanced at her an expression of openness and surrender passed across his features and he closed his eyes. Claire shut hers too and they sat together connected by the energy, both blessed and cherished by a spirit who had long since died yet still possessed the mysterious power to transmit love and healing. Claire realised then that love itself was a power that could transcend death and knew her belief that the outer world hid a deeper dimension was true. She felt humbled and honoured to be a part of something that linked her to that understanding.

The flow lasted for some minutes then faded until they both knew it had gone. Claire withdrew her hand and opened her eyes. Jared sat there looking at her with an unfathomable expression on his face. She noticed his cheeks were wet. "Thank you," he whispered. "I never knew I could feel like that, so, so... loved."

"It wasn't me. It was Eleanora."

"I know," he said. "I know. I felt her distinct from you and yet linked to you, to me. I felt we were all one thing in a way. Does that make any sense?" He ran his fingers through his hair. "No, it doesn't, does it? None of this makes sense. It's all crazy. Things like this don't happen in real life."

"But this *is* real life," Claire said. "I think what we felt was more real than most of what we see and experience in the world."

"I don't understand what just happened and yet I can't deny I felt..."

"Don't think too much about it. You need to be quiet and allow yourself to come to terms with how you feel."

"Mmm, I guess so. I like to understand things, though."

They both fell silent. Claire knew Jared needed time to adjust to what he had experienced. She allowed him to sit with it for a few minutes then said gently, "Don't let Andrea or what happened to your father and mother stop you loving again, Jared. Don't shut others out. Sure, you might get hurt but it's no life being isolated. Not everyone is out to use you."

"Is that you or Eleanora talking?"

"Me," Claire blushed and hesitated, "I think. I'm so sorry, I've no right to tell you what to do, I..."

"It's all right. I'm glad."

"What?"

"That it's you I'm talking to. I think I prefer to actually see the person I'm communicating with."

Claire laughed. "I know what you mean. It's all been pretty far out for me too, you know. I was just an ordinary girl a few weeks ago until I walked into your shop."

"Oh, I don't think ordinary is a word I would ever use to describe you," Jared said. He smiled at Claire with a look of genuine warmth in his expression and, in that moment, she became conscious of something she hadn't admitted to herself before: just how attractive he was, especially when he wasn't angry. She blushed and looked down. In some ways she found the amenable Jared more disconcerting than the disgruntled one. He had gorgeous dark brown eyes and soft lips. For an instant she found herself wondering what it would be like to kiss them, what his hair would be like to touch. She remembered the feel of his hand earlier. Now the barrier of distrust had dissolved, she became aware of him as a man.

Claire squirmed inside, desperate to find a way to get his attention off her. The waiter saved the situation by bringing their food and so she focussed on eating. "I hope we find something out at Castlerigg tomorrow," she said, after a while.

"Although I'm willing to admit there may be something in what you sense, I'm not going to rely on it," Jared said. "While we're in Keswick, I'd like to see if we can get access to what the police found, if anything, when my father disappeared."

"Bella said they found no trace of him."

"I know but it's worth asking. There might be something."

"That's a good idea. Maybe newspapers of the time would be worth a try, too. I wonder if we can find a reference to the attack that killed Eleanora, as well."

"I'm sure there would be one."

"Do you believe your father's alive?" Claire asked.

"I think it's possible."

"Eleanora says he is."

"But why can't *she* find him, though?"

"I don't know, there are obvious limitations to what she can do. I think she needs someone to work through. She said Philip is far away. That would make it very difficult for her."

"Mmm, it's all very intriguing. I hope we can find something out. I don't know much about my father, you know. It always upset my mother to talk about him. She only said he disappeared one day. As a child I used to dream up imaginary scenarios about where he'd gone, you know, secret agent, witness protection... taken by aliens, all quite ridiculous. In one way I'm glad you've come into our lives and brought it all into focus. I've always wanted to know something about my father so I could understand where I came from. Mum did her best but I always felt the absence of a male role model. My grandfather was the closest but, by the time I'd grown up enough to want a proper relationship, he'd become senile.

"What about you?" Jared asked. "I don't really know anything about you."

"There's not much to tell," Claire said, embarrassed by the ordinariness of her life back in London. "I worked, shopped and slept, basically. Boring, mundane."

"That can't have been all. No boyfriend?"

"No."

"Do you have any ambitions? What do you want out of life, Claire?"

"To tell you the truth, I don't know yet. Everything changed for me the day I got the necklace. I always felt trapped and bored by my life but somehow could never see a way out. I mean, I just worked in a supermarket. I didn't do well at school, couldn't wait to leave, in reality, so what else could I do?"

"What about your family?"

"I don't get on with them. They're... not like me."

"You say it all changed for you when you got the necklace?"

"Yes. The moment I put it on I felt as if life held more possibilities. I looked so different wearing it; I suppose I felt I could *be* different. I always dreamed of a better life but had no idea how to even start achieving it. When I put the necklace on, I felt important. I, I don't know, this is silly."

"No, it's not, go on."

"Well, the necklace was so special, a mere shop assistant wouldn't normally own it. I began to think that maybe I *could* change my life somehow, make it match the necklace. It didn't seem so hopeless anymore."

"And what sort of life would you want?"

"I don't know yet but I *do* know it won't be in London. I adore it here in the Lake District. When this is all over with you and Laura, I want to come back. I don't know how I'll do it but I will. There are supermarkets here to work in but I want to maybe train for something. I have no idea what, though."

"Yes, I can see you living here," Jared said. "The surroundings suit you."

"I feel at home somehow. As if I've been here before although I haven't. My experiences with the necklace have changed me, made me realise there's so much more to life than we know, more to *us*. It's shown me we have a depth I hadn't dreamed possible. I used to think we just died and that was it but now I know it's not. It scares me, but I also find it exciting, don't you?"

"I'm not sure. It's all new to me. I don't know what to believe anymore."

"You felt something when Eleanora came through, I know you did. What was that? Don't you want to know?"

Claire could tell by the look in Jared's eyes she had got through, touched some part of him that longed for the kind of loving connection they had experienced with Eleanora. She also knew that, hurt by Andrea, he had blocked off that part.

"When I got the necklace, your mum said something to me. She said, 'It will connect you to the Source of Love.' I didn't know what she meant but now, after wearing it for some time and linking to Eleanora, I do. It's something inside us that is not dependent upon any other person."

Jared looked at the young woman in front of him. Something about her gave truth to her words. She looked peaceful, glowing. He stared into her eyes and found no artifice there. He had misjudged her.

"I'm sorry," he said. "I've doubted you all the way along. I mean, I still find it all far-fetched to some extent, but I don't think you're deliberately trying to trick me, or my mother, anymore. I'm so sorry."

"Thank you, that means a lot." Claire smiled. A feeling of warmth flowed between them for a moment but, all of a sudden, the door of the restaurant banged. A draught of cool air blew through the room and she turned to see a grey cloud surrounding the man who just entered. As she stared, it felt as if all the energy in her body were draining away.

"What is it?" Jared asked and turned to look in the direction of her gaze.

Claire shuddered. "There's something unpleasant about that man over there."

Jared looked. The man, dressed in a suit, looked ordinary to him. He wasn't smiling but not many people did.

"I don't think he's very nice," she whispered. Claire noticed a shadow near the man. "He has a spirit with him," she said, "a man. I think he's affecting him in some way." She looked again. "They're reinforcing each other's negativity." She shivered and rubbed her arms.

"Are you all right?"

"I feel cold. I see quite a few people like that when I wear the necklace." The man walked into another section of the restaurant but Claire continued to look troubled. "There's so much I don't understand."

She felt the presence of Eleanora. "People like that have lost contact with their deeper selves. It makes them vulnerable to the influence of others."

"Are you *sure* you're all right, Claire?" Jared looked worried.

"What I sense connected to your father feels heavy and dark, disconnected from hope. I'm afraid of what we'll discover tomorrow,

Jared. Part of me wants to know what happened but another part wants to leave it alone. I hope I'm strong enough to handle it if I pick up something awful."

"I'm sure you'll be fine. If you're ever unsure about anything at any time just stop, okay? I want to know what happened but it's not worth anyone getting upset."

"But I *have* to do this, Jared. Your father's alive somewhere and may need help. I can't walk away from that. I've got to try."

Jared nodded. "All right but we'll do it together. I won't allow any harm to come to you."

Claire looked at him. "Thank you. That means a lot to me." Jared's concern touched her. This was a side of him she hadn't seen before. It made everything better. Much better. Her spirits lifted. "Let's go."

As they climbed the hill back to the hotel, they chatted for a short while about the Lake District. Claire felt relaxed in Jared's company now, knowing he no longer resented her. They passed Jared's door first. "Thank you for dinner," she said.

"No, thank *you*. I'm glad we talked. Don't worry about tomorrow. It'll be fine."

"Thanks." Claire made her way up the extra flights of stairs to her attic bedroom. Later, as she lay in bed drifting off to sleep, she kept thinking about Jared, remembering the concern in his eyes. Something had happened between them during the evening. A connection of some kind had been forged. She had no idea where it would lead but knew that, if the chance came, she wanted to find out.

Chapter 11

CLAIRE DIDN'T SLEEP WELL. SHE dreamed she stood alone at dawn on the hilltop at Castlerigg surrounded by the stones. Dark clouds gathered in the sky overhead and an eagle circled. A strong wind whipped her clothes tight against her body and she became aware someone stood behind her.

She woke with a feeling of foreboding. Her alarm clock said six thirty-five.

Too tense to sleep again, she dressed in warm clothing and left the hotel. She walked down to the lake, which was just coming into view in the greyness of dawn, and sat on a seat overlooking the water. The scene couldn't be more different than her dream and, as the sun rose and the sky lightened to blue, her spirits lifted. A breeze blew in across the lake and, although cold, she welcomed its gentle touch on her skin. It made her feel alive, more alive and in touch with the present than she had ever felt in her life before.

She caressed the necklace, which hung around her neck. As she did so, she sensed Eleanora. "Stay alert today," the spirit whispered. "Don't be afraid. I will be with you. Remember who you are and no harm can come to you. It is your strength."

The words linked Claire back to what she experienced at Eleanora's grave, the clarity and love she felt deep inside.

"Yes, my dear one, the more you centre in this, the stronger and more peaceful you will become. If you wish, envision a white light of protection surrounding you and your aura."

The road wound through meadows and dark forests, past calm stretches of blue-grey water and through tiny hamlets. They climbed high over passes between barren peaks and from there they caught glimpses of valleys nestling below. It was the most breathtaking scenery Claire had ever seen and yet a feeling of dread grew with every mile closer to their destination. Bella laughed and chattered in the back seat but Claire felt disconnected from her. The good feelings she felt at the lake faded and she questioned her ability to handle what she might find at the stones. She touched the necklace, hoping to draw strength from it.

Jared glanced round and smiled. Although he said nothing, she found reassurance in his look. At least she now had him on her side. Bella watched them with a knowing smile.

When they reached Keswick, they headed along the narrow road leading to Castlerigg. Thank God the weather was good, Claire thought, as Jared drew to a halt beside the field where the stones stood. If the sky had been dark and foreboding like her dream she would have turned tail and run. The anxiety inside her rose yet another notch. She felt tired and heavy as she pulled herself out of the car and stood up.

Feeling vulnerable and overwhelmed by the immensity of the space all around her, Claire forced herself to follow the others as they walked across an area of flat ground towards the circle. For once she felt unmoved by the beautiful views of the surrounding peaks. A few sheep grazed nearby. She moved closer and closer to the circle, feeling more reluctant with every step. The stones were of an irregular shape, some small, some larger, positioned a short distance apart.

Reaching the monument, she stopped and stood still. The others decided to leave Claire alone so she could concentrate but they stayed close by so they could keep a check on her.

Breathing slowly and fully in an attempt to counteract her nervousness, Claire opened out the field of her awareness to encompass the area.

She saw the grass, the sheep, the nearby stones, then the sky and surrounding hills. She felt cold in the breeze and a slight hunger. She heard a sheep bleat but, other than those things, felt nothing.

No images, no sensations, no voice of Eleanora even.

Claire called her name hoping it would elicit some response but heard only silence. She stood for a while but still nothing happened so she walked into the centre of the circle and slowly turned to view the whole area.

Nothing.

Of all the things Claire had been expecting from this moment, nothing at all had not been one of them. Had she lost her psychic ability or perhaps her connection to Eleanora? Bella and Jared came over. "You look upset," Jared said.

"I'm sorry, I don't know why but I can't pick anything up. I feel so bad. I know your mother is desperate for an answer. Eleanora led me to believe something would happen here, that I would sense some sort of clue but," she shrugged her shoulders. "I can't get anything at all!"

Jared touched her on the arm. "Don't worry."

At least he wasn't giving her a hard time and for that Claire was grateful.

They walked around the whole area for about an hour until, feeling like the fake Jared had accused her of being, Claire declared, "We might as well go. I don't think anything's going to happen." She couldn't understand it. Here of all places, she should be able to pick something up. This was where Laura last saw Philip.

The others were walking ahead back to the car when Claire noticed the speck wheeling around and around in the sky and, to her horror, realised it was an eagle. An eagle had appeared to Laura and Philip!

It came nearer until it flew in a tight circle above her head, just like in her dream. Her neck ached from staring up but she could not look away. She felt dizzy and reached out a hand to the nearest stone for support. The moment she touched the cold surface, everything went black!

One moment Claire stood staring up, the next she dropped and slumped against the stone. Bella and Jared rushed back to find her staring up and so still for one dreadful moment Jared thought she'd died. Bella touched Claire's neck and found a pulse. "She's okay, just in a trance."

"What should we do?" Jared asked.

Bella considered. "I don't know. I guess wait and see, at least for a while."

"Are you sure she's all right?"

"No, not really but I don't think she's ill; this is some sort of reaction. Remember the graveyard. She came out of it."

"Yes, but this place is different. This is where my father disappeared. Perhaps the stress of worrying about it has got to her."

Bella looked down. "No, I don't think so. I suggest we give her half an hour. If she's not out of it by then we'll call an ambulance."

Jared nodded. He stared at Claire's face and felt her absence. He had grown to enjoy her enthusiastic appreciation of their surroundings, the gentleness in her voice. He had felt vulnerable when Claire first started telling him what she sensed about his life but, after a while, her caring compassion had eased his awkwardness. He knew now she wasn't in it for money. She *did* care about his mother. Claire had come to Castlerigg to do this even though it frightened her. If anything bad came of it, he would never forgive himself.

Jared and Bella sat beside Claire and waited, grateful they had the place to themselves. Neither wanted to explain what they were doing to inquisitive strangers.

Claire sat immobile, swamped in ink black darkness but, after a while, became aware of a pinpoint of light far away. It grew in her consciousness as she watched.

It flared into brilliance then winked out, plunging her back into darkness. She felt numb and couldn't feel her body. Where *was* she? She couldn't remember. *Who* was she? Somehow all the details of her life had vanished into this void and yet she still felt herself to *be* there. Another light grew, this time an orange glow tinged with dark blue. It grew stronger and she found herself sitting by a standing stone. The whole sky above lightened now and she saw the shining edge of the sun burning on the top of a nearby hill. She watched it as it lifted higher until it broke free from the land.

She scrambled to her feet and, in the light of this dawn, stood still. A cold wind blew. She couldn't remember why she had come to this place. She turned around and out of the lightening sky saw the approach of the eagle and remembered. Jared and Bella, where were they? She looked across to where they had parked the car but saw no sign of it or the road. The sheep had gone too. Reaching up to her throat, she found the necklace and held onto it, hoping Eleanora would come and explain this but she remained absent.

Something made Claire turn around and a short distance away she saw a bearded man aged about forty with long greying hair writhing in the wind. He wore brown robes and crude leather sandals on his feet. He stared ahead, his face devoid of expression, as if in trance. She sensed a coldness about him and it sent a chill through her body. Behind him she saw other men all dressed in the same way walking into the circle of stones. None of them appeared able to see her. They reached the centre and stopped. The first man turned and stood facing Claire.

Their clothing told her it wasn't the present day and knew she was somehow seeing back through time. She wondered how it could have happened then realised she had touched a stone. It had been placed there in the distant past by an ancient people, perhaps by those she now saw. They began to chant and looked at the leader. Still in a trance, his eyes turned heavenward.

The eagle circled. Somehow in that moment, Claire felt herself lifted up into the sky and became one with the great bird with her mind. The countryside stretched beneath her and the infinity of space opened up above. She flew through the air, leaving all human concerns behind. She felt complete freedom in the flight of the eagle but then caught a sense of the bearded man in brown robes and realised that, somehow, he too had become linked to the bird. The moment this thought came, she regained consciousness of her body and realised the man was staring right at her as if aware of her presence!

Claire tried not to panic and remained motionless. Nothing happened. The man looked for a few moments then turned and walked away followed by the others. The thought came that this was neither her time nor place. She had no more business here.

She touched the necklace and felt strengthened so shut her eyes and brought the face of Philip into her mind, hoping his image would link her to what she wanted to find out at Castlerigg. She imagined him standing in the stones with the eagle circling in the sky. She had trouble at first but remembered the photo she found in the necklace box, the one of his face shining with love. She concentrated on the image and, after a while, felt a change in the atmosphere around her.

Claire opened her eyes and saw the men in robes had vanished. A single figure stood in the centre of the stones. Philip. He stared up at the eagle circling in the sky and she sensed his terror as he watched its approach. Why did he fear the bird so much? An image of an eagle perched on a gloved hand being fed raw meat came into her mind. Its beak tore into the flesh and she recoiled. A vegetarian, the sight turned her stomach. She sensed Philip also felt this way but knew he also feared the eagle for some other more terrifying reason she could not tap into.

Philip's fear grew and Claire saw a grim-faced man of middle age who wore a tailored black suit standing behind him. He had brown hair and a full beard. Philip turned and drooped as if he had no strength left in his body, almost cowering. Claire wanted to run to him, lift him up and say, "No, you can be strong," but knew she was witnessing the past and could take no active role in the scene.

More men ran up. Their mouths moved but she heard no sound. Philip could for he put his hands over his ears. The man in the dark suit drew closer and stared at Philip who lifted his head and returned his gaze as if hypnotised. The two men stood connected in this way for about a minute then the man vanished leaving Philip alone. After a few moments, he walked away from the stones and Eleanora's voice cried, "He has him, he has him!"

"What do you mean?"

"He controls his body."

"Who is 'he'? You know, Eleanora, don't you?"

"William," she paused, "my husband." Eleanora fell silent then continued in a voice heavy with sorrow, "My murderer!"

The scene went black and Claire became aware of sitting on the ground. She felt icy cold and could hear voices whispering nearby. She opened her eyes and Jared said, "Thank God. Are you okay?"

"Yes, I think so." Shaken by what she had witnessed, Claire needed help from Jared to stand. She shivered, knowing she had seen the possession of Philip by another person.

"What happened," Bella asked, "did you see anything?"

"Just give me a moment," Claire said. "I think I need to go over there." While the image remained fresh in her mind, she wanted to be where Philip stood in the hope it might connect her to something which would tell her where he had gone.

Claire went to the centre of the circle and Eleanora came in. "Stand firm in your power," she commanded. Strengthened by the presence of the spirit, Claire stood still and opened up her consciousness to embrace the area.

"He walked away from here," Claire whispered as Bella came to stand beside her. "I can see him walking but not back down into Keswick. He went that way," she said, pointing to a valley in the other direction. "Philip, Philip," she whispered, "where did you go? Where did he take you? *Why* did he take you?" She fell silent waiting for some clue. "Wait, I see a house, a large house in the distance." She shuddered. "There's ... eagles... stone eagles... on pillars, two pillars by a gate at the start of a winding driveway. I see Philip standing near the building now. I don't like this place."

A rush of coldness ran through Claire's body and she sensed sadness from Eleanora.

"So, he took him there," the spirit said.

Everything went black and Claire swayed but Jared came over to stop her falling. She welcomed the feel of his arm around her and leant against him for a moment, wanting to let go, lay her head against his chest and pretend dark images did not fill her mind. She could still see Philip's face. All trace of the loving, generous spirit that so animated his photographs had gone, replaced by an empty stare. She shuddered again, sensing the man, William, clinging to Philip, seeking to gain power and control over his body.

Jared, sensing Claire's distress, held her tighter and she relaxed against him, needing his human strength to ground her, to bring her back to the moment. It took her a while until she regained her composure. The connection to Eleanora vanished and the hillside returned to normal. Claire became aware again of the sky and grass and the circle of stones.

She straightened and moved away. "Thank you," she murmured and, for a moment, their eyes locked. Claire sensed his sympathy for her and felt warmed by it. She held on to it for support. The visions she received were hard to handle. No doubt remained in her mind, Philip had been possessed, made to turn aside from his whole life and those he loved to do the will of another!

"Let's go now," Claire said so they returned to the car. On the way down the hillside and into Keswick, she filled the other two in on what she had witnessed.

They found an attractive old stone house which had been made into a restaurant and ordered some lunch. Jared leant back in his seat and said, "Well, what's next?"

"We find the house where Philip went," Claire said. "Maybe I can pick up his trail from there."

"But how? The house could be anywhere."

"We know who is possessing Philip, Eleanora's husband, William, William Waterford," Claire said. "I'm wondering if the house could have been connected to him in life. If so, we can trace it, I'm sure. We have the eagles on the pillars to help identify it. I would know that gate if I saw it. The baptism entry for Charles Waterford at the church listed him as living in a Waterford Hall. That could be the place."

Their lunch arrived so they focussed on eating, Claire grateful to take a break. "You look pale," Jared said.

"I'm exhausted." Claire admitted. Her head ached as well, despite having taken aspirin.

"I want to go to the police station." Jared said as they left the restaurant. "The cashier told me where it was. Maybe you should rest while I see if I can get anything from them."

"Yes, I think I will."

Jared drove them to the police station and parked. Claire lay on the back seat of the car while Jared and Bella went inside.

Grateful for the peace and quiet, Claire closed her eyes. She soon fell into a half sleep and found herself standing between the two pillars on which perched the stone eagles, their wings outstretched. She walked through and along a long gravel road winding through a park filled with trees. Round a bend she saw the house, a large elaborate building constructed in the gothic style. Constructed of grey stone, it had pointed arched windows and a steep pitched roof with several turrets reaching to the sky. Grimacing gargoyles looked out from under the eaves. A wide staircase led up from the garden to an imposing porch with pillars on either side. The setting sun flamed orange in the windows giving the house the appearance of being on fire.

Claire's eyes flew open and she instinctively touched the necklace. As she did so, she sensed the presence of Eleanora and felt a gentle pressure as if a hand lay upon her brow. The headache lifted as if it had never been.

"Thank you," Claire whispered.

"Waterford Hall *is* the place you saw," Eleanora said.

Claire heard the car doors open and sat up.

"How're you feeling?" Jared asked.

"Much better, thanks. What did you find out?"

"It was like getting blood out of a stone but eventually we spoke to this one guy who looked up their records. A search was made of the Castlerigg area but no trace of Philip was ever found. The hospitals were checked, especially those taking care of mental cases as they thought it most likely he suffered some sort of breakdown. Mum told them he'd been upset, you see, and because no body was ever found, they didn't have any cause to believe foul play had taken place. It was assumed he either had a nervous breakdown or simply chose to disappear. People do this all the time, just up and go. Something snaps and that's it, they leave everything behind."

"What about the rest of the country?"

"They didn't circulate Philip's description beyond the Lake District. According to the man we talked to, they didn't do so in the seventies when this happened, unless they had a good reason. Computers hadn't come in much then. The Internet didn't exist so it remained a localised case. Things would be very different now. I don't think they took it seriously, if you ask me."

"That doesn't really help us much, then."

"No." Jared sighed. "Let's go get a coffee and work out what to do next."

They found a café by the side of a river. Jared opened the laptop he had brought with him. "I'll see if I can find out where Waterford Hall is." Claire looked out of a nearby open window and watched the water pour over the rocks. She found the sound of it soothing and it lulled her into a trance. She closed her eyes and the sound of the water increased to a thunderous roar and she had an impression of standing by cascading water in a forested area. She saw high peaks off to one side and felt hot all of a sudden.

"Claire?"

"What?"

"Are you okay?"

"Yes, I'm fine."

Jared scrutinised Claire. Her face looked flushed. She worried him. All this psychic stuff took it out of her. He didn't want her harmed and, in that moment, realised he actually cared what happened to this young woman who he used to think was only out for what she could get. "I think I've found the house. I looked up the name William Waterford and found a few small references. He seems to have been quite a guy in his time, a hot shot tycoon of his era, around the early nineteen hundreds. He owned several factories here in the North but went bankrupt. He died at age forty-six in 1924, hanged for the murder of his wife, Eleanora Waterford.

"Poor Eleanora." Claire felt a deep sense of compassion for her. What suffering she must have gone through in life.

"Anyway, I've found it on a map. It's not that far from Bowness."

"Let's go there now," Bella said. "This is so exciting. To think my brother is alive and we know where he went after he left Castlerigg. I can't tell you how this makes me feel. When are we going to tell Laura?"

"I'm not sure," Claire replied. "I don't want to give her false hope. What if I can't find him? And we don't know what state he's going to be in. Will he still be possessed by this William? If he is, how will she feel?"

"But maybe we can help him break free," Bella said, excited.

"I wouldn't know how." The thought scared Claire. She had no experience of such things.

"You're connected to Eleanora. She will guide you, I'm sure. Or we can find someone who maybe *does* know."

"I guess so." Claire replied, still unsure but at the same time knew she had to tread the path she was following. She wouldn't be able to live with herself if she turned her back on helping Philip and his family. "Okay," she said. "Let's go to Waterford Hall."

Claire took no pleasure in the sunlit countryside they drove through, even when they had to stop for a mother sheep and her two young lambs to get out of the way. Jared kept glancing at Claire in the rear-view mirror. She sat rigid, her face a mask of fear, and he became more and more concerned. Could she cope with what they found?

They passed through a small village then Bella shouted, "Look, there!" Jared went past but backed up and came to a halt beside an ornate wrought iron gate. Claire recognised the two stone pillars on which eagles perched with outstretched wings. Jared got out and, finding the gate unlocked, opened it. As he drove through, she asked,

"What are we going to say to the people here? How will we explain what we want?"

"Don't worry," Jared said. "Let me do the talking. I'll think of something." He smiled at Claire who, lifted by his expression, smiled back. She liked this Jared, she thought, the one who appeared to care. She liked him more than she wanted to admit. For now, though, the thought of what she might find out overshadowed her growing attraction to Jared and she turned to look out of the window to watch their approach to the house.

They drove through the wooded parkland and up the incline Claire remembered from her vision, rounded a bend and came to a halt in front of the house. They all got out of the car and approached the building. Claire stared up. "Oh my God!"

Although the stone walls remained intact, the interior of the house had been burnt out.

"I wonder what happened here?" Bella mused.

Claire walked up the stone steps leading to the main entrance. Jared called out, "I don't think you should go in there, it may not be safe," but she ignored him and passed through the main entrance and into the gutted building. The floor, built of flagstones, looked sound but was littered with debris. Looking up, she saw the roof had gone. Jared moved to follow Claire but Bella stayed him with a hand on his arm.

"She'll be okay. Just wait. I think we should give her some space." They both watched as she moved through the hall, gazing all around, a look of awe and wonder on her face.

To Claire's astonishment, she walked, not into a burned-out shell, but a richly decorated house. Panels of dark wood lined the walls and thick red carpets lay on the floors. She stared into one room and saw a gleaming black grand piano. Sunlight streamed through the bay window. She went over and stared out, sighing at the sight of the lovely garden beyond. A manicured lawn swept down to a small lake surrounded by groups of trees. Near the water stood a round, white painted wooden pavilion. Swathes of bluebells dusted the grass with an intensity of colour matching the sky.

She heard the sound of music and turned to see a beautiful woman with dark hair swept up in an elaborate style on her head. She wore a long white dress and sat at the piano playing a lilting melody with long graceful fingers.

Eleanora.

"Music was one of my saviours," a quiet voice explained in Claire's mind. "It lifted me from the darkness surrounding me." Eleanora vanished and so did the opulent interior.

The blackened stone walls and rubble strewn floor filled Claire with a feeling of profound sadness. An unhappy house, she sensed, moving along a corridor into a large open space, once a ballroom. A broken chandelier lay dirty and wrecked on the floor. She walked to the centre of the room then spun around as she heard an orchestra playing. The sound built and, for a few moments, Claire saw couples dancing around her. The women were dressed in long gowns with jewels sparkling at their throats, the men, in close cut dark suits with long tails. Eleanora stood watching from the back of the room in an elegant full-length navy-blue dress. Although young and lovely, the sorrow in her eyes made her seem older than her actual years. Silence fell and the scene faded.

Claire walked back to the front hall. Something made her look up at the blacked stone steps once leading to the upper levels of the house. As she did so, she saw Eleanora coming down the stairs, this time dressed in a simple long brown skirt and coat with a plain black hat on her head.

"Where do you think you're going?" a harsh voice demanded from behind Claire. Startled, she turned and saw a tall thickset man with light brown hair swept back from his face and a full beard. He was dressed in a dark suit with a vivid red waistcoat stretched over his protruding stomach. She recognised him as the figure with Philip at the ring of stones, William.

"To the hospital."

"Damn you, woman. I'll have no wife of mine dirtying her hands with riff raff. What will people think?"

"They will think that it is fitting we all pull together at this time, even people like us, when so many are injured and dying. You haven't seen them, William. This war is a terrible thing. Some of the men have gone through the most dreadful suffering. They need as many people to nurse them as they can get."

An older man, dressed in a formal black suit, perhaps a butler, came into the hall. "The car is ready, Madam."

"Thank you, Atrell. I will be right out. I'm sorry, William," Eleanora said, turning to her husband. "I don't care what you say, I'm going. Open the door please, Atrell."

The butler moved forward and did as Eleanora asked. She swept out and he closed the door, a slight smile playing about his lips. William's face darkened and he gripped both hands into tight fists then strode away down a corridor into a room, slamming the door behind him.

It must be some time during the First World War, Claire thought, judging by what she had just seen and the style of the clothing. The scene evaporated and she felt a compulsion to walk through a doorway beside the staircase. It led down a corridor and down some stone stairs to what had once been a kitchen for it contained a cracked, stained sink and a large black iron stove covered with dust. Claire stood still and became aware.

The smell of meat roasting came into her nostrils and she heard the sound of a metal lid being placed on a saucepan. Two women tending pans on the stove became visible, then three other women and the butler, Atrell, sitting around a large wooden table. All the women were dressed in black dresses with white aprons. Glancing out of a window, Claire saw it was night.

A high-pitched scream echoed down the corridor and the servants froze.

Everyone turned anxious faces in the direction it had come. A young woman stood but the butler laid a hand on her arm to stay her. "You cannot interfere," he said.

"But..."

Mr Waterford has been drinking heavily today. Don't worry, Rachel. You're new here. This has been going on for years. Madam has her ways of dealing with him. It is not easy for her but she will be all right."

Rachel sank back down. "Poor Madam."

"Mrs Waterford is very special lady. She has a way about her. Waterford's a monster. He doesn't deserve her."

The scene faded and Claire found herself back in the present. Oppressed by the filth in the room, she hurried back to the hall. She cast her awareness around the building and felt the sadness and pain etched into the substance of the walls. The feeling of it grew and she felt dizzy. She leant back on a stone pillar and put her hands over her face. Jared rushed over. "Are you all right?"

"Yes," she whispered, "but I can sense echoes of the past. So much suffering." Claire touched the amethyst necklace. She took a deep breath and centred herself within as Eleanora had encouraged her to do, detaching from the sadness and fear that swirled through her awareness. In a few moments, she found herself feeling stronger. She had to focus, she told herself, not get caught up in what she sensed otherwise she would be unable to discover what happened to Philip, the reason they had come.

Claire heard the sound of the piano playing again and moved towards the sitting room. "I'm okay," she said to Jared. "You wait here. I need to be alone to concentrate better." She walked into the room where she saw Eleanora before and saw her moving her fingers over the piano keys, a rapturous look on her face. All of a sudden, an angry voice broke through the music. William strode into the room followed by the butler Claire had seen before.

"Hurry up and give me my coat, Atrell, you fool. We're late." The butler helped William into a dark overcoat. "Where's that footman, Peters? I asked him to get my case from the study. He's bloody useless, too."

Claire recoiled at the dark anger emanating from William.

A young man entered the room. William glared at the terrified looking servant who handed him a leather case. "And where is Charles? His nanny was supposed to bring him down."

"Oh, don't take him to the factory, William," Eleanora moaned. "He's only six. He needs to be at home with me."

"He's a Waterford and will be carrying on the business. He needs to start young. You don't know what you're talking about, woman." He glared at Eleanora with an expression full of contempt.

His face had a deadness about it, which sent a chill through Claire's heart. What had happened to this man to make him so foul?

A young woman dressed in a long grey dress and white apron came in accompanied by a golden-haired boy Claire recognised as the child from the church, although maybe younger. "Mother!" he cried and ran to Eleanora who put her arms around him. "Do I have to go?"

"Please don't take him today, William," Eleanora pleaded. "Let him stay."

"Charles, come here. We are leaving." At the harshness of William's tone, the boy clung tighter to his mother.

"I've had enough of this nonsense," William thundered and strode over. He pulled the boy's arm so he had no choice but to go with him. The agony on Eleanora's face broke Claire's heart.

As he left the room, Charles turned and smiled. "Don't worry, Mother," he said and smiled. "It will be all right." William pulled the boy into the hall, then they left the house. The sound of a car driving away came from outside.

Eleanora put her head down on her arms and collapsed onto the piano keys, the dissonant sound echoing the chaos of her feelings. She remained that way for a few moments but then raised her head and shut her eyes, taking several deep breaths. The tension melted away from Eleanora's features replaced by a look of great serenity.

Claire felt a feeling of peace move through her own body as she watched, fascinated.

Eleanora sat for a few minutes then rose and tugged on the bell pull, a long strip of embroidered fabric hanging down beside the fireplace. When the butler appeared in response to her call, she said, "Prepare a car for me, Atrell, please, and ask Emily to bring me my blue coat."

"At once, Madam."

When the maid brought the coat, Eleanora strode out of house and waited on the gravel drive.

Claire watched as what to her appeared to be a vintage car with gleaming maroon paintwork drew up.

A driver stepped out and opened a door for Eleanora. "I want to go to the factory," she ordered.

The scene shifted and Claire found herself watching Eleanora walk through a huge building filled with machines attended by weary looking workers, most of whom were women, the men having been called away to war. The wore rough and dirty work clothing. Grime caked the windows and a terrible noise filled the air as people laboured to manufacture what, to Claire, looked to be metal components of various types. She felt Eleanora's indignation at what she saw.

A middle-aged man approached, thinning grey hair slicked across his head. "Good morning, Mrs Waterford. Allow me to conduct you to your husband's office."

"No, Mr Pearce, I wish to stay here. I would like to speak to these good people." She waved her hand to encompass the factory. Pearce, looking appalled, hurried off.

Eleanora stopped by a young woman wearing a dirty cardigan covered with holes over a stained wool skirt. One of her arms hung limp by her side. Eleanora touched her on the shoulder. "Does it pain you very much?" She had to shout to make herself heard above the racket of the nearby machines. The woman nodded.

"May I touch it?"

The worker stared at her with confusion but the expression in Eleanora's eyes reassured her and so the woman nodded. Eleanora laid her hand gently upon the injured arm and began a firm massage. She then manipulated the arm up and down and twisted it a little. "Practise moving it like this every day and it will get stronger," she said. The woman flexed her arm and smiled.

Eleanora straightened up and looked around. A circle of grimy faces looked at her.

A woman came forward, her face so lined she looked far older than her forty years. "Madam, my leg is bad, could you look at it?"

"Sit there," Eleanora pointed to a low stool. Being as discreet as possible, she lifted the woman's skirt, gasping at the enormous ulcer marring the woman's leg. Eleanora lay her hand on the woman's skin and the tension in the worker's face relaxed as her pain eased.

Eleanora continued to move through the factory, seeking out all those suffering in some way but, after about an hour, the figure of William appeared, his face thunderous, although he kept his voice controlled. "Eleanora!" He gripped her arm so tight she winced. "Come with me to my office, if you please. I wish to speak to you." He kept hold as he propelled her between the lines of machines and up a metal staircase to an office.

"Get out!" he shouted to a scared looking clerk then turned to face Eleanora. "Did you not understand when I forbade you to come here again?" he roared. "This is no place for you. How dare you come and make a fool of me by consorting with my workers."

"I came because someone has to do something. How can you force these poor people to work in these conditions?"

"Don't be ridiculous. They're grateful for it, I can tell you. What would they do without the work? They'd be starving or dead. You're as guilty as me of using these people," he sneered. "Where would you be without your big house, all your fine furniture and fancy hats? This," he waved his arm to encompass the factory around them, "is what gives them to you."

Eleanora weakened at his words knowing he was right. How they obtained their wealth weighed heavy upon her.

Sensing he had scored some kind of victory, William smiled. "You can't refute it, can you?"

"No, William, I can't," Eleanora returned, her eyes full of sorrow, "but I can still wish it were otherwise. The women should be home with their children. They need their mothers. Like Charles," Eleanora said pointedly. "Where is he, anyway?"

"He is down in the yards. I sent him with Pearce to learn about the packing."

"Please look after him," she pleaded. "He does not belong here. Not until he's older. Can you not give him his childhood?"

"I accompanied my father. He taught me everything I needed to know. Charles has to learn about the business world."

A tear trickled down Eleanora's cheek. She knew only too well about the business world. She had to be the hostess of dinner parties for William's obnoxious associates: those who also owned factories and those others she dare not contemplate what their business was. She hated Charles being in their company, picking up their uncaring attitudes. "William, what have you become?" she whispered.

He stared at her, a mixture of emotions moving across his face. Something about her expression permeated his consciousness and his face softened but, remembering what she'd done to him, bitterness gained supremacy. "How dare you presume to judge me!"

Eleanora could no longer meet his eyes and sagged, defeated. "Call the car for me, William? I need to go. Can I take Charles with me?"

"No, I will bring him later."

"Please, William. Let him have at least today with me away from here."

"NO!"

Eleanora sank onto a chair, too drained to fight William any longer but hating him in that moment.

The scene faded and Claire became aware of standing in the gutted building once again. A sudden gust of wind ruffled her hair and blew away the shadows of the past. She walked to a room towards the back of the house. A large tree outside the window blocked the light giving the room a depressing feel. As Claire stared around, her attention became drawn to the fireplace and a fire ignited in her mind. She stared into the flames then became aware of people behind her. She spun around and saw about ten men of a variety of ages standing around a table. On it were two candles and a box with unusual patterns on its surface. A large book also lay there.

William, standing off by the window, looked perplexed. "Do you sense anything, Barrett?" Next to him, stood a tall man in his late thirties with straight black hair and a short well-trimmed beard. He scanned the room, his brow furrowed in concentration. "Hmm, you're right. I think we're being watched."

Barrett's dark piercing eyes paused where Claire stood and she gasped in shock. Could he somehow sense her? She felt naked and exposed. These men scared her. She tried to block the scene out but it kept on playing. Barrett continued to stare in her direction

He can see me! Claire panicked. She had to get out of here right now! She tried to move but couldn't. Held in thrall by the vision of the past, she had disconnected from her body. In horror, she saw the man called Barrett walk towards her. "Eleanora!" she screamed out loud. "Eleanora, please help me!"

Chapter 12

Helpless, Claire stared at Barrett as he advanced, his eyes narrowed in concentration, He moved closer and closer but then came the sound of knocking.

Barrett's attention turned to the door. William opened it and Claire saw Eleanora standing in a beautiful yellow gown. She looked upset. "What do you want?" William demanded. "I thought I told you not to disturb me."

"I know, I'm sorry, I just..." she stared at Barrett with fear filled eyes. "I'm sorry. I don't know. I thought something was wrong."

"Everything's fine." William snapped. "I'll speak to you later."

The moment Barrett's focus went to Eleanora, Claire's inertia lifted and she found the momentum to move her body. The past evaporated and her attention came back to the burned-out house in the present. What the hell happened? Her heart pounded in her chest and she felt sick. She took several shaky breaths to calm herself but the face of Barrett remained etched in her mind. She shivered. Who *was* that?

"The Lost One!" Eleanora whispered.

Hearing the sound of someone behind her, Claire spun round, fearful it would be Barrett but found herself staring at Jared. He looked worried.

"Are you okay, Claire? You cried out."

"I just had the most disturbing vision of the past," she replied and recounted what had happened. "Eleanora called this Barrett 'the Lost One.' Claire shivered. What does *that* mean? I felt Barrett could actually *see* me Jared. Thank God Eleanora came in. I wonder if she sensed me in some way. Perhaps my link to her somehow reached her in the past."

"Oh, I expect her coming in was just coincidence."

"Maybe but I'm not so sure. I'm wondering if those men I saw with William were the others I saw around Philip at Castlerigg. William did not act alone. It's so confusing. And, to be honest, very, very frightening."

"Come here," Jared said. He pulled her to him and held her for a moment. Claire relaxed against him, grateful for the physical touch of normal reality. "It's going to be all right," he said with tenderness. Jared wished he could stop all this psychic stuff. He wasn't sure it was a good thing, it distressed Claire. He did not want her to suffer to find his father. "Why don't you take a break," he suggested. "Take off the necklace."

"No, no, it's all right. I'm fine now." Claire moved back. "Honestly. Thank you. I'm going to walk around here some more. I still don't have any sense of Philip and that's what we came for."

"Okay but call if you need me. I won't be far away."

Claire nodded, strengthened by his concern, and wandered through the building again. All too soon, present reality faded to a vision of a white painted bedroom.

Eleanora lay in a large four-poster bed with red drapes. William, wearing a black silk dressing gown entered the room. Claire experienced Eleanora's fear and revulsion as he approached, sensing the poor woman would have no choice but to succumb to the attentions of a man who sought only his own pleasure.

Claire tried to block the vision but it was too powerful and she felt herself violated in sympathy with Eleanora as William threw off his dressing gown and climbed into bed with her. She retched at the smell of sweat and alcohol.

Eleanora knew from bitter experience that to refuse meant pain and so did not resist as William sought to remove her nightgown. But she did not help him, either, and, irritated by her unresponsiveness, he tore it. Eleanora stiffened and William became angry and bitter. In his confusion and suffering, he sought to hurt Eleanora, punish her for not wanting him, so he forced his way into her with no regard for her comfort. Her head knocked against the headboard again and again until he found his release, then William pulled himself away, lay down next to her and fell asleep. Eleanora turned her back on him and moved as far away as possible, tears soaking her pillow, until she too drifted into the blessed oblivion of sleep.

"Dear God," Claire sighed. How can someone have so little consideration for another?

"He lost his belief in love," came the quiet voice of Eleanora. "By then he had sold his soul for money and power. He lived in the darkness of his own shadow and I could not reach him."

Experiencing first-hand the depravity of another human being shocked Claire to the core. Knowing Eleanora lived a horrendous life with William, a man lacking in kindness and warmth of any kind, depressed her. The feeling grew in power until sadness gained ascendency.

The familiar purple haze drifted into her perception. "Draw back from your sadness," Eleanora whispered. "Don't allow it to possess you."

Claire closed her eyes and relaxed.

Eleanora continued, "Remember the sunlight gleaming on the lake, the bluebells in the grass, the feel of Jared holding you, his concern for your wellbeing. These too are real. Don't allow William's darkness to take you over, too, Claire. Remember that it can have no power in the light of your own loving consciousness."

Claire heard the sound of a bird singing and it brought her back to the present. The depression faded and she became aware of a different feeling and realised it came from Eleanora. "How can you have compassion for the man who treated you so badly?" Claire asked, amazed.

"There are things you do not know."

Claire picked up a sense of shame but then the presence of the spirit faded away. Looking around, she saw the charred remains of the house around her again and shuddered. How had this happened? Touching a blackened wall, an impression of anger and revenge came into her mind. The house had not burned down by accident!

Could it be related to what happened to Philip? She had been unable to sense him at all so far so Claire continued her walk through the gutted building, her feet crunching on the debris, alert for any sign of him.

"Philip," she whispered, "you came here, I know you did, but why can't I sense you?" Her attention kept going to the windows and she realised she needed to go into the garden. Walking down the stone steps out of the house, a great weight lifted from her. Such a place of heaviness and sorrow, she thought, glancing back, although once it had been a wonderful house. Her steps led her down a path towards a pavilion built beside the lake. She saw Jared and Bella talking over by a group of pink and white rhododendrons.

At that moment, a shadow passed over the sun and she stopped. Perplexed, she looked up and saw an eagle circling in the sky. Round and round it went, flying lower each time it passed over. She stared, mesmerised, but then it swooped! She heard the flapping of wings and felt the rush of air as it passed close by her face, its talons extended. She screamed and put up her arms to shield her eyes.

When nothing happened, she lowered them and found herself looking at William standing a short distance away, an eagle clutching onto the leather gauntlet he wore to protect his hand. She watched as he reached into a pouch hanging from his side and gave the bird a lump of meat. Claire felt sick. She became aware of other men around her, the same ones she saw in the office at the house. From their manner, it was clear they had been drinking. Eleanora walked across the lawn. She glanced over at the group of men and sped up, disappearing into the pavilion.

The scene faded leaving Claire with a feeling of dread. No wonder Philip had been afraid of eagles. They would remind him of William, perhaps even allow his presence to grow stronger. She remembered how the eagle had flown at her and could imagine being torn apart, the bird's talons tearing into her soft flesh. She shuddered and focussed on Bella and Jared who still stood talking together as if nothing had happened.

Claire decided to head towards the pavilion where Eleanora had gone. Soon she stood in front of the small, round wooden building. Around it had been built an encircling verandah supported by attractive carved beams and posts painted with now peeling white paint. Here she felt a sense of Philip. He hadn't gone to the main house, which would explain why she hadn't sensed him there; he had come to this pavilion. The door stood ajar. She felt loath to go inside but knew she must.

Light streaming through panels of red glass bordering the windows fell on a floor thick with dust and debris but a sense of peace and joy filled her and she saw a vision of a cane chair and table set with a delicate floral tea service on a silver tray.

"My sanctuary," came Eleanora's voice. "William never came here."

Claire heard singing and saw Charles standing by the lake. He turned and waved and she became aware of Eleanora sitting in the chair looking out of the window. A small wooden boat floated on the water and Claire watched as Charles pushed it along with a stick. Her attention fixed on the boat as it bobbed on the water's surface. It felt important somehow, although she did not know why. All of a sudden, the ground moved, undulating and tilting until she became uncertain on her feet and nauseous, as if she herself were on a boat of some kind. She left the pavilion and held onto one of the pillars for support until the sensation faded.

She cast her attention around the lake and the woods beyond. Such a lovely place, she thought, but this wasn't getting her anywhere. Claire had asked Laura for a copy of the photograph she found of Philip in the necklace box to bring to the Lake District. She took it out of her shoulder bag and looked at it. Her heart moved with pity for now she knew something awful had happened to him and could not bear to think of it.

As she forced herself to stare into his eyes and connect to the love that flowed from him, she had a strong impression of Laura. Why had she picked up on her? Claire wondered.

"She knows something," Eleanora said.

"What?"

"She does not know the importance of what she knows."

"That makes no sense, what on earth do you mean?" Claire moaned.

"I cannot sense Laura clearly. She is too far away. It is not always easy for those of us who have passed out of the mortal realm to connect to those of you still living. I have no power to act in the physical realm. I need someone like you. Philip is beyond my ability to sense and yet when we visit the places where he once was, connected to you, my dear, I *can* sense more, help *you* connect with him. Together perhaps we can find and help him whereas alone I cannot."

The necklace is my link to you and hence to the world while you wear it for, when it was mine in life, I loved it. This binds us, clears the channel. It is getting stronger the more you open up."

"Why is all this stuff in riddles? It's so difficult. I do wish I could pick things up more clearly."

Sometimes what you receive will be indistinct and clouded by mental interpretation. You will have to look behind what you see, feel and sense for the truth. This is why I urge you to be still and quiet. It helps open you up.

"Why have you not passed on, Eleanora? I've heard some spirits remain because they don't know they've died but that's not true of you. Why do you want to help Philip?"

Eleanora remained silent for a long while but then said, "I cannot rest until what has been done is undone."

"What is that?"

The connection went blank leaving Claire wondering why Eleanora did not want to say. A more complex story must exist than had yet been revealed. She hoped one day it would all become clear. She stared at the picture. Back in London, Laura too held her copy of the photograph and, for the hundredth time since Claire and Jared had gone, wondered what they would find out.

In the Lake District, Claire felt the love that flowed between Philip and Laura. Surely something so powerful could not be obliterated by evil? The man she looked at in the photo had a brightness of spirit. He had obviously loved with great intensity and been a sensitive person so why then had he drawn darkness to him?

Eleanora spoke again. "There are more things going on in life than we know, deeper purposes and plans our conscious minds cannot comprehend. Philip had no defence as a child. His openness made him vulnerable. For the same reason I am drawn to you, William needed someone he could work through to achieve his purpose. He and Barrett found Philip."

"Barrett?" Claire shivered. "He scared me. I thought he could see me back at the house."

"He probably could. He has great power."

"What!" Claire shuddered, but right away felt the purple haze of Eleanora, soothing and reassuring.

"I am with you and can protect you but know you are safe, always, when you connect to the truth of who you are, dear one."

"Who *is* Barrett? You called him the *Lost One*. Why?"

"Because he has turned his back on love and created much evil in the world. William met Barrett at a party and they became great friends. They spent a lot of time together and William fell under his spell. When I met Barrett, I sensed his darkness and feared for my husband. I tried to tell him many times not to have anything to do with the man but he would not listen. When Barrett introduced William to the Circle, things became much worse.

"The Circle, what's that?" Claire remembered the others she saw around Philip at Castlerigg.

"Yes, you are right. They were members of the Circle."

"They were spirits?"

"Yes, not all spirits pass over to the next realm when they die. Some are anchored to the earth plane and do not want to leave. Barrett and the other members of the Circle are ones such as these. As a result of their experiences in life, they lost touch with their sacred essence, with love, and so are doomed to seek satisfaction through the material world and the manipulation of others. Many hundreds of years ago, they gained the power to remain on the earth, either in disembodied form or by possessing the bodies of others. They have the power to come and go from people at will. This is what they were doing when William met them. They had taken over the lives of those men you saw at the house. Barrett is their leader.

"Life became progressively worse. William and Barrett and the others lived a debauched life with no consideration for the effect their actions might have on others. They held wild parties at the house the like of which I could not condone. We had a child living there and it broke my heart. I entreated William to stop his ways but he only laughed. And then one day I had an encounter with Barrett."

Claire heard music playing and found herself back at the house in the past.

Tired, Eleanora hurried away from the party and down the hall. William had insisted she be present but she could not tolerate it any more. She had nothing in common with any of William's new friends nor with the brash women they brought with them. Turning a corner, she ran into Barrett. "And where are you going?" he asked, looking her up and down in a way that turned her stomach. He never made any attempt to hide his appreciation of her body.

Eleanora pulled her stole tighter around her shoulders and tried to move on past but Barrett's arm snaked out and gripped her wrist. He thrust her into a nearby empty room and kicked the door shut.

"You've been talking against me to William," he snarled, gripping her face with his hand and forcing her to look at him.

"No, I, I..."

"You're lying. I have ways of knowing these things." His hand dropped down to caress her breast." Eleanora cringed away.

Barrett laughed. "I suggest you stop," he continued, "or you might come to regret it."

"What do you mean?" The colour drained from Eleanora's face.

"You're an encumbrance," Barrett snarled. "I don't tolerate those who get in my way. Things tend to happen to them, unpleasant things."

At that moment, William's voice sounded in the corridor. "Eleanora, where are you?"

"Here!" she called out in relief. Barrett moved away as William entered.

"What are you doing in here," he snapped, not seeing Barrett at first who now stood off to one side by the door. "You should be with our guests."

Eleanora looked at Barrett. William followed her gaze. "Oh, Barrett, I didn't see you there."

"Your lovely wife has been entertaining me," he drawled.

William looked suspicious for a moment but then Barrett continued, laughing, "She is such a pleasant conversationalist," and William relaxed.

"Excuse me," Eleanora said and slid past them out of the room.

"I knew then I had to leave and take Charles with me."

Claire picked up a sense of Eleanora's sadness and desperation in that time. "That's awful."

"Barrett taught William how to remain here on earth when he died and how to possess Philip."

"Oh, I see! Do you think these spirits, this Circle, are with William now wherever he is?"

"Yes, I would think so."

"But how can we possibly help Philip if these spirits are with him?" Fear gathered in the pit of Claire's stomach at the thought of Barrett.

"Have courage, my dear. If you stay centred in the truth of your being, they cannot harm you. Know who you are and you will have a strength they cannot stand against. Do not worry, both Charles and I will help you."

For a moment Claire saw the faint figure of Eleanora's child, then he faded away.

"My son died when he was nine."

"I'm so sorry."

"Do not be sad for he is with me. You must have faith, dear one, for I know what must be done when we find Philip."

"I hope you're right," Claire said but her voice lacked conviction. She stared again at the picture of Philip in her hand. "So, what does Laura know that can help us?"

"Perhaps she knows where he went."

"But that's impossible. She doesn't. Why did she send Jared and I here? That makes no sense."

"I can feel her love for him through your connection to her," Eleanora said. "She thinks of him now. You must ask her."

"Okay. I'll talk to her."

The connection faded and Claire became aware again of standing outside the empty pavilion. She saw Jared and Bella looking at a Grecian style statue of a woman over by the rhododendrons and walked over.

Claire filled them in with all she had experienced. "I have to ask your mother, apparently, Jared."

"That's strange," he said. He delved into his pocket and brought out his phone. "No time like the present. Do you want to talk to her or shall I?"

"I will."

Jared brought up the number and handed the phone to Claire.

Claire had no idea what she would say. How much should she tell Laura? She decided on as little as possible. She still felt it would be wrong to get her hopes up until they knew for sure where Philip was.

"Hello."

"Laura? It's Claire."

"I've been thinking about you, dear, wondering how you were going. Have you," her voice wavered, "have you found out anything more?"

"Well, yes and no. I've received a lot of impressions but as yet not much of it makes any sense. We went to Castlerigg today." Claire paused, unwilling to say what must be said yet knowing she had to. "I now know that Philip had a spirit possessing him and it caused him to leave Keswick. My connection to Eleanora has strengthened and she has been able to tell me more about it all."

"Oh my God, poor, poor Philip. Do you know where he went?"

"No, I'm sorry I don't. Not yet but I *do* know he walked away from Castlerigg and came to a large old house, the home of the person we think possessed him. We're at the place now. "I know this is going to sound odd but Eleanora says *you* might know where he went from here."

"But I have no idea," Laura wailed. "Don't you think I would have tried to find him if I had known?"

Claire staggered as a wave of dizziness unsteadied her. Why did she feel like this? It started when she saw Charles with his boat. What did it mean? Did the toy have any significance? On a whim, she asked, "Does a boat mean anything to you?"

"What, when Philip disappeared?"

"Yes."

Laura thought back. "No, he never mentioned a boat."

"What about before that. Did he like sailing?"

"We went on the lake a few times in a boat."

"No, that doesn't feel right. The sea?" Claire asked, hopeful for some sort of connection. "The coast? Anything like that?"

"No, I'm sorry."

This wasn't getting them anywhere, Claire thought, then had another inspiration. Could the boat thing mean a trip of some kind over water? "Did he ever mention anywhere he wanted to go, Laura?"

"No, he didn't. He really loved the Lake District and told me he could never live anywhere else."

"Are you sure he had no interest in any other places?"

"No, oh, but..."

"What?"

"Well, he did have a collection of pictures. They were all of the same place, a river in a forest. He had quite a number, all in a metal box. He would look at them every so often and, now I come to think of it, those times often coincided with one of his dark moods. I think the pictures helped him somehow. He would sit looking at them for a while then after that the depression would begin to lift."

"That's great, Laura, where was this river?"

"I'm sorry, I don't know. He never said, but if you look in his things, I'm sure you'll find the pictures. Do you think they're important? You don't think he went to this river, do you?"

"To be honest, I just don't know, Laura. Anyway, thank you. I'll let you know as soon we find anything more out. Do you want to talk to Jared now?"

"Yes, please."

Claire handed the phone to Jared who chatted for a few moments then hung up.

"What was all that about a river?' Bella asked.

Claire told the other two what Laura said. "Do you remember any metal boxes of pictures, Bella?"

"No, I don't but that doesn't mean anything. We'll have to go and search."

Jared's phone rang so he wandered off to take it. "I think I need a bit of a rest," Bella said, scrabbling in her bag. She drew out a puffer and took two deep breaths of the medication.

"Are you all right?" Claire asked, laying her hand on the older lady's shoulder.

"Yes, yes, I'm fine, love. I'll just sit on that seat over there and shut my eyes for a while. I'm missing my afternoon nap."

Claire wandered away, her mind spinning with the implications of what Laura told her. Yet again nothing had been solved, only more questions created. Could the pictures of the river really be significant?

Her mind gave up and she allowed herself to look around and enjoy the simple beauty of the garden. Not wanting to go back to the burnt-out shell of the house and the bitter memories that haunted it, she walked in the opposite direction, drawn towards a nearby wooded hill. Reaching its base, she noticed some rough stone steps leading upwards between two rhododendron bushes covered with white flowers. Claire could not resist climbing them.

They let her to a little path leading up between more rhododendrons and huge trees burgeoning into fresh spring growth. Beside it, a stream tumbled down over rocks and stones from above. After a few minutes, Claire reached the top of the hill where she saw a stone bench set in front of a gap between the trees. She sat down and gazed at the magnificent view of the lake below and surrounding peaks, her heart lifting at the beauty of it all. How she loved this land. She never wanted to live constrained within a drab and dirty city again. She continued to sit on the bench, her mind silent in rapt attention on what lay before her. Never had she experienced anything so perfect. Swathes of bluebells, in echo of the colour of the sky, spread over the ground below the trees and vibrant clusters of pink and white blossoms decorated the rhododendrons. The sound of the stream bubbling and churning down the hillside, accompanied by the rustling of the trees and an occasional bird song, lulled her mind. The water poured like liquid glass over the rocks, shining with reflected light.

All of a sudden, despite her joy, a sorrow welled up so strong it pierced her heart. She knew right away, however, it was not *her* pain but that of Eleanora whose presence she now sensed nearby.

"I hoped you would not find this place," the spirit said.

"Why, Eleanora, why?"

"This is the place of my shame," she replied.

The light on the falling water burned into Claire's brain taking her away from the present and back to another time. Something made her turn around and she saw a handsome, slim young man she had not seen before. In his mid-twenties, with short straw-coloured hair and a sparse beard, he wore a grey suit with a light blue waistcoat. With a start, Claire realised she was looking at him with the eyes of Eleanora.

"I hoped I would find you here, my darling," he said and came towards her.

"Don't come any closer," she heard herself say. "Please leave."

"You know I cannot do that. I have waited too long for a chance to be alone with you and I know you feel the same."

The truth of it burned through her veins as she stared at Robert Ashworth. She had been drawn to him ever since William's mother introduced them several months ago. They both moved in the same social circle and so encountered each other quite often. She loved their conversations when they met at dinner parties, where they discussed their mutual love of poetry and art. When he read her some of his work it touched something deep inside Eleanora and she knew he had a rare gift, a powerful love for life and the ability to communicate it to others. How could she not feel something for this sensitive soul, so opposite in every way to William.

They had only ever spent time together in the company of other people at social events and yet their love for each other had grown, blossoming in simple moments when their glances met and held across crowded rooms and in the times when he sat beside her and recited his poetry. There had been others present and yet she knew he read it just to her. They had never even touched and yet the love that shone from his eyes as he looked at her stirred Eleanora in a way that she could not help but think of him all the time.

"It does not matter what I feel. I am married to William and so you must go. NOW," she said with all the vehemence she could muster.

"You can't mean it."

"I do, I do."

Eleanora put her hands over her face but gentle fingers prised them apart and she found herself staring into kind grey eyes. "I'm sorry, Eleanora. I don't want to cause you any more pain than you have already. I will leave if that is what you truly want, although it breaks my heart to do so. I hate the way your husband treats you. You deserve so much better."

He pulled her hands down and held them in his. The love and concern in his eyes and the softness of his touch broke her resolve. A wave of anguish and sorrow rose up from within and she slumped in weakness and despair. Robert pulled her against his chest and, although she knew she should not, she relaxed against him and allowed her tears to fall, the result of years of pain at the hands of a man who knew no other way but violence and cruelty.

Robert held her for a long time as her suffering found expression, until the intensity passed. Sensing it, he lifted up her face and kissed the tears away from her cheeks. He stared at her with such love in his eyes she became lost in them and so, when he touched his lips on her mouth, she could not push him away. She yearned so for love—a gentle touch and soft caress. He undid the pins that constrained the hair on the top of her head and it fell around her face in chestnut waves. "You're so, so beautiful," he whispered and she could do nothing but surrender to the closeness she had yearned for and a passion for Robert arose so powerful she could no longer resist him nor he, her. And so, beneath the trees by the sparkling stream, they lay together on his jacket and allowed their passion to find release in each other.

Claire became aware again of the light from the stream burning into her eyes and lifted her gaze away up to the cool peace of the blue sky.

"It was the one and only time I betrayed my husband," Eleanora said, in a voice so quiet Claire found it hard to hear.

"William and I were happy once: when we first married. In those days, he always behaved with respect and honour," Eleanora said in a wistful voice. "He had a sensitive side then, I could sense it, and he loved me. But he could not show it. It was not his way. He had a cold upbringing. We spent the first few months of our marriage travelling in Europe but then William's father died and we had to return home. William inherited the estate and discovered his father, a weak and ineffective man, had brought the family business to the edge of ruin. William determined to rebuild it. He had always longed for wealth and power. He began to work long hours and I never saw him. The business became his sole focus. When it proved to be more difficult that he thought, I began to see another side to him. He became angry and bitter, often falling into a rage and taking out his frustration at life on his mother, Esme, and me. We learned to stay out of his way. At first, he used to apologise but then he stopped.

"Broken hearted after losing her husband and having to witness the terrible effect her son's desire for power had on him, Esme died and I was left alone with William. Life became hell but then Robert came. Dear sweet, gentle Robert who loved poetry and beautiful things like gardens and art. He adored me and, desperate for love, I could not help but be drawn to him.

"Although he never said a word to me after Robert and I made love, it was obvious William knew what had happened. I don't know how but he did. He became so much worse: twisted and cruel, taking his bitterness out, not only on me, but also on all the staff. He made no attempt to hide his contempt for me. Even when we had our son, Charles, William failed to change. I thought being a father would make a difference but, sadly, it did not."

"Charles wasn't Robert's, was he?"

"No, no, the affair happened in 1910, four years before Charles was born in 1914."

"What happened to Robert?"

"I never saw him again after we made love. He stopped coming to the house and I feared for his safety. I asked several people in our circle of acquaintances but they hadn't seen him either. No one knew where he had gone."

"Did you ever hear from him at all after that?"

"Not during my life."

"What do you mean?"

"He came to visit my grave many years later as an old man. He sensed me but could not hear me. We were never meant to be together. He died a long time ago now."

Claire felt another upwelling of sadness coming from Eleanora. "You blame yourself for it all, don't you? That is why you cannot rest." Her words met only silence but Claire knew she had hit upon the truth.

It was some moments before Eleanora replied, "I blamed myself for many, many years. I believed if I hadn't given in to Robert, William wouldn't have become consumed with bitterness and fallen under the influence of Barrett and the other members of the Circle who led him down the path of corruption. I knew I could not pass over until I made it right. William hurt many, many people. He is still doing so."

"Philip?"

"Yes."

"Claire!" She turned. Jared stood behind her. She had not heard him approach. "I wondered where you were," he said.

"How did you find me here?" she asked.

"Actually, by chance. I noticed this path and thought I would see where it led. Now I know." He smiled. "It led me to you."

Claire smiled in return.

"Can I sit beside you?"

"Of course."

Jared stared out at the view. "It's amazing here. I wish..." he fell silent.

"What do you wish?" Claire pressed.

"Oh, that for once I had nothing to do, that I could just stay here in the Lake District. Go walking, look at the scenery, take a breather." He turned and smiled at Claire.

"Things are difficult for you," she said.

"Yes. It's been hard to put things back on track with the business since Andrea betrayed me." He sighed. "I nearly lost everything."

"I can understand why you would be bitter and suspicious of me."

He turned and looked at her. "I'm not anymore, you know that, don't you?"

Claire nodded. "Yes. I'm glad you believe me now. It means a lot to me."

They stared at each other for longer than Claire felt comfortable with. She sensed he liked her now and it made her feel warm inside. It was important that he liked her.

To cover her awkwardness, she turned away first. "We should get back. Bella will be wondering where we are."

"Of course."

Jared and Claire found Bella standing in one of the burnt-out rooms of the house. She looked unhappy.

"What is it?" Jared asked.

"I don't like this part of the house," she said. "It gives me chills. I feel very bad things went on here."

Claire picked her way over the rubble of the floor to stand next to her. She looked around and became aware of crimson velvet curtains at the windows and William sitting behind a dark wooden desk.

Two men stood looking down at William. The first was very tall and thin and dressed immaculately in a well-cut suit. He had a distinctive pointed nose and looked at William with a disdainful expression on his face. The other man, shorter and thickset, was dressed in rough working men's clothes and grinned inanely. William had papers laid out in front of him and looked angry.

"You have one month, after that, well, who knows what might

happen," the tall man said. He looked at his associate who laughed, then they both turned and left the room. William, his face twisted with frustration, picked up the papers and screwed them up into a ball but then sank down in his chair, sorrow and hopelessness playing across his features.

If she hadn't known anything about him in that moment, Claire would have felt compassion but then she remembered the person he was, someone who destroyed the lives of others without compunction, someone who reached out even in death to achieve his ends. She shuddered. How did human beings become so lost? Claire felt depressed at the thought of all the evil things people did in the world, the depths to which they could fall, and for a moment felt she would lose all hope herself but the voice of Eleanora came to her then.

"William suffered greatly," Eleanora said and Claire felt the spirit's sadness for him.

"I don't know how you can feel compassion for him. He abused you, Eleanora. He *killed* you."

"He could never really touch me," Eleanora continued, "not the real me, deep inside. In my despair, my imprisonment, I had to reach beyond the body he violated. In the darkness I found the Light within myself and became one with the power of Love, the true spiritual love that holds all of life sacred in its embrace."

Eleanora stopped speaking and, in the silence, Claire felt an absolute stillness and lightness arise, something beyond the heaviness of her physical body yet not apart. It had a special quality about it her mind could not construct a concept for. The feeling faded after only a few seconds but it left behind a quiet resonance of peace and love.

"Yes," Eleanora continued, "never lose your feeling for, and belief in this, my dearest one, for it will be your anchor against despair. It is our true reality, even William's, only our ignorance blinds us to it."

The velvet curtains vanished as Claire came back to the present. Through the windows she saw the vibrant beauty of the garden and sky, so in contrast to the ruin within the walls and felt a great love arise for the world, even the house around her. The wave of love increased, spreading through the building, through the walls, the floor and even down to the darkest cellars beneath. It was then that Claire sensed the presence of several shadows moving towards her and Bella. As they gathered around them, she saw they were distinct men and women and even a young girl. She counted nine. They looked so sad and lost, Claire's heart went out to them.

"This place is full of spirits," Bella said. "I can feel it."

"Yes," Claire agreed, "I know. I wish I could help them."

"Hey, you two, let's move on," Jared called and the spirits vanished.

As they all walked back to the car, Claire told them both about Robert. "That's why Eleanora hasn't passed over. She feels responsible. And, do you know," Claire continued, "I think she still loves William even though he treated her so badly. It's such a sad story."

"I don't understand why William would want to possess Philip when he was young," Bella said. "Why did a poor innocent child have to suffer because of him?"

"I don't know," Claire replied. "It makes no sense. Anyway, we need to go back to your place. I have a feeling Philip's collection of pictures might help us discover where he went."

Something made Claire look back and she saw the maroon car drawn up in front of the main entrance.

Eleanora and Charles came down the steps followed by the butler, Atrell, and another servant carrying suitcases, which they loaded into the car. Eleanora looked back at the house and shuddered. "Where will you go, Madam?" Atrell asked, sorrow on his face.

"I have a place prepared, a friend has found me a house. I cannot remain here any longer. Barrett has threatened me, told me I have to leave or he will kill me. What else can I do? I tried to tell William but he did not believe it. His heart has turned against me."

"You are doing the right thing, Madam. Good luck. We will all miss you."

The driver helped Eleanora and Charles into the car then climbed in himself. The vehicle disappeared down the drive.

Poor, poor Eleanora, Claire thought. What a terrible life she led in this house, even having to flee for her life in the end, and yet she had remained compassionate and loving.

"Claire!" Jared called, "are you coming?"

"Yes, yes. I'll be right there."

Chapter 13

B ELLA, CLAIRE AND JARED ENTERED Philip's bedroom. "Do you know where he might have kept these pictures?" Claire asked Bella.

"No, they could be anywhere."

The three of them went through everything in the room but found no photos of a river in a forest. "Do you think he destroyed them?" Bella asked in exasperation.

Claire became still and scanned the room. The others saw her and waited, hoping she might be able to pick something up. She walked around the room, running her fingers over the walls and furniture but came up with nothing. "What about the rest of the house, did he have any other places he might have put stuff?"

"No. I'd know it if he had."

"Why don't I give my mother a ring," Jared said, taking out his phone. "She saw the pictures. She might have some idea of where he kept them."

"Good idea. Let's go and have a cup of tea, Claire," Bella said. She led the way downstairs. On the way down, Claire stared around her. She loved the house with its winding staircase, stripped pine woodwork and antique furniture. Bella had filled the place with all kinds of fascinating objects, paintings and photographs. It just stopped short of being cluttered. Claire kept stopping to look at them.

Bella, noticing, laughed and said, "Welcome to my old curiosity shop; the result of a great love of car boot sales. I can't go past them. There's always a treasure or two hiding away and it's such fun to search them out. I always come back with something, often several things."

When they arrived in the kitchen, Claire admired a small collection of china animals on a shelf. She picked up the tiny figurine of a deer. "Oh, this is enchanting. So cute." Next to the animals, a menacing African wooden statue with large eyes stared out into the room. "He's a bit creepy, though."

An entire wall had been decorated with old postcards from Victorian times. Ladies in crinolines with parasols wandered along promenades with well-dressed gentlemen. "I love them," Bella explained. "Snapshots of life in the past."

Claire wandered into the lounge next door while Bella made the tea and noticed an assortment of photos in silver frames gathered together on a sideboard. One caught her eye. A sweet looking lady, with tight curls of blonde hair sat in a chair smiling. Beside her, stood a tall and thin woman with penetrating eyes, her black hair tied back. Claire recognised the two from her vision of the séance. Bella came in carrying a tray with a floral teapot and three matching cups and saucers. "That's a photo of my mother, Helen. The woman standing is her great friend, Elizabeth Templeton, the one who gave Philip the necklace." Bella turned away, put the tray on the coffee table then returned to the kitchen for some biscuits.

Something about the expression on Elizabeth's face held Claire's attention. As she stared into the woman's eyes, she felt herself being drawn down a dark tunnel back into the past.

Claire saw Elizabeth admiring herself in a mirror. She wore a white blouse and a straight mid length blue skirt with hair swept back in the waved style popular in the forties. The amethyst crystal necklace sparkled at her throat. After a while, she removed the necklace and placed it in its silver box. As she did so, the scene changed and Claire found herself looking at a child with ringlets of long dark hair lying in a bed with a floral coverlet.

A grey-haired woman, her face worn with care, dipped a cloth in cold water and wiped the child's fevered brow. She turned to look as a door opened behind her. "Oh, thank God, Eleanora. Please can you do something for Elizabeth? The fever has burned for more than two days now and I am afraid for her."

Eleanora walked over to the bedside and placed her hand on the young girl's brow. She shut her eyes and the minutes passed as the grey-haired woman stood close by twisting the cloth in her hands, her face tight with strain. The child moaned and shifted in the bed then became still. The mother moved forward in fear but Eleanora smiled and removed her hand. "She will be fine. Let her sleep now. It is not yet her time. She has great work to do."

The vision faded and Claire felt Eleanora's presence. "You healed Elizabeth when she was a child."

"Yes."

"How did Elizabeth get your necklace, Eleanora?"

Before I died, she used to come and help me with the healings sometimes and I taught her what I knew."

Another image came into Claire's consciousness, Elizabeth, now grown into a young woman, standing near the grave of violets staring down.

Eleanora continued. "She had the Gift. Her abilities were great and after my death she was able to hear me. She would come and sit at my grave. It gave her strength and peace. I told her where to find the necklace and what to do. She was the only one who I could connect to and I hoped that she could work with me to help Philip but it was not to be."

"What happened?"

"She was not strong enough."

A chasm of fear opened up inside Claire. How could she ever hope to help him if someone like Elizabeth had failed. "Why not?"

"She blamed herself for the death of her first-born child. She left her daughter unattended near a fire and her nightdress caught alight. The guilt weakened Elizabeth. William also had help from other members of the Circle, the most notable one, Barrett. You have felt the power of him before, in Philip's room, when you were pushed back."

"That was Barrett?"

"A psychic energy force set in place by him"

Claire shuddered.

Eleanora continued, "He has great power and is trying to prevent us from finding Philip."

Claire felt sick. What had she got herself into?

"I told Elizabeth to give the necklace to Philip," Eleanora continued, "in the hope that somehow it would connect me to him more or draw aid in some other way I did not know at that time but he put it away and never looked at it again. William ensured he did so and yet, by some miracle, Philip remembered what Elizabeth said about giving it to someone worthy and later gave it to Laura. She could not help him either. Her fear and grief prevented a clear connection with me but, most important, she had a child growing within her. She needed to be protected. Laura, however, gave the necklace to you. You are different. With you there is hope."

"But why, Eleanora? I'm not a natural psychic."

"You are more sensitive and receptive to the world of the spirit than you think. You were drawn to the necklace because you sensed it was important, that in it lay a portal to somewhere you needed to go. You are ready to transcend the limits of your knowledge, open up to a greater understanding of the world."

"But I don't think I'm strong enough, Eleanora. I'm afraid. This is all beyond my ability to understand."

"Dearest one, have faith. Stay aware, awake. Know you are always connected to Spirit. Surrender to it; ask it for guidance. Trust it. Allow it to flow through you and you will know what to do. No darkness can withstand the Light of Love."

"I hope you're right." Claire felt enfolded in a purple haze and relaxed to some degree.

"I am with you and together we will prevail."

Claire sighed. "I wish this all made sense to me. I feel as if I'm in the centre of a giant web following threads I don't understand."

"Try not to worry. It *will* become clear."

"How do you know that?"

"I just know. Stop trying to analyse it, Claire, it will only lead you around in circles. Follow the guidance of your heart. Place your attention there. What does it tell you?"

Claire cast her awareness within her body but felt only the clutch of fear in her abdomen.

"Just be aware of your fear," Eleanora said. "Know that you are not the feeling. Let go of it and centre in the truth of who you are for it is beyond all suffering. At a deep, deep level, my dear, you are always safe."

Although the feeling did not diminish, her ability to perceive it reawakened the sense of a loving sacredness emanating from her heart and Claire relaxed. She continued to stand, allowing herself to rest in the sensation. She felt a sense of flowing as if she were on a river drifting downstream and sensed rhythms and currents within the water.

"Remember, you are not alone. Relax and you will be supported. Tense and you will sink. As I have told you before, there are many forces working at a deep level. People are drawn to be together because there are things they need to do and experience. Have faith and you *will* be guided."

"I will try."

Claire felt the presence of Eleanora fade and became aware of Bella standing nearby.

"Were you getting something?" the older woman asked.

Claire pointed at the photo. "What do you know about Elizabeth?"

"I liked her. She and my mother helped a lot of people."

"How?"

"By connecting them to their loved ones who had passed over."

Claire explained what Eleanora had told her about Elizabeth.

"Yes, she did spend some time with Philip but it never made any difference. William must have had a strong hold on him even then."

"Not completely, though," Claire said. "It wasn't until he went to Castlerigg that William took total control. Before that Philip still retained his own identity."

"My God." Bella said. "It's so sad to think of all those years the poor lad fought to keep William at bay. It says a lot for his strength."

All of a sudden, a loud bang came from above and Jared shouted out. Bella and Claire both looked at each other then made for the stairs. They found him sprawled on the floor in Philip's room covered with soot. "Fucking hell!" he swore. "It bloody knocked me back."

"What?" Claire asked

"I, I don't know, just some kind of force."

"You're not making any sense," Bella said. "A force?"

"Yes, dammit. I felt something push me back, like a physical shove."

"That sounds like what happened to me in here," Claire said. She felt a palpable heaviness in the room and tensed. Eleanora enfolded her in a blanket of purple light to help her stay firm against the unpleasant feeling.

"What's happening," Bella asked, staring around in fear. "I feel as if I want to be sick."

"Something, somebody, doesn't want us in here anymore," Claire said. "What were you doing before you felt the shove, Jared? He scrambled to his feet looking a comical sight with soot all over his face but no one laughed.

"I was looking up the chimney."

"Why?"

Jared looked sheepish. "Well, when I was a teenager, I used to hide things up the old unused chimney in my bedroom."

"What things?" Claire grinned. She couldn't resist asking even though she had a good idea what a young man might hide from others.

"I only ever had one magazine," he said.

"Of course," Claire smiled.

"Anyway, I put my hand up and found a ledge. I could feel something there but then some force pushed me back.

"Eleanora? What shall we do?" Claire asked.

"Tell him to try again," the spirit replied. "I will help."

Claire told Jared what Eleanora said.

Jared looked sceptical.

"I think it'll be all right. She is here with us."

With great reluctance, Jared moved towards the fireplace and reached up. Even though he felt like he was pushing through resistance, he persisted. He grabbed a box and drew it out. He placed it on the floor and tried to prise it open. It resisted his efforts at first but then the lid flew off and papers scattered all over the floor. They found themselves staring at photographs. Most showed a river in the middle of a forest. The pictures had been taken from many sources, some were even drawings Philip must have done himself. They showed roots winding over rocks or scenes of stones in the water. Jared leaned down and sorted through the pictures. "They all look to be of the same area," he said, turning them all over. "How frustrating. There's no writing on any of them so we don't know where this is. Wait, there's a newspaper clipping. Hey, look at this." The article had two photos: one of the now familiar river and forest but also a small head and shoulders shot of a serious looking young woman with long, straight hair. The headline read "MYSTERIOUS DISAPPEARANCE AT MOSSMAN GORGE."

"What does it say?" Claire asked.

> "British tourist, Elaine Clarke has still not been found. She was last seen at Mossman Gorge, a popular tourist destination in North Queensland,"

"That's in Australia." Jared said, looking at the others for some moments before continuing to read:

> "Elaine Clarke aged twenty-seven of no 17, Elmsdale Road, Bowness, in the Lake District, disappeared two weeks ago."

"Goodness, that's next door," Bella said. When the others turned and looked at her, she went on, "Elaine Clarke's address, it's the house next door to this."

"Oh my God! Philip would have known her then," Claire said. "It's too much of a coincidence he should be interested in Mossman Gorge too. What else does it say, Jared?"

> "Her husband, Craig Clarke, reported her missing. Police investigations have uncovered bank statements indicating that, unknown to Mr Clarke, payments were made to John Greggson, a travel agent in Ambleside. Police interviewed Mr Greggson and found Mrs Clarke purchased a plane ticket to Australia and booked into a hotel in Port Douglas.

According to police in Australia, Mrs Clarke stayed at the Palm Lodge Hotel for one night. In the morning she asked for directions to Mossman Gorge and has not been seen since. Investigations are continuing."

"Did you know this woman, Bella?" Claire asked.

"No, I didn't. Can I see the report?" she took it from Jared and scanned the cutting. "This is dated February the fourth, 1965. I didn't live here then. I was in Kendal."

"I wonder if the disappearance of Philip and this woman are linked," Jared said.

"He didn't disappear until six years later, that's a long time," Bella said.

"Let's go and ask next door, perhaps the husband still lives there," Claire suggested.

"No, he doesn't," Bella replied. "I know the lady living there now. She moved in after I came back here to live. Before that the house was rented out to students. I don't think we'd be able to trace Mr Clarke."

"Well, at least we know one thing," Claire said, "the river in all these pictures, the place Philip was obsessed with, is in Australia."

"I wonder if my father was having an affair with this Elaine and they planned to be together in Australia?" Jared suggested.

Claire took the newspaper article from Bella and looked at it. "But if he and Elaine were having an affair why did he not go with her when she left? He didn't disappear for six years and besides he was in love with Laura when he left. That doesn't make sense." As she stared at the article, she had a vision of Philip cutting it out of the newspaper and staring at it. Claire got the feeling it intrigued him, that he wondered what it meant. She didn't sense a strong connection between him and the woman in the photograph. "No," she said, "he wasn't having an affair with Elaine, I don't sense any passion between them, but they knew each other, that's obvious. They were both obsessed with this place." She scanned the pictures lying scattered across the floor. "Mossman Gorge," she whispered.

Another vision came of Philip sitting on his bed, the pictures laid out around him. He picked one up. It showed the river swirling around large boulders. Philip stared at it for a while, a soft smile on his face.

"There's something about this place that's very important," Claire said and fell silent as a sense of an ancient forest filled her mind. It felt as if she were actually standing beside the rushing river herself. The sound of water poured through her consciousness and she caught an impression of a man standing underneath a tree. Philip. As she saw him, Claire became aware of Eleanora.

"Yes," the spirit agreed. "I can feel him in this place."

"Are you sure?"

"Yes. Together with you, my power to sense him is amplified and his energy is strong around these images."

Claire took a deep breath and turned toward the others. "He's at Mossman Gorge," she said.

"Are you sure?" Jared asked, dubious.

"Yes."

Chapter 14

"OH LORD!" BELLA SAT DOWN on the edge of the bed. "Australia. I would never have thought he'd go there."

"I wonder what this place Mossman Gorge is like?" Jared went on.

"We can look it up on the computer," Bella said.

"What I want to know is why Philip put this stuff up the chimney," Jared asked. "It seems a bizarre thing to do. I can't see why he would need to hide pictures of a river in a forest."

"He must've felt he needed to keep them safe," Bella replied, "and it looks as if he was right." When Jared and Claire looked at her, she went on, "You said you felt a force, Jared. What if it was one of the members of this Circle, one of the spirits trying to stop us finding the pictures?"

"Eleanora told me the force I felt in here before was something caused by Barrett to prevent us from finding Philip."

Bella shuddered. "Ugh, that's horrible. Let's go downstairs now. I need a cup of tea. "You can use the bathroom, Jared," she smiled. "It's the next door on the left."

Jared wiped his face and looked at his black fingers. He grinned sheepishly. "I look ridiculous, right?" The others nodded and laughed, lifting the atmosphere in the room. Something had tried to stop them locating Philip's destination but it had failed. It was a small triumph but what would happen, Claire wondered with apprehension, if they located Philip himself? Would she know what to do?

"Be still, dear one," Eleanora said. "I will be with you. You forget I know William. Between you and I, we can bring Philip back."

"Do you really think so?"

"Yes, and you must stay true to this belief. Don't permit worry to take hold for it will weaken you. William and Barrett are not the only enemies here, so too are your fears and doubts, remember that."

"I will try.'

Claire followed Bella downstairs and watched as she turned the computer on in the lounge. "You look, Claire, you young people are so quick on these things. Do you really think Philip is in Australia?"

"Yes."

"He used to tell me he never wanted to leave the Lake District, though. He really loved it here."

"My father was possessed when he disappeared, Bella," Jared said, coming into the room to stand beside Claire. "The question we have to ask ourselves is, why would *William* want to go to Mossman?"

Claire stared at Jared. "You're right," she said and sighed. "None of this makes any sense."

Bella looked puzzled. "But why on earth would William Waterford want to go to Australia so much that the desire persisted after his death?"

"I've no idea," Claire replied.

"And what does Elaine have to do with it? It's all so bizarre."

"I'm sorry, I'm only getting bits and pieces, a brief image here, a hint of a feeling there. My ability to sense things is so variable." Claire sighed. "It's very frustrating."

"Type in Mossman Gorge," Jared said. "I want to find out more about it." Claire did as he requested and a long list of sites sprang up on the screen. She clicked on one at random and an image of water pouring over large boulders filled the screen. Tall trees rose up on either side of the riverbank. She scrolled down and read out loud, "Mossman Gorge, an area of outstanding natural beauty, part of the World Heritage listed Daintree National Park, North Queensland."

Claire continued reading, "An area popular with tourists because of its easy walking tracks through the tropical rainforest. Guided tours, Dreamtime Walks, are available from the Kuku Yalanji, the local Indigenous people." More images of rushing water and dense rainforest appeared as she scrolled down.

Going back to the site list, she clicked on another listing and a tourism page with the words 'TROPICAL PARADISE' in large letters at the top came into view. "'Port Douglas,'" she read out, "the perfect place to stay with its first-class accommodation and easy accessibility to two world heritage listed sites: the Daintree Forest and the Great Barrier Reef.' Oh, I've heard about the Barrier Reef," she exclaimed, excited. A photo of a vivid blue sea dotted with coral atolls appeared then one of people snorkelling underwater looking at brightly coloured fish. "You can go diving to look at the reef," she said. "How cool would that be?" Next came another of a rainforest growing by the edge of the ocean. "Oh wow! Look at that beach, it's so beautiful. What a fabulous place."

"Mmm," Jared murmured. "Look up accommodation."

Claire did as he asked and clicked on a site that brought up small huts set amid trees. "Look, you can stay right in the rainforest," she gushed, her face lit up with enthusiasm. "And here in tree houses! How amazing!" She kept on clicking through the sites, one after another. "You can stay on the beach, too." The words 'romantic getaways in the wilderness' came on the screen showing a young couple sitting together next to a cabin surrounded by palm trees. Other views showed modern resorts with pristine blue swimming pools.

She turned to look at Jared, her eyes shining. He couldn't help but smile at her enthusiasm. He liked that about her, the joy she found in things.

Claire continued moving through sites. An advert for cruises on the Daintree River came up. "My goodness there are crocodiles there. Ugh, I don't like the sound of that."

Jared laughed. "I'm sure you wouldn't get eaten if you were careful. Go back to accommodation." He scanned the list of rooms available for one of the rainforest retreats. "The prices are a bit steep," he said. "It wouldn't be a cheap excursion. God knows what the cost of flights to Australia would be."

Claire sobered. "I'm sorry. I was getting carried away. I'm sure there are some basic hotels that would be cheaper. I'd be fine in a youth hostel or something, if we went. And I wouldn't expect to do any of these tourist things. We'd focus on finding Philip." She gave Jared a sympathetic smile. "We'll find him, I'm sure."

He nodded, appreciating her willingness to do what it took to find his father. He knew she genuinely cared and it sent a warm feeling through him. All of a sudden, he wished he *could* take her to all those wonderful places just to see her reaction. He couldn't think of anyone he'd rather go with.

"Well, if all of this isn't a turn up for the books," Bella said. "*Australia!* I still can't believe it. What are you going to do?"

Claire looked at Jared and waited for him to reply. It was his call.

Whether they went looking for Philip further was up to him. It would cost a lot of money.

"It's a long way to go and we don't really have much to go on, no disrespect to you," he qualified, looking at Claire. "Don't worry, I know there are no guarantees we'd find anything but I don't think I could live with myself if there's a chance my father's alive and I don't go and I know my mother's not going to rest easy about it when we tell her what we've found out. Do you have a passport, Claire?"

"I do, as a matter of fact. I got one because I planned to go on holiday to Spain last year but didn't go in the end, though."

"Good. You're going to need it." Claire stared at Jared in shock as it sank in that she might be going to Australia, a distant place she knew very little about.

Jared laughed at Claire's expression. "You don't think we can give this up now because we have to travel, do you? I mean to search until I find my father and bring him home. And I believe you can help me do it."

"But the cost..."

"I don't care about the cost. I'll work it out."

Claire just looked at him, trying to come to terms with this new development.

"Well, are you willing to go?" he asked.

"Of course, I am," Claire replied. "I couldn't rest easy either, nor could Eleanora."

"Okay, then, we're going to Australia!"

They finished their tea and said goodbye to Bella, promising to keep her informed on their progress in Australia. Jared drove them back to the hotel. On the way, Claire's mind worked overtime. Her whole life had changed. A new path had opened up, one that would lead her away from all she had known to the other side of the world. The thought she had when she first got the necklace, that if she wore it her life would be different, had been right. She hadn't realised then just *how* different, though.

They parked at the hotel but Jared said, "Let's go and have a meal. I'm starving."

After a short walk, they found a small restaurant and ordered drinks and food. "How're you feeling?" Claire asked.

"I don't honestly know," Jared replied. "The world I thought I lived in has gone and been replaced with one I don't understand at all, one where spirits affect the living and the father I thought dead could be alive!" His whisky arrived and he downed it in two long gulps. Claire sipped her orange juice and watched him. He had changed so much over the last few days. The belligerence and sarcasm had gone and she now sensed vulnerability, the effect of having no father. He still had a core of anger, though, a deep resentment of Andrea. Claire longed to help him release it, but knew it was something he would have to do himself. At least he didn't direct it at her any longer.

She sensed Jared had a hidden depth, a side he never showed to others. She thought of what he had created back at the antique shop.

"I love your garden in London," she said.

Jared looked embarrassed. "It's just a hobby of mine. I started out building it for Mum because, with her hip, she couldn't get out much when I was away. She said she hated the drabness of London."

"That was a wonderful thing to do," Claire said,

"Oh, I don't know about that, I enjoy doing it. I find it relaxing. One day I'd like to move out of the city, get a bigger garden." Jared looked uncomfortable and Claire sensed he felt awkward talking about himself. "I'm exhausted," he said, changing the subject. "It's been quite a day."

"It's been quite a few *weeks* for me," Claire said, "ever since I got given this." She touched the necklace.

"It suits you. It's a lovely piece." He stared at it for a few moments then lifted his gaze. Such a beautiful face, he thought, noticing her clear skin and how her green eyes were so full of life. He felt jaded and ancient in comparison although he was only thirty-eight. "How old are you, Claire?"

"Twenty-nine."

"And do you know what you're going to do when all this with my father is over? You mentioned coming to live here in the Lake District before."

"I've no idea," Claire replied, "except for one thing: I *do* know I want to come back here. This place feels like my home. I told Bella about it and she offered me a place to stay while I get myself sorted out. Isn't that great?"

"I'm glad something good has come out of all this."

Without warning, Claire reached across the table and laid her hand on his. Jared looked at her with an indefinable expression on his face. Embarrassed by her show of affection, she withdrew her hand. "We will find your father, I'm sure of it," she said, in an attempt to hide her awkwardness.

Jared looked worried. "But what state will he be in? And are we going to be able to help him?"

"Of course, we are," Claire said, but with an optimism she did not feel inside. His words echoed her exact fear. What if they couldn't help Philip?

Both tired from the long day, they did not linger after their meal. When they finished, Jared said. "There's no point in staying here in the Lake District any longer. We know where we're headed next."

Claire nodded but felt sad at the thought of leaving so soon.

"I'd like to make an early start back to London, if that's all right with you?"

"Yes, that's fine."

Claire left Jared at the door of his room and made her way up to the attic. As she shut the door of her room, she noticed the box with the christening gown inside it taken from the grave lying on the dressing table. With all that had happened in the last few days, she had not given it any thought but now it drew her. It felt important.

She opened up the box and took out the yellowed garment. She now knew to whom it had belonged, Charles.

Claire sat on the side of her bed and unfolded the gown. It had been beautiful once. She gently touched the delicate lacework on the hem, wondering who had placed the garment in the grave. As she did so, she felt a presence with her in the room. It brought with it a feeling of joy at odds with an old relic taken from a grave. She shut her eyes and saw a vision of the church at Oakdale. Eleanora stood next to the stone font, holding her baby son. He wore the christening robe, Claire recognised the distinctive lacework. William and a small group of people stood beside Eleanora. She handed the baby to a vicar who spoke several words Claire could not make out then he lifted a handful of water from the font. As he dripped it over the child's head, the liquid caught the sun streaming in through the window and the glistening droplets became a baptism of light.

The scene shifted then and Claire saw Eleanora sitting before a window holding the baby. He still wore the white gown.

Eleanora rocked her son and sang a quiet lullaby. Charles's blue eyes looked up into hers and a powerful love flowed between them. He was so, so special. "Oh, my darling child, you are so sweet," Eleanora whispered. She bent her head and kissed the velvety brow of the baby and ran her fingers through the downy hair on his head. "You are my life and my hope."

A young woman, perhaps about twenty-five or so, entered the room. "Shall I take him now, Madam? He must be tired after the service."

"No, no, just a while longer, Maud." The young woman smiled and turned to leave, but as she did so, knocked against William dressed in

a dark suit. "Out of my way, woman," he barked, barging into the room. Eleanora stiffened and held the child closer to her body. "Wait, Maud," she called. "Take him. I think he is tired."

Nervous at having upset the master, Maud re-entered the room and took the baby from Eleanora. William paid him no heed but went to stand by his wife. Maud took Charles into the nursery. "Hello, there, my little man," she said in a tender voice and cradled him close to her. She smoothed his hair and straightened the rumpled gown. The child started to cry so Maud rocked him and sang quietly. Claire sensed the young woman's great love for the boy. They felt bonded together.

Claire noticed tears running down Maud's cheeks. "How like my little Martin, you are, my precious," she whispered. Claire felt her sorrow. She saw another baby, this time cold and lifeless, wrapped in a very different cloth, rough and grey. Dirty gnarled hands placed the child in a hole in the ground and she saw Maud turning aside, unable to watch as the gravedigger shovelled earth onto the tiny bundle.

The scene shifted back to the nursery at Waterford Hall and Claire saw Maud had removed the christening gown from the baby. She placed it in a cloth bag and took it to a small dark room at the top of the house where she sat on her bed, cradling the garment to herself, Charles and her own child linked together in her memory. Claire knew Maud would keep the gown and that it would give her comfort to hold it over the years, somehow easing the weight of grief the young woman carried.

Claire touched the fabric of the christening gown, staring at its stained and aged appearance. Her mind drifted back in to the past again and this time she saw Maud several years later standing next to Eleanora's grave, the earth newly turned. No violets yet, only fallen white petals from the mourning wreaths.

Maud glanced around the empty cemetery then knelt and dug with her hands in the soil. When she had created a hole, she placed the tin containing the christening gown inside and covered it over. She stayed for a while by the grave, tears falling onto the earth. "I am so sorry, so, so sorry. I should never have stolen it."

Claire felt the young woman's despair and guilt but then saw Eleanora materialise behind Maud.

Eleanora touched Maud on the shoulder. She turned and looked behind her. Although unable to see anything, her face brightened and she relaxed. The spirit spoke, "Let your sorrow go now. Your child has not gone, merely passed from this physical realm. He is still with you in your heart for in truth you can never be separated. You are one together in Spirit." A wondering look appeared on Maud's face and she smiled.

Maud relaxed and the grief that had weighed her down for so many years lifted.

And so, the first healing took place at the grave.

Claire knew Maud now had received the forgiveness she craved for stealing the gown and in this blessing had also found peace and acceptance of the loss of her own child. The vision continued and Claire saw a man come to the grave, a servant she recognised as being one of those who had worked for Eleanora at Waterford Hall. His face twisted with agony from the pain in his back as he bent to lay some flowers on the grave. As he did so, Eleanora appeared behind him and passed her hands down his spine. When he straightened up, a look of surprise came over his face. His pain had gone!

Claire saw others come at different times to pay their respects and all found more than they expected at the grave, some healing, others simply a sense of comfort and peace. Over the years, more and more people came as the grave's reputation grew.

She sat back on the bed. So much suffering in the world, she thought, a wave of compassion flooding through her. It brought with it a wonderful feeling of peace and love. She shut her eyes and allowed it full expression. On the crest of this uplifting wave of emotion came a sense of Charles. Claire opened her eyes and saw him in front of her as he had appeared in the church, a boy of about nine dressed in white clothes and with the most wonderful golden hair. He moved forward and gently touched Claire on the head in blessing, smiled then disappeared.

"You look happy," Jared said when Claire knocked on his door in the morning.

"Yes." She told him about what she had learned from the christening gown and how she had seen Charles the night before. "I think he was a very special child," she said. "I feel this wonderful joy and love emanating from him every time I see him."

Jared followed Claire down to breakfast. They helped themselves from the buffet and sat down at a table. "I'm all packed so we can leave anytime you want but I was just wondering, can we go back to the churchyard?" Claire asked. "I know you want to get back but I'll be very quick. I want to replace the christening gown in the grave."

"Oh, okay."

Claire waited for Jared by the car while he paid the bill. They had been blessed with yet more fine weather. It was too nice a day to be heading back to the city.

Jared appeared, folding up a receipt. He put it in his jacket pocket and opened up the car. They stowed their luggage and set off, Claire enjoying her last few glimpses of the picturesque town. They soon reached the churchyard and made their way to Eleanora's grave. Jared didn't want to have to explain to anyone what they were doing so kept watch as Claire reburied the christening gown.

As Claire replaced the violet plants over the area and leant back, she felt the presence of Eleanora. "You *will* be with me in Australia, won't you?" Claire asked. "I can't do this alone."

"Your psychic ability has grown and the bond between us has strengthened so I can now be with you wherever you go."

Claire stood. "That's it," she said to Jared. "We can leave now."

As they drove away from the church, Claire looked around at a landscape she had grown to love. She hoped it wouldn't be too long before she returned. "Hey, where are we going?" Claire asked when she saw they had taken a direction that led to Lake Windermere and not towards the motorway leading out of the Lake District.

Jared looked at her. He grinned but said nothing.

Claire watched, confused, as he pulled into a car park near the lakeside. "Come on," he said and got out. She did the same and followed him as he walked towards the boathouse on the lake. "What are we doing?"

Jared laughed. "We're going on the lake." The shock on Claire's face made him laugh even more.

"But you said we had to leave early."

"I know but I got to thinking last night. You deserve a bit of a treat for having to come here and put up with me. We can still make it back tonight."

Claire's face lit up with happiness. "Oh, thank you, but you needn't have."

"I know but I wanted to." It was worth it just to see the look on her face, he thought.

They bought tickets and boarded the next boat. "It's cold," Jared complained when Claire dragged him up to the open-air top deck.

"But look at the view," she exclaimed. "You can see the whole lake as well as the hills and sky. It's awesome."

Jared pulled his jacket closer and stared around him. He had to admit the view *was* breathtaking. The boat pulled away from the quay and he felt himself relax for the first time in a long while. There was nothing more to do in this moment other than sit and look. He found his attention drawn to the shape of the tree-clad hills moving past and the blue grey sheen of the water. He glanced at Claire and smiled at the rapt look on her face. If only he could be more like that, he thought.

Claire turned and looked at him and smiled. "Thank you again for this. It's wonderful."

"It's a pleasure." he returned and meant it for he realised nothing mattered in that moment more than to be sitting with this woman at his side staring at the moving landscape around them. "In fact, I think I should be the one thanking *you*," Jared continued.

Claire looked at him, confused.

"I would never have done this if it weren't for you," he explained.

"You need to get out of your office more," she replied. "There's so much to experience in life and I want to do it all. I'm excited about going to Australia now, even though I don't know what we're going to find. I feel so alive."

Jared thought of the coming trip and realised he couldn't plan this one out. All he could do was hope Claire and her bizarre connection to the spirit of a long dead woman would see them through. He felt worried but at the same time knew what Claire meant for he felt more energised than he had for a long while.

They got back in the car, invigorated from their trip. A lock of Claire's hair blew out of place. Jared leaned across and gently put it in place. "Oh, God, I must look such a mess," she moaned.

"No, you look great," he said. Something in the way Jared said it made Claire look at him and saw something in his eyes that thrilled her to the core. He cared for her, at least to some degree. She blushed and looked away, unwilling to show him the depth of her own feelings, which had been growing ever since coming to the Lake District. An easy intimacy had developed between them now but she still felt it to be fragile. He had so many issues and she did not want anything to come between them as they needed to focus on what lay ahead.

Jared set the car in motion and they drove off through the town. A pleasant perfume wafted through the car. Claire wondered what it was but thought no more about it, instead focussing out of the window, anxious to enjoy as much as possible the last views she would have of the Lake District for a while. They hadn't gone far, though, when she cried out "Jared!" and gripped his arm.

He turned to look at her. "What is it?"

"That lane back there, I had the strangest feeling as we went past. Do you think we can go back and take a look?" Claire sniffed. "And that sweet smell, can you smell it?"

"No, no, I can't." Jared sighed. "Do we have to? I don't want to be too late back."

"Please, I have a feeling it might be important."

Jared braked and turned the car around. "Where do you want to go?"

"There," Claire directed him to a small lane bordered by stone walls. "Can we go that way?"

Jared looked. "It's very narrow and steep."

"Oh, look it's called Honeysuckle Lane. I wonder... I have a feeling I should know that name, and that perfume..."

Jared drove up the lane but soon had to brake and back up when another car appeared coming from the opposite direction. "God, I hate these single-track roads," he moaned.

"I'm sorry. You can pull over, if you like," she said when they reached a wider section. "I think I need to walk from here." Claire scrambled out. "I'll try not to be long." Jared's phone rang so he stayed in the car.

She stood and looked around her, feeling she needed to go further along the road. She walked on a short way, looking at the houses, all built very close together, until she heard the sound of running water. A gravel drive leading up an incline drew her attention and she felt she needed to follow it. She hadn't gone far when she came across a small stone house set in an overgrown garden. Beside it, a small stream flowed, its grass banks dotted with bluebells. A steep hillside covered with trees stretched up behind the house and Claire heard the sound of a waterfall.

On impulse, or perhaps as a result of a subtle nudge from Eleanora, Claire passed through a broken gate in the low stone wall surrounding the garden and went up to the house. The place looked to be empty. Paint peeled from around the dirty windows and the faded wooden front door hung from its hinges. Claire pushed and it grated over the floor a short way then stuck. It wouldn't budge but she managed to squeeze through into the dim interior, which was empty except for dirt and rubbish on the floor.

Claire shut her eyes and stood still, allowing the feeling of the place to move through her. All of a sudden, the temperature dropped and she shivered. She felt a sense of impending darkness and knew, without doubt, something was about to happen.

Chapter 15

CLAIRE OPENED HER EYES AND saw the cottage now filled with a few pieces of simple furniture. A fire burned in an old iron stove. Eleanora sat before it sewing and her son, Charles, knelt on the floor looking at a book. Of course, Claire realised. She remembered Eleanora's burial entry in the church record had listed her as living in Honeysuckle Lane. Yes, in a Bluebell Cottage. Her occupation had been a seamstress. Eleanora had taken in sewing to make ends meet.

Someone hammered on the front door and Eleanor looked up in fear.

"Don't open it," she said to Charles but it was too late, for with childish curiosity, he had jumped up and unlatched it.

The door was thrust back and William strode into the small room, his face darkened in anger. He had two men with him. "Did you really think you could leave me?" he demanded. His eyes flicked to Charles who stood staring wide-eyed at his father. "And take my son?"

"I feared for him," Eleanora said.

"You thought this," he waved his arm around the gloomy cottage, "this would be better than Waterford Hall? Are you mad?"

"Barrett threatened me. How can you let that man influence you, William? Can you not see he is just using you?"

"Don't be ridiculous. He's helped me, I tell you. With his influence I have more money and power than ever before."

Eleanora sighed, knowing William would not see the truth. "I'm glad I came to this house for here there is peace and love and Charles is not subjected to long days in a factory with you and your associates learning cruelty. I want him to know there is more to life than using others. He has had time to play...to be a child. Come here, Charles," she commanded but William put himself in front of the boy.

"He is coming with me. There is no way I will permit my son to live in this squalor. You, madam, may do as you please." With that he turned, took Charles by the arm and hauled him from the house.

"Mother!" Charles screamed. Eleanora rushed to stop them but was no match for the two men waiting outside. They held her until William had walked down the lane to his car. He thrust Charles, crying, in the back seat then got in himself and shut the door.

The men released Eleanora and she ran to the car. The driver cast her a look of pity as he drove off. She caught a glimpse of her son's face pressed up against the window. The two men walked to a second car which followed the first, leaving Eleanora desolate in the lane.

The scene blinked out and Claire became aware of standing in the empty room, although she still felt Eleanora with her. "I tried to return to Waterford Hall to visit Charles but William would not allow it. He gave strict orders I was not to be allowed admittance. I never saw my son alive again."

"Oh my God, Eleanora. I'm so sorry. What happened?" No answer came. "Eleanora?" Claire called out but knew the connection had gone so picked her way through the cottage. The other ground floor room lay empty, as did the rooms upstairs, which she discovered when she climbed the stairs. Looking out of one of the windows she noticed Lake Windermere could be seen in the distance and savoured the view.

Returning downstairs, Claire stood and listened. The sound of falling water coming through a broken window lulled her mind and she found herself entering another trance. Intense sorrow permeated the building but, as she became quiet and even more aware, she also sensed a deep peace.

Confused as to how this could be, she looked around her and saw clean windows and pale blue curtains. A vase of coloured flowers sat on a wooden table and the front door stood open. The fire once more crackled in the grate.

A man sat on a chair. Eleanora stood behind him with her hands on his shoulders. He had a dirty bandage wrapped around his head. Both of them had their eyes shut.

Claire felt the power of a loving energy coming from Eleanora into the man. It flowed on outward, filling the house; such was the power of the healer's spirit. Claire even sensed it embracing her, too.

In time, Eleanora moved back and the man opened his eyes. A look of wonder came over his face. "The pain has gone," he exclaimed. "Thank you, thank you. How can I ever repay your kindness?" She touched him on the arm. "Just go and take care of your family." He nodded and left but it wasn't long before a woman, her face creased with worry, knocked and entered.

"Rebecca. How nice to see you. Sit down." This time Eleanora sat and listened as the woman poured out her woes in a torrent of weeping. As it reached a crescendo, Eleanora reached forward, grasped the woman's hands and sat in stillness with her, and, strangely, it was enough for, after a while, the woman fell silent too, shut her eyes and relaxed in her chair. When she rose a little later, Claire saw she looked happy, lighter. The woman dropped some coins on a table and left. Once alone, Eleanora sat in meditation.

As she witnessed this, Claire felt an even greater sense of peace. She came back to the present marvelling that Eleanora, who had experienced such a difficult life, could be so serene.

"The Source of Love within gave me strength," Eleanora whispered.

Claire touched her necklace, remembering Laura saying it would help her discover the Source of Love. It seemed so very long ago and yet was, in fact, only a few weeks.

"It is our very essence, the place where we are one with that which sustains all life," Eleanora continued. "It is the Light in the darkness that guides our way when the path through life seems beset with trials."

"But what of your son?" Claire asked.

"After I left, he lived at Waterford Hall for three years. I tried many times to see him but all to no avail. However, William could not keep Charles prisoner in the end." Eleanora paused for a moment, an enigmatic look on her face. "Sometimes lives are not meant to be long. When the life purpose is fulfilled, the spirit will move on."

Once again, Claire saw the interior of Bluebell Cottage in the past.

Eleanora sat before the fire sewing. It was early in the morning. She needed to get the dress for Mrs Andrews finished. Soon the people would come for healing and her time would not be her own.

Something made her look around to the door. She gasped and dropped the sewing. It fell to the floor in a heap but she paid it no heed.

"Charles!" Eleanora exclaimed. He stood in the doorway, light streaming from his body.

Eleanora went closer.

"Mother, you must be strong. My time on this earth has come to an end." Charles looked at her with compassion.

Eleanora gasped. "No. No." She reached out to her son but her arms passed right through him.

"Do not grieve for I am with you now and always will be." Charles touched his mother's head and a look of profound peace passed across her features.

The scene vanished. Claire, shocked and saddened, stared around her at the derelict interior. How did Charles die? And what had been the life purpose fulfilled so young? Aware she had been gone a long time and that Jared would worry, Claire left the building, pulling the door shut behind her.

As she came out of the house, she noticed a worn piece of wood lying on the ground. Carved into it were the words 'Bluebell Cottage.' Claire propped the nameplate against the wall of the house and turned as the sound of barking came from behind. A small white dog dashed over into the garden and jumped up at her. Two people approached down the track, a tall young woman with long straight blonde hair followed by a bearded older man.

"Hey, Christie, stop that," the woman called, coming over. "I'm so sorry."

"That's all right. Oh, my goodness, you're so cute." Claire bent down to pat the dog and it licked her hand. "What is it?"

"A chihuahua."

"She's so *tiny*."

"Yes, I know, my son wanted a puppy that never grew up. He picked the right dog for that."

Claire laughed, captivated for a moment by the adorable brown eyes of the small creature, and uplifted by its obvious joy as she stroked the soft domed head. So uncomplicated and trusting, she thought, and wished that she too could be like that.

"Are you thinking of buying Bluebell Cottage?" the man asked in a voice with a strong Scottish accent.

"I didn't know it was for sale," Claire said, straightening up.

"Yes. It's been on the market for years. It's got quite a few structural problems."

"But it's so *lovely*," Claire said, turning to look at it again. "I would if I had the money."

"It has quite a colourful history," the woman said. "There was a murder here. Maybe that puts people off."

"You went and looked it up, didn't you, Eve?" the man said.

"Yes, someone told me about it when we moved in. We live in that house over there. I love anything to do with history, so I had to look up something so intriguing. I went on the Internet and checked old newspapers."

"I did hear a woman healer lived here."

"That's right, in the early 1920's. Eleanora Waterford. She had quite a reputation. Some thought her a saint; others thought her the devil. You know how people are in small towns when they're faced with things they don't understand. Anyhow, she had quite a following. People used to come here in the hope of a cure. Sometimes there would be twenty or thirty people here waiting at any given time. There were several reports of miracle cures. It was a terrible shame; she was murdered by her husband."

"William."

"Yes, William Waterford, you know the story then?"

"A little. But tell me what you found out."

"William Waterford was a very wealthy businessman who owned a big factory in Kendal. He and Eleanora lived at Waterford Hall, a large house near Oakdale. He had a terrible reputation so his wife left him, came to live here. The Hall burned down one night. Apparently, it was arson but they never found out who did it. Anyway, his young son died in the fire. William, I guess crazed with grief, came here right after and killed his wife."

"Oh, the poor, poor child.'" Claire visualised the angelic young boy she had seen. "What a terrible story. Do you know how Eleanora died?"

"Yes, William struck her. She fell and hit her head. Died instantly."

"We should be going," the man said pointedly.

"Oh, all right, Gerry. I'm coming. It's been absolutely lovely to meet you. I hope you buy the place. It would be nice to have you as a neighbour. As Eve and Gerry walked away, their dog at their heels, Claire cast a last look back at the cottage, at its quaint grey stone walls and leadlight windows and the bluebells on the grass. Yes, she thought, it would indeed be nice. She shrugged. It wouldn't ever happen, though. She had no money whatsoever.

Claire turned to leave but noticed an area under some trees dotted with flowers so walked over to take a closer look. Violets. She felt Eleanora's presence and a vision flooded Claire's mind.

Snow lay over the ground. Eleanora stood in the garden taking a breath of fresh air, tired after healing all morning. She looked calm and peaceful. A number of people stood close by. Someone addressed Eleanora and she smiled. "I will not be long."

A figure strode towards her across the snow, pushing his way through the others that waited. Eleanora's smile faded at the expression in his eyes.

"It's all <u>your</u> fault," William shouted, his face contorted with pain, ignoring the interested stares of those present.

Eleanora looked at him, shocked by his sudden appearance and the anguish twisting his features but said nothing.

"I've lost everything. Everything now."

"What do you mean?"

"The house burned down last night. Our son is dead. DEAD! He died as he lay sleeping, while you were here," he spat out the last word, "healing your precious sick people."

Eleanora simply stood there looking at him with a look of infinite sadness and compassion on her face.

"Don't you care your son is dead?" William roared.

"He has not gone'"

"What do you mean? How can you say that? Are you insane?"

"He came to me this morning."

"He can't have."

"His spirit came and spoke to me."

"You sicken me. None of this would have happened if you could have loved me."

"I did love you, William."

"No, no," he shouted. "You loved <u>him</u>."

Eleanora gasped in shock.

"Yes, I knew. I followed you and Robert Ashworth up to the lookout that day and I saw you together. You cannot deny it."

William turned around to address the people watching. "Did you know your wonderful saint is really a whore?" Everyone froze in shocked silence. "No, I thought not." He let out a grim laugh.

"Oh, William, I'm so sorry," Eleanora whispered.

"What good does being sorry do?" he thundered. "It won't bring Charles back." With that he lifted up his hand and hit Eleanora as hard as he could across the face. She fell, knocking her head on a tree root, and lay still. No one came forward, all too afraid of what William might do next. He stared down, all colour leaving his face as the enormity of what he had done sank in.

A man standing nearby crept closer. He looked anxiously at William, still frozen, then knelt down by Eleanora and touched her neck. "She's dead!" he announced. William turned and fled from the garden but, too dazed by what had happened, no one tried to stop him.

The scene vanished and Claire found herself staring down at the tree root where Eleanora hit her head. Violets bloomed around the whole area.

"Oh my God," Claire whispered. She bent and touched one of the tiny purple blooms with her fingers. "We are so fragile."

The tragedy of it all shocked her but then she heard the words, "Our bodies are fragile but *we* are not." Claire straightened up and saw two figures by the tree. Eleanora and Charles. "I did not need to mourn what I did not lose," Eleanora said. "It was his time." She turned and looked at her son. He looked back at her and smiled.

Turning her attention back to Claire, Eleanora continued, "But I do mourn for William, for he is lost in darkness and he has dragged another down with him. You must hurry. Time for Philip is running out."

The words *time is running out* echoed through Claire's mind. What did that mean? She felt so inadequate. How on earth would *she* be able to free Philip from William's influence? It seemed an impossible task, one way beyond her abilities.

"Remember what you are," Eleanora whispered, "Remember what you are."

The words echoed in Claire's consciousness bringing with them a resonance of the sacred stillness she had felt a few times now.

She became aware of the sound of falling water and noticed a narrow path leading upwards through the trees. Keen to locate the waterfall, she scrambled up. She passed around a bend beside a large tree and saw water cascading down from a rocky ledge into a small pool before it overflowed down the hill.

The air, tinged with the scent of bluebells, smelt fresh and clean. As she stood and took in the scene, the sound of the water washed through her, cleansing and opening her up and she knew the place held a special energy. She knelt down and scooped up a handful of the water and drank, knowing instinctively the water came from a clear mountain spring. As the cool liquid slipped down her throat, energy flowed throughout her body and she felt the presence of Eleanora and Charles close by emanating love.

An answering love arose within her. It flowed up and out of her heart, embracing the two spirits, the pool and trees and even the ground beneath her feet. As it did so, she felt a powerful connection to something deeper and wiser than herself on which she could depend.

Eleanora and Charles faded away but the sense of loving energy remained. Claire smiled and whispered, "Thank you," before making her way back down the steep path. She cast one more look at the cottage then walked away down the track back to Jared.

Claire and Jared pulled up outside the antique shop a few minutes past eight o'clock in the evening. They had made good progress during the day, stopping only once and having encountered no traffic problems. The moment they entered the environs of London, Claire felt oppressed. She missed the green hills of the Lake District already. The few trees around had done little to alleviate her sense of loss. Claire had promised Laura she would see her the moment they got back. They had yet to tell her they believed Philip still lived. As Jared turned off the engine, Claire wondered how Laura would take it.

Stiff, Claire climbed out of the car and followed Jared through the shop to the upstairs apartment. Laura sat reading in her armchair. "Oh, my dears," she said, "you're back." She struggled up to embrace Jared and then Claire. They all sat down and Laura looked at one then the other expectantly. "Tell me all about it. I want to know everything."

Claire looked at Jared. He nodded, so she leant forward and took Laura's hands in hers. "Philip is still alive. We believe he's in Australia."

"Still alive?" Laura repeated as if in a daze. She looked over at Jared, then at Claire, her watery eyes wide. "All these years he was alive?" Her voice shook and she began to shake.

"Oh no! Are you all right, Mum? Mum?" Jared moved towards his mother and, to their horror, Laura's face lost all colour. She slumped back in the chair and her eyes shut.

Chapter 16

"OH MY GOD!" JARED EXCLAIMED. He reached into his pocket. "I'd better ring an ambulance."

"No wait!" Claire said. "I think she's just in shock." Claire went over and laid a hand on Laura's shoulders. The presence of Eleanora came to the fore and, as with Jared in the restaurant in the Lake District, energy moved through her hands into Laura.

"I was afraid this might happen," Jared exclaimed, his face white. "That's why I didn't want to tell her while we were away."

"Shh, don't worry."

"How can I not worry?"

"You're not helping. It's going to be all right."

Jared stared at Claire, at the expression of love and peace on her face and fell silent.

"Eleanora will help her." Claire closed her eyes and allowed the energy to flow as it needed. Laura's eyelids fluttered.

"Mum?" Jared leant forward. "Mum?"

Laura shifted in her seat and opened her eyes. She looked up at him. "He's really alive?"

"Yes. He's in Australia."

Laura moved herself more upright. "I'm sorry. It's so hard to take in.

I don't know whether to be happy or sad." She fell silent for a few moments. "I think I'm angry more than anything."

"Don't be," Claire said. "It wasn't his choice." She went on to tell Laura everything they had learned. When she talked about finding the newspaper clipping about Philip's neighbour, Elaine Clarke, going missing at Mossman Gorge, Laura broke in. "Do you think this Elaine was having an affair with Philip, that he left to be with her?"

"No, no," Claire reassured Laura. "I don't think so, she disappeared six years before he met you. It's obvious some link existed between them because of their mutual interest in Mossman Gorge but I don't sense a passionate relationship or anything like that."

"Thank goodness, I don't think I could bear it. You know, I remember Elaine's husband. I used to see him leaving the house with his elderly mother sometimes. He didn't seem like a nice man at all. She often had trouble walking and he was very rude and uncaring. Mind you, she swore back at him. Philip told me Craig Clarke was known in the street for causing trouble and to keep my distance from him. I wonder what this all means. I'm so confused."

"That makes two of us." Jared sighed.

Claire filled Laura in with all that happened at Bluebell Cottage.

"All this is so unbelievable." Laura's eyes brimmed with tears. "Such a waste," she whispered. "Philip and I could have been together all these years. It's been so hard." She looked at Claire with anguish. "How could this have happened to him?"

"I've been wondering if perhaps he just happened to be in the wrong place at the wrong time," Claire said. "His mother and Elizabeth held séances. Perhaps they brought William through and he sensed Philip in the vicinity. Young and highly sensitive, he would have been vulnerable to someone determined. He tried to fight William's influence for many years but that day at Castlerigg he lost the battle."

"How is it possible that someone as loving as Philip, and he *was,* you know," Laura looked up at Jared, "someone so *good* could fall prey to evil?" She shuddered.

"I don't know," Claire replied, "but I think maybe Philip's loving nature is what prevented William from taking complete control for so many years."

"So why did he not find someone else, someone more vulnerable? Why did he fix on Philip? And what happened at Castlerigg that tipped the balance in William's favour and gave him control?"

"Again, I'm afraid I don't know." Claire visualised the scene she had "witnessed" at Castlerigg. "William had help that day. Philip had other spirits around him."

"Why has this William taken Philip?" Laura asked. "What could he possibly want with him?"

Eleanora said that sometimes souls don't want to pass on to the next world and so remain. They can't do much here as spirits but can by possessing the bodies of others. It is the same for Eleanora; she is very limited in what she can do so she is linking with me. The difference is that she's not imposing her will on me. I have agreed to do it."

"But why Australia," Jared broke in. "What on earth would William want to do there? It's so far away."

They all fell silent for a moment. No one knew the answer. Jared spoke first. "Well, we're going to find out. Claire and I are going to go there, Mum. If that's where Dad is, we'll find him."

"Do you really think you can locate him, Claire, from what you've sensed?" Laura asked.

"I can't promise, Laura, but I think I can."

Claire brought out the pictures of Mossman Gorge they found in Philip's bedroom. She had borrowed them thinking they might be useful to have when they went to Australia. While Laura sifted through them, Claire picked up the newspaper clipping, staring at the photo of the river in the rainforest with its rushing water and large boulders. As she did so, she sensed loneliness and isolation. She could feel the presence of the forest around her. She stared at the words "MYSTERIOUS DISAPPEARANCE AT MOSSMAN," the words burning into her brain. She touched the word "MOSSMAN" with her fingers and felt a small electric charge. Claire had no doubt in her mind that Philip had gone to Mossman. She could feel the truth of it.

But what sort of state would he be in? Eleanora had said time was running out. Philip wasn't a young man. Born in 1936, according to Bella, put him well into his seventies now.

"Oh, I wish I were younger," Laura said, "that I didn't have this cursed hip. I would come with you but I know I'd be a liability. But if you find him, *when* you find him, if he won't come back, or can't, then I *will* come. Somehow I will."

Claire found it difficult being back in London. Walking into her shabby little flat felt so depressing. So much had happened since she left a few days ago. She stared around her, no longer feeling she belonged. Having grown so much, the place no longer fit. She touched the necklace and knew it had done its work. Her life had changed beyond recognition. Very soon she would be off to the other side of the world.

She felt unlimited. Even the thought of the adventure ahead did not faze her for Claire knew she would not be alone. Eleanora and Charles would be there to help her with what lay ahead.

And then there was Jared. Her thoughts kept coming back to him. She missed their being together. The thought of going to Australia with Jared excited her. She sensed he liked her now, even felt attracted to her, but knew he kept his feelings firmly in check, reluctant to let go and allow himself to be with another woman. She thought of his dark eyes and brown hair and the leanness of his body. He obviously worked out. She remembered how good it felt when he held her in Waterford Hall and wondered what it would be like to touch him and be kissed by him. She imagined them together at the hut on the sandy palm tree lined beach she had seen on the Internet and coloured at her fantasy's direction.

It took Jared and Claire two weeks to organise everything and leave for Australia. They didn't spend much time together, Jared having business commitments. He not only half-owned the antique shop with his mother but also had various other investments. They only met once to book the travel arrangements.

Claire returned to work. She tried to obtain holiday leave for the Australian trip. When they refused, she gave in her notice and walked out. To hell with it, she thought. Strangely, she did not feel worried by this but liberated. She no longer fit in the supermarket. She had enough money to last her until she went away. Just. Jared was paying all the Australian trip costs so that would be all right. After that, well, she'd be going to stay with Bella. Claire felt sure she would be able to find some sort of job. It shouldn't be that hard to find one in the popular tourist area around Bowness. Something would turn up.

The thought of having to deal with William and Barrett, dark spirits with God only knew what supernatural powers, filled Claire with great trepidation. However, she spent a lot of time wearing the necklace and found herself becoming more awake and aware and the sense she had of her own loving essence strengthened. She tapped into it for strength and her perception sharpened. The world that had once seemed so ordinary and mundane became a fascinating place. Life in all its various manifestations assumed a beauty she had never seen in it before although the suffering she perceived in others caused her great pain. She found herself overwhelmed by a deep gratitude for the richness of the physical world and her love for it grew.

She became more confident and willing to talk to people, sensing their struggles and wishing she could alleviate them. She visited Laura several times, listening as she reminisced about her time with Philip. Claire hoped that when they found him (she did not want to contemplate failing) it wouldn't be too distressing. She tried not to think about how they would remove William from Philip, focussing instead on having faith that when the time came Eleanora would, as she had promised, know what to do.

Two days before they were due to leave, Claire went to visit Laura for the last time. She found her in the sitting room upstairs. Laura rose from her armchair and fetched a large brown envelope. "This is from Bella. You look at it while I make some tea."

Claire sat down in one of the soft armchairs and pulled out a sheaf of photocopies. A note from Bella read: 'I have been doing some research and thought you would be interested in these newspaper reports.' Claire picked up the first piece of paper, a photocopy of a newspaper item dated the 12th of December, 1923. The headline read:

TWO DIE IN FIRE AT WATERFORD HALL.

In the early hours of yesterday morning fire gutted Waterford Hall near Oakdale. Charles Waterford, aged nine, and Angus Atrell, aged 59, butler, were killed. The body of Mr Atrell was retrieved but so far no remains of Charles Waterford have been located. Staff verified he was in the building at the time of the fire and it is assumed his body has been totally destroyed.

Police said today they suspected arson. A man was seen in the grounds shortly before the fire started at around 12.15 am. Police are interested in talking to anyone who may have any information.

The man they are looking for is in his late forties, has grey hair and is short with a stocky build.

Who had wanted to burn the house down? Claire wondered. Her mind flew to the scene from the past she witnessed in one of the parts of Waterford Hall when the tall man with the pointed nose and disdainful expression had talked to William in his study. "You have one month to pay, after that, well, who knows what might happen," the man had said. His tone of voice had been threatening. The man with him, a rough looking character, had laughed in an ugly way. *He* had been short and stocky, Claire remembered.

Another image came into her mind then and Claire saw William sitting with the man Barrett who sensed her. Thinking of him made her shudder. She had the feeling of someone cruel and ruthless who would stop at nothing to achieve his ends. He frightened her. Her fear grew and she felt her attention being pulled back into the past.

"What can I do?" William asked.

"Don't worry," Barrett said with a sickly smile. "I know a way you can get the money. One you might enjoy very much, very much indeed."

"What is that?"

Barrett laughed. "There is someone I want you to meet. She is very beautiful but also very rich."

Barrett's voice made Claire feel heavy and depressed. She felt weak as if all her energy were being drained away. His words repeated in her mind. "There is someone I want you to meet." Desperate, she forced her attention back to the present but Barrett's voice came with her intoning, "I want you, I want you," over and over, then it became, "you... you... you."

The word continued like a chant within her mind, Barrett's voice worming itself deeper and deeper inside. Claire felt sick. She saw his face clearly in her mind, his piercing eyes staring at her and felt dizzy. The room dimmed and she floated in a grey mist. The word, "You," still kept repeating and nothing mattered but the sound of it in her brain.

"Stop!" Eleanora commanded. "Come back!"

Startled, Claire opened her eyes and tried to focus on the surrounding room. A flood of purple washed through her and she felt better. "My God! What was that all about?" she asked Eleanora.

"He took you by surprise. You must protect yourself when you open yourself up."

"But how?"

"Anchor yourself to your inner essence, to your physical body and connect to the earth, the ground beneath your feet. Visualise yourself surrounded by white light, too. But call on me. Remember you are not alone."

"I don't understand any of this, really I don't."

"Don't worry, it isn't necessary to understand it all. You will be guided. Always listen. Be still and listen. Also, be alert and observant. Look for things that seem significant around you. If you do, the path will be made clear for you." For the first time, Claire had a vague sense of several others with Eleanora. It made her feel more protected but also part of something greater than herself. She felt more alive, as if she were plugged into some internal energy source.

"Yes. There are those who can assist us. They will do so when the time is right."

"Thank you, Eleanora," she said. "How is Barrett aware of me?"

"When you sense him, you connect to him on some level. He is very powerful. He will try to stop you helping Philip. This is why you must stay strong within. Keep focussing on your inner strength, your connection to Love, the Love that embraces all things."

Claire felt a surge of fear but also anger at the idea of someone trying to get at her.

"No, no, that is not the way," Eleanora was emphatic. "A greater purpose exists here and we all have our parts to play within it, even Barrett. Try not to judge him. Resentment and bitterness will invite him closer. He will feed off it psychically and it will tie you to him. Your strength lies in the power to forgive, to love."

"Claire?" Laura entered the room with two mugs of tea. She looked concerned. "Are you all right? You look pale."

"Yes, yes, I'm okay," Claire reassured her.

"How are you coping?" Laura asked. She handed Claire her tea then lowered herself into a chair. "This must be a terrible strain on you. I feel so bad about it."

"No, I'm fine," Claire smiled. "I'm excited about going to Australia, I can't tell you how much. It's more than repayment for doing this. This whole thing has changed me, made me realise how much greater we are than we know and that life is not just some meaningless struggle to stay afloat between birth and death. There *is* a meaning and purpose to it all, even if we don't always see it. And another thing," Claire smiled, "that the power of love is real and in it is our strength and our hope."

She reached over and grasped hold of Laura's hands. "It occurs me to say something to you. I don't know why, perhaps it's Eleanora, but you must never lose your love for Philip. Keep it burning bright. Send it to him in any way you know how. Pray for him. Visualise him here with you or being with him. I feel it is important for you to do this for it is our faith and love that will help free him."

"I *will* come to Australia if necessary," Laura said, "if you need me to."

"Okay but let Jared and I go and see if we can find him first. It might be difficult and we can see how things are but, as I said, keep your love for Philip strong. We are all connected at some level and it will not be a wasted effort, even though you are here."

"All right. I will do as you say."

"It'll keep *you* strong too," Claire said.

Laura nodded.

While they drank their tea, Claire looked at the next photocopy. This was dated the 13th of December, 1923.

KILLING IN BOWNESS

Local faith healer dies. Eleanora Waterford residing at No 2, Honeysuckle Lane, Bowness was killed in the garden of her home yesterday at about 1 pm. Samuel Moore, who witnessed the event, said: "The man came right up to her. He seemed very upset and began shouting, then he hit Eleanora on the face. She fell to the ground and knocked her head on a tree root. The man ran off."

It is believed Eleanora's assailant was her husband, William Waterford, and he is being sought in connection with the crime. He has not been seen since the incident. Mr Waterford suffered the loss of his son, Charles Waterford, aged nine, in a house fire just prior to the killing. Joan Clitheroe, who was present at the attack, said Mr Waterford blamed his wife for his son's death. Eleanora had been living apart from her husband in the house and had become well known in the area as a healer.

Claire looked at another newspaper article dated one week later with the heading:

LARGE CROWD GATHERS FOR FUNERAL OF LOCAL SAINT

Hundreds of mourners gathered at St Giles' Church in Oakdale for the funeral of Eleanora Waterford. Many people had to remain outside. Eleanora Waterford was well known in the local area as a healer.

The article went on to outline the events surrounding her death but did not contain anything Claire did not already know. She looked at the next article. It had been written a year after Eleanora's death.

MIRACLES AT ST GILES

Mrs Edna Morton, 42, of Bowness, claims she gained the power to walk again after spending time praying at the grave of Eleanora Waterford, a well-known healer, in St Giles' Church, Oakdale.

Mr Thomas Barnes, vicar, has been quick to refute the claim. "There is no evidence the spontaneous improvement of Mrs Morton's paralysis is connected to her prayers to Eleanora. It is more than likely the condition was hysterical in the first place."

Since Mrs Morton made her claims, a number of other people have also stated they found cures at the gravesite. Mr Jonas Johnson, 72, of Ambleside said he no longer had chest pains and Daisy Melrose, also of Ambleside, said she conceived a child after praying to the healer. She had been childless for all fifteen years of her marriage.

Another article, dated the 12th of March, 1925, read:

GRAVE DESECRATED.

The gravestone of Eleanora Waterford, who died last year aged thirty-six, was desecrated last night. All information on the headstone was chipped off.

Many healings have been attributed to Eleanora Waterford and her grave has become a popular place of pilgrimage with a steady stream of visitors ever since her murder in 1923. However, some claim Mrs Waterford practised witchcraft and have condemned her activities. It is speculated that this may have been the motive behind the desecration.

Claire felt sad that someone had felt this way. They could not have been further from the truth.

"People fear what they do not understand," Eleanora said. "They wanted to prevent people coming to the church and praying on the grave. They thought erasing my name would make it hard to find my resting place. They did not succeed. A vision of the grave carpeted with violets floated before Claire's eyes. It stood out in contrast against the simple grass of the other graves so it drew the eye.

Miracles come in many forms, Claire thought. She reached for her tea and took a few sips. She looked up and smiled at Laura. "Don't worry about finding Philip. We're in the presence of powers beyond our ability to understand but ones that will assist us."

"Yes, I think I can believe that. Looking at you, I can see how much you've changed since you came into my shop with such hesitation. You're glowing."

"Thank you."

"It lifts my spirits." Laura smiled.

One last photocopy remained. This one had the date 15th of October, 1924. Claire picked it up. "My God," she breathed.

Laura looked too. "Oh, yes, he got his just desserts."

HANGING OF WILLIAM WATERFORD

At 6 am in the morning yesterday William Waterford was hanged for the murder of his wife Eleanora Waterford.

The moment she read this, Claire had a sense of a group of people waiting in the sharp chill of an early morning and saw a vision of William, his face set in a mask of pain. She felt his intense anger and bitterness, not only at Eleanora, but at life itself. To support this insight, the report went on to say William lashed out at one of the prison guards before being led to the noose. Claire sensed tightness around her neck. Not wanting to go there, she anchored her attention back in the present.

"How very, very sad," Claire murmured, putting the report down, unable to read any more.

"Yes," Laura agreed, sighing. "We humans create such a mess."

"I know. It's hard to see the purpose of it all sometimes. I think we're all still like little children just learning how to be."

Laura nodded and they both fell silent. The door opened and Jared walked in. He stopped short at the sight of Claire. "Oh, hello, I didn't know *you* were coming." His face lit up with a smile Laura noticed right away. He hadn't looked so happy for a long time. She turned to look at Claire and saw an answering smile on her face. They cared for each other, Laura thought, with amusement, although she suspected they may not have truly realised this yet.

"Not long now," Jared said. "Are you all set?"

"Yes. I've started packing already."

"Good. Good." He stood there for a moment just looking at her. "Yes, well, I have a lot to do. See you Thursday."

"Yes, Thursday."

Jared picked up a pile of letters lying on a table and left the room. Claire watched him go. "What?" she said, noticing Laura's amused expression. It didn't take long, however, before Claire guessed. "There's nothing between us."

"If you say so, dear," Laura said with a mother's knowing smile.

Up in the Lake District, Bella, unsettled, decided to drive to the church at Oakdale. She felt a compulsion to go back to the grave of violets. All the accumulated worry and grief surrounding the inexplicable loss of her brother, now reawakened by Claire and Jared's search, weighed heavy upon her. Her head ached and she felt exhausted by her asthma. She parked the car and made her way up the path towards the grave but found it harder to breathe with each step. The violets still bloomed and she felt uplifted by the sight of them. She sat down on the nearby seat, took two puffs from her inhaler then looked around, relishing the solitude and peace broken only by the occasional bleat from a lamb. Chilled by the overcast weather, she wrapped her large woollen jacket closer around her.

Would Claire and Jared find Philip? She still missed him. His disappearance had taught her that life held mysteries and dangers beyond her comprehension. The knowledge had always overshadowed her life with uncertainty but it *had* caused her to pursue a spiritual path, seeking answers to the puzzle of existence. Through it she had discovered meditation, which had always helped her, so she sat now in simple contemplation of the beauty of the grave.

There had to be a reason for it all, she thought. Her faith in a higher purpose had always sustained her through all the many disappointments of her life. As she sat there, she felt a growing stillness. This spot was sacred, she realised, and surrendered herself to the experience. A feeling of peace enveloped her but then something made her turn and she saw a blonde-haired child behind her.

She knew who he was. He said nothing, just looked at her and smiled. No words were necessary. Love poured from him, bathing her in a living light and warmth, which entered her heart.

That evening Bella rang to tell Claire. "I saw Charles."

"What? Where?"

"In the graveyard at Oakdale Church. As clear as anything." Bella told her what happened then exclaimed, "It's a miracle! I feel so energised and alive. I had a headache at the time and it vanished but, most amazing of all, is that my asthma has gone. It's made me so tired these last few years but now, now I feel invigorated, as if I could climb a mountain. I walked up the hill to visit my friend this afternoon and didn't even get puffed."

"That's incredible!"

The two women chatted on for a few minutes about Claire coming to stay in the house in Bowness on her return from Australia then Bella asked, "When are you off?"

"This Thursday."

"Good luck."

"Thanks. I think we may need it."

Chapter 17

THE ENGINES ROARED AS THE aircraft gathered speed. Claire gripped the armrests on either side. She saw the ground rushing past the window then, all of a sudden, her stomach lurched as the plane lifted off. Jared turned and gave Claire a reassuring smile. "You all right?"

She nodded. Never having flown before, she had been nervous but it felt fine, at least if she didn't think about it too much. She touched the necklace and sensed the subtle presence of Eleanora.

Claire glanced out of the window and stared down at the patchwork of tiny fields and towns of England passing down below. "Wow!" she exclaimed. "I can't believe I'm doing this." All fear fell away in her excitement and she felt a bubble of joy rise within her.

Jared smiled at her childlike enthusiasm. He had flown countless times and no longer gave it any thought but this time leant over and watched the view below too as Claire marvelled at it. He loved being in such close proximity to her. Thoughts of holding her close and kissing her came into his mind but he dismissed them, knowing all too well how messy intimate relationships could be. He didn't want anything to get in the way of their main goal: finding his father. They didn't have much time according to Claire.

The plane lifted higher and broke through the cloud layer into a clear blue sky. This must be heaven, so beautiful, so perfect, Claire decided, half expecting to see angels sitting upon the clouds below. She glanced at Jared who turned and smiled. Their eyes met and held then his gaze flicked down to her lips. Claire moved towards him but he pulled back and the moment passed. She knew Jared had thought to kiss her and it filled her with excitement. She wanted him to.

Claire turned her attention back to the scene outside the window. Everything seemed so simple up here, she only had to sit and watch, but knew, all too soon, they would descend into a strange and different world, one with no certainty of where the trail they were following would lead.

They stood together staring out at the azure ocean. Behind them the dense tropical forest stretched back towards the mountains. Dressed only in a thin sarong, she felt the breeze waft across her shoulders and legs. Jared reached for her hand and pulled her towards him. He stared into her eyes, brought his lips down on hers and something nudged her in the ribs. Startled, Claire opened her eyes.

"Hey," Jared said, "you don't want to miss this." He gestured towards the plane window.

After the long haul to Sydney and now this flight to Queensland, Claire had grown weary of flying. Jet lagged, all she wanted to do was to sleep, an impossibility with the roar of the engines.

She turned her head and came wide-awake. "Oh, *wow!*" Down below stretched a sparkling ocean dotted with small sandy islands highlighted by the brilliant sunshine. Some had clumps of dark trees whilst others shone white and empty. Beyond the sand, the translucent water gleamed turquoise before it merged into ink blue further out. In between the islands, laceworks of coral decorated the seabed.

"We're flying over the Coral Sea," Jared told her. "This is the Great Barrier Reef."

Claire couldn't believe it. She had seen a documentary about the reef but never dreamt she would see the real place. From that point on, she stared out of the window, enthralled, unwilling to miss a moment of it. Jared smiled to himself, though even he had to appreciate it was a fabulous sight.

The plane continued on along the coast of the mainland over forests and grasslands. Every so often, a curving river wound its way to the sea, glinting in the brilliant sunlight.

The plane made its approach into Cairns and, for a moment, Claire saw low mountains swathed in trees before they flew in over buildings and touched down on the airport runway. As the plane came to a halt, everyone stood, grabbed their luggage and jostled for the exit. Claire paused for a moment at the plane door, overwhelmed by the brightness and vibrancy of Australia, so in contrast to the softer light of England, and also the heat and humidity. Dazed, she followed Jared through the airport to pick up their luggage, grateful he knew what to do. While he hired a car, she stood and soaked in the atmosphere of the place.

The process complete, Jared jingled a set of keys at her. "We're ready to go." They followed a thickset man out to the car park where Claire found Jared had hired a large four-wheel drive vehicle. "I'm told you need them round here," he commented as he lifted in the suitcases. "Not all the roads are made up and we don't know where we might have to go."

Claire scrambled up into the front passenger seat. It felt weird to be so high. Jared thrust a map at her and pointed out their destination, Port Douglas, along the coast from Cairns. "This is where we're headed."

They began their journey along a wide road through a built-up area then passed out into the countryside through wide fields full of tall, feathery fronds waving in the breeze. "Sugar cane," Jared explained. "Are we on the right track?"

With reluctance, Claire pulled her gaze down to the map then stared back up at a passing side road. "Yes, we are. We need to turn right soon but not yet. Isn't it amazing? I can't wait to see the beach."

She adored North Queensland right from the start. She loved the wildness of it, the vistas of forest and mountains, vibrant in the bright sunlight and the rich variety of trees and plants so different from England.

Jared laughed at her joy but could not share it. He wished they could just rest and soak up the place, have fun as if nothing mattered, but the thought of his father here somewhere, perhaps even close by, filled him with a sense of urgency. He couldn't allow himself to lose focus.

Claire soon had her wish as the road took them beside the sea, a brilliant expanse of calm blue water lapping soft white sand backed by palm trees.

Sometime later, Claire directed Jared down a side road. After a few other turns, they found themselves driving through Port Douglas past hotels and resorts of various kinds both small and large.

They located their destination, a small hotel down a side road. It looked pretty dismal at first and Claire's heart sank but, as they entered through the main gate, they found themselves in a lush tropical garden. Small paths wound through the vegetation and from somewhere came the sound of falling water. They entered a small foyer and the attendant directed them to their two rooms, next to each other on the ground floor overlooking the garden and, to Claire's excitement, close to a swimming pool. A waterfall cascaded into it at one end.

"This is paradise," she cried but revised that opinion a short while later when Jared suggested they walk into town to get something to eat. They discovered they were not far from the beach. Claire kicked off her shoes and ran down to the edge. She didn't care what Jared thought; it felt so wonderful to walk through the clear water over soft sand. She stared at the expanse of sparkling sea in front of her then back at the palm trees moving in the breeze on the shore. "I was wrong, *this* is paradise."

"I'm hungry," Jared called.

"Okay." Claire ran back to the road. "Sorry, couldn't help it. Isn't it fabulous?"

"Yes," Jared agreed but she sensed his anxiety. "What is it?"

"Frankly, I'm scared," he admitted. "I don't know what we're going to find here."

Claire sobered. "It'll be all right," she said but could not stop herself absorbing his fear. She touched the necklace. It always calmed her. She sensed Eleanora's presence and felt strengthened.

"Let's have an early dinner," Claire said. "You're tired and hungry from the long flight. Then we'll get a good night's *quiet* sleep and start looking for your father tomorrow."

"You're right," he said but his voice lacked conviction. Having been the prime mover in getting them here he now found himself sailing without a rudder. "I'm not too sure what we should do next," he admitted. "How are we ever going to find my father, Claire?"

"We have a place to start, remember," she replied. "Mossman Gorge." The name thrilled her. "Philip," she whispered under her breath, "will we find you there?" She saw a vision of tall trees and the river pouring in white turbulence between rocky banks but failed to sense Philip. She did not mention this to Jared, instead chattering on in a cheerful voice about their surroundings to lift his mood.

They ate in a small bistro on the main street of Port Douglas, a place she found charming, full of restaurants and gift shops. Jared remained quiet and depressed the whole time and nothing she could say shook him out of it. She understood how stressful it must be, hoping to find the father he had never known, and felt compassion for him, and poor Laura, too, waiting at home wondering if now, forty years later, she would be reunited with the man she loved. Why did life thrust such challenges at people?

Afterwards, they paused by an ornamental pond in which a water lily bloomed. Its perfection lifted her spirits. Purple petals radiated around a vibrant yellow centre. Jared went into a shop to buy some sunglasses so Claire waited by the lily. The longer she stared at it, the more she felt connected to the flower, loving its purple colour, which reminded her of Eleanora, and how it glowed in the sunlight as it floated in the murky water of the pond.

Claire stared down into the depths. Hidden things moved down there. She felt repelled by the mysterious world beneath the surface of the pond but it occurred to her that the beautiful lily drew its sustenance from the dark mud of the earth, not only from the sun as a source of light. Dark and light, both bringing forth life, she thought, and wondered if somehow William and Barrett's manipulation of Philip, and all the other terrible things that went on in the world, had a part to play, whether they too could also bring forth beauty. Was it possible that truth, joy, love, spiritual growth, all the things that were important in life, needed the mud of humanity's struggles to sprout? The thought gave her comfort and, in that moment, she felt a deep connection to Laura and Philip, to Jared and Eleanora and her son, even William.

A shadow fell over the pond and Claire turned to see Jared scowling at her. "Let's go. I need some sleep."

She studied him, concerned by the harshness of his tone. He looked haggard and drawn from the strain of the long flight but something else about his manner disturbed her, although couldn't put her finger on it.

"I'd like to make an early start in the morning, if that's all right with you?" Jared said.

"Of course." Claire felt gutted by the coldness in his voice but struggled not to show it. What had got into him?

Claire woke at dawn, opening her eyes to sunlight streaming in through the window of her room. She could hear the sound of the waterfall. Two minutes later, grateful she had thought to bring a swimsuit, she waded into the shallow end of the turquoise pool. Although warmer than England, it was winter in the tropics so the water felt cold. She loved swimming. Last night Jared burst her bubble of joy about going in the ocean by explaining about the poisonous jellyfish. She had found a tourist leaflet explaining they were not around in June but felt reluctant to risk it now.

She sliced through the water, enjoying the feel of it on her skin, unaware Jared stood looking through his window. He continued to watch as she lifted herself out of the pool, appreciating the litheness of Claire's body in her yellow bikini. God, she was beautiful, he thought. He felt so drawn to this young woman. She had an ethereal quality about her, tiny and delicate, so open to life. To him she represented everything he was not. He felt closed off, cynical and afraid.

Claire wrapped herself in a towel, her hair hanging wet around her shoulders, and walked into her room.

He wanted her, Jared thought. Did she want him too? Sometimes he caught her watching him. He had treated her so badly at the start so he wouldn't blame her if she disliked him. Did she know his feelings? She had read him so well up to now. She *must* know and yet said nothing. That spoke volumes, he thought, and sighed, despondent. He got dressed, the heaviness of his mood intensifying as he contemplated the day. Would they find what they were looking for at Mossman Gorge?

A short time later, Claire met Jared for breakfast in the hotel restaurant. As she helped herself to fresh fruit and cereal, she noticed he still looked subdued. He felt remote, detached. "It will be okay," she reassured him but he remained unconvinced. It didn't reassure her either and anxiety took up residence in her stomach.

Used to being in control, Jared now had to trust Claire but felt afraid. He hadn't accepted the idea of William possessing Philip, it went against everything he believed in, but could not deny what he experienced in the Lake District. He feared what they would find in Australia but also wondered how he would feel meeting his father.

They wasted no time before climbing into their car and setting off, Claire with the map on her legs. The route proved to be straightforward and, in no time, they reached a sign indicating Mossman Gorge. Claire and Jared exchanged a glance as they turned down the narrow road. The tree-clad mountains rose dark in the distance as they left civilisation behind and drove into the rainforest.

They passed a sign reading Kuku Yalanji Dreamtime Tours, Guided Rainforest Walks. Claire sensed herself moving into a very different world. She knew very little about Indigenous Australians but the Dreamtime sounded mysterious, mystical. All she did know was that they felt a powerful affinity to the land on which they lived. As she stared around her, she understood why as her senses expanded to encompass the majesty of the landscape.

They reached a car park at the end of the road and Jared brought the car to a halt. As the engine stilled, the density of the trees and undergrowth permeated Claire's consciousness. She clambered out and looked around her. They were alone. The occupants of the two other cars in the car park had been absorbed into the forest.

Her senses heightened by the necklace, she could sense the powerful energy of the area and her nerve endings tingled,

They located a well-worn path and made their way through the trees, so different from the flat photographic images she saw back in England, now half a world away. The sheer physical presence of the forest took her breath away. So much growth, all tangling and entwining in a kaleidoscope of varied forms and she found it hard to adjust to the pungent odour of vegetation pervading the air.

The trunks of massive trees rose up to the light above, overrun by entwining vines and plates of white fungus. Palms spread out their fan shaped leaves. Moss and lichens clung to rocks on the forest floor. A large grey bird picked its way through the clumps of ferns.

They moved on through the dappled light of the forest. All around, tiny saplings thrust themselves up from the earth, ready to take the place of the older trees when they fell. Jared stopped and pointed. "Look."

Claire followed the direction of his gaze and noticed a flash of blue. Creeping closer, she saw it was a stunning butterfly with wings of turquoise edged in black. The creature allowed them to admire it for a few moments then flew off into the forest. Claire noticed even Jared seemed awed by their surroundings.

After a while, they heard the sound of rushing water. Rounding a bend, they came upon a wooden platform reaching out over a narrow river flowing beneath the arching boughs of trees. Stepping onto the planks, Claire gazed at the water, constricted at this point by large boulders, and felt dizzy with the untamed power of it all. In the distance, she glimpsed dark mountains.

Claire clung to the handrail to steady herself as the sheer presence of the place assaulted her senses. It pulled her attention into itself. Jared touched her arm, motioning her to move on and, dazed, she followed him back onto the path. Soon they reached a place where the river became wider and calmer. They scrambled down between large rocks onto a small beach of tiny stones and sand. Here the river took on a different guise. The water moved gently, emerald and crystal clear. Further along, whirlpools swirled where the current flowed strong. Claire moved to the river's edge, almost tripping over one of the many twisted tree roots washed free by the water.

Jared reached out to steady her and she smiled at him. He continued to hold her arm as they negotiated more roots along the bank. She liked the feel of his hand on her arm and drew strength from the human contact. It counterbalanced the impressions crowding in. Things were coming into her awareness she didn't know how to handle. Her instincts told her to block them out yet Claire knew, if she wanted to find Philip, she needed to open up. "I want to find somewhere to sit and be quiet," she said.

He understood, knowing from their experiences in the Lake District she needed time and space to allow insights to come.

Claire noticed a large boulder with a flat top right next to the water. She felt a sudden chill and a pulling sensation as if some unseen energy were drawing her to that area of the riverbank. "Over there," she said, pointing. They clambered over and Jared helped Claire up onto the rock. She settled down and looked around.

It was a great position. To her left, the river foamed down from upstream, passing into a deep section, which lay beneath her where the water whirled around and around. A small beach lay some way off to her right. The mountains lifted into the distance beyond the forest. Jared made as if to walk away. Apprehensive now, Claire asked, "Can you stay with me? I need you close, I think."

Jared felt irritated. He would have preferred to wander by the water than wait while she communed with the place or whatever it was she did. However, he sat beside her on the boulder. He massaged his brow. The strain of it all had given him a headache.

"Thank you," Claire said and gazed around at the river and trees. She kept her hand on the necklace for support and became still. A coil of fear tightened in her gut but she ignored it and took a deep breath. "Eleanora are you here?" she asked, concerned the connection might be weak so far from the spirit's grave.

"I am with you," came the reassuring words. "This is a wonderful place, so different to the Lake District. There is great power here. Remember to stay grounded. You can do this. You have grown strong these last days."

Claire did not feel strong, in fact, she felt small and vulnerable. Impressions from the forest pressed in upon her.

Eleanora fell silent and all Claire could hear was the water rushing down from the mountains. It filled her up and threatened to wash her away with it down the river to the sea. She relaxed her body as much as possible and extended her awareness to permeate the area, picking up on a feeling of sorrow held in remembrance by the stones and watching trees. She remembered the newspaper cutting they found in Philip's collection of pictures of Mossman, the one about the disappearance of Elaine Clarke.

Elaine had come here. She, like Philip, had been obsessed with Mossman Gorge. Why? What was it about this place?

As Claire opened up, she saw a vague figure standing upon a boulder nearby and knew it had been no accident she had been drawn to this particular spot. The image solidified into a slim young woman with long straight red hair, who stood with her head uplifted, gazing at the mountains. Elaine. Claire sensed the pain weighing her down, the unfulfilled dreams and alienation from others. She caught an impression of shyness and sensitivity and knew she had not been able to stand up for what she wanted. No one had ever listened. Rejected and humiliated by those she lived with, she had come to the limit of her endurance.

As Elaine's features became more defined, the image came of an angry blonde man striking her across the face. More visions came of her in a bathroom, weeping, her body bruised and bloody and then of her packing a suitcase and leaving. But she had not only left the house and town where she lived, but her country and travelled thousands of miles to this forest where the river poured down from the mountains.

"Why, Elaine," Claire whispered, "why did you come here?" The young woman stood for a long while staring out over the river. Claire sensed her waiting.

But for what?

The answer floated into her mind. Hope.

She was hoping for something more to sustain her in life. An end to the emptiness she felt inside.

Elaine scanned the surrounding forest, her senses reaching out, desperate for some sort of answer to her intense longing for the love and connection she had never found in her life. Rejected by her mentally ill mother at age three, she had been raised by a string of foster parents too busy to give her much attention. Then she met Craig. He seemed like everything she could ever have hoped for.

At first.

It did not take long for the soft words and caresses to fall away, replaced by angry orders she could never fulfil. She wanted answers as to why things had gone so wrong. Why did everyone hate her so?

Elaine waited but nothing happened. The pain in her heart, the fear and longing, the hoping for something to make everything okay, gripped her tighter. If only she could let go of it all but couldn't. She just couldn't.

A sense of hopelessness flooded though Elaine and her posture slumped. If there weren't any answers here in this special place, then where? She could not go on. Elaine stared down at the river. She felt the power of the water surging past. It held her attention and she could not look away.

Claire found herself watching in horror as the young woman allowed herself to fall into the turbulence, offering no resistance as the river took her into its cold embrace. Claire, identified with Elaine, had the sudden yearning to let go as well, give up the struggle of life, of trying to understand what it all meant, and sink into the water too, allowing it to take her.

She stared down into the river, at the frothing whiteness and the sound of it took over her mind. It became louder and louder. Mesmerized by the water surging and whirling, Claire leant down, further and further, pulled by the lure of the river, wanting peace like the woman in the past. She swayed, dizzy with it, and, in slow motion, inexorably, began to fall.

Chapter 18

A VICE TIGHTENED AROUND HER arm as Jared yanked Claire back onto the rock. "Jesus!" he exclaimed. "Don't do that to me. You could have fallen."

"Thanks," Claire gasped. "I'm sorry. I felt a bit light headed. I'm okay now."

"I'm going to hang on to you, if you don't mind."

"All right."

"Anchor to the earth, it will hold you secure," Eleanora said.

Still shaking from the shock, Claire sensed the solidity of the boulder beneath her and Jared holding her arm, now more gently, and came back into the present moment.

"You *can* let go," Eleanora continued, "not by surrendering to the river but to what you really are, your true being as Spirit. Allow it to guide you. The knowledge of this is what we need to heal the past and make all things right. This is your strength. It exists beyond all suffering, all shadows cast by the mind. Pain is an illusion, a whisper on the wind of your greater self."

Claire gazed around at the beauty of the forest and the swirling water and, as she sat in silence, became aware of a growing sense of sacredness. It was all around her, murmuring in the trees and flowing in the river, moving with the wind and shining in the sun. It spoke of the power of nature, so raw and obvious in that place and the beauty of what it was to be alive, to experience life as a human being and she knew, without doubt, behind it all there *was* something greater, something infinite and eternal, in which all the perfection around her rested. Then, with a shock that ran through the whole of her body, she became aware it was also her own true essence and knew that it shone throughout all creation and would never fade or die.

Claire sensed the young woman once again, as if they were both united in the spirit of the gorge, and found her attention being drawn down into the water below.

Elaine swirled around and around in a deep part of the river. Bubbles washed over her skin and a rushing filled her ears. Tightness gripped her chest but then, just when she thought her lungs would surely burst and the end would come, she saw the blue sky and green forest flickering through the silver surface of the water, a last glimpse of the world in which she could not live. But then something strange happened. All resistance left her body and she felt as if she were being held by an energy or force. It felt soft and gentle, like a loving caress and she knew, without doubt, she was not alone there within the river.

An overwhelming sadness flooded over her as if the whole world was mourning the tragedy of her wanting to kill herself and, in that moment, Elaine knew something existed that cared whether she lived or died, the spirit of life itself. It came to her then that she had been created for some reason, even though she herself could not see it, even if those she had sought love from did not see it. She had a worth to the universe or why else had it brought her into being?

It was wrong that she had allowed her life to be shaped by the violent dictates of her husband. What right had Craig, or his bitter, angry mother, with whom they lived, to determine her value, her worth? Elaine looked through the shifting surface at the blue sky and trees above and it was all so beautiful. Why had she not seen it before? A loving energy flooded her body and, in that moment, she wanted to live. The life she had sought to cast aside was far too precious to be denied. She felt an overwhelming regret for all the experiences of living in the world she would not now ever know.

The knowing also came that, although existence so far had been filled with pain and suffering, a definite purpose existed behind it all, a gift to be found she would never find if she turned aside from the world now, a thought she could not bear. Elaine strove to move her body, desperate now to resist the current of the water. Pain searing her lungs, it took all the strength she had to swim towards the light above.

Her face broke through the water and she took a blessed breath but sank back down. She refused to give up, however, and struggled to the surface yet again, this time managing to swim closer to the bank. Her toe touched the riverbed and she found her footing. Somehow, she waded up and out of the water to collapse, exhausted, on the riverbank.

She lay there for some time staring up, feeling the beating of her heart and the blood flowing through her veins and, as she did so, sensed again the sacred energy she felt before under the water but this time within her.

And in this she knew was strength and love but also peace, which would sustain her through whatever happened, however challenging things might be.

Claire felt this too as she connected to Elaine back through time. It was a sense of their own eternal nature, one with life itself.

After a while, Elaine stood. She made her way along the bank to where she had left her bag. She reached in and drew out a battered book with a painting of a river flowing through a forest on the torn dust cover. She clutched it to her chest for a moment and whispered, "Thank you, Philip." then replaced it in the bag, which she slung over her shoulder.

Claire gasped. Jared turned to look at her but she looked deep in meditation so he turned his attention back to the river and his own thoughts.

Although motionless, Claire felt anything but peaceful as her mind sought to come to terms with what Elaine had said. "Thank you, Philip!" What did it mean? Claire sought to sense more but only got an image of the young woman walking away through the forest. Claire knew she would not return to her husband, would simply disappear and leave them all wondering. She hoped Elaine found the better life she deserved.

Casting her gaze around her, Claire wondered what had made first Elaine, then William, want to come to Mossman Gorge? Eleanora said it was an area of great power and Claire could believe it after what she had just experienced. Did Elaine and William know that, and, if so, was it why they came? It was such a long way from home, there had to be a very good reason. And the book, what was *that* all about? She wished she had been able to make out the title.

No answers revealed themselves so Claire stilled herself and began to open out again, hoping to sense Philip. Her consciousness ranged through the water then the trees, touching them, sensing their life. She felt the forest and river within her awareness and relaxed even further to allow whatever impressions that came freedom to reveal themselves. When she failed to sense anything related to Philip at all, a wave of disappointment flooded through her, threatening to distract her, but she managed to stay with it and wait.

The water poured between the boulders and the trees rustled. Jared coughed and Claire's awareness sprang in his direction. She sensed a strange heaviness around him. Looking at him, he appeared tormented, as if struggling with something in his mind.

"Are you all right?" she asked but Jared didn't answer.

"Eleanora!" she called in her mind. "What's going on?"

"He is afraid," came the answer, "angry and hurt. All the sorrow around the loss of his father has been locked inside him. It is coming up here seeking release and can no longer be contained."

"How can I help him?"

"Just stay close and hold him in your heart, in your loving consciousness."

Jared felt sick. What had come over him? Sitting there waiting for Claire to tune in to what they needed to know made him feel helpless, impotent. Somehow it brought all the latent frustration of a life trying to succeed, to accumulate wealth, to the surface. The betrayal of the one person he had allowed himself to trust still burned and he wanted to lash out at someone or something. Part of him felt angry at Claire for bringing him on a wild goose chase across the world, wasting his money, money he didn't have much left of after that bitch Andrea cheated him. When Claire leant out over the water, he hadn't wanted to help her, even for a second, hoping she would fall! At the last moment, his reason had taken back control and now he felt appalled. How could he have thought of doing such a thing?

Claire sensed the negativity in Jared and felt concerned. Something wasn't right. She sensed darkness and moved her attention towards it.

"No!" Eleanora exclaimed. "Don't be drawn into Jared's pain. Focus on your breathing and feel the rock beneath you. Stay connected to how you felt a moment ago, to what you now know you are, to that which is free and clear in you. Remember it, do you hear me?"

Eleanora's voice became fainter as Claire connected to Jared. She wanted to help him, heal his suffering. With a shock that ran through her whole body, she realised she loved him. She yearned for him and needed him. He must not get lost; she would not allow it.

"No," said Eleanora. "Step back! You have to let go of him. It is not your battle. You can help but not if you're in it too."

Claire took a breath and pulled back into her own body sitting by the river. The moment she did so, a weight lifted from her chest and she felt the presence of Eleanora and Charles upholding her. "If you fight it," Eleanora said, "you will give the spirit power."

"Spirit?"

"Yes, one of the Circle is with Jared. He has been since you arrived in Port Douglas. He entered him because he has become lost in his pain and anger and been broadcasting this. William is somewhere in this area, as are other members of the Circle. Barrett is very powerful and has sensed our presence, that we want to help Philip and he has sent this spirit to prevent us.

"Did you know that something like this might happen?" asked Claire.

"Yes, but it would not have helped you to know it. You would have been filled with great fear."

"You're right, I would," conceded Claire. "But what can we do, Eleanora?" Claire looked at Jared. Her heart sank when she saw his eyes focussed on nothing.

"Don't worry. It might work to our advantage. I believe he may lead us to Philip. I don't think the spirit will be able to do much as he not yet got total control of Jared. It will take him some time to do so and, in the meantime, will not want to betray his presence too soon. You *must* step back," Eleanora repeated.

"But how?" Claire moaned inwardly.

"Remember what you have experienced here today and stay with the knowledge of that. William and Barrett, and those others drawn to be with them, have turned away from their true essence, no longer even believing in its existence. They are imprisoned in their belief they are separate individuals in a hostile universe and cannot see beyond the shadow world created by their fear and pain, their need to control and manipulate." The words were tinged with a subtle sadness and something else.

"You feel sorry for them, don't you, even Barrett!" Claire said, aghast.

"Yes, I do. In no way do I condone their actions but we must have compassion. They will suffer from the consequences of what they have done, make no mistake about that. We reap what we sow. Evil will draw evil to itself. They are to be pitied.

"But who are we to condemn, anyway? In our blindness and ignorance, we also often hurt others and so we must have compassion for ourselves too. Mistakes are inevitable as we struggle to understand our place in the universe but all things will work out if we live life with the honest intention to do the best we can, rectify any suffering we cause if we can and look for the lesson in what happens."

Eleanora paused and an impression of Eleanora and Robert together flashed into Claire's mind.

"I no longer blame myself for my affair with Robert but I *do* know that it is my responsibility to do what I can to release poor Philip and bring William back. I have to help him turn from the shadowland in which he now lives so he can remember there is more and come with me into the Light. Then I can rest.

"We must also not be so quick to judge. Things are more than they appear. Behind all that happens runs a hidden purpose. We are all playing our parts in a larger drama.

"Was what happened with William ultimately good or bad, right or wrong? Much suffering arose but out of it also came a powerful yearning in me to know the truth behind life. I spent many hours alone in contemplation and discovered my oneness with Spirit. In this I found the true love I always craved and sought through William then Robert. From this spiritual connection also came the power of healing. If William had not rejected me, I would never have been able to heal the suffering of others. There are always blessings."

On reflection, Claire had to concede the truth of this. Searching for Philip was pretty scary but she now knew she was more than just her physical self. She had connected to something powerful and amazing, and this was setting her free in a way she might not have learned in any other way. Would she want to return to the restricted view of life she had before? Would she have not wanted to meet Jared who she now realised she loved? No.

Eleanora continued. "Laura also grew in love and strength in a way she would never have done without the rough edge of circumstances to hone her development."

"But Jared?" Claire asked. "What should we do?" Looking at the anguish in his face, her heart went out to him knowing he couldn't see anything but his fear and pain. She touched him on the arm and he came back to himself.

"Claire, sorry, I was miles away. I..." He looked confused. "I felt, I don't know, something." He shrugged. "It's all right. It's nothing. I'm so sorry. Are *you* okay? Did you sense anything?"

She stared into his eyes and knew he had no awareness of the spirit that had been drawn to him. As she sensed him, she felt the presence of a shadow in his aura and shuddered.

"What is it? Have you discovered something?" Jared's brow creased with anxiety. When Claire hesitated, unsure what to say to him, he continued, "You *are* all right, aren't you? I wouldn't want anything to happen to you." Concern for her dominated his consciousness now, Claire thought, with relief. Jared was strong but would he be strong enough to survive possession?

"I'm fine," she reassured him and described what she had experienced with Elaine. "It was amazing, she and I were so connected, and not only to each other, but to this whole place. There is a depth to life, another dimension, beyond normal experience. I felt it, Jared. I really *felt* it.

"I'll just have to take your word for it," Jared replied, cynical.

"This place healed Elaine." Claire continued. "She came suicidal but left feeling she could live her life anew."

"But what about my father?" Jared asked, impatient.

"I don't know where he is yet but I *do* know he is close. Eleanora told me we must just wait for the right moment, that we will be guided." She did not mention that Jared himself would guide them. He did not need to know this. Perhaps we should go back to Port Douglas and have some lunch," she suggested. "I need a break. I'm starving."

"Good idea," Jared said. "I have the most terrible bloody headache."

Claire remained subdued throughout the drive back to Port Douglas. So much had happened. Part of her still felt a powerful connection to the landscape behind them. And Jared worried her. She hadn't expected a spirit to attach itself to him and it scared her. She didn't know what she had expected but this whole exercise was so far out of her experience it defied all attempts to understand it.

She was having to revise her whole concept of life and death knowing now the spirit remained when the body died. In most cases, it moved on to its next phase of existence beyond the physical world to continue its evolution but in certain circumstances this did not happen and spirits remained connected to the earth and other people. Some became attached to them or took possession of their bodies. Claire looked at Jared gripping the steering wheel, his teeth clenched and shuddered. One of the Circle had entered him. The thing was; could she trust Jared now? He looked at her and smiled but it lacked conviction and she knew he felt unwell.

Sensing the presence of Eleanora, Claire asked. "What can I do?"

"Just love him. Hold him in your heart and it will help to anchor him to you."

Claire thought of what she had experienced with Elaine at the river. They had connected with something sacred, an ineffable presence within them that also permeated the landscape. The sense of it grew again and it lifted her mood. It gave Claire hope that somehow, even though it all seemed so impossible, everything would turn out all right. It had to. The thought of losing Jared was unbearable.

Claire leant back in her seat and closed her eyes. She needed to rest.

They had lunch in a small café on the seafront near their hotel then walked along the beach. They wandered along the sand listening to the waves. How lovely it was, Claire decided. How could anything harmful exist in such a paradise but then remembered that at certain times box jelly fish lurked in the water ready to inflict pain on any unsuspecting swimmer who ventured too close.

She kept a careful eye on Jared but he seemed okay. He had taken some medication for his headache but remained subdued, content to allow her to take the lead now. Still feeling the effects of the long journey from England, they lay down under a palm tree grateful for a chance to rest. Claire's eyelids grew heavy and her eyes closed.

Sometime later she opened her eyes, at first unable to take in her surroundings, but then it all came crowding back into her consciousness. She turned to look at Jared but saw he no longer lay beside her! Alert, she scrambled to her feet and scanned the beach but saw only a young couple walking along the water line. A horrible feeling grew in the pit of Claire's stomach. This didn't feel right.

Claire walked all around the area and back through the town to the hotel where they had left the four-wheel drive. It wasn't there!

He could have just gone to some shop or perhaps a bar for a drink, she reasoned, but knew it wasn't true. Jared had always shown great consideration for her safety, even when he didn't trust her, so wouldn't leave her sleeping alone on the beach. Not if he was in his right mind! Christ! How could she have been so stupid as to leave Jared unattended when she knew he'd been affected by a spirit? She was a fool, a complete fool.

Claire sat down on a seat in the hotel garden overwhelmed by doubt. She couldn't *do* this, she thought. How could *she* deal with powerful spirits? She was far too weak and useless. A terrible dread gripped her chest, draining her of hope, of all courage. She saw herself losing Jared and being taken over herself, Laura waiting in vain at home in England.

"Stop!" came Eleanora's voice. "Let go your fearful thoughts and lurid imaginings right now; they are not true. These projections will enslave you if you pay attention to them. You will not be taken over if you centre in yourself, the power of your own living Light, for it is the place where true peace and power may be found. Return to awareness of your physical body and notice what is around you. This will bring you back to the present moment."

Claire tore her attention from the images filling her mind and focussed on the sound of the trickling water. It washed over her and she felt herself relax.

"Yes, now centre in your body, the feeling of it, the aliveness. Find the stillness, the clarity, which is your essence. You know now in this you will always find strength and peace and guidance.

Claire *did* know. She wished she could remember it more, though, stop herself from slipping back into her former ways of thinking. She focussed on a bright green insect crawling along a leaf. It moved slowly, yet with purpose, one hinged leg in front of the other. She stared fascinated and the tightness in her chest lessened.

"Good," Eleanora said. "Now, you love Jared. Feel it, allow it to grow. Focus on that. Bring him into your awareness and into your heart." Claire did so, connecting with the image of his face and remembering how caring he had become before the spirit came. A vision of the rainforest and the sound of flowing water came into her mind followed by a view of the car park they had been in earlier. "He's gone back to Mossman. My God! Why's he done that?"

Eleanora sought to gain a sense of the situation. "I believe he may be trying to resist the control of the spirit," she said. "The spirit could be trying to influence him to do things he does not want to do, maybe even harm you. The spiritual energy at the Gorge is very powerful and I think he may sense that so has returned there to try and free himself. He does not know what he is doing. We must help him. It is getting late and will be dark soon. You must hurry." For a moment Claire felt immobilized then realised she could get a taxi there. She remembered seeing a place in town where taxis waited. Claire set off in that direction.

Don't think, she told herself. Don't think. It will be all right. It will be all right. She repeated this phrase over and over as a mantra to prevent her fearful thoughts from gaining dominion in her mind.

It did not take long to find a taxi and she directed it to Mossman Gorge. The driver looked at her with curiosity but said nothing. The trip passed in a blur during which Claire continued to recite her mantra to herself until they pulled up about half an hour later in the now familiar car park. Two cars waited there but neither of them was their rented four-wheel drive. Claire's heart sank. Jared hadn't come here after all. As she took a few deep breaths and cast her awareness through the surrounding forest, a feeling of peace arose, a sense of rightness about her decision to come to Mossman Gorge. It was important to be here and she felt it definitely had something to do with Jared.

Claire felt nervous about being in the forest alone but knew she had to follow this lead. She did not know what else to do. She felt sick as she paid the driver. He handed her a card along with her change. Claire looked at it without comprehending. "It's our firm's number for when you want to come back," the driver explained. "This is no place to be at night," he warned.

"Oh, yes, thanks." She hadn't thought of getting back. Grateful, she tucked the card in her bag.

As the taxi drove away, the sound of the forest intensified. Now alone, she felt vulnerable. "It will be all right, it will be all right," Claire whispered to herself and hurried down the path towards the river as fast she could. It would be dark soon.

She fancied the light was dimming already. How long did she have? Fumbling in her bag, she found the small torch she always kept with her for emergencies. She stayed on the path, knowing it would be easy to find her way back. A rustling off to one side made her jump but she relaxed at the sight of a bird moving away.

Her heart beat fast as she made her way to the river's edge. She stopped and cast her awareness around the area, hesitant at first, but then remembering she had Eleanora and perhaps Charles with her, with more confidence.

Nothing came, only a feeling of living energy from the forest and river. The rapids gleamed white in the dusk. Claire moved on along the path until she reached a lookout built over the water itself. She stared down into the foaming turmoil below and felt something building in her awareness, the power of unbridled nature. Taking a deep breath, she took strength from it and felt somehow the land welcomed her, perhaps would even aid her.

"Where are you, Jared?" she whispered. "What are you doing?" She felt an echo of his presence but sensed he had now gone. But where? Claire glimpsed a faint light down by the water but it winked out, then she saw another off to her left. Spirits. Her heart rate increased even more but she tried to stay calm, sensing they would not hurt her. They only came drawn by wonder that someone should be there at nightfall. In fact, she felt the welcoming feel from the environment increase until she felt blanketed in peace. Up in the darkening sky, a single star shone. It gave her hope, something bright to focus on, the knowing that normality existed outside the bizarre situation she found herself in and that one day she would return to live in that world.

But not yet.

She continued on into the forest again, sensing around her. The peace in the place intensified until she felt absorbed by the forest, a part of it like one of the trees. She stopped and felt her roots burrowing down into the soil. Down and down, yet her branches touched the beauty of the night sky. Held in thrall, she could not move. Darkness fell and the moon rose. Bats flew through the trees but even they did not faze her as she stood, held fast by the spirit of the place. She felt as if she could stand there a thousand years, a million years, like the mountains, but she had to find Jared.

She called his name into the night hoping to get a feel for him but nothing came. The bizarre idea came to ask the forest for its help. "Where did he go?" she whispered and listened. When again, nothing came, Claire became despondent. This was ridiculous. She couldn't stay here in the dark, she decided, but, at that precise moment, heard the sound of someone walking towards her!

Claire tensed. Jared had gone so it could be anybody. She was alone in the forest at night. Rigid with fear, she waited, her senses hyper alert. Clicking her torch on, she circled, sweeping the light through the trees.

Third time round, she saw it.

A face.

Staring at her!

Chapter 19

"YOU ALL RIGHT, MISS?" THE man standing in front of her asked. Claire stared at him. He had dark brown skin, shaggy greying long black hair and a beard. She recognised him as an Indigenous Australian, one of the original inhabitants of Australia living there way before any settlers arrived to plunder their land. He looked to be in his late forties and wore a white T shirt and jeans. His feet were bare. He had stopped a short distance away and stood looking at her.

The moment she saw the man, the knowing came she need not fear him. He had come to help her. Her parents, thousands of miles away in London, would be appalled if they could see her in what looked to be so risky a position—in a forest at night with a strange man, but they did not have the necklace, they could not see beyond the limits of their normal world.

They thought the physical universe was the only one.

The man stared at her for a few moments then moved closer to look at her necklace. He reached out and lightly touched the amethyst crystal with one finger before stepping back. "The lady with you says you're searching for someone."

"You can see her?"

"The lady in white, yes," he gestured to Claire's left.

"Who are you?" she asked.

"You can call me Jack. I live in these parts."

"My name is Claire. I'm looking for my friend. He's about thirty with dark hair and..."

"Yes, your lady already asked me about him."

"Do you know where he is?"

"He's with the old man."

Claire gasped and thought of Philip. "What old man?"

"Tugger."

Claire's heart sank but then the thought came that perhaps it still might be Philip.

"Is that his real name?"

"Shouldn't think so but it's what he's known as round here."

"Is he ever called Philip Harcourt?"

"Dunno."

"Do you know Tugger well?"

"Me and him have had a few beers."

"Can you take me to him?"

Jack nodded. He turned and walked away through the forest away from the river. Claire followed but became nervous when they left the well-defined path. What if he left her alone? She would have no idea how to get back. What if there were snakes? All kind of things lurked in the forest. She knew this from the Internet and tourist literature she read at the hotel. Jared in his typical way had focussed on the dangers and teased her with ghastly comments about leeches and insects dropping on people walking in the forest, the bastard! She hadn't worried at the time but now she was walking through it and couldn't even see! The tropical rain forest was a wilderness and so very far from the tame woods of England.

But she didn't have any choice and felt this man meant her no harm; the forest had sent him. Hopefully, he wouldn't want to get bitten by snakes either and would know what to do.

It will be all right, she told herself and followed Jack deep into the forest. It will be all right. It will be all right...

Claire stumbled and almost fell. They had been going through the forest for what seemed like hours. She felt hot and tired. Jack set quite a pace, dipping and diving through the undergrowth, turning this way and that to avoid trees and other pitfalls along the way. Every so often he stopped and motioned her forward more cautiously. She did not like to imagine what he was trying to avoid. It didn't seem like they were following any path the way they wove in and out but Jack seemed very sure of the direction they were heading.

The mantra had fallen away as Claire struggled to keep up and negotiate the roughness of their route. A bright moon now hung in the clear sky so she could just make out the surrounding forest although it remained veiled in shadow. They stopped once, why Claire could not tell. Jack appeared to be listening. She glanced upward and stared in amazement at the vast sweep of night sky filled with millions of stars. Never had she seen so many in one place, the clouds and street lights in London prevented them showing up but here...this was wilderness, far from any city sprawl.

Jack moved on and Claire followed, still worrying. Jared wouldn't have found his way through this, she thought. Her intuition told her he hadn't and yet she still had the strong sense that following Jack was the right thing to do. It will be all right. It will be all right. It will be all right...

Sometime later, Jack stopped. "Tugger's place," he said and Claire saw a soft light gleaming through the trees ahead.

Whatever she expected to find, it was not this.

A wide stretch of green grass swept up to the edge of a floodlit swimming pool. A big, white painted modern building with large plate glass windows stood beyond. Whoever owned the place had money. Was Jared here? She felt unsure and afraid but Jack walked across the lawn towards a doorway at the back of the building. Claire pulled herself together and followed, her heart pounding.

As they moved closer to the house, an external light flashed on. Caught in the spotlight, Claire felt exposed and vulnerable. Jack knocked on the door and so, sick with fear, she had no choice but to hurry up and stand at his side. In moments, the door opened and Claire found herself looking into dark brown eyes, familiar dark brown eyes. Although the skin around them had aged and his hair had turned grey, she recognised him.

Philip!

Despite his advanced years, he still looked vital and held himself in a good posture, although he carried some excess weight around his middle. "Jack, mate, good to see you," Philip said then his gaze fell on Claire and his eyes widened in surprise. "And you are?"

"Claire," she said, her voice high pitched in fear, unprepared to be confronting Philip so soon and all too aware she was also in the presence of William. She felt sick at the thought but sensed she had no choice but to go along with what was happening for the moment.

"Come in, come in." Philip said affably, standing aside and allowing them to pass into a tiled passageway. The instant he shut the door, Claire felt trapped and oppressed by the heaviness of the atmosphere.

She couldn't believe she was looking at Philip. He did not seem possessed. He acted normal. She had expected to find a wreck, someone only half alive, but this man looked to have a good life, be in control of his faculties and be successful. They followed him through the house to a lounge overlooking the pool. Claire looked around for any sign of Jared but found none. "Sit down," Philip said, motioning to a couch. "Can I get you a beer?" he asked Jack.

"Sure."

"What about you, Claire?" Philip looked at her and she met his gaze for a second, trying to see what she could sense but anxiety made it impossible to relax. Nothing. "I'm fine...thanks."

Philip fetched two cans of beer and handed one to Jack. "So, what brings you to my door so late at night?" he asked.

Jack said nothing, just stood there so Claire mumbled, "I'm... I'm looking for a friend of mine."

"And who might that be?"

"His name is Jared. He's in his thirties, tall, dark hair, thin. Have you seen him?"

"Can't say that I have," Philip replied smoothly.

He was lying. Claire could feel it. Her stress levels shot to the roof.

"Why do you think I might have seen him?" Philip asked.

"I... was told he came here." It sounded so lame and she looked at Jack but he ignored her, intent on drinking his beer.

"Oh? By who?"

"Er, a friend," she said, for some reason reluctant to say it had been Jack. She decided to try something. "Does the name Laura mean anything to you?"

Philip's eyes narrowed. "Laura," he repeated. Quickly, Claire shot in with, "Have you ever been to the Lake District? In England," she emphasised when Philip's face remained impassive. "Bowness by Lake Windermere?" Claire's mind sought to find some key to reach him and struggled to think of something, anything.

"The Grave of Violets" she said, on impulse. "At St Giles' Church there is a grave where violets grow. You loved that place. You took Laura there." It was a long shot and she knew it would sound weird to anyone listening but it had been a special place for Philip. It was worth a try.

It hit home! Philip's eyes widened in shock and a subtle change came over his face. The calm assurance fell away and Claire caught a glimpse of another persona, a confused hesitant one. He looked pained, as if he were trying to remember something. "Violets?" he repeated, "Laura?" He looked wistful but then it was over. A shutter came down and he pulled himself together. "No," he said. "I'm sorry none of that means anything to me. I've never met you before so why do you think I would know this Laura? I think you've got the wrong person."

But Claire knew she hadn't. Just for an instant there had been a hint of recognition, a glimpse of the real Philip. Deep down he was still there and remembered something, she could tell. But William had control. She could sense him now, *feel* his different presence. The longer she sat in that lounge, the more she recognised the man she had seen visions of at Waterford House with Eleanora. He did not look like William, for he had taken over the body of another, but she sensed his energetic resonance in a way she did not fully understand yet felt. She had an impression of hardness, of determination, an intention to achieve his ends come what may, and suppressed a shudder.

Philip scrutinised her and something told her he could tell she knew who he was yet on the surface he remained completely normal. He smiled but it held no warmth.

Jack finished his beer and stood. "Well, if you can't help us, mate, I reckon we'll be on our way. Sorry to trouble you." He looked at Claire and she stood too, realising she wasn't going to get any further. They had entered the house by the back door. Now Philip led them to the front. As they walked down the hall, Claire glanced into another lounge and could not suppress a gasp. A large picture dominated the room: an eagle with outstretched wings and talons extended, coming in for the kill. Claire shuddered. "Do you like my painting?" Philip asked. "It's so life-like, don't you think?"

"Yes," Claire said feeling as if she were going to vomit as they walked past. Philip opened the door and they passed outside. Before they left, on an impulse she would regret later, Claire said. "If you *do* remember anything, I'm staying at the Paradise Lodge in Port Douglas."

"I don't think I will," Philip said. "I'm sorry I couldn't help you. See you, Jack."

"Night."

The door shut and Claire realised they stood in a street with several other large, expensive looking houses like the one they had just left. Philip had obviously done well for himself to be living in such an area.

Jack started walking.

"Hey wait, where are you going?" Claire ran to catch up and asked, "Why did Philip, Tugger, deny seeing my friend? What made you think he went there?"

"'Cos I seen him."

"My friend, he's tall, dark hair, clean-shaven. He's wearing dark trousers and a blue shirt."

"Yeah, that sounds like him for sure."

"So, you saw him with Phil... Tugger? When, where?"

"About two hours ago when I passed earlier this evening. They were stood in the garden."

"So why didn't you say anything to Tugger just now?"

"Thought you could handle it."

"But..."

Jack started walking down a track back into the rainforest.

"Where are you going?"

"Home."

"You can't just go."

Jack stopped and looked at Claire. "I don't want to get involved."

"But you *are* involved. Why did you talk to me in the first place?"

Jack sighed. "I work in the tourist centre. I heard you in the forest and came to see if you were in trouble. Most tourists have left by nightfall. When I found you, I saw your lady."

"Eleanora?"

"Yes."

"You see spirits?"

"Sometimes. She asked me if I'd seen your friend. I told her I had and she asked me to take you to Tugger. That's it."

"And how do you know Tugger?"

"I see him around. He likes a drink, doesn't care where he gets one. He's a big man in these parts, I think. Owns a lot of hotels but he likes to rough it. Gambling, women, you name it, he likes it. Everyone knows Tugger round here. Been picked up off many a bar floor. I fetched him out of the forest once, too. I took him home."

"What do you mean?"

"Found him passed out by the river. Been drinking heavily. I reckon he was lucky he didn't fall into it."

"What's he like?"

Jack looked awkward. He glanced towards the forest and shifted on his feet.

"Please tell me, Jack," she implored. "It's very important."

Jack remained silent for a while then said, "He has darkness with him."

"What do you mean?"

"Sometimes I see stuff around people. Light an' that, but he has a dark cloud around him. And he's tense. Man, you can feel it when you get close. It's as if he's trying to hold something back. I reckon it's why he drinks. Then there's the fella always with him."

"Who?"

"A young man. Now he's a bad one." Jack shuddered.

Barrett. It had to be Barrett, Claire thought, in a young man's body.

"Why would Tugger deny seeing my friend?"

"I dunno."

Claire felt the reassuring presence of Eleanora. "Let him go," she said.

"Okay, Jack, thanks. You've helped me so much. You get home."

"Are you gonna be all right?"

"Yes, I think so. I'll go to my hotel, maybe Jared's gone back there." Claire fished in her bag. "I have the number of a taxi company somewhere." Locating it, she continued, "Now if I could work out where I am..." She glanced around and noticed a street sign. "Oh good, Cascade Road. That's okay, I'll call them now."

Jack watched her while she called.

"They said they wouldn't be long," Claire said when she hung up. "Do you need a lift?"

"No, I like walking at night."

"You go, then."

When he hesitated, Claire continued, "Honest, I'll be fine. I'm not alone."

"All right, night then," Jack said.

"Goodnight, oh, and Eleanora, my lady, said to tell you 'don't worry about your back. It'll be okay now.'"

Jack stared in amazement. "What did she do? It *does* feel better."

"Eleanora is a healer."

"Thanks." He paused then said, "I guess if you need any more help just ask for me at the tourist centre."

"Okay."

Claire watched Jack walk off into the forest. She was lucky and didn't have to wait long before a taxi arrived.

As they turned into the hotel car park later, Claire noticed the four-wheel drive. Jared had returned!

Chapter 20

C LAIRE PAID OFF THE TAXI driver and hurried over to Jared's room. She hammered on the door, hoping he would be there, but it remained shut. What the hell was he doing? As she hovered, unsure what to do next, the door swung open. Claire looked at Jared and felt sick. The heaviness she sensed earlier had intensified and he looked as if he didn't recognise her. This wasn't the man she knew.

"Jared?" Claire whispered.

He continued to stare at her with a cold, blank expression but then his face slowly softened and he looked lost and bewildered, as if he didn't even know the time of day, like someone drugged. The heaviness receded and she knew Jared had returned. At least for the moment.

Jared moved aside to allow her to come in. "I'm sorry," he said, "I'm not feeling too well. My headache has worsened and I've had to take some strong medication for it."

"Why did you leave me on the beach?" Claire demanded.

"What? I told you I was going to go and rest at the hotel." He looked unsure. "Didn't I? I... I... meant to."

"Oh, Jared," Claire whispered. She reached out a hand and touched his face. "Jared," she repeated. "You don't remember anything else?" she asked. "Driving? Going to Mossman Gorge? Meeting someone?"

Jared looked exhausted and sat down on a couch. "I... I did have some sort of dream like that."

"Tell me," she said, sitting next to him. "What did you dream?"

"I... I was in the forest, by the river... just walking... then I was driving to a house... there was a man. I saw a bird... yes, it was an eagle... I can't remember the man clearly but he seemed familiar. I knew him. This is crazy, why do you want to know?"

What should she tell him? Claire wondered. "Did the man do anything?"

"He... touched my head... I'm sorry. That's it. Why are you asking me all this?"

"Just curious," she said. "Don't worry. You look like you need some sleep." She stood. "I'll see you in the morning." She walked to the door but then turned.

"I care about you, Jared. I really care about you. Don't forget me."

He looked confused. "What the hell are you talking about? I'm not going to forget you."

Claire's heart broke at seeing him in such a state and she longed to let Jared know how much she had grown to love him.

"He needs to know," Eleanora said. "It's important."

Claire walked back to the couch. "I more than care for you, Jared, I love you. I *love* you," she repeated. Shock spread all over his face and he opened his mouth to speak but she put her fingers on his lips. "No, don't say anything. Just remember it, all right? I'll see you in the morning."

Jared remained seated, with a dazed expression on his face, as Claire walked out of the door.

The moment it shut behind her, tears came, knowing she had felt the presence of the shadowed entity who had possession of Jared. Claire rushed to her own room and threw herself on the bed, her mind reeling. Jared had gone to the forest but then the spirit made him drive to Philip's house. But why? What happened there? She knew Jared still struggled to retain control and hoped saying she loved him would help him hang on.

"Eleanora, Eleanora, how did this happen?"

"When the members of the Circle seek out someone to possess, they find those whose frequency they resonate with, those who follow a similar path. Like tends to attract like. Those who seek to control and manipulate are open to being manipulated themselves. This is why Jared has been affected. He has been hurt, first by the loss of his father, having to witness the struggles his mother went through coping with her grief and loneliness, then the betrayal by his fiancée. His bitterness and anger made him vulnerable."

"My God!" Claire breathed. "That's awful. Poor Jared. What will the spirit do with him? What can we do?"

"Don't worry," Eleanora answered, "the light of your love will stop him being dominated by the darkness. This is the key. He is unconscious of his true nature so you must hold the Light for him as you do for yourself. That is why I told you to tell Jared you love him. Jared loves you too. If you can connect with that it will help keep him safe. The spirit that is seeking to use him will not succeed."

"It's so scary. Does this sort of thing happen to many people?"

"Not very often, most people haven't lost touch with their hearts, with love, at least not completely, and therefore do not attract such souls."

"But what of Philip?"

"We have to somehow reach him, help him reconnect with his heart and with love, the truth of who he is, then William will lose his power."

"But how can we do that? It seems so impossible."

"We will find a way. The main problem we have is Barrett. He is helping William stay in control of Philip. Barrett is a darker soul who has been lost to the Light for many, many generations."

Claire shuddered, remembering her encounters with Barrett. She felt a surge of anger and fear as she thought of him.

"Remember he too once suffered, he just sought answers in the wrong direction," Eleanora said gently.

"I still don't know how you can have compassion for someone who takes over other people's bodies?"

"What would you have me do? To hate and condemn would make me no better than him. It would make me weak. No, our strength lies in our ability to forgive, to have compassion, for it connects us to the sacred unconditional Love within, and it is that which will draw those we care about back to us."

"I hope so. Oh God, I really hope so."

"You must do more than hope, dearest, you must *believe,* then you will be strong and can help Jared and Philip. You have Charles and I to assist you, and others too. Together we can bring them back. This is why you were chosen. This is your destiny in this life."

"Chosen?"

"Yes. As I have told you before, it was no accident you saw the necklace that day and were attracted to it. Events are more than they seem on the surface. There are things that need to be worked out, experienced by us, in order for us to grow, for all of us to grow. Remember the water lily at Port Douglas?"

"Yes," Claire remembered the vibrant purple blossom arising from the hidden depths of the pond, blending the nutrients from the mud and the light of the sun into beauty. As the image of the sun came into her mind, she had a strong sense of Charles. Yes, a golden child, she thought. Then the realisation came, more than a child.

An image came: of him with his father, William, walking through the dirty, crowded and noisy conditions of the factory. Charles smiled at everyone. Old men doffed their caps at him or touched their forelock in respect and women looked at him with adoration. He had an unworldly quality, an inner light and a strength and beauty the darkness of his father's world could not extinguish.

Claire felt it now. Although she could not see him, his presence spread around her in a golden glow, brightening her own light and chasing her fears and forebodings away. The thought came that some are born ancient, endowed with the wisdom of the ages. He chose to maintain the image of a child for her perception but, in reality, could take any form.

"Yes, you are right. I was so blessed that he came to me as my child," Eleanora said. At that moment, a vision came to Claire of Eleanora with Charles, who looked to be about five or six, walking in the long grass by the lake at Waterford Hall.

Charles stopped and held out his hand. A white butterfly landed upon it. "Look how beautiful he is, Mother." Eleanora smiled to see the fascination on her son's face. He found everything interesting. The butterfly flew off and they continued their walk. A little later, they came across an injured swan. It lay limp by the edge of the water, barely breathing, its white feathers darkened with mud. "Oh no," Eleanora cried. Charles ran forward and knelt down. With great gentleness, he stroked the graceful neck.

"What are you doing, little one?" she asked.

"I am loving it better," Charles answered.

"Oh, my dear, he is too broken. There is nothing you can do."

She tried to ease him away but he would not move.

Eleanora sighed. He looked so peaceful she did not have the heart to make him stop so sat down beside him and watched as he caressed the bird. She sensed great love emanating from him and it moved her to tears. A pool of sacred stillness surrounded Charles and she felt drawn into it. In time, the bird stirred and Eleanora watched in amazement as it struggled into an upright position. Charles helped it to the water and it floated away.

"From him I learned so much. I believe he came to me because I had opened up to Spirit and longed to help others. He showed me how to heal. He taught, not with words, but by his presence. Charles came to illuminate the lives of others, show by his example the power of the Light of Love that shone so bright within him. This was his sacred purpose on earth, fulfilled in just the few years of his earthly life. Even William could not remain immune from Charles's influence which was why my husband was so devastated when our son died."

"That's amazing," Claire said, in awe.

"Rest now," Eleanora said. "We will watch over Jared."

Claire opened her eyes the next morning and lay half asleep listening to the sound of the waterfall in the swimming pool outside her room. But then she remembered the events of the previous day and came wide awake. How would Jared be today?

Impatient to find out, although fearful, she showered and dressed as fast as she could. In minutes she stood at Jared's door. It opened before she could knock and he came out. "Are you ready for breakfast?" he asked.

Claire studied him. He appeared normal but his eyes lacked animation.

"Yes." She sighed and followed him to the restaurant where they ordered breakfast.

"What shall we do today?" Jared asked.

"Perhaps we should go and see Philip." Claire looked at Jared, wondering how he would react to this suggestion.

"Philip?" Jared looked at her as if he didn't understand. "Actually," he said, "I did wonder if we could go on Sky Rail." He took several leaflets from his pocket and handed one to Claire. It showed a photo of a cable car hanging over the rainforest.

"Don't you want to find your father?" Claire asked.

"My father? I don't have a father," he said. "You know that, I told you, I never knew him."

Claire sighed but said nothing, sensing the spirit in Jared was blocking his memory, affecting his behaviour and preventing him from wanting to help Philip. What should she do?

She looked at Jared eating and, as she did so, felt an overwhelming love for him flow through her body. She couldn't bear the thought of losing Jared but sensed him receding away from her. Claire knew she had to be strong, that if she could somehow reach the real Jared and show him he could have faith in her, in love and life, maybe he could repel the spirit affecting him.

Philip would have to wait. Jared needed healing first.

"Okay," she said. "I'd love to go on the cable car, where is it?"

"Let me see." Jared rifled through the other leaflets and picked out another one. "Hmm. Look, we can get this train up to Kuranda, a village up in the highlands on the plateau where the cable car runs from, that way we can see the rainforest from below and then from above. What do you think?"

In any other setting, Claire would have been ecstatic at the adventure but at this moment only felt apprehension and sorrow.

The soft presence of Eleanora filtered into her consciousness. "Don't allow your sadness to possess you, it will weaken you. It is not who you are. Find the joy in today. Show it to Jared. It is what he loves best in you, for it counterbalances the bitterness that stops him loving fully and completely. Charles and I will help you when we are needed."

Be joyful in this situation? That would be challenging, Claire thought, but knew she had to try.

"Okay," she said, with a bright smile. "I've finished. I'll just get my things and meet you by the car."

He nodded.

It didn't take them long to get underway and, as they began the drive to the railway, Claire's spirits lifted as she gazed at the view through the windows. They soon left the built-up environs of Port Douglas and passed into wilder country. "Oh, my goodness, how stunning it is here!" she exclaimed as the road wound along the coast overlooking a turquoise sea sparkling in the sunshine, purple hills in the distance. The sand looked so pristine. She leant forward, anxious not to miss a second of it.

After some time, they came across a café by the roadside near the sea. "Oh, let's stop for a break," Claire exclaimed. They bought takeaway coffees and walked across the road through a group of palm trees to the white sandy beach, which stretched away on either side. So early in the day, they had the place to themselves.

They sat down under a tree and sipped their drinks. "Isn't it beautiful?" she said to Jared. "Look at the amazing colour of those hills and the purity of this sand." She scooped up a handful and watched it fall through her fingers. "It's so soft and clean. And the air, it's so fresh. It's a long way from the stony beach at home in England where I last went swimming."

Jared had not turned to look but sat without moving, his gaze focussed far out to sea. She felt his distance and it made her sad. But that, she knew, would not help. She touched him on the arm. "Hey, you, come back. What are you thinking?"

"I'm not really thinking; I just sort of feel light headed." He turned and looked at her and the emptiness in his eyes shocked Claire to the core. More drastic measures were needed, she thought. She had to reach him, draw him back.

"I wonder how your mother is doing. Have you spoken to her?"

"My mother? Er, no, not since we arrived."

"I'll ring her later," Claire said. "She must be very worried. You know how desperate she is to get news of your father."

Jared looked at her with a blank expression.

"Your father, Philip. It's why we're here... to find him? Remember?"

"My father? Why do you keep bringing *him* up?" he retorted, annoyed. "He's gone, dead, I tell you. My mother's living in cloud cuckoo land, thinking he isn't."

Claire gasped. The spirit had blocked Jared's memory of their purpose in coming to Australia. "Is she? Do you really believe that? I've met him, Jared."

"Who?"

"Your father, Philip."

She lay her hand on his briefly and, for a moment, Jared looked confused, as if he was trying to remember something but it soon faded. "Stop it," Jared retorted. "Don't get into all that psychic stuff with me. Don't you think life is hard enough without having to deal with dead people as well?"

Sensitised by the necklace which she now wore all the time, the force of his anger drilled right into Claire's heart. "He's not dead, Jared. I saw him alive." She didn't mention that she knew he, Jared, had also seen Philip. What had gone on during the time Jared had been with him? The memory of that had been blocked out too.

"I've had enough," he shouted. "I don't want to hear any more about it."

Tears sprung into Claire's eyes but she smiled bravely, feigning a happiness she did not feel. She had to keep it together or all would be lost. "Okay, okay, I'm sorry. Let's forget it, shall we?" She touched Jared on the arm and his face relaxed a little. "Look at that yacht out there. That would be great to do, wouldn't it? Sail over the reef. I'd love to see the coral. It would be so marvellous."

"We could do it, if you like," he said, although without enthusiasm.

"Could we?"

Jared nodded. "We'll look into it. Anyway, let's get a move on. We have to get to a place called Freshwater. That's where the railway starts."

They headed back to the car and continued their drive, Claire doing her best not to allow Jared's coldness to pull her down. She felt Eleanora's gentle presence. "Can't you do something?" Claire pleaded.

"I have already tried but his bitterness is a wall I cannot get behind. It is up to you."

Oh, great, Claire thought, annoyed. Why did it all have to be up to her?

Despite the fear of losing him gnawing at her, she tried to focus on the real Jared, the man of caring she had seen glimpses of in the Lake District. She knew he had genuine feelings for her and sensed he wanted her physically.

"All of us long for Oneness," Eleanora said. "that is why we reach out to others and feel so hurt when they betray us. It underlines the isolation we all feel. Reach out to him. You are strong because you know you already have that Oneness and Love within you. And what you are, you cannot lose. But he does not know this. If you can get him to respond, then Charles and I can help you."

Grateful for Eleanora's presence and the inner connection she had with her, Claire focussed on enjoying the scenery as much as possible as they progressed on their way. They drove inland through green countryside and pulled up by a small railway station. A field of sugar cane stretched away towards the forested hills where they were headed. A sign read 'Kuranda Scenic Railway.'

They wandered around the quaint old-fashioned station building. Claire bought some post cards in the gift shop to send to each of her parents. They had been very concerned at her decision to come to Australia with a man she barely knew. She had rung them on her arrival but knew they would enjoy receiving postcards.

Jared found her and they headed out to the platform. They did not have too long to wait before a diesel engine arrived pulling some old-fashioned wooden carriages.

"You can sit by the window," Jared said, when they located their seats. "I know you'll appreciate it." He smiled and Claire's heart lifted at the show of consideration, knowing she needed to build on it. "No, you sit there. You're too jaded," she teased. "You need to do more looking. Reawaken your sense of wonder."

He smiled and did as she requested. However, every so often she leant over him to peer out of the window, exclaiming at the wonderful views of the forest that stretched to the valleys below. Once she put a hand on his knee to help support herself. She hoped that the closeness of their bodies would perhaps ignite some feeling in Jared but, if it did, he did not show it.

Although bound for the village of Kuranda, the train stopped for a short while on the way for passengers to view Barron Falls. Claire and Jared stood side by side on a lookout point staring at the water pouring down the mountainside. "Thank you so much for bringing me here," she said, taking his hand. "It means more to me than you know." Jared looked at her and then Claire did something she would never have imagined herself having the confidence to do. She touched his cheek then kissed him gently on the lips. He did not respond and so she pulled away but an indefinable expression moved across his face and he stared at her for a long time. Claire held his gaze, hoping to show him in her expression that she cared for him, really cared for him.

"I love you," she whispered. Shock passed across his features then bewilderment. "Don't worry," she said, touching her fingers to his lips. "You don't have to say anything. You don't have to say you love me back. There are no strings. I just want you to know."

He nodded. "Come on, we need to get back on the train."

They reboarded their carriage and Claire returned her attention to the view to give her strength. Jared had not responded to her show of affection, giving no indication of his feelings. Every so often, though, he pointed out some feature of the landscape or a bird and even laughed at the antics of a small child on the seat opposite so she fancied he had relaxed to some extent and it gave her hope.

However, as they pulled into Kuranda station, Jared retreated into himself. He remained silent as they followed the other tourists up a hill to a small village. Claire had picked up a leaflet about Kuranda from the station shop. She read through it whilst they ate lunch at one of the many cafes in the main street.

"Can we go to the wildlife centre they have here," she asked Jared. "I'd love to see a kangaroo. Oh, and a koala bear."

"They're not bears," Jared said.

"Oh, they're not? How did you know that?"

"I read it somewhere."

"Oh, but they look so cute. It says you can hold them." She smiled at Jared but he seemed miles away.

He still had an appalling headache. It had not lessened since the previous day. He had tried everything and now felt depressed, as if he had something heavy weighing him down. He couldn't think straight and everything irritated him. He was making an effort but it felt forced. He had a feeling he had to remember something but it eluded him so he became more and more frustrated. He stared at Claire. She had told him she loved him, but Andrea had said that all the time. Why didn't he feel anything? Claire was an attractive woman but he felt frozen, as if he were not in control of his body. It must be the migraine; it was the worst he had ever experienced.

"Butterflies! They have a butterfly sanctuary," exclaimed Claire.

"That sounds nice," he replied but it felt as if it wasn't him speaking. He shook his head to clear the fog in his brain. "Yes, let's go there next, then."

Claire stood, knowing Jared was only going through the motions. This simply wasn't working. How could she reach him? She felt him becoming more and more distant.

In any other circumstances, Claire would have been ecstatic walking through the glass building that housed the butterflies. Full of lush tropical vegetation, butterflies of many different shapes, sizes and colours flitted through the air. "Look," she said and pointed, "it's one of those wonderful blue ones we saw at Mossman Gorge." She consulted the guide. "It's a Ulysses butterfly."

Jared moved close to get a good look at it. "Hmm, lovely," he said, his voice flat.

Claire held out her hand near a bush and an orange and black butterfly with spots of white landed on her forefinger. "Oh my God," she whispered so as not to alarm it. "How amazing it is." She turned but Jared wasn't even looking. He looked unsettled as if he wanted to leave. She allowed the insect to fly off and said, "Let's go, then."

They visited the small wildlife park next and Claire loved looking at the kangaroos with their large incongruous back legs and long tails. They saw cute little wallabies and stubby wombats, even a crocodile, although Claire could not warm to this. She even got to hold a koala. That did get a laugh out of Jared and her spirits lifted at the show of normal human emotion.

They looked around the shops then headed to the Sky Rail terminal for their trip down the mountainside. They had to wait for a while before being able to get a seat in a small cabin dangling from a cable stretching over the rainforest to the lowlands below.

Claire clutched the handrail as they swung out and over the rainforest, but soon lost her fear in excitement as she gazed down at the treetops spread out below. Even Jared looked mildly interested. The cable car stopped at a small station halfway down so people could walk along a trail through the rainforest itself. They climbed out of the cabin and it moved away. Jared and Claire followed the path and found themselves in a different world to the one they had seen from above only moments before. Now they walked through dense foliage beneath the forest canopy shifting in the wind far above. Light flickering through the leaves danced on their faces and the pervasive scent of vegetation filled the air. Claire glanced at Jared and her heart constricted at what she saw. He looked closed in upon himself, his expression blank.

Neither Claire nor Jared spoke as they moved along the designated trail. All they could hear was the sound of the wind through the trees and the occasional call of a bird. They came to a point where the trees thinned out by the side of a cliff and paused to admire the forest spread out in the valley below. Claire felt a growing unease, which even the magnificent view did not dispel. As she looked down, her stomach clenched and her knees weakened at the height of the drop. She wouldn't want to fall. It flashed into her mind how it would be, the sensation of dropping then the unimaginable pain of smashing into the trees, perhaps over and over again until she came to rest, mangled and broken, skin cut and bruised, bones shattered, below. She shuddered and stared up at the blue sky but the vision intensified. It wouldn't let go and, all of a sudden, she felt gripped by dread.

"Turn around!" Eleanora commanded. Claire did so and found herself staring into the eyes of a man she did not know, although he looked like Jared. It was then she knew why she had seen herself fall. This man, into whose eyes she looked and saw only hate, wanted to destroy her.

Chapter 21

Here in the forest alone with Jared, poised above a precipitous drop, it would be all too easy for him to push her over. She had to think fast. Claire edged away but he reached out and grabbed her arm in a vice like grip so tight she cried out. She could not break free and felt herself being propelled nearer and nearer to the edge of the cliff.

"Jared!" she screamed. "Don't let the spirit who has attached himself to you take you over. Resist him. Come back to me. Please. I know you're still there. He wants to kill me. Look into my eyes. Do you, Jared, want to do that? How will you feel if you do?

"I love you, Jared. I love you!" Claire pleaded, frantic now. "Please try to believe that. Is killing me what you really want? And what about your mother? She's waiting at home for you. She needs you. Come back to me, Jared," she implored. "Please."

She cringed at the coldness in his face. As she tried to squirm away, his grip tightened. "You're hurting me," she cried.

But Jared felt only hate for the woman he saw in front of him. In that moment, he saw her as an obstacle. Somehow, for reasons he could not remember, he knew she wanted to use him, take all his money, destroy him.

Claire felt the full force power of Jared's hate directed at her and it broke her heart. She tried to break free again but he held her in a powerful grip. Jared pushed her closer to the edge. In desperation, she tried to grasp an overhanging branch but her hand only pulled away leaves. As they fluttered down, Eleanora's voice sounded loud in Claire's mind, "Don't resist him!"

"What?"

"It is the only way. Trust in me."

"Are you sure?"

"Yes."

Terrified, she had to force herself to speak. "All right, Jared," Claire gasped. "Do it, then. If that's what you truly want, then do it. I won't resist you." She stopped straining for release and instead relaxed and moved closer. "Push me over. Go on. I love you, Jared. I want you to be happy. If this is what it's going to take, then so be it." Fear gripped her heart. She was going to die! Now, in this place. She forced herself to continue, "I don't want to live without you, anyway, so if you hate me that much then it doesn't matter anymore."

Jared stared at her as Claire prepared herself for what was to come. She shut her eyes. She knew now it would not be the end if she died and the thought gave her peace. The feeling grew and a profound calm overtook her. If this was how it was meant to be then she was ready.

Claire waited.

Nothing happened!

The moment stretched for an eternity but then, all of a sudden, Jared pulled her back from the edge and held her tight. He clung to her, sobbing. She put her arms around him as he cried. "Jesus, what have I done?" he moaned. "I nearly killed you. Oh my God, help me. I, I don't understand. Please, oh, God, please, someone help me." As he said those words, Claire sensed Eleanora and Charles. They encircled them with Light and drew the possessing spirit from Jared. Claire felt it go. There was a moment of resistance, a sense of a clinging dark shadow, but then all of a sudden it went. Eleanora and Charles vanished with the spirit leaving Claire and Jared alone in the rainforest crying and holding each other.

They stood there for a long time, neither able to speak until Jared pulled away and looked into Claire's eyes. "I'm so sorry. I, I, don't know what came over me. I, I could have killed you. I wanted to, I..."

"Shh, it's okay. It wasn't you. It wasn't you. A spirit had control of you. One of the Circle."

"No, you don't understand, a part of me wanted to do it, too. I felt so angry, so bitter and afraid. Andrea, she..."

"It's all right. That is how the spirit could take you over. He was magnifying those feelings in you, using them to motivate you to do his will. On your own you would never have let your feelings find expression like that. And, Jared, you *didn't* act on it. You broke free."

"Yes, yes, I did. It was when you were going to let me do it, let me kill you. I couldn't believe you cared for me that much. I could see the love in your eyes, the surrender, the trust on your face. It touched me deep inside and I knew I couldn't destroy something so beautiful. And in that moment, I became aware of the thing inside me."

Eleanora spoke, "We could not help Jared until then. The spirit had complete control of him but when you triggered his love for you by your surrender it broke the spirit's hold just enough so that, when Jared called for help, it connected him to us. Then we were able to draw the spirit away and guide him to his rightful place."

"Thank you," Claire said.

"It was your love for him that reached him in the end." With these words, the spirit vanished.

"Do you forgive me?" Jared asked.

"Of course, I do."

"Even after what I put you through?"

"It's strange, the moment I stopped struggling, I felt only love and peace. I know now we're not just physical bodies and that death is not the end, Jared. I knew Eleanora would be there, and Charles too, to help me if the worst happened and I had to die so it no longer mattered. I felt free. I trusted the power of love."

"Thank you for loving me. You saved me, brought me back from certain ruin." Jared reached for Claire's hands. "I love you, too. I think I have right from the start when you came to Mum's shop, even with your outrageous talk of spirits. In the Lake District I came to realise you were coming from truth and I've been hard pressed to resist you ever since."

"I know."

"Oh, Christ, of course you bloody would. So, when I imagined taking you in my arms and kissing you, you knew?"

Claire nodded, smiling.

"But you didn't do anything."

"It wasn't the right time, Jared. We needed to focus."

"Oh, Claire." He pulled her too him again and they held each other tight, as if they never wanted to ever let go. Jared drew back first. He bent his head down to hers and they kissed, gently at first but then with increasing passion, as all the pent-up emotion of the previous weeks flooded through them.

It was some time before they broke free and then only because a group of people came down the path.

"Let's go." Jared said. They returned to the station and waited until the next cable car came along. They continued their flight over the rainforest, sitting close to each other holding hands. The view passed in a blur for Claire. All she could focus on was the feel of Jared's hand in hers and the warmth of his body beside her.

Somehow, they ended up at the final station and boarded a bus for the trip to where they left their car. On the journey back to Port Douglas, Claire suggested they stop at the café on the beach where they had coffee earlier.

Ravenous, they devoured two burgers. Later, they wandered down to the water's edge. Claire kicked off her sandals and walked over the sand, enjoying the feel of it beneath her feet. Surely there wouldn't be any harm in paddling? The gentle waves rippling in from the ocean beckoned to her so, lifting up the hem of her long blue skirt, she stepped into the crystal-clear water. As she did so, the enormity of what happened only an hour or so before hit her. She had almost died!

But she hadn't. She stood there with her feet in a turquoise ocean on a white beach backed by verdant rainforest. The breeze ruffled her hair and the sun warmed her face as it sank down towards the horizon in an orange pink haze. She felt an intense, delicious aliveness and a gratitude and appreciation for life. Jared stood at the edge watching her.

She held out her hand. "Come walk with me."

Jared glanced down at his trousers and shoes. Even in this tropical paradise he still looked as if he had just come from an office. "Roll them up," Claire said. "Let your hair down, you know you want to." Playful, she scooped up a handful of water and threw it at him.

"Hey!" he protested, laughing. She did it again, then again. "All right, give me a moment." He sat down on the sand, undid his shoes and dutifully rolled up his trousers.

"That's better," Claire said as he joined her in the shallows, holding his shoes. She took his hand and they ambled along the beach as the sun sank lower and lower in the sky. When night fell, they stopped. Jared took Claire in his arms and they kissed deeply, a powerful passion stirring within them. They had come some distance from the café so had the beach to themselves.

Jared led Claire away from the water and they settled down on the sand under some palm trees. Hidden there, no one saw as they kissed again and again then slowly removed each other's clothing. Claire took off her necklace, even though she felt sure Eleanora would respect their privacy. The sand shifted beneath their bodies, as they lay down in the sand, oblivious to anything other than being with each other until Jared moaned and moved away. "My God. We have to stop but I want you so much, Claire."

"We *don't* have to," she said.

"But we have no protection."

Claire reached for her bag and searched through it, bringing out a small packet.

"Good God, woman, you thought to bring contraception? Did you know we would need it?"

"I've felt the passion between us building for a long time, Jared. I didn't know if anything would happen. I thought we should keep our distance so we could focus on Philip, but I knew you wanted me and that I would find it very hard to resist, so I decided to be prepared."

"You're bloody incredible." He laughed. "You never cease to amaze me."

"That's good."

"Mmm." They fell silent. Neither moved and they lay there looking at each other in the fading light. Claire became aware of the hypnotic sound of the sea washing the beach. A breeze moved across her naked skin and she shivered.

"Are you cold?" Jared asked. "Come here, let me warm you." He enfolded her in his arms and she relaxed against him, enjoying the feel of his naked chest against hers. He kissed her, then moved down to kiss her neck, then her breasts. She moaned and they lay back again on the sand. "Claire, Claire," Jared whispered. A single star twinkled into existence in the sky above as the veil of darkness descended to enfold them and they became oblivious to everything else except each other.

Sometime later, their passion spent, they fell asleep there on the sand. As the grey light of dawn permeated the sky and brought them into visibility, they came awake. "To think I could have lost you," Jared whispered. "I couldn't have borne it. I can't tell you how much you've come to mean to me." He ran his fingers through her hair then cupped her face with his hands before kissing her. "I love you, Claire. I really love you. Hey, you're crying. What is it?"

"It's all right, they are happy tears. I can't believe all this has happened and we've found each other." She returned his kiss but then drew back. "We have to get back to Port Douglas, Jared. We can't forget what we came here to do. I have a strong feeling something is going to happen. Barrett will soon realise, if he hasn't already, that you've broken free. I don't know what he'll do."

Jared became serious. "This Barrett is a pretty nasty character, isn't he?"

"Yes. I think he has a very powerful influence on William."

"You're right. Let's go."

They walked along the beach in the direction they came the night before. Despite overshadowed by the unknown, both felt they were walking through paradise. On one side a calm blue sea as clear as glass stretched out to eternity, on the other, palm trees edged the gleaming sand. Hazy mountains lifted up to the sky in the distance. Jared reached for Claire's hand. "One day, when this is all over, we're going to come back here," he said. "I'm going to take you to do all the things you want to experience: the reef, the forest, everything."

"I'd like that." Claire smiled.

They stopped for breakfast at the café. They both knew they would need their strength for what might lie ahead. During the meal, Claire filled Jared in on what had happened since he had come under the influence of the spirit.

"I have no recollection whatsoever of going to visit my father. It's scary."

"I know. The spirit had complete control at that moment."

Jared touched Claire's hand. "He didn't bargain for you. I still can't believe you did what you did at the cliff edge."

"It was the only thing I could do to reach you, I guess. But I trusted Eleanora and so, when she told me to do it, I just could and the funny thing was, I felt complete serenity." Claire gazed at him with a light in her eyes. "There's something so beautiful about life. I know it now. Although things seem so hard and frightening on the surface, with death and illness, poverty and wars, I know that underneath of all of it, is peace; love and peace. I can't explain it but I feel it."

As Jared gazed at Claire, he felt the love and peace she talked of pouring from her. It triggered an answering resonance inside him and a surge of energy coursed through his body, healing and cleansing. He felt his heart open and a reciprocal love flowed from him to her. She, sensing it, smiled and squeezed his hand, knowing how hard it was for him to open up.

"Eleanora has told me we have to have faith and forgive others, Jared," she said. "Other people can't help what they do. In fact, I think in some ways they're our allies, for, in all the struggle, we're forced to search for what is real and, in that, we can find the love that transcends all suffering."

"You mean I have to forgive Andrea, don't you?"

"I think it's something you need to do to be free. It's not a question of right or wrong. It happened. She did what she did because of what happened to her in life, the way she was treated and the ideas she picked up. I doubt using you the way she did made her truly happy."

"No, you're right."

"And sometimes, too, I think that what we dislike so much in others are things we don't want to recognise about ourselves."

"What do you mean?"

"What is it you hate about Andrea?"

"She lied and cheated. She pretended to love me, yet all the while only wanting to use me."

"And have you never done any of these things?"

"No! Never." Jared retorted.

"You're a businessman. You sell antiques. Are you always completely honest when you buy things off people?"

Jared thought to refute this idea but then a memory arose out of his past, of sitting in the lounge of an elderly lady's house. Ruby her name had been. In those days, he often knocked on people's doors to see if they had anything to sell. She had invited him in and given him a cup of tea. When he saw the porcelain figurine of a shepherdess with a lamb at her feet on the mantelpiece, he grew excited and offered her five hundred pounds for it.

"No, I love that," she said. "My husband gave it to me." The old lady paused and covered her face with her hands. "I lost him a year ago now."

Knowing the figurine to be extremely valuable, Jared returned every so often to see if she'd change her mind. Always she gave him tea and they chatted. He knew she enjoyed his company. Living alone, she had little contact with people.

In the end, she agreed to sell it for seven hundred pounds and he auctioned the figurine. It made him three thousand pounds. He always meant to go back and give Ruby some more money for it but, somehow, life became busy after that.

"Well..." he mumbled, sheepish now.

"It's all right. We all do such things because we don't know any better. We must have compassion for ourselves and, when we do, we can more readily access the love inside us. We can heal, Jared. Then we can change how we act. Forgive yourself and you can forgive Andrea and be free." The more Claire spoke, the more insight welled up, as if she were tapping into some realm of knowledge deep within her.

"Hmm." Jared looked sceptical.

"Once you learn to love yourself, Jared, you'll find it easy to accept and love others in their fallibility. In love is peace."

"I suppose I *can* let it go now." Jared gripped Claire's hand tighter. "But I can't let go of the fact that some bastard has control of my father. We *have* to set him free."

Claire felt a compulsion to share what Eleanora told her. "It's important to remember the possessing spirit is suffering too, perhaps far more than you and I could ever know. Eleanora told me spirits like that are trapped in ignorance and fear. We have to have compassion for William, Jared, for in that is our strength. Hate will weaken us and make us vulnerable.

"I believe we also have to forgive life too," Claire mused. "We fight it and the more we do, the harder it gets but I think that everything happens for a reason and that is to make us connect to our deeper selves, the part of us beyond the physical."

"You're so wise."

"No, Eleanora is. I'm so lucky to have her with me."

"Yes. So, what are we going to do now?" Jared asked.

"I need to get back to the hotel to shower and change then I think we need to pay your father a visit. Philip needs to know he has a son."

Claire walked into the hotel foyer first. She stopped in surprise and laid a hand on Jared to make him pause. "It's Philip," she whispered.

A mixture of emotions flooded through Jared as he stared at the man he had never thought to meet.

Philip sat in a cane chair staring out at the lush tropical garden beyond. "I wonder what he's doing here," whispered Claire. They didn't have long to wait for the old man turned his head and looked at them. He stood up.

Claire went over. Jared stopped and stared, showing no sign of recognition despite the fact she knew he'd been with Philip before. Jack had seen them together.

"Tugger," she said, "this is Jared, the friend I was looking for the other night. I believe you've already met."

Philip looked at Jared. Philip nodded his head at him then turned back to Claire. It was then she noticed he seemed odd. He looked confused and, with a shock that ran throughout her whole body, knew she was not looking at the same person she met in the house on the edge of the rainforest with Jack.

The man in front of her looked so much older than before. His whole body drooped as if carrying a great weight and he looked exhausted. Gone were the arrogance and disdain, the sense of power and control, she had seen in him. But what impressed her the most was his expression: he looked as if he did not know where he was.

"Are you all right?" she asked.

"I, I..." He hesitated for so long Claire wondered if he had lost the power of speech but then he continued. "I don't really know. Something you said the other night, it's been bothering me. You mentioned the Lake District in England and a grave... a grave with violets on it."

Claire could not suppress a small gasp. She had got through to Philip after all, despite the presence of William.

"I thought you were crazy," he continued, "but then I remembered. I don't know why I would have forgotten it but I *have* been to the Lake District... a long, long time ago. There was a place I used to visit and there were violets on a grave like you said. And I began to wonder why you would come to my door late at night and tell me that." He looked at Claire who felt a wave of pity for him. "I want to know how you knew I was in the Lake District," Philip asked. He swayed and Claire reached out a hand to stabilise him.

"Are you okay?" she asked.

"Yes, yes. I'll sit down, though, if you don't mind." He lowered himself into the cane chair again. Claire and Jared also sat down, on a settee opposite.

Philip composed himself then looked at Claire. "I want to know who you are and how you know these things?"

Claire had to think fast. What could she say? It looked like, somehow, for the moment at least, William's control over Philip had waned. It seemed like a miracle. Perhaps the losing of one of the Circle had affected William in some way, weakened him. She could only imagine but she *did* know she had to make the best of this opportunity and now, before William gained the upper hand yet again.

Philip spoke again. "The name Laura... I have a feeling I should remember her but I..." He seemed lost again and put up his hand to massage his brow as if by doing so he could prise open his memory.

"She's your wife." Jared's words sliced through the air. Unable to hold back and say nothing any longer, the words rose up from within him and would not be stayed. He used them now like a weapon to attack the man he saw in front of him. He could not stand to see his father deny his past, the woman he had loved, Jared's mother, as if she had not existed. It made him angry and he forgot the man in front of him had been unable to control what happened to him. Jared's bitterness over never having the father he longed for and anger at his mother's grief rose to the surface. He wanted to shake this man, *will* him to remember. If he had really loved Laura, he would have remained strong. Claire shook her head at Jared but he ignored her.

Philip turned to look at Jared. "I don't understand," he said. "I don't have a wife. I've never had a wife."

"You did." Jared spat out the words. "You had Laura."

"Jared," Claire said. "I don't think this will work."

Philip struggled to his feet. "I... I don't know what I'm doing here. This doesn't make sense. You're confusing me with someone else." He swayed again and Claire felt concerned. Philip was in his mid-seventies and he looked every one of those years. The energy had drained from his face and he looked pale and weak.

"Laura was your wife," Jared repeated, "and I should know."

Philip stared at Jared. "Why?"

"Because I'm your son!"

Philip sank back down in the chair and stared at Jared in shock. "No, no."

Claire reached out and laid her hand on his arm. "It's true." Philip looked at her and her heart moved with compassion for this wounded soul. Reaching into her bag she drew out the necklace from where she had put it during the night on the beach.

"Do you remember this?" she said and showed it to him. He gazed at the shining amethyst as if in a daze. Claire handed the necklace to Jared. "Help me put it on."

Jared placed it around her neck and Philip stared at the necklace. "You gave it to Laura when you were together," Claire said. "It was a long, long time ago when you were young. You met at a wedding. Your home was in the Lake District then and you took Laura there. Do you remember the lake, Lake Windermere? You loved it there, the bluebells in the spring and the church you used to visit. You took Laura there to show her the grave where the violets always bloomed. A place you loved. And it was there you gave her the necklace. Look at it. Try to remember."

She laid a hand on Philip's arm and a healing flow of energy from Eleanora coursed through her.

"You didn't know," Claire continued, compassion in her voice, "but Laura conceived a child." She looked up at Jared.

Claire reached again into her bag and drew out something she had packed before leaving England, sensing it might be needed. She handed Philip a photograph of a smiling Laura standing beside Lake Windermere. Around her neck hung the necklace. "You took this, shortly before you disappeared."

Philip held the photograph in his fingers and gazed at it in silence. "She was so beautiful," he said at last. Claire and Jared held their breath as he went on, "I do remember..." Philip's eyes narrowed in concentration. "I, I remember..."

"What?" Claire encouraged.

Philip touched Laura's face with his finger. "My butterfly. I used to call her my little butterfly." Claire and Jared exchanged triumphant glances. Jared's eyes filled with tears he made no attempt to hold back.

"She had a child?" Philip looked up, his eyes full of wonder.

"Yes, yes," Jared said. Philip turned his attention to him and stared at Jared in stark disbelief. Claire couldn't believe it. She felt a wave of elation run through her but it was short lived for a shadow passed across Philip's face. "I remember the stones." Philip became agitated. "I took her to the stones. The eagle came. The eagle came."

Claire felt the presence of Eleanora. "Don't allow him to dwell on the eagle," she said but it was too late and, in seconds, Philip transformed. He became more animated as strength flowed into his body. He straightened and colour returned to his cheeks. He laughed and stood up, now appearing taller and more powerful. It was obvious the spirit of William had now surged forward and taken back control of the man in front of them. "Forgive me," Eleanora said, as a purple haze flooded through Claire, "but I have to do this. Will you let me?"

"Yes," Claire replied, intuiting what Eleanora wanted to do. Claire felt a pressure then sensed herself dislocate from her body and retreat back inside herself.

"This is between me and him," Eleanora said. "I have waited for too many years.

"Hello, William," she said using Claire's voice although, to Jared, listening, it took on a different quality.

"So, you follow me here, Eleanora," William bellowed in a voice quite different to Philip's. "It *is* you I'm speaking to now, isn't it?"

"Yes."

"So, we are together again."

Claire realised he had deliberately stepped back, waiting for Eleanora to show herself. Philip had never been back in control at all.

"It is time," Eleanora continued.

"What do you mean, time? Time for what?"

"You know what I mean. You have destroyed Philip's life for long enough. Release him so he can know peace and find the love he has been denied all these years."

"And why should I do that? I have a good life here."

"A good life? Is it really? And where will it all end? What about when Philip dies?"

"Then I will find someone else." William turned and looked at Jared. "Philip has a son. That's very convenient."

Claire, although not in control of her body, still retained awareness of everything going on. She felt appalled at the idea that Jared could be at risk.

"You would ruin his life, too?" Eleanora cried. "For what? Does the life you lead through Philip give you what you really want?"

"Yes," William replied without hesitation. "I have money and power. I live in a house with everything I could wish for."

"But what of love, William?"

"Love?" he sneered and laughed. "I have had many women."

"And where are they now?" Eleanora asked. "Do you share your life with anyone? Is there someone there to listen to you in the dead of night when the fast cars and the fancy clothes are put away? Is there anyone to hold you and soothe away your troubles when the body you live in begins to suffer and weaken?

"Did they care about you or was it for what you could give them?" Eleanora continued. "*I* cared about you, William."

"No, you didn't," he spat.

"Back at the start when we first met. Think of that time."

"I won't. It is pointless. It meant nothing. You never loved me. No one ever did. No one ever could."

"That isn't true. I *did* love you. I still love you, William, even now."

"You lie. I know what you're trying to do. You only want to release Philip. You don't care for me. You never cared for me. I won't listen to you."

"William, despite it all, even though you took your anger and pain out on me, I still loved you, felt for you, wanted to help you, but you chose the road into darkness and I could not follow you there. You know deep inside yourself this is true. You chose to listen to Barrett."

"Nothing can undo the enormity of your crime. You betrayed me. It was because of you I became bitter and sought to find consolation in making money. It was because of you that I would do anything to achieve it and became involved with those who sought to destroy me. Because of that Charles died and I lost everything. How can you say you love me? It is ridiculous."

Jared did not know what to do. It had become obvious it was Eleanora talking to William, but what about Claire? Would she be all right? Could he do anything?

Without warning, William made the body of Philip stand up and grab Claire's arm. He pulled her along with him and out of the hotel foyer. Jared sprang up and followed but, the moment he passed through the doors, a large bulky man placed himself in front of him. Jared dodged around but saw another taller, thinner man helping William bundle Claire into a large black car. The door slammed shut. Before Jared could do anything, the man who had stopped him dashed around and flung himself into the car, then it sped off.

Jared watched them go. He thought of trying to follow but knew by the time he got into his car they would be long gone. Jared felt sick, William, twisted with rage and pain, could do anything!

# Chapter 22

J ARED STOOD HELPLESS AS SILENCE descended over the car park. He knew they would, in all likelihood, go to his father's house but, although Claire had told him he had been there, he had no conscious recollection of it. The spirit possessing him at the time had suppressed his memory of the place. What the hell could he do?

He thought back over what Claire had said. Of course! He could find this Jack she met in the forest. He knew where his father lived. Wasting no more time, Jared ran over to the hire car and roared down the road towards Mossman Gorge.

It didn't take him long to find the Tourist Centre, they had passed it the first time they went to Mossman Gorge. He screeched to a halt in front of it and rushed inside. Mindful not to appear as distraught as he felt, he took a deep breath and walked over to a counter behind which sat a young man writing in a notebook.

"Hi, I was wondering if Jack is about?" he asked, as casually as he could although inside gnawed by anxiety. What would happen if he couldn't locate this person? How would he find Claire?

"Who wants to know?" the man asked.

"My name is Jared. Jack doesn't know me but he knows a friend of mine, Claire. Tell him she needs his help." The man, as if sensing Jared's agitation, studied him for a while, considering whether he was to be trusted or not. After a while, he nodded. "Okay. Come with me."

Jared followed him out of the centre and down a short track to a small building. A middle-aged man sat reading under a verandah. "Hey, Jack, this bloke wants to talk to you." The young man turned and walked back to where he came from as the man in front of Jared looked up and eyed him quizzically.

"I know you," he said. "You're the guy Claire was looking for."

"Yes, yes I am. I'm sorry to bother you but I need help. Claire needs help. Philip, Tugger, he's holding Claire against her will."

Jack put down his book and slowly rose to his feet.

"What do you want me to do?"

"Can you tell me where he lives? I've... been there, apparently, but I wasn't... *myself* so I don't know how to find it."

Jack stared at Jared, assessing him. "I'll take you."

"Well, I'd be grateful if you could. I don't know what else to do."

"I knew there'd be trouble," Jack said. "I felt it. Come on. We'll take the ute."

He led Jared over to a beat-up looking truck and coaxed the reluctant engine into life as Jared climbed into the cab beside him. They set off, jolting along a rough track, until they reached a proper road. Anxious, Jared stared out of the windows. On the way, he told Jack as much as he could about what they had come to Mossman Gorge to do. Claire had mentioned Jack also had the *Sight* and so Jared knew he would understand.

They reached an area of expensive looking houses. Here Jack slowed down and drew up beside what looked to be some sort of mansion. "Is this it?" Jared asked.

"No, it's down the road there but it won't do to attract too much attention until you know what you want to do." He eyed Jared who realised he didn't know. What would happen if he went to the front door? They weren't going to just let him in. He remained silent, uncertain.

"Let's take a look around the back," Jack suggested. "Come on." He climbed out of the cab. He waited for Jared, then led him along the road to a small track beside two large houses. Within minutes, they were walking through rainforest, pushing through dense undergrowth. After a short while, Jack stopped. "We have to be quiet from here," he whispered. They crept on until they could see the back lawn and swimming pool behind Philip's property. The black car stood in the driveway.

"I think they're inside," Jared whispered. "That's the car they took

Claire away in." Unhappy, he stared at the garden. What should he do? "I'm going to take a closer look," he said but Jack pulled him back.

"They'll see you."

"So, what can I do?" asked Jared in despair. "I can't leave Claire in there. This William is pretty nasty but it's not only him I'm worried about, it's this spirit, Barrett. I think he's been behind a lot of what's happened over the years and he's capable of anything. I know Claire has Eleanora but I'm not sure even she, and I know she's pretty special, is a match for Barrett." He looked at Jack in desperation.

Jack touched Jared on the shoulder. "Take it easy, mate. It'll be all right."

"How can you say that?" Jared retorted. "These spirits have no compunction about killing. *I* know." He described nearly throwing Claire off the cliff. "I have to get in there somehow. You go. There's no need for you to be involved. Thanks for bringing me here."

Jack sighed, "No way. I can't leave you alone. Anyway, I *am* involved. I owe her, Eleanora, that is. She fixed me back." He flexed his body. "I can't believe it; the pain's all gone."

"Okay, well, thanks," Jared said, grateful to have Jack with him. He liked the man, sensing his power and wisdom. "So, what *should* we do?"

"Wait, I reckon," Jack replied.

"But what good will *that* do?"

"I dunno, but it's what *he* says to do." Jack gestured to a spot in front of them. Jared looked but couldn't see anyone. "Who?"

An expression of awe came over Jack's face and he looked as if he might cry. "The child," he whispered.

Jack sank down onto his knees, looking straight ahead as if listening. Jared sighed, he should be used to this sort of thing by now after spending so much time with Claire but it still irritated him. He felt so excluded.

"He says his name is Charles," Jack said.

"Oh, William's son. Claire saw him, too. Tell him I can't just wait."

"You must. It's important."

Jared stared where Jack focussed his gaze but saw only the fronds of a palm. However, as he watched, the area brightened as a sunbeam shafted down through the trees and bathed the two men in light. Jared felt a sense of wellbeing as if something, or some*one*, were reassuring him. Moved, he knew he was in some way sensing the presence of Charles. Jared had the impression of someone ancient and wise, not a young boy at all.

The light faded. Jack relaxed back and sat cross-legged on the ground. "We wait," he repeated. Jared followed suit but remained tense, his gaze on the house across the lawn but it gave nothing away.

It had all happened so fast. When Philip grabbed her, Claire found herself back in control of her body as Eleanora withdrew but, powerless to fight off the superhuman grip on her arm, Claire had no choice but to allow herself to be propelled to the car. "Try not to worry," came the reassuring voice of Eleanora.

Easier said than done, Claire thought. She sensed the darkness inhabiting the large man who helped Philip bundle her in. The feeling built when his body pressed up against her in the next seat. He felt as cold as death.

"It is the denial of Love you feel," Eleanora said.

That did nothing to relieve Claire's mounting fear. Her head jerked back as the car accelerated away. The interior reeked of leather and sweat. Claire glanced nervously at the younger, thinner man who sat on the other side of her. His face was devoid of all expression. He appeared blank, dead, but as she stared at him, he turned his head and an expression of contempt and triumph came into his eyes. Claire shuddered and tore her gaze away, staring down at her hands clasped tightly in her lap.

"Stay centred and conscious. Remember your truth, the love you are." Eleanora said. "They cannot handle that. It weakens them. If you find it difficult, think of Jared and Philip, both innocent souls. We have to stay strong for them, for Laura too, waiting at home desperate to be reunited with the man she loves. If you do this, Barrett cannot harm you."

"Barrett?"

"Yes, he has taken over the man next to you."

"Oh my God! Him! What can we do, Eleanora?"

"We have to reach Philip, help him return to the Light. We have to make him want to come back then William will lose his dominance."

"What do you mean, *want* to come back. He didn't ask to be taken over by William."

"Not consciously but like draws like. Philip must have resonated with William on some level or he could not have gained admittance."

"I don't believe it."

"We are all struggling to make sense of our lives, to deal with the world, and it is through this that we become more conscious and can begin to dispel the darkness of separation and ignorance, the illusion of ego, and realise our oneness with the Light of Spirit. But the way can be hard. We become caught up in pain and suffering, believing the physical world is all there is. It makes us weak and sometimes open to influence from others who have fallen by the wayside like the members of the Circle.

Claire sensed a strong feeling of sorrow from the spirit. "It's been difficult for you, Eleanora, hasn't it?"

"When William fell prey to Barrett after my betrayal with Robert, I could do nothing. William's bitterness towards me prevented him from listening to my warnings; it only fuelled his determination to follow the path he had chosen. When William died for murdering me, Barrett was there waiting to guide him further into darkness. Together they created terrible suffering, then later Barrett helped William take control of Philip. I tried to get him to leave him alone but my power was limited. And so, I had to wait, for I knew I could not pass over until I had righted the wrong I had done to William and, in turn, to Philip.

"Fortunately, Elizabeth could hear me when she visited my grave and at the séances to which I was drawn. I asked her to bring Philip to the churchyard but, although he felt my presence, William had begun to influence him too much for me to connect with him fully.

"I told Elizabeth where to find the necklace. It was my most treasured possession, the thing that helped keep me sane through the years living with William for it always gave me comfort and hope of a brighter future. It had a power about it. The crystal is a special one, full of healing energy and it enhances connection to Spirit. It was given to me when I needed it and I always knew it would be important.

"Even wearing the necklace, Elizabeth could not help Philip so I asked her to give it to him so he and I would always be connected in some way.

"You haunted the necklace."

"Yes, I hoped that he would give it to someone who would be receptive and able to help me save him. He gave it to Laura but she was weak and fearful then became pregnant and I could not risk exposing a child to the influence of the Circle. When William gained full control of Philip and took him away from the Lake District, they passed beyond my reach completely.

"I made Laura put the necklace on display in her shop many times, hoping that it would draw someone to it who could help me find and bring William back to the Light and release poor Philip. Although several people wanted to buy it, no one came that I could connect with, who felt right.

"Until you.

"It was not easy in the beginning. My power was weak and you were closed but over time our link has strengthened. Now, together, you and I will bring William back from darkness and free Philip."

"But what if we can't?"

"Then he will go on hurting and using people."

"And Philip?"

"He will die and there is a danger he too will become lost, unable to pass over to the next dimension, or worse be sucked into the Circle by the powerful spirit of Barrett."

"Oh my God!" Claire didn't dare ask what might become of her but she had a very good idea. Her stomach twisted with fear at the thought of being taken over or perhaps even killed.

"No! Don't allow your fears to gain ascendency in your mind. Together we can be strong and Charles will help us. We *will* prevail. Feel your connection to spirit, the sacredness of it within you and focus on seeing Philip safe and reunited with Laura. My dearest, dearest one, in reality you are a Divine Being of Light, and as such are always perfectly safe even though the appearances of the world may suggest otherwise."

As Eleanora spoke these words, Claire felt the truth of them resonate inside her.

"Always stay in awareness of this and no one will be able to take you over. It is your source of power and strength. If we can bring the Light of Spirit to this situation, it will heal it and those imprisoned will be released."

Claire remembered how she felt at Mossman Gorge, the sense of being one with something so much greater and more powerful than herself, and the sense of it rose up again. She visualised herself glowing with light and felt stronger. It came to her to pray. Please heal this situation, she repeated silently several times, then added, for the highest good of all of us.

The car slowed and turned into the driveway of Philip's house coming to a stop in the rear garden. The man driving turned off the engine and there was a brief moment of silence. For an instant, no one moved then the two men accompanying Philip got out. They pulled Claire from the car and hustled her inside to the lounge. She stared at the painting of the eagle. Its predatory glare sickened her but Eleanora enveloped her in a reassuring blanket of purple.

The two men stood impassive by the door. The minutes passed and Philip did not appear. Where had he gone? What would happen? When he entered the room after a while, Claire knew William had full control. "Take a seat," he said, his voice deadly cold and indicated a large leather armchair.

"Allow me to come forward again," Eleanora said to Claire.

"Okay."

"You must stop all this," the spirit said to William.

"And why, my dear Eleanora, should I do that?"

Claire found herself standing up and walking forwards.

"See how you are using this poor woman. You and I are really no different."

"She is allowing me to of her own free will," Eleanora said. "There is a big difference."

William scoffed. "If you say so."

"It is good to see you," Eleanora said.

"Of course, it isn't. You only want to release Philip."

"That is not true. I *do* want to release him but I also want to help you. I still love you, William."

"You only want to help me because you feel guilty. That isn't love."

"We should kill the woman now," the tall man inhabited by Barrett said. "Then she cannot harm you."

"Yes, all right," William said. "I don't have time to waste arguing about the past."

"Wait!" Eleanora broke in. "This woman I am with is innocent."

"No, she isn't. She will stop at nothing to release Philip. She must be destroyed, then I can make use of Jared. He waits, as we speak, in the garden. You can have Philip back, Eleanora. He is worn out and tired, of little use to me now. Jared is still young and, as Philip's legal son, he can inherit all the assets I have accumulated. If I take over his body, I can carry on living the life I have been." William gestured to Barrett and the other man. "Fetch him and Jack in." The two men left the room, leaving Eleanora and William confronting each other.

"Is this really what you want, the blood of yet another person on your hands?" Eleanora asked. "I am so sorry, William, for hurting you."

"It does not matter now."

"It *does* matter because this is not the way to find what you truly seek, William. All this," she waved Claire's arm to encompass the building, "is it really satisfying? Here in Australia, you obviously have the success you always craved but, tell me, does it make you happy? Do you even know what happiness is, true happiness?

"We were happy once, William. Do you remember? When we first met."

"I know what you're trying to do and it won't work," William shouted. He lurched forward and raised his hand to strike Eleanora. "I will silence you myself."

"The rose was so beautiful, William," Eleanora said, her voice calm. "White and soft, with such a wonderful fragrance."

William froze then slowly lowered his arm. The white rose! Unbidden, the memory surged into his mind of a bright day way back in time, the summer of 1907. The day he met Eleanora. He had been walking through the garden at Waterford Hall when he came upon her standing looking at some rose bushes.

"Hello, and who are you?" he asked, stopping beside her. She turned and he found himself drowning in the most extraordinary violet eyes. Never had he seen anyone more lovely. She had a creamy complexion and long dark hair swept back in a bun but a tendril had come adrift and curled beside her face. She had soft pink lips that curved in the most entrancing smile he had ever seen.

"I am Eleanora Hartnell," she said and blushed. "I thought I would take a walk in this enchanting garden while my mother talks to Mrs Waterford in the pavilion."

"Allow me to introduce myself, I am William Waterford."

"I am very pleased to meet you, Mr Waterford."

"William, please, if I can call you Eleanora?"

"Yes."

"I did not know my mother was entertaining today." William could not take his eyes off Eleanora. Her blush intensified and she lowered her gaze. He took the opportunity to glance down at her slim body dressed in a long light blue gown decorated with fine lace over her chest, cinched in tight at the waist then flowing over her hips to the ground. Instantly he felt as if he had violated her. This wasn't one of the women with whom he usually associated, with their brash sexuality. From Eleanora he received an impression of chaste purity. She raised her amazing violet eyes to his and, in that sublime moment, he was captivated. Such innocence and gentleness. Here was something special, something he had never thought about wanting but want her he did. Normally he simply had his way with women he felt attracted to but this time knew that what he felt drawn to in Eleanora was infinitely fragile and, if he treated her with roughness, it would be destroyed.

"I was looking at this rose," Eleanora said, pointing to a white blossom. "Can you see the Light inside it? It is so beautiful."

"Not as beautiful as you," William could not help murmuring.

Eleanora blushed deep red.

"Forgive me. I could not help myself." William realised he had to be careful not to frighten her away. "Yes, the flower is indeed enchanting." He looked down at it and, to his astonishment, the world

around him vanished and he saw only the bloom, vibrant, and, yes, like Eleanora said, glowing with light. He blinked and looked again but the flower still gleamed as if illuminated from within. And, in that moment, his whole life up to that point felt tarnished and empty and he wanted nothing more than to look at the flower with Eleanora by his side. A profound happiness rose up from within him, something he had never experienced before, and he knew that this simple love and appreciation was what he craved more than anything in his whole life. He felt such an up-welling of joy he could not help but turn to Eleanora and whisper, "I never knew a flower could be like this."

She saw the look in his eyes and knew he too saw the blossom as sacred, as she did, and, in that moment, her heart was lost to him, for she had never known anyone to take her fancies seriously. Most people laughed when she told them she saw the world shining with beauty and smiled with indulgence when she danced with happiness at the sheer pleasure of being alive. But William, he understood. Their eyes held and a love flowed between them, binding them together for eternity.

William knew then he would marry this vision by his side, that with her his life could be something worth living for and not the dissolute, selfish existence he now led.

"Eleanora!" called a high-pitched woman's voice from close by. "Where are you?"

Neither wanted to look away but, when the query came again, Eleanora said, "I must go." She turned and began to walk away.

"Wait! May I call upon you?" William asked.

Eleanora stopped and looked back. "Yes, I would like that. Very much."

Then she was gone, but William still felt uplifted. He sat awhile upon a bench overlooking the lake. He would marry her and make this house a palace. For that he had to make a success of the family business. More concerned with drinking and carousing to the small hours with his gentlemen friends up until now, he hadn't paid it much attention, but now all that would have to change.

"What happened to what we shared that day with the rose?" Eleanora asked and William stared again at the body of the young woman in front of him, so young and full of life, just like his Eleanora had been.

As if guessing the line of his thoughts, Eleanora said. "Claire is in love with Jared, the man you mean to take over, the birth son of Philip. They are just starting out like we were the day we met. Do you really want to destroy all that? They have a chance, William.

"What you saw in the flower still exists. You sensed its sacredness and beauty, the spirit of it, just like me, you know you did, and we were united in that magic moment. It is all still true but you lost sight of it. It became obscured, William, but not destroyed. True love can never be destroyed. You can connect with it again.

"You brought me a rose from that bush when you asked me to marry you. You even broke off the thorns so I would not hurt my hand. I kept it all my life, William. I even took it with me, pressed into my Bible, when I left Waterford Hall.

"You kissed it before you handed it to me all those years ago and I never forgot the look of love in your eyes. I longed for that look again and again over the years but it never came. Yet the rose always gave me hope that one day you would realise trying to create a great empire of wealth would never bring you true peace. I never needed those things, William, but it is not too late. I can help you find what it is you really want."

"No, you lie," he shouted. "Don't you think I have longed to know such joy again but now it can never be, not after all I have done." William's face twisted with grief in remembrance of his unspeakable crimes.

"That's not true."

"I have to find what pleasure I can in the world. And I have made a great success. I have businesses, an empire. And I created it all, *me.*"

"Yes, you have indeed, but for what, William? Do the businesses help people or do they use them? To whom do you give all your money? Who do you share your bed with at night?"

"I have had many, many women. I told you that before."

"Yes, you did, but why did they not stay with you?"

"I... I..."

"They wanted more than expensive gifts, cars and clothes and the like. They wanted love, William. Something you turned aside from all those years ago. But you can turn back."

"How," he spat, "when I have hurt so many? Give it up, Eleanora. I have no soul left to save."

"You say you have no soul but tell me something. Why have you done this?" With these words, Eleanora walked to the window and pointed. "Look at your garden, William. Tell me what you see."

In the centre of an area of grass were a number of bushes covered with white flowers.

Roses.

William turned to look. His roses were his pride, a challenge to grow in the tropical climate and yet he had done it. Tears came into his eyes and Eleanora realised she had reached him, knew she now had a chance of pulling him back from the brink but, at that moment, shouts came from outside; Barrett and the other man had captured Jared!

Chapter 23

E LEANORA KNEW SHE ONLY HAD a few minutes before Barrett returned and his attention would once again be on her and William. She looked at him, her heart twisting with pity for she could see the battle raging within. "Why white roses, William?"

"Yes, it is true. I did love once. I held someone sacred but what did you do? What did you do?" he accused, his voice rising in anger as he thought back.

"Yes, I betrayed you, William, and it is to my eternal shame."

"You openly admit it yet you say you still love me. Did you love me on the hillside with Ashworth? Be honest. Did you love me then?"

"I have always loved you, William. I have always had faith in what I saw in you the day we met but I was only human and when your obsession for money and power took control I felt so alone. You never had time for me but when you *were* there, I irritated you in some way. You never wanted to walk with me by the lake or listen to music. You never took the time to caress me with gentleness, hold me or tell me you loved me. All you wanted was your own pleasure, taken but never given.

"All you cared about was proving you could be a success. I always came second to that. But still I never gave up hoping and trying to reach you, that is, until your father died."

William interrupted, "I had the sole responsibility for the businesses then. It was hard, so hard and there were debts. I... I..."

"I know and I tried to tell you I did not mind if we had to move away from Waterford Hall but you would not have it. You wouldn't let me help you. Your pride stood in the way."

"Your way of helping was to leave me," he spat.

"When you met those lost to the Light, Barrett and his friends, their shadows encircled you, William, and I could no longer reach you. Life became intolerable. Barrett threatened me, told me he would kill me if I stayed so I knew I had to leave, to protect myself and Charles. I left to wait and pray that one day I would be able help you."

"You lie."

"No. Look at me. Look at me." Eleanora moved across the floor and with both of her hands reached up to his face to make him look into her eyes. "I never forgot you, William," she said. "I have been unable to rest these long years because I vowed I would not enter the Light unless *you* came with me.

"I have waited a long time, William. You say I do not love you but that is not true. Yes, I cared about Robert, he was there for me when you were not, but I always hoped you would turn back from darkness and remember the part of you I saw the day we met. That is the real you, down underneath, the part that built the rose garden outside despite all your bitterness. Don't let Barrett win, William. His way cannot bring you peace. Come with me into the Light. There you will find forgiveness and healing, we both will."

"You have waited all these years to help me?"

"Yes, it is true."

William looked at his wife in the young woman's body. He had spent so many years hating Eleanora, ever since the day he came upon her and Robert Ashworth on the hillside. They hadn't seen him, too focussed on their passion for each other. He returned later and stared in desolation at the bluebells lying crushed where she and Ashworth lay. After that the hate began to grow. It corroded everything and his finances fell into ruins as his businesses began to fail. It even affected his relationship with his son and he raged at the world for not obeying his commands.

He met and became friends with Barrett who offered William power and control over others. Barrett's esoteric practices frightened William at first, how he talked with spirits and used hypnotism to mould people's will to his whim, but when Barrett said he could bring him wealth, William submerged his misgivings.

But it had not happened. When his debts increased, he fell prey to a powerful moneylender introduced to him by Barrett.

"He will give you the money," he said.

"But I don't know how I will repay such an amount."

"It's all right, I can persuade him to forget all about the loan."
Barrett laughed.

Except that it hadn't worked. The man had other associates and they threatened to burn William's house down if he did not pay. In fear, he had gone to Barrett.

"What can I do?" he asked.

"Don't worry," Barrett said, smirking. *"I know a way you can get the money. One you might enjoy very much, very much indeed."*

"What is that?"

Barrett laughed. "There is someone I want you to meet. She is very beautiful but also very rich. You are handsome, I will help convince her to invest in you."

William had enjoyed his dalliance with Vera. It always gave him pleasure to get back at Eleanora with other women.

One night after he had spent the night with Vera, she told him she would give him the money. But it was too late! Triumphant, he had arrived back in the morning to the smoking ruins of Waterford Hall and knew it was the end of his dream, the great empire he had hoped to build.

A constable picked his way across the charred remains towards him. "Mr Waterford. I am sorry. Two people perished here last night. One was your butler, Mr Atrell, but I am afraid I have to inform you the other was your son, Charles."

William's world darkened. People came and went, sorting through the charred remains of his life, but the devastation outside was nothing compared to what occurred inside him. As he stood, immobile in shock, his grief and anger exploded into blind rage. He had lost everything.

Everything!

The darkness built within him and he raged at God who had allowed all this to happen, but most of all he raged at Eleanora. It had all gone wrong the day he found her and Ashworth together. And now he had lost his son, his heir, the only good thing his wife had ever done for him. And in that moment, the darkness of hatred and anger closed around William's heart. He turned away and climbed into his car. All he could think of was getting back at Eleanora somehow and that bastard Ashworth. They would pay for what they had done.

And pay they had. He looked at Eleanora now, knowing she had been unable to rest, tormented by what had happened, to him and then to Philip. Yes, she had certainly paid for what she had done but, unbelievably, he felt sorry.

William gazed at Eleanora staring at him with love and compassion. "Don't look at me like that," he moaned.

"Why not, William, it is the truth of how I feel."

And with her look, she tore him open again, just as she had all those years ago when he first came upon her in the garden. She touched the part of him he had thought dead forever, the part that still believed in, yearned for, beauty, for love, the part that had put in the effort needed to make roses grow well in his tropical garden because he loved to look at them. He felt tired. If only he could travel back in time to when they first met, he would do it all differently. But he couldn't go back, the weight of his past, the evil he had done, couldn't be obliterated. He no longer deserved love. Too many had suffered because of him.

William heard a noise in the hall outside and Jared and Jack came through the door. They were followed by Barrett and the other member of the Circle. Both of them had a gun.

"Claire!" Jared cried out, but, when she looked at him, he saw Eleanora had control of her.

"I'll take care of this woman for you, William," Barrett said, pointing his gun at Claire, "so she can't cause us any more trouble. Then you can have Jared. I don't think he'll give us any problems." Barrett gestured at Jared, whose eyes burned with hate, knowing the woman he loved was at risk. "His mind is ripe for us," Barrett said. "Take his body, William, and live on. He is young and strong. Think of the life we can still live."

William stared at Barrett, knowing he wouldn't give the destruction of Claire a second thought.

"Stop him, William!" Eleanora cried out. "Give Claire and Jared the chance to have what we could not."

Barrett's finger tightened on the trigger but in that instant William made his choice. He leapt forward and knocked Barrett's arm. The gun went off, ripping into the painting of the eagle and passing through the plasterboard interior wall. In the commotion that followed, Jared threw himself at Barrett, forcing him to the ground, and Jack punched the other man direct in the face with such force he fell unconscious to the floor.

Jared pinned Barrett to the ground. "You bastard," he snarled but Barrett laughed. He didn't care, Jared realised, and raised his fist, desperate to smash that jeering smile from his mouth.

"You want to, don't you," Barrett sneered. "Go ahead. It'll make you feel good. Powerful." Jared realised it was true. This man had threatened Claire, the woman he loved. He wanted to destroy him, to take out all his deep-seated frustrations on the man.

"No, Jared, no!" Eleanora cried. "Don't do it. It's what he wants. If you do, he will enter you. Let him go! Let him go! Don't be like him. He will pay the price for his crimes, don't worry. It will not be easy. Have pity on him."

Jared hesitated, realising the truth of Eleanora's words. Claire's face came into his mind, the beauty and gentleness of their time together the previous night. If he allowed himself to vent his anger on Barrett, he knew he'd lose her, lose the love he had rediscovered in himself and he couldn't bear that. He didn't want to follow the path of bitterness and revenge any longer. It would only lead to more suffering. Then he remembered he couldn't really hurt Barrett anyway. He was only using the body he held pinned down. Barrett would leave and find another. Him probably! The only one who would suffer was the person whose body Barrett now possessed. Jared felt a wave of compassion for him knowing how it felt to be unable to control what happened.

"What can we do, Eleanora?" he screamed. "Please help me. How can we get Barrett to leave this man?"

Eleanora came across to kneel beside Barrett. She laid her hand upon his heart and, as she did so, he arched his back. He shuddered and sought to lift himself off the floor, his face contorted with hate. "Don't let him go!" Eleanora said but Barrett managed to get one hand free and gripped Jared's throat. Gasping for breath, Jared released his hold and Barrett rolled aside. As he struggled to stand, Jack rushed over and, with all the force of his weight, knocked him down. Jared, now recovered, grabbed Barrett's arms again but he kicked out with his legs so Jack flung his body over them. Together, Jared and Jack somehow managed to hold Barrett down although he strained and swore at them.

"So much darkness," Eleanora exclaimed. "It is time for it to end. There has been too much suffering."

Barrett continued trying to break free then went limp. Eleanora, knowing he would try to leave the body he inhabited, called out in a loud, clear voice, "I invoke the power of the Light." As she did so, the room filled with an ethereal glow and several figures materialised. They looked human yet shone from within.

"No!" Barrett shouted.

"Be still," Eleanora commanded. "The Light will not harm you."

"You lie," Barrett shouted. His body shook and his eyes filled with terror, as he felt the power of the glowing beings encircle him, preventing him slipping from the body he possessed and making his escape.

"You have forgotten," Eleanora said in a quiet voice. "It is time to remember."

"I will not," Barrett whispered. "The Light will destroy me!"

"That is not true. It is a falsehood given to you by the dark ones you sought to aid you in the past. They told you that so you would not discover the truth. The Light does *not* destroy, it creates, gives true life. Look inside yourself. What do you see?"

"There is nothing."

"Keep looking."

"There is nothing, I tell you!" he yelled, angry now. "There is only darkness. Terrible darkness..." then he gasped. "I see people, they're crying and shouting."

"They are the souls you have harmed. Allow them to show you the way. Follow them back to the beginning. Feel their pain."

"No," he moaned, "no."

"Yes, you must."

"I cannot!" Barrett moaned and his face contorted with agony.

"Go back through time," Eleanora commanded.

Faces came and went in an endless procession, all those who had suffered from Barrett's evil. Each time he saw someone, he experienced their agony as if it were his own and witnessed the devastation he created in their lives.

"I cannot go on."

"You must. Go back further."

The terrible flood of suffering rolled on. Barrett could not keep it back. The people kept on coming and coming but then, after what seemed like an eternity, he saw the child, *his* child, lying outside the burnt-out shell of his home. His first-born son, just ten years old, lay in the dirt, his throat cut, murdered by the invading horde that had swept through the countryside. Then he saw his wife sprawled out, the back of her head caved in, his beloved, her blue dress splattered with the blood of the dead baby, his daughter, she still held in her arms. Her sightless eyes stared back at him and, in that moment, he knew God did not exist nor could he ever love again. He swore vengeance, that he would not rest until those responsible had paid for their crime.

And so, he had sought them out, one by one, until so much death and suffering warped his mind and he forgot there had ever been any other way to be. The darkness took possession and he took apprenticeship with masters of evil powers and learnt to manipulate and possess others. Death could no longer gain dominion over him then for, when his body began to weaken, he found another and another after that. And so, he had lived on through time, for generation upon generation, becoming more and more corrupt.

"Go back to the very beginning," Eleanora commanded. Now Barrett saw his wife again. This time she stood before him. She wore a long gown of blue wool and a wreath of small white flowers in her soft, brown hair. It was their wedding night. Barrett reached out a hand and with the tip of his fingers caressed the smooth skin of her cheek, so soft, so perfect. He had sworn then to love and cherish her with all of his power.

They stood in a garden before the small wooden building that would be their home. A single star shone in the night sky.

"What do you see?" Eleanora asked.

"My wife. She is crying. No, don't cry," he whispered. "Please don't cry…"

She held out her hand. On her smooth pink skin lay a smear of bright red blood. Looking into his eyes, she said, "Even one drop of blood lost for our deaths is one too many."

"What else do you see?" Eleanor asked.

"There is nothing. I can't see anything, it's all dark now."

"Keep looking," Eleanora commanded.

Barrett looked up. "Oh, there is a star."

"Look at it."

"So distant, so small," he murmured, "but so beautiful.

"Yes, it is. Keep looking at it. Is it harming you?"

"No, it's… No."

"It is your Light."

"No, it cannot be. I have no Light."

"You have been led astray. It is the source of your life."

Barrett stared at the star. It brightened the more he looked at it. Then he felt himself being drawn up towards it. He tried to resist again but felt the beings of Light gather around him and knew he had no choice. He let go and they drew him from the body of the man he possessed.

Claire, enmeshed with Eleanora, watched as the beings of Light encircled the spirit of Barrett. The light intensified, then they all vanished and the room snapped back to normal.

The man beneath Jared and Jack sighed and lay still.

"He sleeps now," Eleanora said. Jared stood up and Jack followed suit.

"It is done," Eleanora continued. "Barrett has been taken by those who know how to deal with him. He will bother us no more."

"What will happen to him?" Jared asked.

"He will continue to experience the suffering he caused until he learns there is a better way. It will not be easy."

"What about the other man?" Jared gestured towards Philip's other associate lying unconscious on the floor. "He will be fine. The spirit possessing him has been taken away also. Like Barrett, he too will come to understand the effects of what he has done."

After he knocked the gun from Barrett's hand, William had fallen to his knees on the floor. He maintained this posture, unable to find the energy to stand. It was all over. He couldn't carry on, didn't want to carry on. He felt so tired, exhausted by the effort to manipulate and control. Eleanora, still in the body of Claire, went over and knelt beside him.

"William, you must leave Philip now." William looked at Eleanora, saw the love and compassion in her eyes and it broke him. Tears coursed down his cheeks as he reached out and touched her face. "I'm sorry," he whispered. "I'm so sorry." Then he saw the spirit of his son standing beside him. Charles held out his hand and William moved away from Philip's body.

Jared saw his father sway so rushed over and guided him down to the ground where he lay still as if sleeping.

Claire felt Eleanora pull away and found herself once again in control of her own body. In front of her, she saw the spirits of William and Charles. Claire, although in the *back seat* the whole time had been aware of everything and felt a wave of compassion for William, who had saved her from Barrett. It would go a long way to redress the wrongs he had perpetrated throughout his long years of hate and bitterness. He had opened himself back up to the Light of Love so she knew he would now have a chance to finally heal. They all would.

Eleanora moved to stand next to William and looked over at Claire. "Thank you," she said with a soft smile then turned to her husband and held out her hand. He took it and for a few moments Claire watched them as they stood there, a united family at last, until they turned and walked away. As they reached the wall, an area of brightness engulfed them and they vanished.

Turning to look at Jared and Jack, Claire said, "They've gone," and burst into tears.

Jared rushed forward and enfolded her in his arms. "It's all right."

"I know. It's all just so...beautiful."

"You're okay?" Jared asked with concern.

"Yes, I'm fine. What do we do now?" They both looked around them. Philip still lay sleeping but the two other men showed signs of coming to.

Jack spoke, "Your lady spoke to me before she went," he said. "She told me these men will be fine." When the taller one who had been taken over by Barrett, opened his eyes, Jack went over and said, "Come on, mate, let me give you a hand." He helped the man onto a large leather settee where he stared around him in confusion.

Claire came over and laid her hand on his arm. To her surprise, healing energy flowed from her to him despite the fact she no longer had Eleanora with her. The man looked startled but then relaxed. "It's all right," she soothed. "You've had a spirit possessing you but it's gone now. Do you remember anything?"

The man frowned. "A spirit? Christ, I thought I'd gone bloody mad. I knew what I was doing and it wasn't what I wanted but I just couldn't stop it. I felt this heaviness in my mind." He rubbed his forehead. "But it's gone now." He smiled. "I feel so light."

Jared had helped the other man up and also guided him to the settee. "It was the same for me," the man said. "I'm so sorry I hurt you," he said to Claire.

She smiled, "It's okay, please don't worry about it." She laid her hand on him next and felt the tension leave his body as the healing energy flowed through his body. "Just take it easy for a few days," she said, "but you'll be fine."

She went over to Philip. He lay inert on the floor and Claire, concerned, knelt beside him. To her relief, she saw his chest rise and fall gently. She touched his forehead and allowed the energy to flow into him too, but he did not stir.

Jared came over. "Do you think he is going to be okay?"

"I don't know. He's sleeping. We have to remember he's not a young man and had William with him for many years. I think we just have to let him rest for the moment." She stood and walked out from the room returning a minute later with a pillow and a blanket. She made Philip as comfortable as possible then looked around at the others. "I'm going to make some coffee."

Claire disappeared off to find the kitchen. She returned a short while later and handed round mugs. Whilst they sat drinking, Claire told Jack and the two men, whose names were Josh and Ryan, the story of Eleanora, William and Philip.

"But what about the man who possessed me?" asked Josh who had been taken over by the spirit of Barrett. "What if he comes back?"

"He won't," Jared reassured him. "I felt him being taken away. When Eleanora called on the Light, I couldn't see anything but I felt as if I was encircled with a loving energy. I felt incredibly peaceful. It was like that for quite a while but then I sensed a dark shadow leave you and the energy went. I've never experienced anything like that before. It must be because I'm spending a lot of time with you," he said, turning to Claire, smiling.

"You've become more open to it because you accept it as a possibility now. You didn't before. I was the same until I got the necklace."

"This all blows my mind, man," Josh moaned in anguish. "I just can't believe what I did while that, that... *thing, spirit,* was in me." He shuddered. "I was sort of half aware but I couldn't do anything at all about what was happening."

"You, therefore, are *not* to blame," Claire smiled. "Please understand that."

Josh stared into her eyes then nodded. "Okay, I guess so. Anyway, I'd better get going. I've got some explaining to do to my family."

Ryan looked tortured. "I doubt my wife is going to be there when I get back. I left with no explanation. I haven't been back for three months. She wouldn't understand all this."

"Try her," Claire said. "You never know, more people are open to it than you might think. And it's up to you to show her you love her. That's what will help her understand. Love is the key to a lot of things."

"I will."

"I don't have a wife," Josh said, "but my mum and sister will be worrying. I never saw them much but I did ring them every so often. I was so rude to Mum the last time we spoke on the phone, though. It wasn't me doing it but she doesn't know that."

"Why don't you go and see her." Claire saw the image of an elderly woman with a sad face.

"She lives in South Australia."

"It's just a thought. I think you need time to come to terms with all this and I am sure it would mean a lot to your mother. Have you got anything here?"

"No. I was just bumming around Australia on my bike, going where I could get work. I guess, it would be good to go home for a while. Things were feeling pretty pointless when all this happened."

"I think that's how Barrett gained control over you, your energy was low."

Josh looked anxious.

Claire guessed his concern. "Don't worry; it won't happen again, I'm sure. The spirits in you and Ryan were pretty powerful and had possessed many people for years. We apparently all have guides with us from the spirit world. If you're afraid you can call on them and they will help protect you. You only have to ask." A picture of Josh with a glass in his hand came into her mind. "Maybe not drinking so much might help?" Claire suggested gently.

Josh looked sheepish. "I'm gonna go," he said.

"You need a lift anywhere?" Jared asked, then remembered he had left his car at the tourist centre. He would have to go back in a taxi and get it when things were more settled.

"No, thanks. My bike's in the garage here. I don't think I'll take any of the clothes I had while I lived here." He looked down at the rumpled suit he wore. "The spirit that took me over had the most terrible taste in clothes." Everyone laughed.

"I feel the same," Ryan said.

"I'll give you my mobile number," Jared said. He wrote the number on two pieces of paper and gave one each to Josh and Ryan. "Ring us if you need to talk or are worried."

"What will happen to Barrett?" Josh asked.

"I don't know," Claire replied.

Josh nodded and left. A few moments later, they heard the sound of his motorbike revving up and moving away down the street. Claire went over to Philip who still lay unconscious. Jared followed. "How is he?"

Claire stared down at the man lying on the ground. Although he had aged, she still recognised the face she had stared at in the photograph so many times. "William has been affecting him from such a young age. I don't know what that would do," she said. "I can't ask Eleanora, she's gone."

"What do *you* think?" Jared asked. "You still seem pretty powerful even without Eleanora."

"Hmm, Eleanora did say the necklace had power in itself, something about the amethyst."

She sat beside Philip and laid her hand on his chest. Nothing happened for a while but she sensed a stillness in the room, as if everything had paused, so waited and after a minute felt the healing energy flow through her arm. It helped for Philip murmured something indecipherable and shifted. Claire and Jared looked at each other.

Claire kept her hand on Philip's chest. "He's very far away," she said, "so small and lost. And afraid. He's like a child hiding in a cupboard."

Her voice gentle, she tried to reassure him. "It's all right now, Philip. William has gone and will not return. It is safe to be with us here, now. There are people who love you and who will help you."

To Claire's disappointment, Philip remained immobile. "I don't know what else to do," she sighed. "I don't want to leave him like this, though."

Jared looked down at the old man. He had finally found the father he never had, the man he had hated and despised all these years but who he now knew had been blameless, a puppet in the hands of a more powerful soul. He didn't want to find his father only to lose him. "What about taking him to hospital? He's old, perhaps it's been too much for his body."

"I don't know," Claire said. "That might make things worse."

"But we can't just do nothing."

"Look, you guys, I'm going to go," Ryan said, standing. "Good luck with him. I'm sure he'll be okay." Ryan began walking to the door.

"I can give you a lift," Jack said.

"Thanks."

Jared went over and shook Jack's hand. "Thanks for everything." Jack nodded then went over to Claire. He looked into her eyes and, as she stared into his, she sensed him at a deeper level and knew they both shared the experience of the sacred stillness within life, that with him it manifested in a deep love and communion with the rainforest, his ancient home. "You don't need your lady, you know," he said, "you got it yourself."

"What do you mean, Jack?"

"The wisdom of your own soul. Ask it for guidance."

"But how?"

"Listen to your heart. Open to it, trust and rely on it. The more you do, the more the connection will grow. Just love and be yourself, Claire, doing and being what resonates within you. Have faith in who you are," He smiled. "It's pretty special." He reached out a hand and squeezed her on the shoulder then glanced down at Philip. "Let me know if you need any more help." With that he turned and walked away, joining Ryan by the door. Claire and Jared went with them down the hall and watched them drive off in Jack's truck.

Claire shut the door and turned to look at Jared who pulled her into his arms. "Oh, my love, I thought I was going to lose you," he whispered. He tightened his hold, wanting to meld himself to her. "I don't *ever* want to lose you," he murmured, burying his face in her hair.

They stood for some moments, each drawing strength and joy from the physical closeness of the other. They kissed passionately, neither wanting to pull away, but knew they must. They had to take care of Philip.

"Okay," Jared said. "Let's see how my father is. If he doesn't get better soon, we'll have to call an ambulance." They headed back down the hall. Reaching the lounge, they stopped in shock. Philip had gone!

P HILIP OPENED HIS EYES TO white.

A blank. Nothing.

A hanging thread of cobweb came into focus and he realised he was staring up at a ceiling. He turned his head and saw a room full of furniture. It looked familiar and yet he felt detached from it. His body felt heavy, as if it did not belong to him. With a great effort and the support of a nearby table, he heaved himself to a standing position. His head swam and his legs threatened to give way but, slowly, more strength came into his body. He straightened up and turned around.

The eagle came swooping down out of nowhere, its claws outstretched to tear at him as painting and memory merged into one terrible reality in his shattered mind. Philip put his arms up to protect his face and moaned. He would never know freedom, always be the prey, the pursued. Turning, Philip staggered from the room, through the back door and onto the open lawn.

He felt exposed, knowing he could be seen for miles. The forest beckoned. He would be safe there. The eagle couldn't come at him through the trees.

Philip hurried across the grass and into the enclosing protection of the forest. Despite the pounding of his heart, he had to get further in. Fear gave him unnatural endurance and he pushed through the undergrowth for a long way until shortness of breath forced him to stop. He looked around for somewhere to rest. The sound of rushing water penetrated his mind so he moved in that direction. He had to get to the river. He would be safe there. Philip stumbled on and a few minutes later came across it.

He cowered back under the trees, afraid that the eagle might see him but noticed a rocky overhang. Crawling under entwining roots into a tiny cave behind two large boulders, he curled up into a ball on the earth floor. He watched the river swirling past and the sound lulled him into a more restful state. He loved the sound of falling water. It reminded him of somewhere else, a place where the grass was green and the water tumbled down a hillside scattered with blue flowers.

Everything felt mixed up in his mind. He knew the place was a long way away but he wanted to go there. There was something important there but the memory eluded him. Maybe when he felt better, when his heart stopped pounding in his chest, he would try to get there. But for now, he had to rest. The eagle could not find him in this protected place. Philip's eyes closed and he fell asleep to the sound of the water gurgling and pouring over the rocky river bed.

"Bloody hell!" exclaimed Jared. "Where's he gone?" He and Claire separated and searched the whole house but found no sign of the old man. They met in the kitchen and stared at each other in disbelief. "The garden," Jared said. They dashed outside and checked the whole area, in all the outbuildings and the black car which sat on the drive, but found no sign. Philip had vanished.

"Where do you think he could have gone?" Jared asked. Claire gazed towards the rainforest.

"In there?" Jared rushed to the end of the garden and a short way in. He listened but heard only the normal sounds of the forest. Claire joined him. "He could have gone in any direction," Jared said in despair. "There's no path here. Where the hell would he go? Claire, can you sense anything?"

"Wait." She closed her eyes and became still. A warm breeze caressed her face as she listened, not only with her ears but also with her heart. All her senses alert, she tried to get a feel for the old man. Nothing happened for a while but, as she waited, she sensed water, pouring water. "The river," she whispered. "I feel the river. I think he's near it."

"So which direction is it in?" Jared asked, looking around.

Claire still had her eyes closed. If the forest could speak, she thought, it would tell her the way to go. But perhaps it can. She swivelled around and looked at the trees. One in particular caught her attention. Ancient beyond reckoning, it bent over under the weight of time. Creepers grew in a tangle all over an odd shaped branch and a picture came into her mind of Philip passing beneath it. "He went that way," she said, moving forward.

"I hope you know what you're doing," Jared said. "I don't want to get lost." He had heard news stories about British holidaymakers losing their way in the Australian bush and wandering for days.

"That branch is pointing the way," she said

"Oh, for God's sake! That's ridiculous even for you."

"I know, but I honestly feel we should go in that direction. Come on. We have to find Philip. He may be ill."

"All right. Just watch out for snakes."

Claire walked on, her senses probing the forest. A large tree looked to be glowing in a patch of sunlight so she moved in that direction then towards a creeper swaying in an unusual fashion in the wind. She increased her speed as she became more attuned to subtle nuances of pattern or shape that felt significant or drew her attention.

After fifteen minutes of walking, Jared began to panic. "Where's the river? Are you sure you know where you're going?"

Claire stopped. "Look." They saw a small building left to decay into the forest. Most of the wooden walls had long since gone except for a few upright timbers supporting a corroded metal roof. Creepers and other plants had claimed the place for their own.

She moved inside followed by Jared. "Philip isn't here," he said. "Let's move on."

"No, wait. I was guided here." Claire looked around her. "I want to know why."

She stood still and shut her eyes, touching her necklace with one hand whilst holding a wooden beam with the other. A shaft of light fell on her face and she opened her eyes again. This time she saw a building filled with a few rough items of furniture. A man sat writing at a small battered looking table on which many pages of writing lay. "Who are you?" Claire whispered. She moved around to take a look at his face. He looked familiar but she couldn't place him at first then realised; he was Eleanora's lover, Robert.

"My God!" she exclaimed. "Why did *he* come to this place?" Robert covered the paper before him with a flowing script then reached for another sheet. As he did so, the scene faded to the present ruin.

"What is it? What do you see?" Jared asked.

"Robert, the man Eleanora had an affair with. Eleanora told me she never heard from him again after they made love on the hillside. He just disappeared. He obviously came here to this hut, another one who seems to have been drawn to Mossman. This is so bizarre. Australia is such a long way from the Lake District. In those days, not an easy journey by any means, and life must have been pretty rough here in the early nineteen hundreds."

"You're sure it was Robert?" Jared asked.

"Yes."

"Then this is very important. This might explain why Dad came here, why he had such an obsession with Mossman Gorge."

"What are you getting at?"

"Sorry, I should have said why *William* wanted to come here. He controlled Philip who wouldn't have had any say in it. Perhaps William sought Robert out. After all, he seduced his wife. He would have hated him. Maybe he wanted to get back at him."

"Oh, I see what you mean, but wouldn't Robert have been long dead by the time William made Philip come here?"

Jared screwed up his face in concentration. "Let's see. My father disappeared in 1971. We know Eleanora died in 1923 aged thirty-three. If this Robert was a similar age to her that would make him eighty something in '71. It's just possible he *was* still alive if William brought my father here then."

"But that means William had to wait almost fifty years to get his revenge, though, that's a very long time." Claire's mind reeled with the implications of their discovery.

"Some things people never forget. Maybe it took him that long to find Robert, who knows."

"Hmm. There's so much we don't understand."

"Anyway," Jared looked outside and saw the sky glowed pink between the trees. "We must press on if we're to find my father before it gets dark."

"Yes, of course," Claire agreed. The mystery of Robert's shack in the rainforest would have to wait. Going outside, she felt drawn to a small clearing. "This way," she said and, in a similar fashion as before, Claire led Jared through the forest until they heard the sound of rushing water in the distance.

"The river!" Jared exclaimed.

Claire continued to lead the way and a few minutes later they stood on a small gravel bank staring at the river pouring past through the rocks. She looked left and right. Trees overhung the water on both sides. The sky opened out above, now a deep blue, darkening with approaching evening. Jared remained silent, knowing she would be tuning into the place.

They stood for some while, Claire watching and listening, open to any signs or sensations. She closed her eyes and followed the sound of the flowing water. It bubbled, gurgled and trickled, so many sounds, all overlaying one another in a symphony of river music. She became captivated and felt herself losing definition. As this happened, Claire sensed again the spirit of the place she experienced the last time they visited the area. A rush of cool energy swept around her and her consciousness opened out until she felt herself to *be* the river and the forest, even the sky. She found herself able to feel the living energy in the trees and the myriad creatures living in the forest and also in her and Jared.

And Philip!

She became aware of his presence nearby, closed and tight, curled in a ball, hiding, and sensed his anguish. All the years of William's domination had taken their toll and he had become lost deep within himself. "This way," she said and set off, edging her way along the side of the river as best she could.

It did not take her long to find Philip's hiding place. She noticed an overhang on the bank of the river which looked a likely hiding place so she and Jared crouched down to peer inside.

Dirty and dishevelled, they saw the curled-up figure of Philip. Seeing them, he recoiled further back into the hollow, his eyes staring like a cornered animal. "No, it's all right," Claire soothed. "We will not harm you."

"Oh, Eleanora, I need you now," she appealed but, although she waited and listened, the spirit did not answer. Claire sighed. This was up to her.

She touched the amethyst necklace for reassurance then tentatively lay her hand on Philip. He shrank back further. "It's all right," she soothed. "I am here to help you." Claire sensed the circling bird waiting to pounce in Philip's mind and moved nearer. "Come," she said. "The eagle has gone now. It will not return."

Philip slowly uncurled but Claire knew he still felt afraid. "Let me help you," she said, reaching for his hand. Jared came closer and together they helped Philip from the cave. He staggered but they supported him until he regained some strength. He scanned the sky with anxious eyes.

"It has really gone," Claire affirmed and stared into his watery eyes full of confusion. "It will all become clear. Try to relax."

Jared helped Philip sit on a nearby boulder and, as Philip stared at the young woman in front of him, fragmented images whirled though his mind. "William has left you now," the woman said. "There is no longer anything to fear. He will not return. Listen to the water flowing.

It is washing you clean, taking your fear and pain away... far, far away...
Let it move through you."

Claire set a firm hand on Philip's shoulder and sent healing energy
into his body. He relaxed somewhat but she sensed a reluctance to
relinquish his fear. Something more was needed, she thought and,
closing her eyes again, tuned into the spirit of the land around her
falling into a stillness so complete it took her breath away. The sense of
herself as a separate individual faded into an infinite peace. And, as she
became aware of this, the two others in her presence could not help but
feel it too. Even Philip, his mind tired and afraid, felt the resonance as
it bathed him in peace and love. Jared's awareness opened out and
became one with Claire and his father and the forest but, more than
that, with the essence of life itself. Tears flowed down his face as, for
the first time, he became aware of his soul.

"Look up now," Claire commanded Philip. "See, the sky is clear."

The old man raised his gaze to search the sky. He saw no eagle circled
and a heavy weight fell from his body leaving him clean and empty.

"He has truly gone?" he asked.

"Yes," Claire affirmed.

"Where am I?"

"Mossman Gorge."

"Mossman," he whispered. "Yes. Yes." He looked around him,
staring first at the trees, then at the river. He looked down then and
noticed his hands, gnarled with age. "I am old, so old. Where has my
life gone? I don't remember."

"Please don't worry about it; we will explain everything," Jared said.

Philip turned to look at him. "Who are you?"

"My name is Jared. I am your son and I have come to take you
home."

Philip's eyes widened.

"My mother is Laura. She gave birth to me after you left."

"Laura?" Philip repeated.

"Do you remember her at all?" Claire asked.

"I... I..." He looked at the river. The sound of it ran through him and
he remembered the other stream in that place far away where he
wanted to go. He saw the banks of green grass dotted with blue. A young
woman ran up to him laughing then darted away across a meadow
through the flowers. He began to shake so Claire and Jared took hold
of him again.

"Come on, we have to get him out of here," Jared said. "It's all too much
for him. He needs proper rest. Can you get us to the house?"

Claire looked around her to get her bearings. "Yes, I think so."

They set off back through the forest, Claire and Jared each supporting Philip. They made good progress until they passed Robert's shack where, without warning he stiffened and nearly fell.

His face contorted and tears welled up, overflowing down his mud stained cheeks.

"What is it?" Claire asked.

"I am sorry," the old man moaned. "I am so very sorry."

"What's going on?" Jared asked Claire.

"I don't know. Something happened here, I think. Whatever it was, Philip must blame himself for it."

Claire quietened and tried to tune in to the old man but he became more agitated.

"We have to get him away from here," Jared said. "It's getting late and I don't want to be in the forest at night."

"Okay." They pulled Philip away from the building and focussed on guiding him back to his house. Even with both of them supporting the old man, it took them a long time and it was nearly dark before they made it through the back door. They found a bedroom and helped Philip onto the bed. He lay there moaning to himself. "What are we going to do?" Jared asked. "Do you think we should take him to hospital? I'm so worried."

"Give me a minute," Claire said, lowering herself into the chair next to Philip. She placed a hand on his shoulder and closed her eyes. She sat in stillness and expanded her consciousness to embrace him. Right away she sensed confusion and pain. Something was upsetting him, preventing him from wanting to re-engage with life. She no longer felt it had to do with William. The power of the gorge had cleansed away the fear of William. Philip's reaction at the shack told her it had something to do with Robert. But what? Claire felt a wave of concern. If Philip became too lost in pain, he could lose the will to live and slip away out of life.

Something made her decide to scan his body and it was then she felt the constriction in his chest. Fear sprang into her consciousness. Was this a serious problem? She didn't know what to do. If only Eleanora was here, she thought.

Jack's words came into her mind then. "You don't need your lady, you know. You got it yourself, the wisdom of your own soul." Claire knew he was right. She *did* know what to do, just needed to have more faith in herself. She focussed on her breathing then became still. She laid her hand on Philip's chest and centred herself within, becoming aware of her unity with the power behind life itself. Right away she received a sense of being supported and remembered other beings in spirit would be with her. "What should I do?" she asked.

As she listened within, a conviction intensified in her mind. With medication, he would be okay. "I think he has pills he should take," she said to Jared. "Take a look around, will you?"

Jared disappeared and came back with a small bottle. "Here, these are dated last week. It says he should take one twice a day so he's missed one tonight." Jared fetched some water and, with both Claire and Jared supporting him, Philip managed to swallow one of the pills. Claire laid her hand over his heart and felt energy flow. Philip relaxed and fell asleep.

"I think he'll be all right, physically, that is," she said to Jared, "but mentally is another matter. He hasn't been interacting with the world properly for many years. It's going to take a big adjustment but on top of that I feel something else is preventing him from wanting to become truly present."

"I don't think we should take him to the hospital. They'll think he's got dementia or something and we won't get him out of the medical system." She fell silent and looked down at him. "No, I think the only chance we have of helping Philip is to take him home...as soon as possible."

Jared gazed at his father, a stranger to him, and felt a wave of compassion for the old man. "You mean, take him back to where he lost control of his life to William?"

"Yes, reconnect him with the things he held dear, the Lake District, his house, Bella, but, most of all, Laura. I believe she has the most chance of helping him."

"Hmm, I think you're right. But how in hell are we going to do it?"

"Let's check through this house. See if we can find out about his life here, then we can see if it's possible. We will need to find his passport. He must have one."

Jared stood. "I'll get right on it. I'll also give Mum a ring. She needs to know what's happened."

"Be careful what you say. Philip is very changed from what she knew and, to be honest, I just don't know how he's going to be long term."

"Okay. You stay and keep an eye on my father. We don't want him wandering off again."

Claire looked down at the old man. His regular breathing told her he had fallen asleep. She glanced outside. Night had fallen. Her stomach contracted with hunger. She went to the bedroom door and called out, "Ring a pizza, will you?"

"Good idea."

As she stood by the door, she noticed the painting of the eagle in the room across the passage, a bullet hole through its body. "Oh, and, Jared, could you take the eagle down? It will remind Philip of William and we don't want that."

"Okay."

Claire sat down on a chair next to Philip, gazing at him. Light coming through the open door illuminated his face. He looked peaceful but she knew he hovered on the brink of turning aside from life. She touched his hand. "Come back," she whispered. "It will be all right. There's someone who needs you."

In sleep he looked more like the man she had first seen all those weeks ago in the photo she found in the necklace box. She remembered the love in his eyes, the joy. William had not had full control then. Philip had been looking at Laura when the photograph was taken. Claire had no doubt of the depth of love between the two. If anyone could bring him back, Laura would. But what if even she failed? What if it was too late, if the thing Claire sensed holding him back from life could not be healed? Laura would be devastated if she had to lose Philip a second time.

Claire cast her awareness through Philip. He had retreated far, far back inside again. His spirit felt weaker than the last time she sensed him. Claire hoped her plan would work. Two lives hung in the balance.

Chapter 25

CLAIRE'S EYES FLEW OPEN. WHAT had woken her? Moonlight flooded the room where she lay. She sensed something on the edge of her consciousness but couldn't define it so got up and went into Philip's room. Jared sat in a chair by the bed. They had agreed the old man needed to be watched the whole time. "I don't need a break yet," he said.

"I can't sleep anymore."

Jared stood up and pulled her into his arms.

Claire relaxed against him, her body longing for the closeness they had shared the night on the beach but now was not the time. But it would come. She touched his cheek and moved away. "I think I'll get some fresh air," she said, "but then I'll take over so you can get some rest."

"Don't go far."

"No, I won't."

Claire left the house and walked out into a magical world. A full moon hung in the clear sky above bathing the lawn with a silver glow and casting the surrounding rainforest into shadow. Acting on an impulse demanding expression in that moment, she danced in slow motion across the lawn, lifting her arms and twirling around, loving the feel of the cool air on her skin and the sensation of moving.

A faint light caught her eye. Curious, she stopped and looked. It came from within the forest. Claire crept towards the edge of the trees. Something about the light drew her and she walked towards it but it drifted away and kept moving. Knowing it was somehow significant, she followed it through the forest until it stopped and hovered near the shack they found earlier. As she approached, the light coalesced into a human form. Robert.

"Why have you have brought me here?" Claire whispered.

"I loved her without reason," came the words, coming not from his lips but direct into her mind.

"Eleanora?"

"To me she was life. Without her I wanted to die."

Claire waited, wondering what this was all about.

"The day we made love on the hillside at Waterford Hall was the last time I spoke to her." An image of Robert walking along a country lane surged into Claire's mind and she felt his essence as a quiet, sensitive soul, in tune with nature, wanting only to be a poet and artist.

Robert made his way through a gate into a field and stood to admire the view. The waters of a lake stretched in front of him mirroring the sky. Lost in rapt attention, he did not hear the man come up behind him and so the blow to his head came out of nowhere, throwing him to the ground. "I have a message for you," a rough voice snarled. "Stay away from Eleanora." Robert just had time to see a bearded face scowling down before more blows rained down upon him and he lost consciousness.

"I did not listen and one day waited until I thought William would have left for the factory. I wanted to persuade Eleanora to come away with me but, when I rang the doorbell and the butler showed me in, William himself strode across the hall."

"Ah, Ashworth, so good of you to call," William sneered. "What is it, pray, do you not understand about never seeing Eleanora again?" The coldness in his voice sent shivers down Claire's spine.

Drawing on all the courage he possessed, Robert spoke. "Eleanora deserves better than this."

"Is that so and, of course, you are the man to give it to her?"

"I..." Robert quailed and fell silent.

"There is something I want you to understand," William moved in close. "If you come within fifty miles of her I will have you killed. Do I make myself clear?" The depth of hate in William's eyes shocked Robert to the core. He still ached from his brutal beating. He nodded but his heart bled. The thought of his Eleanora, so beautiful and gentle, in the hands of this animal blazed through him and ignited a burning

anger despite his fear. Yet he remained silent, knowing he could do nothing in this moment.

"Good day," William said, turning away. He rang the bell to call the butler and Robert followed the servant to the front door.

He stood for a moment on the gravel outside looking up at the house as the front door closed. Where was she? How could he live without her? He choked back a sob but had no choice but to walk away down the drive and past the sinister eagles poised with outstretched wings on the two pillars. He could not bear to return home to the confinement of his lodgings and so walked for many miles through the countryside, his mind burning with hatred for the man who held his goddess prisoner.

It became an obsession that ate into his very soul. He did not eat nor sleep and all the fine words of his poetry fell away so he could no longer write. Instead, he hatched plots to rescue Eleanora. As the second son of a wealthy family, he had access to a fair amount of money and so it was he conceived of an elaborate plan.

One day he climbed over the wall at the rear of Waterford Hall and made his way to the far side of the lake, a wild area of natural woodland where Eleanora had told him she walked alone every morning. He had everything organised. He had arranged passage for them both on a ship bound for Australia. They would have no chance of living in England, for he knew William would not rest until he had sought them out. Their only chance was to flee a long way away. Robert's younger brother had gone to Australia two years before and so they would have a place to stay.

He hid himself behind a tree where he had a good view of the lake so he could see her coming. He had arranged a car and driver to wait in the road beyond the wall. To his good fortune, the day dawned fine and so, in all likelihood, she would keep to her usual practice. Indeed, it wasn't long before he saw her coming. His heart lifted with joy. It had been several weeks since their time together and he could not wait to hold her close again. He would make everything right. They would flee far away and find a sanctuary where they could live out their days in love and peace.

Robert waited as she approached. She looked so beautiful. He could not take his eyes off her. And this was his mistake.

He did not see them coming. Without warning, a hand covered his mouth and two men dragged him far back through the trees. Eleanora strolled past, oblivious to the terrible drama being enacted just out of sight. The men held Robert fast until Eleanora had gone well beyond hearing, she to return to a house filled with bitterness and hate while Robert struggled for his very life.

He resisted with every ounce of his strength but, restrained by the two men, he could do nothing. Fear coursed through his body for he knew, without doubt, the moment Eleanora passed they would kill him. A small man, unused to physical labour, he stood no chance against brute force. He had to use his wits. Robert went limp. All resistance left his body and his eyes closed. It had the desired effect. The men relaxed their grip a little, thinking he had fainted in fright. They laughed. Rough men, drawn from the streets by Barrett, they despised people like Robert: weak and pampered and, in their eyes, undeserving of wealth.

They dragged him further back into the trees. One punched him on the face then kicked his side. Using all his inner strength to accept the pain, Robert continued to act like a rag doll and it fooled them, for they let his body drop and he fell, limp and lifeless, to the ground. "Let's just knife 'im and get out of here," one said.

Robert knew he only had seconds to make his move. Although physically weak, he was agile and quick. Without warning, he rolled and, before the men could react, rose to his feet. One almost caught him by the jacket but Robert ducked, twisted and ran. Light and fit from walking long distances through the countryside, as he loved to do, he sped ahead of the men.

Fear fuelled his feet; he had never run so fast in his entire life. He heard them close behind him but soon the distance between them widened. After a few minutes, he saw the wall ahead, fortunately quite low at this point. He flung himself over and ran for the car he knew waited nearby. The driver had orders to leave quickly when he returned. The man had been paid well and so he had the engine running. Robert came bounding up and threw himself in beside the driver. "GO!" he shouted.

Seeing the two ruffians approaching, the driver wasted no time and the car accelerated away. One of the pursuers grabbed onto it but lost his grip and fell to the ground. Robert almost did faint then as the shock of it all hit home. His face and side throbbed but the knowledge that he had failed and lost his lady hurt more. He cursed himself for not realising that, of course, she would be watched. Robert knew he had been a stupid fool. What chance did he have now? William would never let her go.

Robert boarded the ship bound for Australia alone, a broken man, mired in guilt at his inability to save the woman he loved. He tried to block her from his memory for he could not stand to imagine her life with that man.

"I arrived here in Australia in 1910," Robert explained. "I stayed with my brother in Sydney for a while but could not rest easy, haunted by my failures. I tried to write but the words would no longer come so I travelled all over Australia for a few years, trying many things but then, by chance, I arrived in Port Douglas and I knew I had come to paradise: the sea, the reef, the rainforest, the colour of the sky in all its moods and the pale sand, so, so beautiful. Then I happened to meet an Aboriginal man. It was strange, but I believe we were destined to meet. I came upon him sitting on the beach early one morning. As he turned to look at me, our eyes met and held and it was as if I was seeing back through time to an ancient past in which we had known each other. He nodded and motioned for me to sit and, from that moment, we knew we had a purpose to our meeting. It was Daniel who guided me to the Gorge and there I found my soul.

Claire had a vision of Robert, his face alight with interest, walking through the forest, a man at his side. She could sense the same deep affinity to the land in him that Jack had.

"Daniel guided me through the forest and the moment I walked through the trees, I knew I had come home. Everything touched me in a way I had never experienced before."

Claire found herself watching as the two men made their way through dense rainforest to the river. They found a large boulder and placed themselves upon it and she found herself right there with them as if it were all happening in that moment. All sense of darkness vanished in the majesty and brightness of this vision and Claire felt an indivisible link with these two men who sat in companionable silence for a long time as they connected to the landscape.

The river surged between the rocks and the trees rustled in the wind. Behind them, the mountains rose, immutable and vast. They breathed in the life of the place and fell still, so still it was as if they had transcended time. And, in that moment, each came into a realisation of the reality of their soul as the spirit of Life moved into them, became them and they knew without doubt they were one with it, one with the infinite essence behind all things.

And Claire knew it too as she stood in the forest, her awareness and knowing back in the past with Robert and Daniel. She felt humbled and blessed by this joining through time but then the sense came that time was an illusion anyway.

The vision faded and Claire came back into the night with Robert in front of her.

"After that day, I felt inspired to write again. Words poured from me in a torrent like the water in the gorge itself. I felt cleansed, open and free in a way I would never have dreamed possible. I had touched the heart of life itself and now it wanted to speak through me."

Claire noticed Robert now had a book in his hand. He held it out to her and, on the cover, saw an illustration of a river flowing through trees. The title read *In the Forest by the River* by Robert Ashworth. He smiled and vanished.

She recognised that book. It was the one Elaine had taken from her bag after she came out of the river. She had had a copy of Robert's book! How weird all this is, Claire thought. She stayed motionless for a few moments, in awe at the strangeness of events, then turned and hurried back to Philip's home. It did not occur to her to worry about finding her way in the dark, she could sense the direction, so attuned was she now to her surroundings.

She slipped back into the house and hurried to Philip's room. Jared looked concerned. "I was beginning to get worried about you."

"You had no need," she whispered. "Come into the room opposite. I want to tell you something." They sat on a couch where they could still see Philip and Claire told Jared what she had experienced. "Elaine had a copy of it," she finished.

"Let's look Robert up on the Internet to see if we can find out more about his book." Jared fetched a laptop he had discovered looking around Philip's office. The password had been written in a notebook he found and so, sitting through the night with his father, he had spent the time sorting through the files and trying to build a picture of his life as William.

He sat back down and typed in the words "*In the Forest by the River*" and "Robert Ashworth."

A whole host of websites came up. Jared clicked on the first one, an online bookshop, and they saw an image of the book next to a brief advert. "It's still in print today, look." Claire read the text out loud: "The story of the author's adventures in the Daintree forest with an Indigenous man known to him as Daniel, with whom he struck up a deep and lasting friendship. In it, he describes the spiritual awakening that changed his life. Although first published in 1914, it still has the power to move the reader today. A must read for every seeker of the truth."

"Hmm, intriguing," Jared said. He clicked on another site. This one showed a photo of a young man standing by the small hut Claire found. They read through and found it described how the man, inspired by Robert's writing, had journeyed to the place where it had been written.

They scanned through a few other sites, either adverts for the book or numerous accounts of how the work had touched people. It had been reprinted many times and they discovered that, despite the commercial success of his book, Robert Ashworth had remained living in his shack until his death in 1973.

"How amazing," Jared said. "*In the Forest by the River* obviously had a profound effect on a lot of people's lives. We must get hold of a copy. I'd love to read it."

Claire didn't say anything for a while but then stood and walked off. "Just give me a moment." She roamed through the rooms in the house, her intuition leading her to a bedroom cupboard. Opening it, she saw a box. Pulling out some old papers, she found what she was looking for. She leafed through it before hurrying back to Jared, waving her trophy.

"I had a strong feeling I'd find this here," she said. "This is Robert's book. William had a copy."

"This is too strange," Jared said. "Why would William have a book written by a man he hated?"

"I don't know." Claire fell silent and held the book between her hands. It felt cool to the touch and smelt old. She stared at the cover and a sense came of Philip holding it as a boy, reading it over and over again, loving it, the book lifting his spirits, helping push away the dark thoughts that haunted his mind, the effect of the presence of William who returned time and time again and, all of a sudden, she knew! Turning to look at Jared, she exclaimed, "This book belonged to Philip! William had it because Philip *wanted* him to have it. We were wrong. It wasn't William who wanted to come here to Mossman Gorge, I think it was Philip."

"My father!"

"Yes."

"But...I don't understand. William had control of him."

"We thought Philip was overpowered but I think maybe he came back into control or semi control sometimes." Claire became still again so as to allow the answers she sought to reveal themselves. "This book definitely belonged to Philip. Somehow, he managed to get William to bring it with him. Perhaps he had it on him when he disappeared although that doesn't feel quite right. Hmm, interesting." She fell silent and flicked through the book, reading passages here and there.

"This book tells of the power of Mossman Gorge, how it transformed Robert's life. I wonder if Philip hoped he could influence William to come here to Mossman believing that, in this special place, he might be able to break free. Perhaps he sensed, like Eleanora did, that William still had some remnant of conscience and awareness of spirit at a very deep level, that, in the powerful energy of Mossman, it might be reawakened.

"Elaine had a copy of this too. Living next door to each other, she and Philip must have talked about the book. It all makes sense. That's why she thanked him. I think she came here to find healing when she left her husband and it changed her life. I bet she told Philip about what happened to her here."

"Yes. If he knew this place had healing power, he *would* want William to come here," Jared replied.

"And it worked to some extent," Claire went on, "for William came to live close to the Gorge and built the rose garden but Philip didn't take into account the power of Barrett and the others. They kept William focussed on his desire for material power and success, things he could achieve with ease in this land ripe with business opportunities, except that, as Eleanora pointed out to him in the end, it never brought him true satisfaction and so she was finally able to reach him here."

"Through you."

"Yes. It's humbling to think she never gave up on William, always believed in him despite the awful things he did. That's true love for you. It shows the power of it to heal and transform."

"So, if William was affected by the power of the Gorge, why has Philip not been healed?" Jared asked. "Even *I* felt something when we found him by the river."

"I don't know. It doesn't feel right. It did help to some extent; it was why he was drawn to the Gorge. I feel he's been cleansed of the effects of William. Philip knows William has gone but something else is bothering him. I know he felt the sacred energy by the river, I could feel it, but he drew back from it. I wonder why he would do that? We're missing something important, I know it." Claire shut her eyes and sat without moving. The image of Philip, agitated, at the old shack came into her mind. "I wonder if it's to do with Robert." On impulse, Claire said, "Does it say anywhere how Robert died? I'm wondering if maybe William *did* get revenge on him and Philip feels guilty."

Jared scanned through a few pages on the computer. "Let's see. It says here he died in 1973."

"That's two years after Philip disappeared so he could have been here then."

"Yes, you're right." Jared carried on reading. "This says Robert was found dead in his bed by a guy who read *In the Forest by the River* and came to visit him. Hmm, this is interesting, there was a police investigation but no clear cause of death was ever determined. In the end it was assumed Robert had simply died of old age in his sleep. He *was* eighty-seven." Jared read on then tried a few other sites. "No, there's nothing more."

"I wonder what happened?" Claire said looking over at Philip. "I feel there's more to Robert's death but I don't know what."

Jared yawned. "I'm sorry. I can't keep my eyes open any longer."

"You go and rest. I'll watch Philip now."

"Thanks." Jared gave Claire a quick kiss and went off to one of the other bedrooms while Claire remained on the couch. She stared at the book she held in her hands. A tingling ran through her fingers and she knew the book was special. A beautiful painting of the Mossman River flowing between overhanging trees had been used for the cover. Turning the pages, she found many more paintings of Mossman. Robert had been a talented artist as well as writer. Going back to the first page, she began to read.

Every so often, she lifted her head to check that Philip still lay sleeping but did not stop reading, power and energy moving through her body as she connected with Robert's words. As she lay the book down, she glanced out of the large plate glass window. Above the darkness of the surrounding rainforest, a pink haze glowed in the sky, presaging the coming of dawn.

Jared came in and looked at her with concern. "Claire, why are you crying?" He sat down next to her, put his arm around her shoulders and pulled her close.

She twisted round to look up at him. "I've been reading Robert's book. It's incredible. It makes me feel... so ... so, I don't know, in touch with what I am, what we *all* are. It's hard to explain." She fell silent then began again. "The power and energy of Mossman Gorge opened him up, allowed him to experience the depth of himself and life. You felt it too, didn't you, when we found your father by the river?"

"I did. I'll never forget it," Jared murmured.

"Robert was profoundly affected. It's so clear. He has a wonderful way of putting into words the mystery and beauty of his experience. This book has real power. You can sense the sacredness as you read and now I feel connected to him, to the Gorge and to the living Spirit we all share. It's in our very consciousness, the Light that we are." Claire's eyes shone.

"What a gift to the world this book is. No wonder it's remained in print for so long. It *is* special here in Mossman. I'll never forget this place, Jared," Claire said. "I have discovered so much here I never ever dreamed of."

"I feel the same, but it's not only because of this place." He took the book from Claire, put it down and took her in his arms, "but it's because of you. Without you I would never have broken free from my mental prison. Now I know there is so much more. Thank you." He kissed her gently.

"I can't take the credit, Jared," Claire replied. "I've merely done what I think I was destined to do. We're all part of the unfolding of something so much greater than we know. I'm certain of it now, especially since we found out about Robert being here.

"Everything is linked, Jared. Think of all that's happened. If Robert hadn't had an affair with Eleanora and had to flee from William, he wouldn't have come here and written this incredible book, something that obviously touched a lot of people. I don't know how Philip got a copy but I believe it had a profound influence on him. That's why he became so obsessed with Mossman Gorge. Even though overshadowed by depressive moods, he knew there was something more and it gave him strength. And so, when William took control, Philip still stayed present at some level and influenced him. He encouraged him to come to Mossman Gorge where he hoped they both might be set free."

"And it worked. Philip *is* now free of William," Jared said.

"Yes, but something is still wrong. I know it. I'm very worried. Claire got up and went in to stand beside Philip.

Jared closed the filing cabinet in Philip's study and went in search of Claire. He found her sitting with his father on the back verandah of the house. She spent most of her time with him whilst he sorted through paperwork in an attempt to piece together Philip's life in Australia. Jared noticed Claire reach across and gently lay her hand on the old man's arm but he simply stared ahead. He blinked but otherwise showed no response to anything around him. He had been like this during the three days since they liberated him from William. Luckily, he had been very compliant and seemed content to be guided. Claire worried about him, though. He remained locked inside himself, despite all her efforts to engage him in conversation.

Philip's eyes slowly closed and his head slumped forward. "Is he all right?" Jared asked. Claire looked at the old man. "Yes, he's just fallen asleep. He finds everything an effort."

"William certainly managed to achieve his dream of wealth and power." Jared commented. "These are papers relating to six businesses. And I know he has off shore interests. I haven't got into those yet. I've been checking reports and all of them have been pretty successful.

"I found a British passport and it's still current which is going to make life much easier. I also found papers relating to Philip's arrival in Australia. He came in 1973."

"The year Robert died. Hmm, I find that very interesting."

"Do you really think my father could have killed Robert?"

"I can't help thinking there was more to his death than just old age. No clear cause of death was ever ascertained. What if there are ways to kill that are hard to detect? I am afraid I *do* get the strong feeling Philip had something to do with his death."

"But why would he want to harm the man who wrote the book he loved?"

"I don't know. I admit it makes no sense."

"I think you're wrong!" Jared was vehement.

Claire, knowing he didn't want to accept that his father had been involved in someone's death, dropped the subject. "Your father went missing in 1971 so it means he was in England for two years before coming here. I wonder what he was doing all that time?"

"I have no idea. He must have been doing something."

"He would have needed paperwork, like birth certificates etc. to apply to emigrate. I'm wondering how he would have got those? Was he using his own name?"

"Yes."

"So why did he never turn up on records?"

"Computers were only starting to be used in the early seventies. Things weren't linked up like they are now. And no one thought he'd do something like go to Australia. He always said he'd never leave the Lake District."

"What about the formalities of emigration?"

"Well, I think that they would have checked to see if he had a criminal record but it obviously never showed up that he'd been reported as missing. When I spoke to them in Keswick, the police said they kept all their enquiries localised so his name wasn't distributed nationwide. They never took the case seriously enough to do anything much about it."

"I know he came here on a boat," Claire said. "I felt it at Waterford Hall."

"He has a boat now. I found papers relating to it. He bought it last year, cost him two hundred and twenty thousand dollars. I tell you, he's got some serious money. He's also the owner of a small aircraft. He has a pilot's license."

"My God! That's amazing."

That afternoon they took Philip with them to a marina in Port Douglas, hoping perhaps it might trigger some response. They found the sleek white motor launch he owned and helped him on board. He, however, remained disinterested, a shell of a man. Claire felt him slowly receding from a life he could no longer connect with, having been suppressed for so long.

"We have to get him home." Claire said. "I don't think he'll last long like this. Maybe in the Lake District, the place he loved so much and with Laura, he'll find a reason to come back to us."

Jared looked at his father, at the sadness in his face and weary stance. "I hope you're right. I don't think we'll have any problem, not now we've found a passport."

They stood on deck and stared at the wonderful view of sea and shadowy rainforest clad hills. "It's so beautiful here," Claire whispered.

"We'll come back one day." Jared smiled at her. "I promise."

As a result of his research into Philip's life in Australia, Jared contacted a young woman, Rowena Greene, the CEO of one of the businesses. The moment he walked into her office and introduced himself as Philip's son, she impressed him with her calm and pleasant manner. Tall and slim with her long black hair tied behind her in a neat ponytail and dressed in a simple blue shirt and black skirt, she looked the epitome of an efficient businesswoman but, the longer they spoke, the more her honesty shone through. He had spent the last few days visiting Philip's other businesses and hadn't liked what he saw, most run by people like William himself with scant regard for ethical practices. Rowena made a refreshing change.

"I had no idea he had a son," she said.

"I live in England."

"So, what has happened to him? You mentioned some sort of breakdown."

"Yes. He needs to take a complete rest. In the meantime, I'm taking over."

They spent the morning discussing Rowena's management of a chain of health resorts and, at the end of it, Jared had made his decision.

"I like the way you work," he said.

"Thank you."

"How would you like the job of overseeing all my father's business interests for the next few months. I'm taking him to England to rest and recuperate."

"I'm afraid, I wouldn't be interested," she said. "To be honest, I really don't like the way he operates."

"That's precisely why I think you are the person to do it. I want to change how we do things, to become more ethical, to take into account the effects of what we do on people and the environment."

"I can't believe I'm hearing this but I have to admit it sounds exciting."

"So, you'll accept?"

"I'd like to think about it, get more information about the companies I'd be working with but, if that checks out, then, yes, I would definitely be interested."

"I'll see to it."

Despite worrying about his father, Jared felt buoyed up. He liked Rowena a great deal. She had a good business sense but also integrity. He felt that with her, and others like her, if he could find them, he could turn around the empire William had created in Philip's name and undo some of the harm that had been done, maybe even channel some of the profits into charitable causes. He felt comfortable leaving Rowena in charge while he returned to England with Philip. Jared felt inspired and alive, filled with purpose. Claire had been right, there had been so much more going on under the surface of events. Even *he* could see now that what had happened between Eleanora, William and Robert, and now he and Claire, was having a much wider effect than he would ever have imagined before. Jared knew that he had been radically changed for the better as a result of all that had happened.

It had taught him to be less judgemental and more open and receptive to the flow of life, to use his inner sense of what felt right to guide him instead of relying on his mind alone. He had learnt a lot from Claire and her intuitive way and felt a deep gratitude.

That night, Jared helped Claire get Philip into bed. He lay down but stared up at the ceiling with a vacant expression. Life no longer had any power to touch him, nor did the presence of his only son. Jared sniffed. Claire looked at him and saw the sadness in his eyes. She put her hand on his arm. "What is it?"

"I can't bear to see him like this. It's like a living death."

Claire stared down at Philip then placed her hand on his shoulder and shut her eyes. He felt distant and a vision came to her of him sitting alone on the ground in a barren landscape with his head in his hands. He did not want to come back, she realised, shocked, and sensed him becoming weaker and weaker.

"Please don't give up," she whispered but the figure stood up and walked away. "Philip, come back. There are those who love you here, who need you."

It made no difference. He had gone too far away to hear.

Her eyes moist with tears of compassion, Claire came back to the room. "We have to hurry," she said to Jared. "Get him on the first plane we can. Philip is dying. He has lost the will to live."

Chapter 26

J ARED CHANGED LANES AND ACCELERATED. They were heading up the M6 bound for the Lake District. He glanced in his rear-view mirror at Philip sitting next to Claire in the back seat of the car. He looked lost and confused. His father's condition had deteriorated considerably in the week it had taken them to bring him back to England and Jared feared for him. He caught Claire's eye in the mirror. She smiled and her look of love and encouragement lifted his spirits. Their relationship had gone from strength to strength and now he couldn't imagine his life without her.

Claire glanced at Philip. He stared ahead with a blank expression. He looked shrunken in on himself and it broke her heart to see him like that. She gently squeezed his hand but he did not respond. He rarely spoke. At least he remained calm and, thank God, content to be guided.

He hadn't been in charge of his own life for so long, Claire wondered if he had lost the power to do anything of his own volition. Luckily, he ate when encouraged to do so and had been capable of writing a signature on papers, much to Jared's relief, as he struggled to sort out his father's affairs. Philip did so without question, like a child.

Philip's weakening physical condition scared her. The journey from Australia had been hard on him. Every time he fell asleep, Claire feared he would slip away.

After they found medication in Philip's house, they knew they could not risk the trip to England without getting a medical check done, so had arranged an examination with one of the doctors from the practice they discovered he attended. They had not taken Philip to his usual one but another in the group who they hoped had not known him personally. The doctor checked his records and examined him. To their relief, he did not question his state of mind too much as the old man remained compliant. They found out he had a mild heart condition but they got the go ahead for the trip, provided he did not overdo it and took regular medication.

She and Jared had agreed that the reunion between his father and Laura had to be handled with great care and thought it best to take him back to his old childhood home and Bella first. It had been decided Laura would make the trip from London by train the next day and join them there. They thought being back in the environment Philip had once loved so much would help him reconnect with the world although Claire worried it might also bring back his fears even though he was no longer possessed by William.

For the hundredth time, she wished Eleanora would return. Claire missed the gentle spirit's wise and loving counsel but as yet she had not reappeared. Having now helped William, Claire assumed Eleanora had moved on to the next plane or phase of existence.

When they reached the Lake District, she scrutinised Philip, alert for any sign he recognised the countryside but he remained impassive. It was late in the day when Jared pulled up outside Philip's old home. Claire rang the doorbell while Jared helped his father from the car. If he recognised the house, he did not show it. Bella came down the garden path and flung her arms around him, tears streaming down her face, but Philip held himself rigid and did not return her embrace. When she pulled away, they looked at each other. "Philip, do you know me? It's Bella. *Bella,*" she repeated louder, "your sister."

A look of confusion came over Philip's face then he turned to Jared and Claire, who he appeared to trust, at least to some degree. Claire smiled. "Yes, she is your sister." He nodded and Jared guided him into the house. Philip stumbled as he walked through the hall. "He needs to rest." Claire said.

"What about taking him to his room?" Jared suggested.

"No, I don't think he can do the stairs at the moment," Claire replied. "Sit him in the lounge and we'll have a cup of tea."

So, this is what they did. Bella sat holding Philip's hand, unable to let go of him. He seemed happy enough to allow her to, although did not speak. At one point she got up and found a framed photo of herself with Philip as children with their parents. He looked at it as Bella pointed, "That's you and me. He's Father and this is Mother." Philip ran his fingers over the glass but did not respond. Her face creased with anxiety, Bella looked at Claire. "He doesn't remember."

"Give him time," Claire replied but she had to admit she was disappointed. She had expected him to show some reaction. What if he did not respond to Laura? How devastating that would be for her.

As Claire became present to this thought and its implications, the answer revealed itself; this was out of her hands. The mysterious and powerful forces she had sensed before were in control. She needed to have faith and allow her intuition, her soul, to guide her as Jack had told her to do at Mossman Gorge. And her soul told her Laura needed to see Philip. If he did not recognise her then there had to be a reason.

It would not be long before they found out. Laura would arrive tomorrow.

Claire reached into her bag and handed Bella the copy of *In the Forest by the River* written by Robert. "This is the book I told you about." Bella reached out and took it.

"Yes, I remember him reading this when we were young. I had no idea it was something so powerful otherwise I would have read it myself." She flicked through and read a few pages. "Yes, it's beautifully written. I'm right there in the forest with Robert. I'll read it later. I think it's about time we ate. I have a meal prepared. I'll go and dish it up." Bella put the book down on the coffee table.

Claire went with her into the kitchen where Bella started to cry. "Why won't he recognise me? I don't understand. William has gone."

"I don't know. I think he just needs more time. Don't worry. I am sure it will be all right."

Unable to suppress her grief any longer, Bella's shoulders shook. Claire put her arms around the elderly woman. "I, I can't get over the way he's changed," Bella sobbed. "It's been so many years. I know it's him but it isn't."

Claire held her tight. "I know, I know. I wish I understood what was bothering him. I think it's to do with Robert. Philip became agitated at Robert's shack and now he's retreated far back inside. He's like a little child again. But he *is* still in there somewhere. I can feel him. Try not to lose hope."

"Can you really tell that?"

"Yes. I can. I'm hoping that Laura will be able to draw him out and he will be able to heal. Then he and Laura will have a chance to maybe rebuild something together again."

"I do hope so." Bella pulled herself together and moved over to the sink to wash her hands. "Okay then, let's eat."

The two women busied themselves for the next half an hour until everything needed for the meal had been completed and laid out in the dining room. "I'll get the other two," Claire said and went into the lounge.

"Oh my God!" she exclaimed.

Jared eyes flew open. He had fallen asleep in one of the armchairs. "What?"

"Where's your father?" Claire cried. Jared swivelled around and saw the couch where the old man had been sitting was empty.

"Oh no," he moaned, jumping up. "Where's he gone?"

Claire wasted no time. She had a feeling where he might be and bounded up the stairs to Philip's bedroom. Jared, reading her mind, followed. At the top of the stairs, she stopped and listened, motioning him to be quiet, then pushed open the door.

Philip sat on the bed, crying. A book lay open on his lap. "It's Robert's," Claire said. "Your father must have taken it from the coffee table downstairs."

Jared looked at Claire. "Help him," he pleaded.

"No, he needs *you*," she said.

Taking a deep breath, Jared approached his father who, so far, had not acknowledged his son, despite being told who he was. Intense bitterness welled up within him, the sum total of all the buried grief and hatred he had carried for this man most of his life but, as he stared at Philip weeping before him, it transformed into compassion and, in that moment, all he felt was love.

Jared sat down beside his father. Philip continued to stare down at the book, his tears falling onto the pages.

"Dad?" Jared said gently. At first, he received no response but then Philip turned and looked at him. Claire marvelled at the likeness between the two men. They had the same shaped nose, eye colour and hairline.

Jared took the old man's gnarled hand in his own smooth one and gripped it tight. Surprisingly, he felt an answering pressure.

"You are really my son?" Philip asked in a quavering voice.

"Yes, yes, I'm your son."

"I am sorry," the old man whispered. "I did not know of you."

"It's all right." Jared's voice broke and tears pricked Claire's eyes.

"I have been ... a long way away," Philip murmured.

"I know. It wasn't your fault."

"She isn't here," Philip announced all of a sudden.

Jared looked at Claire then back at his father. "Do you mean Laura?"

"Laura," the old man repeated as if he had never spoken the word before.

"Yes, my mother," Jared said, softly.

Philip looked over at Claire. "You're not Laura," he said, his eyes full of confusion. "But you're wearing the necklace I gave her."

Claire came forward. "Yes. Laura gave it to me. She is a dear friend of mine. I will return it to her if you wish."

"No, it looks... right on you." Philip looked up into Claire's eyes and she knew somehow, a miracle had occurred. The block within him had dissolved. By reading something in the book, he had been able to connect with the truth of his deepest being. Philip had been awakened by what Robert experienced at Mossman Gorge coming through in his words. She felt the resonance of it herself as she realised this and tears came into her own eyes at the beauty of it.

She smiled. "Laura is coming," she said. "She is longing to see you." Philip nodded.

Claire turned to Jared. "He has been healed. It was the power of Robert's book."

Jared smiled with relief, "Thank God."

To Philip she said, "Your sister, Bella, is downstairs."

"Let me help you, Dad," Jared said. He took the open book and handed it to Claire who stared at the pages, wondering what part Philip had been reading when his awakening occurred.

Jared gripped his father under the shoulders and helped him to his feet. Philip stumbled so Claire placed the book, still open, on the bedside table so she could help Jared. She resolved to come back later and read what made Philip come back to himself.

Together, she and Jared helped him downstairs. They met Bella in the hall coming out of the lounge, her expression full of questions. "I wondered what had happened to you all." Her gaze moved to Philip.

He looked at her and smiled. "It's been a long time, Bella."

After his awakening, Philip continued to say very little but he seemed at peace. They ate their meal then sat in the lounge. Bella showed Philip photos of their life as children and told him how she became a headmistress after he left. He sat through it all with a bemused look on his face and an occasional soft smile drifting across his features, but then he closed his eyes and fell into a light sleep as if it were all too much for him. Claire still worried about his physical condition; he had become so frail over the last few weeks. William must have given a power and energy to Philip's physical form he himself did not possess. Or perhaps the stress of it all, the release and trip to England, had taken its toll.

When Philip woke a short time later, he seemed stronger and Jared told his father about the businesses he was involved in and the antique shop he ran with Laura. "She is coming?" Philip asked when Jared finished.

"Yes, Dad, she is coming."

Philip gripped Jared's hands. "I am sorry, son," he said. "I was not there for you or your mother. It is my greatest regret."

"You're here now, that's all that matters." Jared said. Claire smiled, knowing what his father's words would mean to him.

After an evening meal, she had the idea to take Philip on a drive down to Lake Windermere and so they did, helping him walk down to the shore where he could get a good look out over the water to the surrounding peaks as the sun set. Claire could tell Philip was moved to be in this place, the countryside he had always loved. Joy shone on his face as he contemplated the view. He took several long, full breaths as if he were absorbing the environment into himself. It gave him strength for his steps were surer as they returned to the car. Throughout it all, though, he still said little.

Back at the house, Jared and Claire took Philip to his old room and helped him prepare for bed. He lay down, smiled at them then closed his eyes. Soon they heard the regular rising and falling of his breath and knew he had fallen asleep.

"Do you think it will be all right to leave him?" Jared asked.

Claire looked down at Philip, peaceful in sleep. "Yes. I think so." Jared took her hand. "Let's go to bed," he said. "I want to hold you close." Claire nodded. Bella had been more than happy to allow them to stay at the house, a broad smile lighting up her features when they told her they had become a couple. "That doesn't come as a surprise to me," she said, laughing.

As they left the room, Claire saw Robert's book. She hadn't had a chance to see what Philip had been reading when he reawakened. She looked at Jared. He needed her. Now was not the time.

Claire woke at six in the morning and, leaving Jared sleeping, went to check on Philip. She knocked and opened his bedroom door to find his bed lay empty. "Oh no!" she gasped. "I wish he wouldn't keep doing this!" Remembering what happened in Australia, she dashed through the house looking for him.

To her relief, she found Philip standing in the garden. He smiled at her. "It's so beautiful here," he said. "I used to spend a lot of time working in this garden."

They heard the sound of a door opening and an elderly woman came into the garden next door. "Lovely morning," she said.

"Yes, yes, it is," Claire replied. The woman hung up a towel on her washing line then disappeared back inside. The incident reminded Claire of Elaine.

"When we were searching for clues to find you, we found a

newspaper clipping about a woman who used to live in that house next door. Can you tell me about her?"

"Elaine."

"Yes, she went to Mossman Gorge some years before you did."

Philip didn't answer at first, instead reaching out to touch the wall as if to steady himself before he spoke. Once he started, the words flowed out as he reconnected back, "I heard her crying in her garden one day. I didn't need to ask why. I often heard shouting through the walls and sometimes saw bruises on her face when I met her in the street. I asked if she needed help and we began to talk. She admitted her husband abused her. I told her to leave him. She said she would but somehow it never happened. We continued to talk sometimes, when her husband and mother-in-law were out. I know it helped to have someone to listen.

"One Christmas I bought her a copy of Robert Ashworth's book *In the Forest by the River*. It had always given me a sense of peace and connection to something greater and more meaningful than just myself when I read it. I hoped it would help her as it had helped me.

"Elaine loved that book. She told me she would go to Mossman Gorge one day. It became a dream, something to sustain her, but she never did. The years passed but then I went away on a trip for a few weeks. When I returned, she had gone. I reckon she just snapped. There was a bit of a fuss at first. People thought Craig Clarke had killed her, you know how people talk, but it turned out she had flown to Australia and gone to Mossman Gorge. She booked a return flight but didn't come back.

"Two months later I had a phone call. It was Elaine. She said Mossman Gorge was a place like no other. She said she had tried to end her life in the river but the sacredness there drew her back and gave her hope. It opened her up to a deeper truth behind the appearance of the world and set her free.

"She went on to say that now she had found peace she was staying in Australia to make a new life for herself and that I should make the trip to Mossman Gorge myself.

"I did not have the money then but I never forgot what she said." Philip took a deep breath before continuing. "William sought to suppress me, drain my light, but he could not destroy me and so, when he took control at Castlerigg, I whispered in his mind and infiltrated his dreams as he had done to me. I spoke of Love and Light and the clear waters of the river washing us both clean. He did his best to block me out but part of him longed for that of which I spoke although he would never admit it to himself.

"His conscious mind was filled with thoughts of hate and revenge but his soul longed for something else, what all of us long for: love, not just human love, but the sacred love of our true nature. I could feel it but he could not. Eventually I succeeded and we ended up near Mossman Gorge. I never intended for Robert to die, though." Claire noticed Philip's hands trembled and he fell silent.

She laid her arm on his. "I'm so sorry. I didn't mean to bring it all back for you."

"It's all right. I am at peace with it now." Philip touched her hand. "Thank you," he said, "for helping me come home."

Claire longed to know what happened, how Robert came to die and what Philip had to do with it, but before she could ask, the back door opened and Jared appeared. "Oh, there you are. Thank God. I was worried."

"Everything's fine," Claire told him. She turned to Philip. He looked tired. "Let's get some breakfast." He nodded and smiled. Her questions would have to wait.

Laura's train not being due until two in the afternoon, they took Philip out for a drive after the meal. He stared out of the car window, his face now alive with interest as they passed through the countryside.

Claire suggested they visit Eleanora's grave. It looked the same as it did before, the swathe of violets blanketing her resting place. They sat on the seat and she told Philip Eleanora's story, and described all that happened to her and Jared.

Philip sat without moving and listened, staring down at the grave. Every so often he glanced around him, an indefinable expression on his face. "They are together now."

"William and Eleanora? Yes, I guess so."

"How do you feel, Dad?" Jared asked. "Do you remember much of what happened when you had William with you?"

A look of pain passed across Philip's face. "More than I would wish to." He shut his eyes. "I'm feeling tired. Perhaps we could leave now."

They took Philip home before going to pick up Laura, thinking the public area of a railway platform not the best place for their reunion. Bella stayed with him, happy to spend time with her long, lost brother.

Claire and Jared stood on the platform. A cool wind blew Claire's hair over her face. Jared moved it aside with his fingers then bent and kissed her tenderly. He pulled her into his arms and they stood like this, drawing peace and strength from each other's presence. After about ten minutes they heard the rumble of an oncoming train and drew apart. They watched as carriage after carriage passed by. "She should be near the back," Jared said, hurrying along the platform, knowing that, with her bad hip, his mother would need help to get off with her luggage. A family friend had assisted her in London.

Jared disappeared into a carriage but soon reappeared carrying a small suitcase with Laura behind him. He helped her step carefully onto the platform.

Claire came forward to hug her. "I can't believe all this," Laura said, her face alive with excitement. "It's a miracle! I can never thank you enough for all you have done."

"It's been a joy," Claire said. "It's changed my life in so many ways I can't even begin to tell you." She looked at Jared and smiled.

Laura saw the expression in their eyes. "Oh, my dears. Something's happened between you two, hasn't it? I'm so happy for you both." Claire and Jared looked at each other and laughed.

They loaded up the car. As they were about to leave the station forecourt, Claire's mobile rang. "Hello Bella."

"I think you had better get back here quick. It's Philip. He suddenly went pale and keeled over. I've called an ambulance. The medics are with him now."

"Oh, dear God, no!" Claire exclaimed. The others looked at her questioningly. "Philip's had some sort of turn," she told them. This couldn't be happening, she thought. He must hang on.

"I'll talk to you again as soon as I know what's going on," Bella said and hung up.

Jared accelerated out of the station forecourt. Laura put her hands up to her face. "No!" she moaned.

"I am sure it will be all right, Laura. Philip will be fine. He knows you're coming." Claire gripped her hand tight and sent healing energy to her.

A few minutes later Bella rang again. "I'm going with him in the ambulance," she said. He's had a heart attack. They're taking him to Barrow in Furness General Hospital." Claire relayed this to the others.

"Let's hope it doesn't take long to get there," Jared said. "Hang on." He put his foot down and sped through the curving country lanes as fast as the speed limits allowed.

Jared slowed as they reached a bend in the road. His mind, focussed on what they would find when they reached the hospital, Jared didn't see the truck until it was too late. Claire saw it a split second before they hit but then everything went black.

Chapter 27

LAURA HEARD A VOICE TALKING in the darkness but could not make out the words. She felt tired, so tired she did not want to wake. But sleep did not come for she became aware of a dull ache throughout her body. Where was she? *Who* was she? She couldn't remember her own name. As if in answer to her question, a voice said, "Laura?" A silence fell and all she heard was the sound of her own breathing. Then it came again, more insistent this time, pleading, "Laura!"

That voice. She knew that voice. But it couldn't be! He was dead, gone, lost to her. But then a memory came. The sound of Jared saying, "He's alive, Mum. We found him. Philip's alive." The day Jared called from Australia to tell her that Philip had been found came back, the shock, the disbelief then the longing for that which had been lost. With the memory came the rest. She had been on her way to see him. Something had happened.

Her eyelids felt too heavy to raise but she forced them open. She couldn't see him at first, only the fluorescent light on the ceiling, but then a shadow came between her and the light, a face so aged she almost did not recognise it except for the eyes. They were just the same and the love in them warmed her through and through like it always had.

"Laura," he whispered, caressing her with the love in his voice like he used to and she smiled although it hurt her face. A hand grasped hers and the warm pressure anchored her.

Another voice spoke, "Oh, Mum, thank God! We've been so worried." Laura turned her head to see Jared and Claire sat beside her.

"I'm so happy you two are together," Laura whispered then looked back at the man she had never stopped loving, even though she had been so angry with him when he left, not understanding he had been gripped by forces neither she nor anyone else had been able to do anything about until now.

"I'm sorry," she said.

"What for?" Philip asked.

"I hated you for a while. When you left. When I had to bring Jared up alone. Can you forgive me?"

"There's nothing to forgive."

Laura closed her eyes, unable to stay awake against the tide of tiredness that consumed her body, but she felt the pressure of Philip's hand in hers and it drew her back. She had to look into his dear face again. Somehow, she opened her eyes and lifted her other hand to touch his cheek.

"You're real," she said. He looked younger to her now. The lines had fallen from his face and to her he seemed as he had all those years ago. "Kiss me," she said.

When she felt his lips touch hers, she closed her eyes again, relaxing against the pillow, a smile on her lips. "I love you," she murmured.

"I love you, too," he answered.

"We should leave them alone," Claire said to Jared. "We'll be right outside," she told Laura then she and Jared left the room. They had been lucky, only suffering a few minor cuts and bruises. Laura, in the rear of the car, had been nearer the point of impact when the truck that hit them failed to stop at the intersection. She had suffered extensive damage to her back and internal organs.

Philip, once stabilised, had thrown off his covers, pulled away the wires connecting him to a monitor and walked off, determined to find Laura in intensive care. Jared persuaded him to at least sit in a wheel chair but Philip insisted on standing by Laura's bed.

Claire and Jared left the room and went over to a window overlooking a garden, grateful to find a moment of peace and quiet. Claire put her hand on Jared's arm. "Are you all right?"

"No!" he bit out, his brow creased with worry and bitterness. "How could this happen? Why?" he demanded. "Why? I can't believe it!"

"You're not blaming yourself, are you?"

He looked at her and sagged, his body reflecting how dejected and helpless he felt. "I... Yes, how can I not? I shouldn't have driven the way I did."

"You were trying to get to the hospital. We thought Philip might die."

"I know, I know, but that doesn't make it right. My mother has serious injuries."

"At least Philip is okay."

"Yes, thank God."

"And they are together now."

"Yes."

They saw Bella approaching along the corridor. Feeling faint, she had gone to get something to eat. "How is Laura?"

"She's awake!" Jared said. "Her condition's stable at the moment but long term? We just don't know. Philip is with her. He recognises her and they're talking."

"Oh, that's wonderful." Bella smiled. "It'll be all right; I know it will."

Claire touched the amethyst necklace round her neck and turned her head toward the entrance of intensive care. "I think we should go back in," she said.

Someone came out of the unit as they approached and, before the door could close, Claire slipped through and held it open for the others. The three of them made their way to Laura's bed to find her surrounded by doctors and nurses. "No!" Jared moaned. They approached only to be held back by a nurse but not before they saw Philip lying slumped on the floor beside the bed!

Laura lifted the hand Philip had been holding a moment before. He's gone again, she thought and felt his loss as a pain around her heart but, as she did so, found herself back in the bluebell wood she and Philip had so loved. In fact, she sensed him close behind her now and so, to tease him, she started to run, soon taking the lead. She was always one step ahead of him, she thought, and laughed, feeling wild and free and joyous with the wind in her hair and the earth beneath her feet.

After a while, she stopped and looked back but couldn't see him. Where had he gone? She knew he'd catch up so she stood by the lake and waited. It took a short while but then she saw him—as he used to be, young and strong. He didn't see her at first but then she waved. He waved back and ran towards her. They fell into each other's arms and he spun her around, laughing and laughing. When they stopped spinning, Philip kissed her and said. "Let's go home now."

"Yes. I'd like that," Laura replied. Philip took her by the hand and they walked off together through the bluebells.

The others stood waiting, their hearts full of dread, as they stared at the activity going on. All of a sudden, Claire saw a glow hovering over the bed and gasped. It waited there for a while then another joined it. The two merged into one and faded out. Unable to hold back tears, she watched in shock as one of the doctors came towards them. Knowing what he was going to say, Claire gripped Jared's arm. He would need all the support she could give him.

They returned to Bella's house as the first light of dawn spread a grey light over the countryside. It had been an endless, indescribable night: first, waking up in hospital and being treated then enduring questioning by the police, followed by the unbelievable shock of losing both Laura and Philip at the same time. At least the truck driver had escaped injury.

Bella and Jared collapsed, exhausted, on the couch. Claire made them all mugs of tea. Bella sipped hers but Jared sat motionless staring at the floor. All the lifeforce had drained from his body.

Claire sat beside him and took his hand. "Please don't feel so bad. You know they haven't really gone. Death is not the end. I saw them go."

Jared looked her. "You did?"

"Yes. It was beautiful. Laura left her body first and I saw her waiting then Philip joined her. They left together." She paused for a moment then continued, "They finally found each other, Jared."

He looked at her, agony on his face, "But *I* lost them," he moaned. "*I* killed them. I *killed* them, Claire. If only I'd been more careful."

"You didn't kill them, Jared. You had right of way. The truck driver didn't stop. It wasn't your fault. It was something over which you had no control. And your father had a heart condition. It was their time to go, Jared, and nothing you, nor anyone else, could have done would have prevented it."

Jared stared at her with an agonised expression. "You really believe that?"

"I *know* it." Claire turned her attention to Bella and asked. "How are *you?*"

"I'm all right," she replied. "I saw them go too and I can feel them around me now, can't you?"

Claire smiled, "Yes." She turned back to Jared, "That's how I know it's all right." She fell silent and waited. To one side of her she saw the faint impression of Laura who looked at her and smiled. She put her hand on Jared's shoulder and he shivered. "Your mother's *here*, Jared. She's touching you. She says she's happy and so is Philip. He is here with her." Claire could just make him out behind Laura. "They want you to know they love you and that you must not blame yourself."

"Tell them I love them, too," he said, unable to hold back his tears.

"They heard you," Claire said, smiling and the two spirits faded away.

"They've gone, haven't they?" Jared asked.

"Yes."

"I think I *could* feel them," he said. "Just near the end. I felt Mum touch me. It was very subtle." Jared lifted his hand to his shoulder for a moment and managed a slight smile but it could not hide the exhaustion and pain in his face.

"I think we should get some sleep," Claire suggested.

"Yes." Bella stood. "I'm going to bed now."

Claire hugged her and helped Jared up the stairs to their room. She pulled back the covers and he collapsed on the bed fully clothed. Claire took off his shoes and pulled up the bedcovers. She kissed his brow, whispering, "I won't be long," but Jared didn't hear. He had fallen asleep the moment his head met the pillow.

Although drained by a day she never thought she would have to live through, Claire felt agitated. She went downstairs, made herself another mug of tea and sat on the couch, relaxing her body and allowing all that had happened to settle within her.

The image of the purple lily flowering from the murky pool in Port Douglas came into her mind and the horror of the day fell away. How much she had changed, Claire thought. A few months back she would have been devastated by what had happened, the seeming senseless deaths of two wonderful people who needed to be together, but now she knew they *were* together—in a fuller sense than she could ever have conceived of before. They had left their physical bodies behind but were together in love and in spirit for she had seen it with her own eyes.

She remembered her intention to look at what Philip read when he began to remember his past. What had reached him? Claire tiptoed up the stairs to Philip's bedroom. The book still lay open where she left it on the bedside table. She sat on the bed, picked up the book and began to read.

> *The knowing has come to me in a vision that one day someone will be involved in taking my life from me, but I want that person to know I do not blame them, for I know they will only be doing what they think is right. All things have their purpose in the scheme of things, even if to our minds it all seems crazy. In Mossman Gorge I learned there is no need to fear death, that only my body will be destroyed, not who I truly am.*

Claire sat, stunned. She remembered wondering about this passage when she read the book in Australia but soon forgot it in the beauty of the writing that followed. But now? Robert had experienced some sort of a premonition that he would one day be killed and, through his words, was reaching out to the perpetrator with forgiveness. Could that perpetrator somehow have been Philip? It explained his reaction at Robert's shack and his reluctance to reconnect with life. No clear cause of the poet's death had ever been found and it had been attributed to natural causes but this was definitely the page Philip had been reading when he came back to himself. His tears crinkled the paper. Claire sat for a few moments lost in awe at the powerful forces at work in Robert and Philip's lives then continued to read.

It is now time for you to bestow forgiveness on yourself. Look within and in the sacred stillness that is your very centre you will find what you have been seeking all your life, unconditional love. This is what you truly are in the depth of your being. Know it is alive within you and can never be lost for it is the power behind the universe. Surrender to it and you will know the truth. Have faith in love and you will be guided.

It does not matter the path through life you have led. Even if you have caused great evil, the deeper truth of yourself is love. In this is peace, joy, healing and forgiveness!

Let go the stifling grip of judgement. You have only ever done the best you knew in your limited understanding. You thought you had to do it alone, carry the weight of responsibility for it all upon your shoulders, but that has never been true. It is time now to surrender and relax into the majesty of your true being. Allow it to flow through you and make all things right.

When I came to the forest, I thought I was not worthy, that I had caused such harm I did not deserve to know love, forgiveness, peace or beauty. And, in that judgement, I cast myself out of the gates of heaven, far, far out into the wilderness. Dear reader, know that you do not have to be perfect to know the love within you. Embrace your imperfections, allow them to be like the stumbling of a child learning to find their feet in a wondrous universe. Know that, whatever happens, there is no death and so nothing real can ever be lost.

Live your life with the honest intention to do the best you can, to bring as much love as possible into the world. Let it flow out through all the hate, the confusion, the anger and sadness you feel. Know there is no end to that love. Allow it to embrace you as you are so that you may be made whole and then let it encompass all others, whatever they may be doing in their own struggles to understand themselves and life. Let your love flow and it will heal not only you but the whole world for the world is you.

So, when it all seems confusing, when there is senseless violence and suffering all around you, find the stillness within, the place where unconditional love resides, the peace underlying our experience. So often we become caught in the mind and are dragged by its ceaseless machinations hither and thither. But here in Mossman Gorge I discovered another way of being, one I had always dreamed of but never conceived would be made real within my experience in this lifetime.

I had thought my life ended when I lost the only woman I ever truly loved and came to Australia, first to the outback, a barbaric place, so harsh and unrelenting. I believed I would die with the heat and the pain but then I came to Queensland and entered the forest with my friend.

He took me to where the cool waters flowed from the mountains and it washed me clean and I could at long last let go of my suffering. And, in the peace that followed, I realised I was not who I thought I was at all. My focus shifted from my mind and the tumult of my emotions to a different place within me, somewhere clear and free, empty yet also full. Full of life for it was life and realising this allowed me to embrace my human existence in a different way, directly and consciously in the present. And out of this a miracle occurred for I knew then I was not alone as I had always feared and that true peace was possible despite the circumstances around me.

I thought I had to make things right in my external world but that was not the way. I had to find my true self first and, in that knowledge, in that centring, the world transformed. I found the strength to carry on and even find joy. I would exhort you, dear reader, to never give up even though it seems as if the darkness surrounding you is complete. The darkness isn't out there but in your mind. You are merely standing in front of your own light, casting a shadow on the world. But it can all change in a moment as it did for me that day in the forest by the river.

You, dear reader, do not need to go to the forest to experience this. No matter where you might be, even in the darkest of places and in the darkest of times, just remember that the love and peace of God exists everywhere but, most important, in you too and you can come to know it.

Claire turned the page and found a poem.

REMEMBER

Fear not the trials of life for they are but illusions
which, in time, will fade away as the Light within you grows.

The path seems hard, the way obscured, when suffering takes control,
but only wait a little while and things will always change.

Be still and remember that, whatever happens, however dark it gets,
the Divine is in you now and never can be lost.

Although everything around you, even your own body,
may seem to pass and fade,
Spirit is eternal, beyond the grip of death,
and always it holds us gently, you and I, and those we love,
safe in Immortal life.

Spirit will always guide you if you listen to your heart.
Simply follow the path of love and you will never lose your way.

So, don't be misled by appearances when things seem bad.
Open your eyes and look around and you will begin to see
Life is flowing to a plan.

Allow Spirit's loving consciousness to shine out through your eyes
and the world will be transformed
into a place of Love and Beauty,
of living Truth and Light.

Claire stopped reading, yet the power of the words continued to move through her, connecting her to Robert, not with him as a person but with the presence of sacredness he had experienced at Mossman and which she now knew to be her own true reality.

How amazing, she reflected, that something so infinitely beautiful and precious as this book, which obviously had the power to open people up to the deeper dimension of themselves, had flowered out of all the tragedy. Claire resolved to be more open-minded and non-judgemental, for who knew what might arise out of apparently senseless suffering.

Was that what all the struggle in life was all about, she wondered, to somehow help people move beyond their identification with the material world, throw off their limitations and find peace and healing and a connection to the essence of life itself?

Claire smiled and lay down on the bed. She relaxed. The book fell from her fingers and her eyes closed. As they did so, she found herself standing by the river at Mossman Gorge in her mind. The wind rustled in the trees and the water rushed and poured around the rocks. The sounds moved through her and a feeling of infinite peace settled all around her. She had a brief impression of Jack sitting by the water but then fell into a deep and dreamless sleep.

Chapter 28

A FEW DAYS LATER, AFTER the joint funeral of Jared's parents at St Giles' Church, all the participants returned to Bella's house for a light lunch. Later, when the other people left, Bella retired for a rest. Claire and Jared sat holding one another in silence on the couch in the lounge. Exhausted, they both fell asleep.

An hour later, Jared came awake. He looked beside him. Claire had gone. He searched through the house and found her sitting on a seat in the garden staring into space. "Hey, are you all right?"

Claire looked up at him, her face troubled so Jared sat down beside her. "What is it?"

"William keeps coming into my mind. I don't know why. It's as if he's around me yet distant. I know that doesn't make sense. I've tried to communicate with him but couldn't pick anything up. It's so strange. What do you think it means?"

"I don't know but William was pretty bad. Think of what he did. You shouldn't have anything to do with him."

"Don't worry. I don't think he'd want to take me over, not now he's turned back to the Light. No, it's nothing like that, it's... I just have the strong feeling it's not over yet and that somehow it's connected to William."

"What do you mean, *not over yet?* I don't like the sound of that."

"I feel there's still something that has to happen but I don't know what."

Jared looked concerned, "Is it anything to worry about?"

Claire remained silent, opening up to what she could sense. The amethyst necklace gleamed at her throat. She lifted her hand and caressed it. Although it no longer connected her to Eleanora, now the spirit had gone to the Light, Claire still liked to wear it. She had come to rely more and more on her psychic abilities. "I'm not sure. I sense it's something we have to do... but not now. Hopefully we'll know when the time is right."

"Good, I'm glad because..." Jared paused and looked into Claire's eyes. His face took on a serious expression. "I have to return to Australia, as you know, to sort out my father's affairs but I want you to come with me. Will you?"

Claire smiled. "What do you think, of *course,* I will. I can help you with everything but I'd also love to go back to Mossman Gorge and do all the other things we didn't have time for."

"I was hoping you'd say that. It'll be wonderful to spend some time together. I love you, you know." He fell silent and gazed into Claire's eyes. "I *really* love you," he murmured and pulled her close.

"I love you, too," Claire whispered before his lips came down on hers.

Claire and Jared flew out to Australia a month later. They stayed at one of the rainforest retreats they saw on the Internet before. When they weren't working on managing Philip's affairs, they spent time exploring the fabulous Daintree Rainforest. Claire got to see crocodiles in their natural habitat, from the safety of a boat, and both of them discovered a love of snorkelling when they took a trip out to the Barrier Reef.

It was on one such trip that Jared asked Claire to marry him. They sat on the deck of a small boat sailing back from the outer reef, enjoying the beauty of the blue, sparkling ocean and the clustered emerald trees along the coast. She had never felt so happy and free and it showed in her expression as she looked up at Jared. "This is all so wonderful."

Jared stared into her shining eyes, so full of life. He loved her excitement and enthusiasm. Some of it had rubbed off on him and he felt so grateful to her for she had awakened him to a fuller experience of life and a real appreciation for the richness and beauty of things.

He had found the death of his parents hard, in particular, knowing he would never now know his father, but Claire had helped him find peace with his grief and move gently through it. She did not realise how important she had been to him, Jared thought, and he didn't want it to ever stop. Overtaken by a sudden impulse, he gripped her hands and asked, "Will you marry me? Here, now, in Australia?"

Claire smiled. "I've been waiting for you to ask."

"Oh, I know," he groaned, "you knew I would, didn't you? I can see I won't be able to keep any secrets from you." He laughed. "I suppose you brought a dress to wear too."

"Actually, I did."

"What? You didn't?"

"No," she laughed. "I was only joking."

"So, we need to get you one, then."

"Well, I did see this lovely white dress in a shop in Port Douglas. I think it would be a terrible shame not to get it, don't you? It will go so well with my amethyst necklace."

"Is that a *yes?*"

"Of course, it's a *yes,* you idiot." They both laughed.

They were married on the beach at the retreat a few weeks later, witnessed by Jack and Rowena, the only people they knew in Australia. Claire wore a sleeveless white gown that flowed down from a bodice decorated with a subtle tracery of seed pearls and sequins. She wore her hair down and the amethyst necklace hung around her neck. To match it, she carried a small bouquet of purple flowers. Jared wore a white shirt and blue trousers. Neither wore any shoes.

They chose to marry at the end of the day and a magnificent sunset streaked the darkening blue sky as they exchanged their vows. A few of the other people staying at the retreat hovered around to watch and at the end Jared invited them and the celebrant all back to the resort for a party. The eating and drinking went on until late but then Jared whispered to Claire, "Let's just slip away." She nodded and they walked away from the bright lights of the bar over the sand into the welcoming darkness.

They walked until the resort lay far behind them and all they could hear was the surf washing in and out over the beach. Jared stopped and pulled Claire into his arms. A canopy of stars spread their twinkling lights above them as he gently kissed her lips then they sank down together onto the soft sand.

Claire came awake to the sound of falling water and, for a moment, thought she was still in Australia but then remembered. It was the waterfall next to the cottage. Excited, she eased herself away from Jared, who lay sleeping on the bed beside her, and stood up. She dressed quietly and left the room. They had arrived late last night, shattered by the long journey from Australia. They had gone straight to bed but now she wanted to explore their new home. She could not believe how incredible it all looked as she walked through the old building, caressing the surfaces and furnishings. Reaching the front door, she let herself out. A gentle rain fell but, undaunted, she left the house, bracing herself against the chill of the late spring air. The garden still needed some work to bring it back after the mess created by the builders but Claire knew, with a little help, nature would soon soothe the scars and cover the wounds with new growth. As she moved outside, she smiled at the nameplate now replaced on the wall, 'Bluebell Cottage.'

It had been almost exactly one year since she had last been here and everything looked so different now. So much had happened. Her life had changed beyond recognition.

Philip had a great many business interests and sorting out his affairs had proved complex, necessitating Claire and Jared spending most of the last year in Australia. During their time there, they became close friends with Jack and also Rowena who proved invaluable in the running of Philip's businesses. Some went to the wall, unable to operate with more ethical practices and some Jared got rid of as they were enterprises he had no wish to be associated with. During their time in Australia, they returned once to England for a few weeks to sort out Laura's affairs, which had included the sale of the antique shop as Jared no longer had time to manage it. As a surprise for Claire, Jared purchased Bluebell Cottage and, before they went back to Australia, they organised the place to be renovated.

Now they had returned, intending to live in the Lake District. Claire gazed at the cottage, now newly refurbished. She would love living here, she thought, and hoped Eleanora would approve of the renovations done to the home where she lived the last years of her life.

The image of William came into her mind. For some strange reason he often came into her thoughts but now she felt as if he were close. She realised she stood under the tree where Eleanora died. Claire looked around, half expecting to see William standing there. She saw no sign of him but something made her look up. A bird circled high up in the sky.

An eagle! It had to be.

Claire watched its flight for a few moments then made her way back into the house and up to the bedroom. Jared turned and looked at her as she entered the room. "What have you been up to?" he asked.

"Enjoying being here," she replied.

"What would you like to do today?" Jared asked.

"I want to go to St Giles' Church. I have a strong feeling we need to go there."

"Okay," Jared said smiling. He reached for her hand and pulled Claire down onto the bed with him. "But in a little while!"

After breakfast, Claire and Jared drove the short distance to St Giles' Church. They made a brief stop on the way at a lookout point that gave them a wonderful view of Lake Windermere. "I'm going to love living here," Claire said, excitement shining in her face. The earlier shower had now passed and the sun shone, flooding the surrounding countryside with emerald brilliance. They drove on to the church and parked by the nearby stream. Climbing out of the car, Claire breathed in the peaceful atmosphere.

Jared and Claire had the place to themselves. They passed through the gate into the churchyard. First, they headed to where Laura and Philip lay together and Jared placed the flowers they had brought on the graves. Claire took Jared's hand and waited with him in silence as he honoured his parents. A few tears ran down his face. Although he knew they had not truly gone, he missed their physical presence.

"Time will heal your pain," Claire reassured him. "And you will always have your memories of them alive in your heart. Think of them and they will be there. Your parents would not want you to be sad, Jared. They would want for you to cherish their memory but to live your life, the best life you can, and find joy."

"Yes, you're right." Jared sighed then smiled. "Thank you."

They stood for a few minutes more but then Jared turned away.

"I want to visit Eleanora's grave," Claire said and walked towards the group of yew trees where it lay. Would there be violets? The season was right. She was not disappointed. Around the defaced headstone bloomed a blanket of the familiar purple flowers. She stared down at them and became still, opening up her awareness for any sense of Eleanora. Claire had come to love the spirit during their time together and missed her gentle presence.

"Eleanora?" she whispered but received no response. The spirit had obviously moved on now her mission to bring William back to the Light had been completed. Claire turned aside and took a few deep breaths. She noticed Jared had wandered a short distance away to look at the headstones.

"There doesn't seem to be a grave for Eleanora's son, Charles," he said.

"No, the fire at Waterford Hall was so intense no trace of his body was found. It's why his nurse put the christening gown in Eleanora's grave."

"Of course." Jared remembered how Charles had appeared to him while he waited with Jack outside Philip's house. It had been one of the most beautiful things he had ever experienced. He really *felt* the presence of Charles. "He was a special child," Jared murmured.

Claire pictured Charles in her mind, his face glowing with love and joy but also great compassion.

"Much more than a child, Jared, I think he was an old soul."

"What do you mean?"

"Eleanora told me once that we have all lived many lifetimes on earth. Some have lived more than others and gained much wisdom. Charles was one of these. He came to earth only for a brief time but he illuminated the lives of all those he came into contact with, teaching them by his example and the power of his presence."

"Yes, I felt that myself." Jared remembered the love emanating from Charles and he wiped a tear from his eye. He sniffed and continued to walk through the churchyard trying to hide his emotion but Claire felt it. She smiled. Jared had opened up enormously in the time she had known him.

"I don't see a grave for William, either." Jared said after a while. "There are other Waterford's over here, obviously relatives, but no sign of him."

Claire cast her gaze around the graveyard, at the countless graves where those who once lived now lay at rest. Where would William's body lie if not here? She gazed up and scanned the clear blue expanse of sky above. She was not disappointed. In the distance, a dark speck appeared and drew closer. Somehow, she had known he would come.

Jared, noticing Claire staring up, followed her gaze. "It's an eagle," he observed.

The two of them watched the bird circle lower and lower until it came to rest on a nearby tree.

As Claire stared at the bird, she became aware of a sense of dislocation and felt light headed. A wave of darkness washed over her and she lost consciousness of the graveyard.

She found herself standing in a bleak room surrounded by stone walls. It was cold, so cold, and her body shook. An overwhelming grief flooded through her and she knew she had lost everything she had ever cared about. Close on the heels of this, came anger. It was all Eleanora's fault. Everything went wrong after the discovery of her with that bastard Robert Ashworth. The anger turned to a burning rage and she hated Eleanora in that moment, hated the world and even God for creating such conditions in life that had brought her here to stand on a bitterly cold morning, knowing that death was moments away.

"No!" Claire shouted out loud. "It shall not be!" Jared looked at her in concern. It hadn't sounded like her voice. He hurried over and saw her face contorted with an agony that was not hers so knew she had entered a trance state.

What should he do? Bella had always said not to touch Claire when she went into trance but he couldn't stand by and look at her in such distress.

Claire saw a door swing open and a man came in. "It's time," he announced. He waited but she could not move so the man hauled her roughly to her feet. "Don't touch me!" she yelled and flung the man aside with such force he staggered back against the wall. Two other men rushed in and gripped her by the arms. They led her down a long corridor to another, but larger, grey stone room where several people waited.

A voice whispered in Claire's ear. "It does not need to be, you know that." Barrett. "Think of me, think of me, and you shall not die." The people scrutinised her, their expressions sombre. She felt their tension, their distaste for the proceedings yet also the morbid fascination that kept their gazes upon her. One of the men stepped forward and placed a heavy cloth bag over her head and a moment later she felt something around her neck. She reached up to loosen her jumper but found a thick rope there. Without warning, the floor beneath her feet dropped away and, with a terrible wrenching, she was flung into darkness.

She felt the presence of someone with her and knew that, somehow, she still lived and yet everything she had ever known had fallen away. She felt numb and yearned for the light, for the feel of blood coursing through her veins, to feel the earth beneath her feet. She thought she would go insane but the presence with her pulled her back and she felt herself travelling somehow, moving without going anywhere. She lost all sense of time but then the sensation stopped and she found herself floating above a rectangular hole, gaping like a wound in an area of grass near the walls of a large stone building with bars over the windows. Four men stood near the hole looking down. One, a large man dressed in a suit, nodded and another man, dressed in a dark uniform, started shovelling earth from a nearby pile over the rough wooden coffin that lay within the grave.

So, this is where I end, she thought, bitterness burning like acid through her chest but also hate for Eleanora and Ashworth. It intensified, consuming her very soul.

"But you do not," came Barrett's voice. "This is where your new life begins." The scene faded into blackness and Claire once again had the sensation of travelling. It went on and on but then she felt a touch on her shoulder.

The darkness evaporated and she became aware of standing in the churchyard, breathless and disorientated.

Claire stared at Jared who stood next to her, tense with fear. He had decided to try and bring her back from wherever she had gone. Seeing the recognition in Claire's eyes, he pulled her to him and she relaxed into his warm embrace, thankful to be back in her body. She shuddered, knowing that, somehow, her mind had connected back through time to William as he died.

She looked over at the eagle. It still sat in the tree. Its eyes bored into hers and she nodded, sensing its connection to the spirit of William. "Let's sit," she said to Jared and motioned to the seat Joanna had put near Eleanora's grave. "Just hold me," Claire said and relaxed against him for a moment before pulling away. "I have to find out what happened." She looked at the eagle again. "William needs to tell his story."

"Claire, no! He was a nasty piece of work," Jared cried, thinking of what happened to his father. "For God's sake, don't let him get into your mind."

"No, no, it's all right. It's not the same as possession. I need to do this," she said. Grudgingly, Jared nodded, desperately hoping his wife was right. She lay back against him and closed her eyes.

Stephen Gray stared at the ruin of Waterford Hall unable to believe what he saw. Only just returned from two years abroad (damn his father for sending him to that hellhole Pennsylvania) he had decided to call upon his friend, William. He had not expected what he found. Although early in the day, he felt in his jacket pocket for the silver flask he always carried. He unscrewed the cap and downed a few gulps of the whisky he favoured.

What happened? he wondered. He took a few more swigs and wiped his brow with his handkerchief, feeling hot and unsteady on his feet all of a sudden. A wave of tiredness overcame him, the result of staying up late the night before drinking. He hoped nothing had happened to William. He enjoyed their association: the wild parties, the beautiful women his friend always managed to gather around him, so in contrast to the boring life his parents led.

Stephen had met William two years before in 1922 at a wedding—he was some distant cousin on his mother's side. Always a rebel, the twenty-year-old Stephen had been drawn to the unconventional William, then in his mid-forties and the subject of many a rumour throughout the family concerning his wild ways. Stephen, keen to get to know the real person behind the gossip, engaged William in conversation. Barrett joined them and said, "William, this is so tedious. Do you fancy a drive, old man? Give your new Rolls a spin."

Obsessed with cars, William had just purchased a new Rolls Royce Silver Ghost. Barrett, noticing the interest on Stephen's face, said,

"Bring your young friend. We could pick up some women and broaden his education, ours too." He grinned at Stephen.

William drove them all far too fast through the countryside to a house owned by Barrett. They picked up three women on the way from some place Stephen learnt later was a brothel in a poor area of Kendal. The women removed some of their clothing and began dancing. When one of them, a young brunette, draped herself over Stephen, his face turned crimson thus revealing his inexperience. William and Barrett laughed and egged the girl on.

That night had been Stephen's initiation into the pleasures of the body and the first of many similar escapades until his father, sickened by his son's drinking, cut off his allowance and sent him off to stay with relatives in America. His aunt and uncle, staunch Protestants, gave him no opportunity to continue his debauched ways. They set him to work in their clothing business but now, two years later, his father had relented and allowed him to return home.

A cold wind blew dead leaves, the last remnants of autumn, across the gravel path. Stephen felt depressed. What should he do now? Go back home?

The idea repelled him. His father would be there, just waiting to give him another lecture about his inadequacies, the old bastard. At twenty-two, Stephen still had no intention of being dragged into the family business but it was harder and harder to find excuses. He wondered where William would have gone. His face came into Stephen's mind. As it did so, he felt cold and a tightness in his chest. He sensed someone behind him and turned, thinking it was his driver, but saw he still sat waiting in the car some distance away. He looked to be asleep. All of a sudden, Stephen felt vulnerable and exposed standing there in front of the burnt-out building.

As if he was being watched!

He spun around several times but saw no one. Then he heard the voices whispering.

Walter Gray heard the front door open. "Stephen!" he called. "Is that you?" Now was his chance to talk to him again. He needed him to take a more active role in the business and he wouldn't let the young wastrel put him off any longer. A knife of pain sliced down Walter's back and his heart thudded in his chest but he struggled up out of his chair to confront his son.

Stephen entered the room. "What do you want?" he asked.

Walter looked at his son. He seemed different somehow but he couldn't put his finger on it. "I want you in the office on Monday at eight sharp and I won't take no for an answer this time." Blood rushed to his face as his anger found an outlet. "It's time you started facing up to your responsibilities as my son. You need to think of your future. I'm not getting any younger, and with my back I just can't..."

"Of course, Father. I understand completely. You are right. It is time for you to retire. I am happy to take over."

"You are?" The older man stared at his son. Something about his voice disturbed Walter; it sounded flat. Cold. What had happened to him? He had expected his usual resistance but Stephen's impassive face gave nothing away. He smiled but in a way that did not reach his eyes.

Walter sank down in a nearby armchair. "Well, good." His son's agreeableness took the force of Walter's bluster away. He didn't know what else to say. He felt weak and tired. "Good," he repeated.

"If that's all, Father?" Stephen asked.

"Yes, yes, that's all. You may go."

As he walked away from the old man, Stephen looked around the hall, at the ornate ceilings and imposing chandeliers, the opulent vases that stood beside the front door, the red velvet curtains and thick carpeting on the floor. He was enjoying walking and breathing again, the feel of the soft fabric of clothing against his skin. Yes, it was good to be alive. He flexed his hands, strange unfamiliar hands, and yet they did as he bid them. How strange. Barrett had been right. It had been so easy.

A maid came out of a nearby room and headed off down a corridor. Stephen watched as she walked away, his attention on the provocative motion of her hips. Yes, William thought, as he followed the young woman, he would enjoy being Stephen.

Claire looked up at the eagle. It sat in the tree looking at her with a gaze of infinite sadness.

"William inhabited someone before Philip," she told Jared.

"That explains the long gap between William's death in 1924 and his possession of Philip in 1945."

"Yes." Claire told Jared what she had sensed about Stephen Gray.

"Poor bastard. I wonder what happened to him."

"Perhaps William will tell me," she said. Claire closed her eyes and fell silent. Jared looked down at her, an expression of peace and trust on her face, and smiled. He loved this woman. He couldn't stand it if anything happened to her.

Claire relaxed back against Jared's shoulder. Soon she heard a quiet voice. "I took over the Gray family business and destroyed it, like I did the one in my life as William. I sought only my own pleasure, determined to take what I could from my stolen life. I remained in association with Barrett, still living in the body I first met him in then, and we continued much as we had done before. He appeared to enjoy my company and so he helped me. I used to wonder at this sometimes but I knew Barrett never liked to be alone. The truth was, he and I had been inexorably drawn together to play out our destiny.

"Tell me more about Barrett," Claire asked, curious.

"He was a dark soul, far removed from the Light, who took pleasure in pulling others down into the darkness with himself.

Claire had a sudden vision of the circle of stones and a group of men in brown robes standing nearby. One turned to look at her. "I think I may have seen him as he was in the past when we were searching for Philip at Castlerigg," she whispered.

"Yes, you did indeed see the man whose spirit would later go on to be known as Barrett. Highly skilled in the occult arts, he found a way to move into other bodies instead of passing on to the next realm at death.

"When I met him, he had done this for many, many hundreds of years, enjoying the power to live any life he chose on the earth plane. He taught selected others, those who would become the members of the Circle. I, of course, knew nothing of this when I first met him at a party in 1910, only a few weeks after I discovered Eleanora with Robert Ashworth."

They moved with graceful precision around the dance floor yet Eleanora held herself stiff. William felt her resistance to him in every fibre of his body and it maddened him. It always did. They danced to preserve the facade of their marriage for the eyes of the world, the elite society they moved within, but he knew he repelled her, that she hated him. Oh, she never said anything but he felt it. He saw it in the way she looked at him, the sad expression in her eyes when she thought he wasn't looking. She despised everything he did but you had to be hard in the business world. Her judgement angered him. He had done it all for her.

And now, damn it to hell, she had turned aside from her vows and betrayed him with that fool Ashworth. William pushed the vision of them together on the hillside away but it remained like a lump of stone in his heart. The music ended and Eleanora moved away to talk to a woman she knew.

William glared after her then made his way over to a hovering waiter. "A whisky," he barked, "and quick." When the man brought his drink, William pushed his way through the crush of people and out into the garden. Placing his drink on a stone wall, he fished in his pocket for his cigars. Putting one to his lips, he next sought to find his matches. He heard the sound of one being struck and a sudden light flared in his face. "Allow me," came a silken voice.

"Thank you," William replied and took a deep inhalation of his cigar. He blew out a cloud of smoke and stared at the man in front of him. Impeccably dressed in a dark suit, black hair slicked back and with a well-trimmed beard, he looked the epitome of style and wealth.

"I don't believe we've been introduced." William held out his hand. The man gripped it with his own and William was struck by the coldness of it.

"My name is Richard Barrett."

"Pleased to meet you and I'm..."

"William Waterford."

"How do you know my name?"

"Someone told me."

"Oh." William stared at the man in front of him. He had the most penetrating dark eyes. They made him feel uncomfortable.

"That same someone also told me you might be in need of a little cash."

Embarrassed, William glanced into the house. He saw his associate, Hubert Manning, staring at them before he turned away. "I see. Well, he had no right to do so," William replied. "Everything is fine. My businesses are doing perfectly well."

"Oh, I'm so glad to hear that," Barrett replied in a voice that made it quite clear he didn't believe William. "Do forgive me for mentioning it." Their talk turned to the politics of the day then Barrett said, "I must leave now. Here is my card. I am having a dinner party next Thursday at eight. I would be honoured if you would attend. And, in the meantime, if you think you find yourself in need of some financial assistance, then I hope you will allow me to be of service to you. I have some influence." With a slight incline of his head, he left.

William turned to look out over the darkened garden and chewed on his cigar. Damn Manning. How dare he talk about his affairs with a stranger and yet... He stared at the card. Things <u>were</u> tight. He did owe a great deal of money and the worry of it weighed heavy upon his mind. Something about Barrett made him feel uncomfortable but perhaps he should go to his dinner party. One shouldn't allow feelings to interfere with business.

A week later, William found himself standing before a roaring fire in a sitting room laughing and talking with six other men. The atmosphere had turned hazy with cigar smoke and the whisky flowed freely. Dinner had been very agreeable, very agreeable indeed for he had sat next to a very lovely woman who Barrett had introduced as Naomi. It hadn't occurred to William to bring Eleanora and he was glad of it.

"She has been invited for your pleasure and your pleasure alone," Barrett, sitting on William's other side, murmured meaningfully. William glanced at Naomi and she flashed him a seductive smile.

William sipped his whisky by the fire and knew she waited for him in the drawing room. Barrett clapped him on the back and said. "You will, of course, stay the night, old man. It's too cold to venture out again on a night like this. Everyone laughed heartily."

"And so began our association," William said. "Barrett loaned me money. He was everything I craved to be: rich and powerful, others always at his beck and call. Barrett introduced me to the other members of the Circle. I had no idea at first who they were or, should I say, *what* they were. They were all prominent people who helped me in my business, told me I could achieve the wealth and power I craved, and we spent a lot of time together.

"And I, in my foolishness, thought that was what I wanted. For the first time, things began to go well. Barrett told me we had to take what we wanted, make what we could out of a life that would give us nothing unless we took it by force. And, I in my blindness, believed him. If only I had paid attention to the unease I felt when I first met him but, full of bitterness against Eleanora and frustration with my failing businesses, I turned my back on everything important and so my path to doom was set.

"Eventually, I found out Barrett didn't have as much money as I thought. He had an extravagant lifestyle and so it began to fall to me to hold the parties, pay for the women. My businesses began to crumble but I did not stop. Barrett showed me things, ways I could get people to do what I wanted. We hypnotised them, bent them to our will. I felt important and powerful. What did it matter if those ways might hurt people? All I craved was my own pleasure; money was everything. Life had hurt *me,* why should I care?

"Even when the war came we did not allow it to dampen our lifestyle. Barrett was with me when I received my call up papers."

William handed the documents to Barrett. "What shall I do?"

"Don't worry. I have the ability to leave my body. I will merely put it to sleep then come with you in spirit to the medical examination. With my assistance, the doctor will soon see how impossible it would be for you to fight with your most awful disability." He laughed.

"Eleanora pleaded with me to change my ways," William continued, "but I would not listen. I hated her for what she had done but also for the way she looked at me, with such pity and sadness. Eventually, in 1920, she left me and took my son with her. *That* I could not tolerate. I took him back, of course, and made sure she never saw him again.

"Barrett and I continued our lavish lifestyle, but it backfired in the end. We gained a bad reputation, and no one would do business with us anymore. Everything went wrong then, several companies I owned failed and I went into debt with those who did not care how they recovered their money. It was they who set fire to Waterford Hall so I lost my home but I also lost my son, the only thing I cared about although, God forgive me, I was never the father I should have been. And I blamed Eleanora for it all. It all began to go so wrong when I found her with Robert Ashworth, when she turned to another man. I could not stand it and took it out on her and everyone else who had the misfortune to associate with me."

Claire had a vision of William standing before Eleanora at Bluebell Cottage. "She looked at me so calmly when I told her Charles had died," William said, "as if she did not care and it maddened me."

William lifted his hand and struck Eleanora with all the force of his pent-up frustration then watched her fall as if in slow motion. He stared in disbelief as she lay lifeless on the ground, a line of blood oozing from the wound on her temple. He heard gasps from those standing around him and fled.

"It was then I began to hate God himself for how could he have allowed all of it to happen? I lost everything. I could not return to my life and went on the run. With the help of Barrett and other members of the Circle, I found a refuge in a house in the country near Lancaster. Unfortunately, a few weeks later someone recognised me going into a public house, such a fool I was for going in there, and I was arrested. The months in prison whilst awaiting trial added fuel to my already simmering rage against Eleanora and life.

"Barrett visited me in prison. He assured me it would be all right even though there were several witnesses to my attack on Eleanora. He told me he would help me, that he could influence the judge, but something went wrong and the man turned out to have a powerful faith in God so he could not be possessed. Then all my staff testified against me, telling how I had abused Eleanora over the years.

"When I was sentenced to hang, Barrett assured me all still would be well, death would not be the end, that he and other members of the Circle had lived many lives already and so could I. He told me what to do and so it was that I found myself able, with Barrett's help, to enter the body of Stephen Gray. Weak and dissolute, he offered no resistance."

Chapter 29

"I REMAINED WITH STEPHEN GRAY for over twenty years," William continued. "His life suited me well, very well indeed. The wealth of the Gray family, with its lands and businesses built up over many generations, provided a rich resource, not only for Barrett and I, but other members of the Circle. My hatred of Eleanora and bitterness at life fuelled my selfishness and I determined to devote myself to power and pleasure. And I was supremely successful for a very long time.

"Barrett and I took everything we could from life. We sucked it dry. We enjoyed the exuberance of the Twenties, so in contrast to the austerities of the First World War and we lived a life of decadence. All through the Thirties, we continued our lives of luxury and excess. Even the shadow of the Great Depression did little to dampen our lifestyle for, once Stephen's father died in 1927, as the only son, I inherited everything and so we had access to all of his considerable wealth. Although some of the Gray businesses suffered, much of the wealth was in land and property that we could sell. There were no other members of the Gray family left then to care what we did.

"Not even the coming of the Second World War stopped us. We were not going to be cannon fodder in the trenches, no, not Barrett and I. Why would we concern ourselves with the insanities of men? We were beyond such considerations. Our egos knew no bounds. When Stephen received his call up papers it was, oh, so simple for Barrett to enter the body of the doctor at my medical like he had for me before and find an ailment that precluded conscription. And so, we continued to bleed the Gray estate dry.

"However, with all things comes a price and, in time, karmic forces came into play and I began to suffer the consequences of my actions. Although I evaded the carnage of fighting itself, at the very end of the war, suffering found me anyway."

Claire had the sudden vision of Stephen lying in a hospital bed staring at the ceiling while two nurses moved around the room. His face was contorted by pain and anger and despair filled his eyes. "Paralysed," William said, "from the neck down. My penchant for fast cars cost him dearly. I took a corner too fast. When I found myself disabled, not a life I wanted to lead, Barrett helped me to leave Stephen's body and seek another.

"It was then that destiny played its hand and I found myself drawn to Philip."

Claire sensed being in darkness, in a cold and empty place once again. She couldn't breathe and yet this did not seem to matter. Again, she had the feeling of being pulled through space and found herself in spirit form in the dining room at Philip's family home with Barrett.

A group of people sat around a table, their hands clasped. She recognised Elizabeth and Philip's mother. Although no words were actually spoken, she had the sense of Barrett saying, "Look at these fools, they do not know what they tamper with. Let us give them something to think about."

All of a sudden, the candle in the centre of the table, the only light in the room, blew out and everyone gasped. A picture fell off the wall and a woman screamed. "Don't worry," came the voice of Elizabeth. "Keep your hands together. They cannot harm us if we remember the Light."

The people began to glow faintly. Barrett drew William away and up. They passed through the wall and there on the ground in the hallway sat a boy crying. Claire realised she was looking at nine-year old Philip.

He had a newspaper, taken from his father's study, on his lap. Claire could see he was looking at photographs. One showed bodies lying piled up, another, lines of skeletal people dressed in striped clothes, their shoulders slumped in exhaustion. The last was a close up of a man. His fingers gripped a metal fence as his shrunken eyes stared in bewilderment at the camera. Claire had seen many such pictures herself—Jewish people in concentration camps. She realised it must be 1945, at the end of the Second World War.

Claire felt Philip's confusion and despair fuelling the dark shadow of depression around him. He did not understand the world in which he had been born, a place so full of cruelty and suffering. How could it happen that people killed others simply because they did not conform to someone's idea of how they should be? Why was life so unfair? His anger and bitterness turned towards God. How could he have allowed such things to happen?

"Something about this boy drew me," William said. "I felt his pain and resentment against life, and it echoed mine. His questions were *my* questions, his anger my own, but it was more than that, he had something about him that attracted me like a moth to a flame although I did not know what, only that it resonated deep inside me, and I became fixated on Philip. I longed to *be* him, to steal his life.

"And so, our association began. I entered his body but found I could only stay with him for short periods. Try as I might, I could not remain. Always Philip's spirit repelled me for he had not yet lost contact with his true essence then, his deepest soul. He, unlike myself, yearned for truth and beauty, love and goodness. Philip tried to connect with these qualities, cultivate them in himself, and at times he was successful but then something would happen he did not understand, that did not fit his ideal of the way things should be, and he would doubt. That doubt would erode his peace and depression would take him over. He stopped believing he could ever attain peace and happiness, that perhaps they were illusions, tricks of life that would turn out to be meaningless in the cold, hard light of day. He found it very difficult to continue then. He had intense periods of despair and confusion. They weakened him and it was at those times I could gain entry, for a while at least.

"But Barrett did not want me to stay with Philip, for he said a child's life was too limited, so I found another body to use in a house nearby, a man newly returned from the war. He was the first of several over the next few years and Barrett and I, with other members of the Circle, flitted from person to person, living the way we pleased with each one until their life had been destroyed, then we would move on but always I was drawn back, time after time, to Philip for he had become my obsession. I spent as much time with him as I could, either within, or just near him, if I couldn't gain entrance, drawing his energy, trying to make it my own. I also enjoyed being a child sometimes. It amused me to encourage him in mischief.

"The woman, Elizabeth, sensed my presence and sought to repel me but I was far too strong. I would always return later but then one time I came to find Philip and discovered that, unbelievably, she had taken him to the churchyard where Eleanora lay buried.

"It turned out Elizabeth had always known and loved Eleanora after she saved her life as a child and had the power to communicate with her in the spirit world. Knowing something was very wrong with Philip,

Elizabeth thought to take him to Eleanora's grave in the hope she could heal him.

"When I found Philip there, I encountered the spirit of Eleanora. She begged me to leave him alone but I would not listen. Her interference fanned the flames of the bitterness and hate I still felt over her betrayal. She had killed my belief in love. I grew even more determined to have Philip. I intensified my attempts to possess him after that, but because Barrett wanted me with him in an adult body, I still could not spend much time with Philip. And so, I could not prevent him from returning to visit Eleanora's grave when I was elsewhere and it was at one of those times, in 1950, that he met Robert Ashworth."

"Eleanora's lover."

"Yes. Fate had decreed our paths would cross again. There are those with whom our lives are destined to entwine and no one can prevent the effects of these encounters from playing out. We all have lessons to learn in life, karma to release, thus it was, he once again tried to take something I desired from me."

Noticing a sudden movement in the corner of her vision, Claire turned her head to the left. She saw Philip, aged about fourteen, sitting cross-legged on the ground drawing in a sketchpad.

Up the path through the graveyard, walked a man. His grey hair hung to his shoulders and framed a bearded face darkened by years in the sun. He looked to be in his sixties. As he stared around him at the softly moving trees and the pale blue sky behind the surrounding grey peaks, he looked as if he were breathing in the landscape itself and had a faraway expression in his eyes.

He moved closer and noticed the violets. "Of course," he whispered. "It has to be this one." He moved under the group of yew trees and stopped by Eleanora's grave. The man appeared not to notice Philip or, if he did, ignored him, focussing only on the grave. He nodded and smiled, then slowly bent down to touch the delicate purple flowers. He picked one and placed it in a buttonhole on his jacket. He stood staring down for a long while then he turned and looked at Philip. "A good morning to you, young man. It is a very lovely day, do you not think so?"

"Yes, sir it is," Philip replied.

"And what are you drawing?" The man approached and looked down at Philip's sketchbook. He stared for a long while at the drawing of a woman in a flowing white dress.

"You have a talent for drawing," he said. "But she was far more beautiful in life."

"Who?"

"*She was everything to me,*" *the old man went on enigmatically. He looked down at the grave covered with violets again. "But, alas, I could not save her. And so, she has lain here all these years."*

"*That's so sad,*" *Philip said.*

"*Maybe, maybe not. Who can tell when all things are counted?*"

"*What do you mean?*"

The old man did not reply but instead cast a speculative gaze around him as if listening. "I can feel her here," he murmured. "We do not die, you know. We are more than our bodies. Never forget that, whatever happens in your life."

Philip stared up at the old man and watched as a myriad of emotions played across his face. He felt in awe of this person for he had a dignity and grace he had not seen in anyone before and it impressed him.

"*What is your name, young man?*"

"*Philip.*"

"*And what are you doing here, Philip?*"

"*I like to sit here. It makes me feel happy when I'm sad.*"

"*Do you come here a lot?*"

"*Yes, I do.*"

"*That's good, good.*" *The man looked at the grave covered with violets. "It is indeed a very special place. He stared at it for several minutes without moving, a wistful expression on his face, then sighed. "Well, I must be off. I came a very long way to get here. All the way from Australia, you know."*

"*That is a long way, sir.*"

"*Yes, indeed, it is. Indeed, it is. And now I must return. Perhaps you will go there one day."*

"*I should like that, I think.*"

"*Perhaps you will permit me to give you something.*" *The old man delved into the canvas bag slung over his shoulder. He drew out a book, handed it to Philip then walked away through the churchyard. Philip watched him reach the gate and get into a car waiting in the road nearby. When it had driven off, he looked down at his gift. A painting of a river surrounded by a tropical forest adorned the cover. The title read: In the Forest by the River by Robert Ashworth.*

Claire saw Philip open the book and begin to read. He did not stop until he reached the end. Halfway through, his face underwent a change and a slight smile creased the corners of his mouth. When he finished, he stared around him and took a deep breath. Claire could tell he felt uplifted, she sensed the quietness of his mind. The feeling remained with him as he set off down the path to return home.

"After that I found it harder to be with Philip and it maddened me," William said. "Ashworth's book opened him up and gave him a sense of the indwelling Spirit. It was this connection that gave him the power to resist me and yet at the same time drew me more. He had a beauty of soul I had long since despaired of ever having for I had turned aside from God, from all good. I felt cast out, separate and alone, truly damned, yet part of me longed for what he had. I became more determined than ever to *be* him. It angered me that Robert Ashworth, through the power of his book, was, once again, preventing me from taking something I wanted and I vowed he would not succeed.

"I intensified my efforts but Philip continued to resist me so I had to content myself with partial possession when I could. Barrett began to tire of my obsession, however, and encouraged me to stay with him most of the time as we moved our way through several members of the aristocracy, including two politicians in parliament. We played havoc there for a while but then it became tedious. And so, the years passed. I spent time with Philip every so often, when it pleased me to do so, but then he met Laura.

"Her love for him was like a beacon in the dark. It cleansed him of many of his doubts. She evoked in Philip the yearning to be more, the best he could be, but it made me even more angry and jealous of him. Why should he have love when I could not? I, in the depth of my darkness and hatred, sought to destroy it. Barrett encouraged me then. He thought it great sport to play with other people's lives. I intensified my efforts to take Philip over. Barrett no longer objected to me possessing him for now Philip was a man.

"But, try as I might, Philip's connection to Spirit and his love for Laura gave him even more power to resist me. That is, until Barrett helped me persuade Philip to go to Castlerigg."

Claire found herself at the circle of stones. From a position high up in the sky she saw two tiny figures down below. "I sometimes possessed an eagle," William said. "I had always loved them, enjoyed the challenge of their training, getting them to fly to my command. When Barrett showed me how I could merge with an eagle, I relished the joy of flight. It gave me a sense of power and control I did not possess as a human."

Next, Claire saw Philip close-up, standing in the centre of the stones, watching as William circled down in the eagle. Claire saw the fear in his face. Laura came over and touched him on the arm but he did not respond.

Once near Philip, Claire became aware of others around him but her gaze fixed on the dark figure of Barrett. "He thought that in the circle of stones, a place of intense energy, his power would be amplified," William said.

Laura hurried away, looking back in fear, and Claire's heart went out to her knowing the devastation of her life that would follow. "When Laura had gone, I finally entered Philip's body, assisted by Barrett and others from the Circle. I did it with such force his spirit was crushed, suppressed right back, yet not destroyed. He continued to resist me and it looked as if he would be successful but then something strange happened. Philip surrendered. After all the years of resistance he just gave up, almost as if he welcomed me."

"How was that possible? It makes no sense," Claire asked, aghast. "Why on earth would he do that?"

"Because on a very profound level he wanted it although he tried to deny it. I had always sensed this and it was why I could not leave him alone. Even though I had access to many suitable lives for my purposes, his was the one I wanted."

"I don't understand? How could he want you to possess him? Did he not sense your darkness?"

"Oh, yes, he knew it. He sensed the evil in me very well."

"And yet he wanted you in that moment?"

"Yes, for he was more like me than he knew. Like attracts like. Everything happens for a reason, even the things that make no sense to the limited human mind. There is a powerful intelligence running through life and it is this that orchestrates. We two souls had business together on the earth plane and so were inexorably drawn to each other."

"I don't understand."

"He sensed the darkness within me and came to recognise it had an echo in his own being. He had always sought to destroy it in himself, seeking to crush those impulses that did not fit his idea of a perfect man: the anger he felt when things went wrong, the hatred he had for those he saw as evil, the fear that so often robbed his life of joy. But repressed impulses have a way of finding their way to the surface and he realised at a deep level he needed to embrace the darkness he knew existed within, the parts of himself he sought to deny.

"Philip thought that, if he stopped resisting, he would be able to bring us both into the light, that he would be free of his dark impulses and of me. His soul hoped that, even though I had gained entrance and taken control of his body, somehow the connection he held to his essence, even though tenuous, would be enough perhaps to pull us both back from the brink of ruin."

Claire saw William, now within Philip, walking away from Castlerigg to a car on the other side of the hillside where a member of the Circle waited.

They sped through the countryside, their intention to obtain the documents William would need to live Philip's life. On the way, the car rounded a bend and Waterford Hall came into view. "Slow down and turn into the driveway," William commanded.

The gutted ruin of Waterford Hall loomed before them, a monument to his past failures and William could not stand to look at it. However, he ordered the driver to stop beside it. What perverse impulse made him want to stop here? he wondered. He walked past the house and down towards the lake, passing through the rose garden where he and Eleanora first met. A brief moment of sadness arose in his chest but then his gaze fell upon the pavilion where Eleanora loved to spend her time. As far away from him as possible, he thought with bitterness and remembered again her betrayal. The pain of the memory seared into his heart, burning and corroding.

As he passed the pavilion, William felt himself drawn in. Eleanora had loved the small building but now it stood empty and cold. A patch of red light from the stained-glass windows spread across the floor, reminding William of the blood on Eleanora's brow when he took her life. Filled with horror, he left the building. Why had he gone in there? He'd put all that behind him. He had a new life to live now.

He stared out at the lake. Here he had flown his beloved eagles, his great passion. He went over to the small building where he used to keep them. Although empty, a few things remained. He picked up an old leather gauntlet, stiff with age. He had enjoyed his union with eagles in between flitting from person to person but knew he dare not lose his grip on Philip now for it might be difficult to return. More mechanical means to experience flight were required. The idea of learning to fly a plane appealed to him and he determined to achieve it soon. There was so much he wanted to do and he would do it for his and Barrett's power knew no bounds.

William threw the gauntlet down into the dust as if in challenge of God. He had no need of love. With a grim smile, he thought of the large luxury yacht waiting for him. He and Barrett had tired of England. They would make the whole world their playground. William turned and walked from the building. He did not look back at the rose garden.

Returning to the car, he commanded the driver to drive to Philip's house, which lay empty. William let himself in with Philip's key, which he found in his coat pocket, and quickly located all the papers he needed, placing them in a cloth bag he found. He paused to pick up one of Laura's petticoats draped on a chair remembering how it had been to make love to her as Philip. Unaware of William in her husband's body, she had given herself generously, with loving enthusiasm, unlike Eleanora. He let the undergarment fall to the floor where it remained, crumpled in a heap, until Laura, distraught, returned, hoping to find some trace of her lost lover.

As he passed through the sitting room, his gaze fell upon the book by Robert Ashworth. William's mind filled with blinding rage, for the book of hope and inspiration had made Philip stronger, more difficult to possess. Hatred for Ashworth rose like burning lava. This time the bastard could not stop him taking what he wanted. The idea came to seek Ashworth out and pay him back for what he had done.

He picked the book up, intent on tearing it into shreds, but at the last moment something stayed his hand. He felt a strange sense of loss as if he were about to destroy something precious. Impatient, William thrust the book into the bag full of papers he carried. He had no time for such feelings but would keep the book. It might help him locate Ashworth.

"I had only vengeance in my mind but the other spirit that existed with me, the one I thought crushed and put aside, had another plan. One I did not, could not, understand then, lost as I was in the darkness of my shadow."

"Philip wanted to go there, didn't he?" Claire asked.

"Yes, it was he who fed my desire to seek out Ashworth, not for vengeance, but because he lived at Mossman Gorge. Philip believed we might both be healed by the sacred energy existing there that Ashworth spoke of in his book.

Philip sensed, like Eleanora, that, at a very deep level within me, lost to my conscious mind, there remained a yearning for sacredness, for love, and that perhaps it could be rekindled into life. He believed that, if I connected with it, I could, like him, become whole.

"I was unaware of all this. When I discovered that Ashworth still lived and was to be found in Mossman Gorge, I thought only of destroying him, to pay him back for what I believed he had taken from me, Eleanora's love. Barrett agreed for he thought nothing of ruining the lives of others and, anyway, Australia seemed like a place ripe with opportunities.

"Gaining all the necessary paperwork was easy. Barrett or one of the other two members of the Circle who came with us, simply possessed people who could organise what we needed. They did this often, continually on the look-out for those whose lives gave them something they desired to experience.

"We felt like Gods. We could do anything we wanted, go anywhere we pleased.

"Barrett kept my conscious mind directed on the search for more and more material success and power. He fed my anger and bitterness, told me that we had to take what we could from a life that did not care, as evidenced by all the things that had happened to me. He said that, because of all the evil things I had done, I was damned, beyond redemption, but that it did not matter. We had no need of goodness or love. We were invincible.

We took up residence in the luxury yacht Barrett obtained for us and left England. We visited many countries on the way to Australia; Barrett had always wanted to travel. Eventually, in the winter of 1973, we arrived in North Queensland and set up base in Port Douglas.

"Right from the start, Barrett and I loved the place, the weather and the lifestyle. We slid easily into the lives of the elite who lived in this tropical paradise and lived like kings.

"All this distracted me for a while but then my compulsion to seek out the man I hated grew and one day I had a dream."

He woke, his head throbbing from the excessive drinking of the night before. He stared at the woman who lay beside him. He couldn't even remember her name. He groaned and rolled aside. He fell back into a half sleep and an image flitted through his mind of Eleanora and Robert Ashworth making love on the hillside. She gave herself with total surrender. Why could she not have been like that with him? The fact seared into his heart as he remembered the stiffness of her body when he came to her at night in their bedroom and it filled him with bitterness. The dream continued and he watched as Robert Ashworth turned aside from Eleanora, looked right at William and smiled in mockery.

William came fully awake and knew this was the day. Although they had been in the area six weeks, he had hesitated from seeking Ashworth out, afraid of what it might mean, but this morning, the pain of the betrayal alive within him, he knew he had to do it. He eased his way out of the bed and dressed. He walked through the luxury hotel apartment they had as their base for the time being. As he passed the half open door of Barrett's room, he saw two women sprawled out on the bed with him. Barrett had taken over the body of an attractive young man and been enjoying the opportunities this brought. Coming back from the bathroom a few minutes later, William noticed his friend had woken. "Where are you going?" Barrett asked.

"I must find Robert Ashworth."

Barrett sat up. "I will go with you."

"I want to go alone. It is between me and him."

"No, I must come with you."

"Barrett had a feeling, I think, that I would find Ashworth difficult to handle."

The heat of revenge burned hot within William as he left the hotel.

Barrett drove and it did not take them long to locate the track into the forest William had discovered would lead to the shack where Robert Ashworth lived. It looked well worn, for many came to visit the author.

They drove for some distance then continued on foot along the narrow path which led to the shack. Turning a corner, they saw the small wooden building they sought and stopped. It looked deserted. Would Ashworth be there? William wondered. He looked at Barrett and the two of them moved forward.

William felt an increasing heaviness in his body and found it more and more difficult to walk. He knew Philip was trying to prevent him harming Ashworth but realising this only fuelled William's determination more and, with great effort, he forced himself forward.

The shack was a crude construction of wood with an iron roof. It had a small verandah over which creepers hung, making it almost look like part of the forest itself. Barrett took the lead and pushed open the door. As they entered, they saw a small table and chair then a crude bed on which an old man with a long grey beard lay sleeping. As they approached him, his eyes flicked open and he turned his head.

"Robert Ashworth," William said, going close, "it has been a long, long time."

The man in the bed lifted himself into a sitting position and surveyed his visitors. "Do I know you?" he asked.

"Oh, yes, I think you do."

"Forgive me but I..."

"I am William Waterford."

"Waterford?" Robert scrutinised William. "No, you cannot be, he died. Even if he hadn't, you are nothing like him. You are too young."

"You are right. William Waterford did die," William snarled. "All because of you."

"I don't understand."

"No, you never understood. Neither of you ever understood. She loved you, wanted you. How do you think that made me feel?"

Robert looked confused.

"I saw you... on the hillside, you and Eleanora making love."

Robert winced as if struck. "But you could not have done. Are you mad? William Waterford is dead, I tell you."

"Yes, you are right. I died on the scaffold but my spirit lived on. I took over the body of another, many others, but I did not forget what went on before."

Robert stared up at William and saw the truth in his eyes. "My God," the old man whispered. He looked over at Barrett who stood watching the scene with amusement. Robert, sensing no support there, returned his attention to William. As he did so, Robert touched his heart before allowing his hand to fall to his lap. "I knew this time would come," he murmured as if to himself. A look of sadness came over his face but he remained motionless.

Claire sensed Robert's powerful connection to Spirit.

"So, you have come to find me," he said, his voice quiet and even. "And what is it that you want now that you have?" Robert gazed calmly at the man in front of him.

But William could not answer for he saw something in Robert's eyes he had not predicted, something that had more power to stay his hand than anything else could ever have done, compassion. All the angry words of hate and accusation he had carried within him for so long froze on William's lips.

Robert continued. "You seek to kill me, is that it? Like you killed Eleanora?"

William flinched and looked up at the ceiling, uncomfortable under Robert's gaze. Barrett put a hand on his arm. "He is playing with you," *he said.* "Don't listen to him."

Robert simply carried on staring at William with a calm almost pitying expression. "You think to blame me but you abused her. What did you think would happen? She came to me seeking the love she did not receive from you. Look at me, what do you see?" *Robert asked.*

With great reluctance, William returned his gaze. Although greatly aged, he still saw a resemblance to the young man who had taken his wife's love from him, who used her body for his selfish needs. Suddenly the paralysis in his mind lifted. "I see someone who talked pretty pleasantries, who beguiled Eleanora with soft words of poetry just so you could take your pleasure with her. You cared for no one except yourself. You did not think once about how your actions would affect others, that you were destroying a marriage. You talked to her of love and beauty but what you did came out of lies and deceit. You are evil.

"I found out there were others before Eleanora. You were just using her. Yes. I talked to my friends and found out I was not the only one whose wife had succumbed to your charms."

"Did you not have other women, William?"

"That was different. They did not mean anything. My wife hated me. A man has needs. You have written a so-called great book and everyone loves you but I can see through you. They are empty words, meaningless words. You talk of love, but how can you when you took it away from me?"

"No, William, I did not take it from you. You took it from yourself."

Robert paused for a moment before continuing. "You are not talking about me, but of your own self. I am simply a mirror. It is why you hate me so."

"No, you lie!" William shouted. "You lie." He moved forward and raised his hand.

"You seek to silence me but if you kill me you won't silence the part of you that knows I speak the truth."

William's hand fell back by his side.

"We are not so very different, you and I." Robert maintained his unwavering gaze upon William.

"Don't play his games," Barrett snarled but William ignored him.

"What you said about me was true," Robert went on. "I discovered that women loved my poetry, my soft words of love, the adoration I could give them, so lacking in their rigid husbands. Yes, I enjoyed taking my pleasure from them but with Eleanora it was different. She had something special about her and I fell deeply in love. I wanted only to be with her all the time. She became my obsession. I could no more have stayed away from her than stop breathing. She had so much love inside her, so much beauty and gentleness.

"When you tried to kill me, I fled here to Australia. I travelled the country for several years, my soul dying. I felt as if I did not deserve to live, for I knew I had failed her. I knew if I had been more determined, not so weak and afraid, I could have saved her from you. I hated myself for what I had done. But then I came to Mossman Gorge and, in this place, I found peace. I sat by the banks of the river in torment day after day berating myself but the powerful energy here, the spirit of the river and of the mountains, washed through me and cleansed my soul, and, finally, I found not only peace and forgiveness but a powerful connection to the spirit of life itself, my own true being.

"I realised I had not meant any harm, that in my inmost heart I wanted only love, and that from my struggles in life had flowered wisdom and hope. I sought to share what I had found and so began to write. From this came my book In the Forest by the River. It was published and I know it has helped many people. Maybe one day it will help you, William, for, as I am the mirror for your shadow, so too I am a mirror of your Light. Look inside yourself and you will find the truth." Robert smiled gently. "Allow it to set you free."

"Let's end this now," Barrett broke in. "I am tired of all this pointless talk."

William continued to ignore him, standing motionless, staring at the man he had hated for so long and, as he did so, felt an overwhelming sadness. It rose unbidden from some dark recess within him and suddenly he turned and walked out of the shack.

"You fool, you should have killed him," Barrett said, following him out. "He got to you, didn't he?"

"Shut up!" William shouted and strode off down the track to the car. He climbed into the driver's seat, put his foot down hard on the accelerator and roared off, leaving Barrett standing in the forest. William drove like a madman along the track, his only thought to find oblivion from the torment in his mind.

Chapter 30

"I STAYED OUT DRINKING ALL that day, seeking to numb the confusion I felt, but eventually returned to the apartment. Barrett was there. He said nothing to me and I said nothing to him but, in the morning, it was in all the papers. Robert Ashworth had been found dead in his shack in the forest, police were investigating.

"Barrett did not deny it when I confronted him.

"*I was doing what you wanted. You hated him. He stole your wife. He deserved to die. I simply applied a little pressure in a certain place and it stopped his heart.*" Barrett laughed.

"*But what if the police find out we were there.*"

"*Don't worry. They will not discover how I did it. They will think he died of old age. I have used the technique several times.*"

"In that moment, I felt as if all hope had gone from my life as I realised I had caused the death of someone who had given something important to the world. Someone who, even though he knew I had come to kill him, looked at me with love and compassion in his eyes. It... touched me in a way I had never known before. It... reminded me of the power of love, something I had long since lost."

"But you *didn't* kill him," Claire said.

"I left Barrett there. I knew what he was like. He had killed many times. I was as guilty as if I had done it with my own hands. I knew then

I could never find forgiveness like Ashworth had done. I really *was* damned, beyond all redemption. Barrett picked up on my thoughts."

"It is true, you <u>are</u> damned." He laughed with glee. "When you followed me, you turned your back on the world of love and now it is lost to you forever. But it does not matter. Love is for the weak, those who depend on others, but we are strong, we have the power to do as we please, mould the world to our whim. We do not need love or forgiveness."

"And I believed him. I knew then I had no choice but to make what I could of the life I had. I tried to bury what happened with Ashworth and turned my attention even more ferociously on living the life I had created for myself.

"Philip became weak then, for he too blamed himself for causing the death of the man he had revered for so long, who had given him so much. Most people I possessed became unconscious whilst I inhabited them, but Philip never did. Always he had whispered to me of going to Mossman Gorge, of finding a better way, but now he went quiet. His presence became so faint I almost felt he no longer existed.

"And so, I tried to make the best of life that I could. I sought distraction and threw myself into creating a business empire and experiencing what the world could offer. I learnt to fly planes and found pleasure in soaring the skies over the barrier reef. I had women aplenty and all the luxuries I could ever want. I told myself Barrett was right, I could live without love and peace, or, at least, I thought I could.

"Barrett wanted me to leave the area but I always refused. We travelled to many places throughout the world but wherever we went, or for however long, something always compelled me to return. Strangely, even though I felt guilty about what had happened to Ashworth, I always felt better in myself near Mosman Gorge and so I built the house by the forest and made it my home.

"I did not know it, but the energy of the sacred place where Ashworth had found peace spread wider than anyone thought and so it could not help but have its effect on me. It continued to do so over the years until one day, when Barrett had left to pursue other business, where I did not know, I found myself driving to the river."

William climbed out of the car and looked up at the clouds gathered around the distant mountains. He felt odd, dislocated and ill at ease. What was he doing here? Barrett had told him never to come to the Gorge, that he would find it too disturbing. William rubbed his brow. He had a bad headache and his back ached. The thought came that if he walked it would ease the stiffness in his joints. He wouldn't go near the river, he decided, just stay in the forest but his steps somehow inexorably led him to a sandy beach right beside the rushing water.

The torrent sounded loud in his ears. Feeling dizzy, he sat down on a rock and utter desolation and desperation descended upon him, enveloping him in profound loneliness. Alone and beyond all hope, he knew he had lost something infinitely precious when he turned his back on love.

Once it had surfaced, the grief and guilt would not go away. They grew in his consciousness until he could bear it no longer. He stood and hurried back to the car where he had whisky. After a draught of the strong liquid, he slammed the door and drove off. William went to the apartment of a woman he knew, Susannah. She attempted to distract him with all the skills of her art, which he paid so much for, but the sadness would not go away. "Damn it to hell," he muttered and flung aside the bed covers.

"Where are you going?" Susannah asked.

"I have things to do," he growled. Anxious to quell the feelings that had taken hold of him, he sought more comfort in a nearby bar. Even though drunk by the time he left, he drove home. Feeling sick, he stopped at a shopping mall. Lurching out of the toilets a few moments later, he saw a garden centre. By the entrance, he saw a pot containing a white rose and something unfathomable drew him to stand before it. He caressed the flower and, for a moment, a feeling of subtle joy came over him and everything became still as if time had ceased to exist. The petals were so soft, the colour so clean and white. It reminded him of something but his mind, fuddled with drink, could not remember what.

A few moments later, he returned to his car and placed the rose bush on the floor beside him. He planted it that same day. He loved to look at it and bought more bushes. It became a challenge to make them grow well in the tropical climate. He nurtured them and spent time with them. Somehow, they made him feel better when the sorrow he fought so hard to keep at bay returned.

"Why do you sit here by the roses?" Barrett asked William once.

"I like them. They remind me of Waterford Hall."

"Why do you think of there? It does no good to dwell on the past. Haven't I given you a life worth living? We are invincible, eternal. We can do as we please. Perhaps you should move on, find a new body. Leave Philip. It does you no good being with him. Find a young man like I have." Barrett never stayed in the same body for long. He liked the vitality of youth. "Yours is older now, it's slowing you down. You need someone fit and vital again, in their early twenties."

Yes, William thought, perhaps that was his problem. He should find someone new. "But all the businesses are in Philip's name."

"We can arrange it so that the assets are transferred to the new person we find."

"We went searching," William said," but no one fit. I still felt a strong need to be with Philip. Every time I found a possible replacement, I would discover a reason why they would not do.

"And so, I stayed in Philip but the sadness grew and so did the hate I had for myself and what I had done yet I knew I had no choice but to continue, to do what I could with life. I had turned my back on love. I had possessed people, ruined lives. I had killed. I knew I was evil and beyond all redemption.

"I started drinking heavily and hung round bars all night, got in with a rough crowd. That's when I became known as Tugger."

"That's a strange name."

"I tried many things over the years. When I was younger, I had a period during which I became interested in wrestling. I was good at it. People called me Tugger after the time I pulled down six men singlehanded in a tug of war and it kind of stuck.

"Anyway, the years passed and I took what pleasure I could from the life I had created but then you and Jared came. Barrett sensed your arrival.

"We already knew of you. We were concerned that Eleanora might try to do something to interfere with my possession of Philip even though her powers were weak compared to Barrett. At the time of my disappearance, he set up a blocking energy in Philip's house to prevent people being able to locate him. When you and Jared came to investigate, it activated and alerted Barrett who then tried to frighten you off. When that did not work, we called on other members of the Circle in England to track you."

"Are there many members?" Claire asked.

"Yes, there are many who have been corrupted by the lure of power over others."

"My God, how awful."

"I have since learnt they have their purpose in the greater scheme of things. If all were paradise here on earth there would be no challenges, no one would learn, no one would seek to realise their true selves. Our lives are all integral threads in the fabric of life. Even lost souls have the Light within them. They do not believe it, trapped as they are in their darkness, but one day even they will have the chance to walk the path of Love and Light.

"And so, we knew when you and Jared came to Port Douglas. Barrett thought to destroy you both at first but then conceived of a better plan. I would take over the body of Philip's son. It was perfect. Kill Philip and his son would inherit the assets and I, as him, could continue with my life of power and pleasure. One of the Circle took Jared over to draw him to us. But when Jared came to my house and I tried to possess him, something happened.

Jared walked into the lounge and stood still, his eyes glazed over. William surveyed the man before him. Philip's son. He could see the resemblance.

"Let's get this done," Barrett said. "As Jared, you'll have no problem dealing with the woman, Claire. With her gone, Eleanora will no longer have the power to interfere in your life."

The possessing spirit slipped out of Jared and William attempted to leave the body of Philip. But he could not do it. Every time he sought to leave Philip's body, William found himself back. Jared opened his eyes and looked around in confusion.

"You fool," Barrett shouted. "I told you, you shouldn't stay too long with one person. It just leads to problems. I will help you." He came over and William knew he had only moments before Barrett would find just the right spot that would stop Philip's heart.

William again prepared himself to leave but a knocking on the back door stopped him. Barrett moved away and scanned the house with his psychic senses. "It's that man you hang out with sometimes, Jack. He's with the woman, Claire."

Jared, left alone for a few seconds, became more aware of his surroundings. "Claire? Is she here?" he asked, looking around. "Where is here?"

Barrett spoke to the spirit who had control of Jared before. "Take him over again and go back to the hotel. We will try again in a day or so. In the meantime, when you get the chance, kill the woman. William, you go and greet your guests. You are, after all, the person Claire came all the way to Australia to find." He laughed. "Not that it will do her any good." He left the room, still laughing, and walked down the hall. Jared followed. Barrett opened the front door to let him out.

"I could not leave Philip, even though I had passed from body to body many times," William said to Claire. "He had been my obsession for so long, we were too enmeshed. Lucky for Philip, you came. If it had not been for you, he would have died and I would have possessed Jared.

"My God, I didn't realise how close we came to losing them."

"Yes, and I would have remained trapped in the darkness I had created. To you I will be eternally grateful."

"It was not I who was your salvation but Eleanora." Claire said. "I was merely the vehicle. It was her love and belief in you that did not allow her to rest until you returned to the Light."

"Yes," William said. "You are right. You know, I had many, many women and yet none of them ever came close to the beauty of Eleanora.

She had something I always craved, something so rare and precious it spoiled me for all those others, a connection to her sacred essence, to true love, something I believed I could never, ever have. I hated her because she would not give it to me, *could* not, even though I tried to take it by force. All I did was drive her further and further away. When I believed she had given it to another, it was more than I could bear and so I took it out on her, on everyone around me.

"As a child, I wanted to succeed, to do well to please my father but somehow I never could. Something always went wrong and he never hid his contempt for me. In the end, I gave up trying but when I met Eleanora, I longed to be different, make a life worthy of her. I worked long, long hours but, no matter what I tried, everything went against me. I made bad business decisions, people cheated me, deals fell through. I became determined to succeed at any cost so stopped worrying about the ethics of what I did to obtain the wealth I craved.

"I had continual bad luck. I became angry and frustrated and, to my shame, I took it out on Eleanora. But she always made me feel so damned small, lecturing me all the time, unfairly, I thought, about being a good person and loving others, not using them for my own ends. But loving people didn't pay the bills. She had no idea about the realities of life. It made me mad. I could never be good enough for her, just like my father.

"When Eleanora turned to another, I thought the universe was against me, that God must surely hate me and so I began to hate him. Yes, I hated him almost as much as I hated myself and I took my anger, my bitterness, out on the world and on Eleanora, more and more. In the end, I believed I was beyond redemption, cast out by God, so why not take what I could from the life I believed had treated me so badly.

"You had her love all the time, though."

"But can't you see that wasn't what I *really* wanted? I thought it was but I was wrong. I wanted something far more precious than that."

"But if not Eleanora's love, then what?"

"I wanted my *own*."

"Ah, I think I understand." Claire smiled.

"Yes, I told you I never felt good enough. I hated and despised myself even before I met Eleanora. I thought it was human love I craved but I know now it was the sacred love of my own true self, my deepest essence, one with the Divine Love of creation. I did not see that then but Eleanora could and she never gave up on me all those years. She saw something in me worth waiting for. She waited, even after death, hoping to bring me back to myself ..." William paused then continued, "and she succeeded."

Silence fell and both felt embraced by sacredness in that moment. Moved by the beauty of it, a tear trickled down Claire's cheek. Jared, still holding Claire where they sat on the seat next to Eleanora's grave, saw and wiped it away with his finger, aware something important was happening.

"She saw what I could not see, that what I craved I already had," William continued. "The more I sought it, the more it became obscured. I thought I needed to get it from her but I was wrong. I had it deep within me all the time. I only needed to recognise it and know myself as Love but I did not know I could." William sighed, "All those years and all those lives I touched with selfishness and greed were more than I could bear to think about. And the longer I hurt people, the less I felt deserving of what I craved.

"Strangely, in the end, she *did* give me what I longed for above all else. She showed me that in the hatred I had for myself lay the seed of what I craved."

"But how can hatred contain love?"

"Don't you see? I hated who I was, who I had become. I hated myself for all the evil I did. I hated myself for the anger and resentment I had against God. But *why* did I hate myself? I hated myself because I did actually care. Deep, deep down I *wanted* to end the suffering I created, I *wanted* to love. I *wanted* to be able to love *myself,* I wanted to connect back to the sense of sacredness I felt when I first met Eleanora and she showed me the rose, something far more precious than any of the material things I thought I wanted. I longed for that connection and it was why I cultivated the roses, for they reminded me.

"The wanting to know love, to help others and not hurt them, was in itself the love I longed for. It was the seed of my salvation. All I needed was to give it a chance and so when Eleanora showed me it was there, it opened me up and I no longer wanted to hold on to Philip and pursue the life I was living. And, in that moment, I realised I was *not* lost, that even though I had done the most awful things, in my inmost heart there existed a tiny flame of love, that my repentance could reconnect me back to it. As I realised all this, I felt the truth of my being, the sacredness that had been there all along only obscured by my bitterness and hate.

"Ashworth said he was my mirror and he was right, a mirror of the darkness within me but also of the Light, which I never truly lost, could *never* lose. When I was finally able to embrace myself as I was, *be* with myself, accept all aspects, both good and bad, I became whole.

"Philip too needed to embrace himself in his truth, to accept his shadow, bring Light to his dark side so in this we were united. It was why we were drawn together—to discover the truth of who we were. It took him a little longer than I for, when Ashworth died, he lost hope."

As William said this, Claire felt the presence of Philip nearby. She turned and saw him standing behind the headstone of Eleanora's grave. He looked young again, as he had before his possession by William. "Yes, I blamed myself for Robert's death," Philip said, "even though it was done by Barrett's hand. I drew William and Barrett to Mossman Gorge, to Robert. He who had brought such beauty into the world through his writing did not deserve to die like that.

Philip continued, "It weighed heavy upon me, so much that I did not want to live, but then when you returned me to my childhood home, I read Robert's book again and came across the words of forgiveness he wrote to the one involved in his death and the true meaning of the passages I had read so many times finally made sense and healed me. Robert reached out from beyond the grave and helped me see I did not need to be perfect to connect to my Divine essence, that it was my sacred birthright, and, with that recognition, I became whole."

The eagle launched itself from the tree and soared up into the sky. Claire watched as it circled and a sense of clarity and peace arose within her. She saw Philip also watched the bird.

"I always feared the eagle," Philip said. "For in it I felt only hate and revenge and the dark impulses of power and control, death and destruction, the things that motivated William which I sought to deny in myself. I see it in a different way now. I know now it also has the ability to soar above the trials and tribulations of everyday life, to look down upon them and see clearly. It can fly free in the knowledge of Spirit, the peace and freedom behind it all."

Claire turned her attention back to the churchyard and saw Philip and William standing side by side.

"Thank you for all you have done," William said. "I am sorry it has been difficult, that you too have suffered."

"But out of it I found a profound fulfilment," Claire replied. "Without all that has happened I would still be living on a shabby street in London dreaming of a different life. I wouldn't be with a man I love. I wouldn't know the treasure I have within me."

"Tell him I love him," Philip said, gesturing at Jared.

"I will."

William and Philip smiled, then both of them disappeared.

"Are you all right?" Jared asked. "I was getting concerned. You were gone so long."

"Yes, fine." Claire told him what she had learned and that his father loved him. She looked up and saw the eagle descending again. It swooped and passed close by above their heads.

"I think it's trying to tell us something," Claire said, watching it.

"Oh, don't be ridiculous," Jared retorted but then noticed the look in Claire's eyes. He knew better now than to question it when she made these kinds of statements."

"We have to go to Waterford Hall," she declared.

"Why?"

"I've no idea. I just know we have to go there."

"Okay," Jared said, trusting Claire's decision.

It did not take them long to drive to the house and they soon found themselves passing between the stone eagles adorning the pillars at the entrance. Jared drove up the gravel drive and pulled up in front of the burnt-out ruin. Shocked, they saw the garden on one side of the building had been torn up. The tracks of several heavy vehicles snaked through the exposed soil. "Something's been going on here," Jared said. They climbed out of the car and Claire made straight for the house. So much had happened since she came to this place, she thought.

Claire stopped in what had once been the hall and opened up her awareness to sense through the building. Why did William want them to come here?" she wondered. Up above, she saw the eagle circling. "I don't understand. What do you want?" she asked but received no answer. She left the building and walked into the garden that led to the lake. Jared followed.

"My God! Look," Claire gasped. A purple haze dusted the whole lawn. Claire ran forward but knew what she would find. "Violets!" she exclaimed. "Violets everywhere!"

Chapter 31

C LAIRE LOOKED AT JARED IN amazement. "They weren't here last time even though it was the right season," she said.

"I know."

"It's so beautiful." They stood looking for a while but then Claire noticed something else.

"Hey, there's someone over there." They hadn't noticed the elderly man digging in the rose garden when they first arrived. "It could be the owner," Jared said.

"Let's find out."

As they approached him, the man straightened up and leant on his spade. "Good morning," he said. "And it *is* a good morning, a *very* good morning," he repeated and smiled.

Claire looked at Jared then back at the man, noticing the shabbiness of his clothes. "Are you the owner of Waterford Hall?"

"Lord, love you, no." He chuckled. "In fact, I shouldn't really be here."

"How come?" Claire asked.

"Well, I just visit this place."

"But you look after the garden," Claire said.

"Yes."

"Are you employed by the owner?" Jared wanted to know as an idea started to form at the back of his mind.

"Nope." The old man chuckled again.

"So, if you're not the owner, why are you here?" Claire asked.

"Well, I live by the estate walls. I grew up in the area," he glanced around him, "and I love it. Always have. The house has been empty for as long as I can remember but what a place it was to explore. I spent all my time here as a boy."

"But why do you work here?"

"It used to make me sad how the garden had gone to wrack and ruin so, when I retired, I said to myself it would be nice to restore the formal part. I don't have much garden at home, you see, and it keeps me busy." He sighed and leant on his shovel. "Although it plays havoc with me back at times."

"Why hasn't anyone bought this place? It's so lovely," Claire asked.

"Oh, many have come over the years but no one ever stays."

"Why do you think that is?" Jared asked. "It's got so much potential."

"I guess they weren't the right owners."

"What do you mean?"

"The house didn't like 'em."

"What an odd thing to say. How do you know?" Claire asked, intrigued.

The old man chuckled again. "I've talked to one or two over the years. They don't like the feel of the place. They feel uncomfortable in the house. It's sort of spooky. There're stories about it being haunted, you know. Odd things have happened here. Not surprising really, the chap that owned the place before it burned down, William Waterford, was a pretty nasty character by all accounts. He had a terrible reputation. My mother used to be in service up at the big house. She told me he practised black magic. Things went on that scared her so much she had to leave."

"You said things happened here?"

"Oh, yes. Just this last year some bloke wanted to build a housing estate on this land. He brought in his contractors but, when they started work, they found their equipment kept going wrong or even disappearing. Sometimes it would turn up again in the oddest of places. People got scared and some refused to work. In the end, he lost his finance through all the delays and it's up for sale now."

The old man chuckled. "Personally, I was glad. I didn't want them to ruin this place. But seriously, even I don't like it up at the house. It feels heavy there and I've seen things myself, shadows, and heard noises, so I can understand why people don't like it." He shuddered.

"But here in the garden, I've always felt at home." He looked around. "Here it's different." He waved his arm to encompass the pavilion and the lake and up on the hill. "It's special. I always feel wonderful here. It's why I come, why I tend this garden, especially my roses."

With great tenderness, he reached out and touched one of the bushes in front of him. As he did this, Claire gasped out loud. The other two turned to look at her. "William always loved roses. He grew them in Australia because he always remembered meeting Eleanora here in this spot. It was here, Jared, where they fell in love and shared a sense of something sacred, an experience that, against all the odds, William, deep down never forgot and neither did Eleanora. Knowing he felt that way once gave her hope she could reach him one day."

If the old man thought it odd Claire knew so much about William and Eleanora, he didn't show it. "It's peaceful here," he went on with a wistful look. "I came here when my Angela died, my wife," he explained. "Somehow I always found solace in this place. I used to feel as if I had someone with me, caring for me."

Eleanora, Claire thought.

"It was overgrown then," the old man went on, "and it seemed a shame. That's when I knew I had to tend the garden, especially the roses, and so I have for many years."

"You've done a wonderful job."

"I love it."

"You mentioned that those who tried to buy the place weren't the right owners, what did you mean by that?" Jared asked.

The man studied Claire and Jared for a few moments then he stared around him at the garden, at the violets growing under the trees. "When I first came here..." he hesitated.

"Don't worry. I don't think anything you say will shock us," Claire reassured him. She had an idea what was coming.

"Well, I came to the rose garden the day after Angela's funeral. I sat here," he motioned to an old wooden seat nearby, "and I heard a voice. I couldn't see anything but I felt someone was with me. A lady, a beautiful presence. I couldn't describe her to you. Anyway, she told me Angela was fine where she had gone but the spirit also told me to look after the garden until the right owners came."

Claire looked at Jared, at the expression on his face, and guessed his thoughts. He wanted to buy the place. It *was* possible, for William had made Philip a wealthy man. Jared, as Philip's son, had inherited it all.

"Did the spirit say anything else?"

"Yes, she said the right owners would be the ones who knew what to do here. She said there would be a sign when they came."

"Oh, what sort of sign?" Jared asked.

The old man looked over at the lawn covered with the tiny purple flowers. "I reckon, I just might be looking at it right now."

"The violets," Claire whispered in awe.

"I've never seen them in this garden in all the years I've been coming here." The old man turned his head and stared at Claire and Jared. "Not until this morning."

A few days later, Claire and Jared returned to Waterford Hall. Jared had already set purchasing the property in motion. He found the estate agent involved in selling the place on the Internet. As Jared suspected, the unsuccessful developer was desperate to sell. An offer had been submitted and accepted.

Claire and Jared, however, did not know what to do with the place. They talked about it for hours but neither could come up with anything. They did not want to live in the house themselves. It needed rebuilding and would be far too large. They decided to take a walk around the property and see if anything came to them. When they arrived, they saw the old man, whose name he had told them was Arthur, in the distance. He raised his arm in acknowledgement and they waved back.

They walked up the hill to the lookout spot where all those years ago Eleanora and Robert made love, an occurrence which set in motion a chain of events destined to have huge repercussions in the lives of countless people through Robert's book.

Claire and Jared sat on the wooden seat and gazed out at the glorious view of the lake and the peaks beyond. "Eleanora said we would know what to do here so why don't we?" Claire asked.

"I don't know," Jared replied and fell silent. Claire's thoughts turned to Eleanora and Robert and the love they had shared in this place. It reminded her how much she loved Jared. She turned to express this to him and saw a tear trickling down his face.

"Hey, my darling, what is it?"

"I miss them so much."

"Your parents?"

"Yes. I lost them too soon. I hardly knew my father and then he was gone. Just like that. Why, Claire, why? What is it all for? How do we find the strength to go on when those we love pass from us? I know there's more to it all, and I really felt that at Mossman Gorge and through reading Robert's book, but it's so hard to remember when I think of my parents. Sometimes the pain is too great and I lose touch with the peace I felt."

"I know," Claire replied. "It's hard when things happen we don't understand."

"Why did they have to go? Why?" Jared fell silent but, as they sat together with the question hanging between them, they both became aware of a growing peace, a sense of rightness and they knew that, although they couldn't understand it with their minds, it had all been meant to be. All of a sudden, they felt embraced by sacredness. The feeling held them and yet also *was* them and they sensed the presence of Laura and Philip, Eleanora and William then Charles, their child, and Robert. They also slowly became aware of the presence of countless others around them, an almost infinite number, all held within that one spirit, essence, in which they were all joined as one.

"They're here," Claire whispered. "All of them. They are never lost to us, Jared, not completely. Can you feel it?"

He nodded. The feeling lasted for some minutes before it faded, leaving them awed, aware something important had happened.

"I know what we're meant to do here," Jared whispered. "I can see it so clear in my mind."

"What?"

"I want to build a hospice for the dying, a special place where they can come and have all the medical facilities they need but in an environment of peace and beauty and with counselling to assist them, and those who love them, through the transition. If we could help others see what we have seen, feel what we have felt, or, at least, give caring and support, it would make all that has happened worthwhile. We have far more money than we could ever want from Philip's estate. What better purpose could there be than to take what William created out of his bitterness and greed and use it for healing?"

"I love it," Claire whispered. "It's perfect. I know Arthur will approve."

"Yes, he will. It was his story of finding peace in the rose garden here after his wife died that just came into my mind."

"We can create a wonderful place where other people can find peace." Claire smiled. "I think I know someone else who will approve of our decision."

"Oh? Who?"

"William. I think it's why I've sensed his presence this last year so much. He wants his house to be used for something good. I wouldn't be surprised if he hasn't been behind things going wrong for the contractor here. He didn't want a housing estate on this land."

"I reckon you're right."

Excited by their decision, Claire and Jared hurried down the hill to tell Arthur. They found the old man standing looking at the ruined house. He looked afraid. "Arthur, are you all right?" Claire asked.

He took a while to answer. When he did his voice shook. "We need to get rid of this building. There're bad things here. I can feel 'em."

Claire looked at where his gaze rested and saw the shadows. As she stared, they became defined as people. A wave of sorrow and fear gathered around them. The sense of it expanded, reaching out to draw her into its dark embrace. She trembled and swayed. Jared, who could not see anything, looked at Claire and grabbed her arm to prevent her falling. "Claire! Claire! What is it?" he cried, afraid, but she ignored him. Her eyes remained fixed on the building.

They stood on the stone steps looking at her. More gathered within the broken walls, the spirits of those who had lost their lives there in the past and remained trapped. She felt their suffering, their confusion. The strength of it threatened to overwhelm her for a moment but then she remembered the necklace. Claire reached up to draw strength from the amethyst but her neck was bare! She had not put it on that morning!

For a moment, fear rose up to overwhelm her but, to her relief, she felt the familiar presence of Eleanora by her side. "You no longer need the necklace, my dear. You now know who you are and nothing can take that away. You are one with the Source of Love and always have been. Rest in that knowledge now and you will find the strength you need."

Claire took a deep breath and centred within, feeling her holy essence, existing in unity with all of life. As her awareness of it strengthened, power and love sprang into her consciousness and her body tingled as if alive with electricity. "No," she said to Arthur, "those you sense are not bad, they just need healing. They can't feel their connection to the Light, to Love."

She walked forward up the stairs and into the ruined hallway. She came to a standstill and the shadows gathered around her. She could read their energy. Some were simply lost, caught in isolation and despair, unable to find their way home, but others, in their blindness, wanted to harm and cause disruption. The activities of Barrett and William had drawn several such beings to the place. Claire knew these intentions were a result of their struggles in life and the disconnection from their own being of Light.

Claire shut her eyes and sensed them waiting. At first, she didn't know what to do but then connected to the Divine Light within her heart. It grew in intensity and flowed out of her to encompass the whole building and all the suffering souls. She held them, every single one of them, in a wave of loving compassion and asked that they be healed. As she did so, she felt the presence of Charles join Eleanora, then several beings of Light like those who had helped before came. They moved among the lost souls and guided them towards the back of the building where an area of brightness came into being. One by one, the spirits walked into the Light. It did not take long. A few souls seemed unwilling but in time all allowed themselves to be guided away. The light beings disappeared into the brightness then it disappeared. A strong wind blew through the building and Claire felt the last vestiges of the heaviness she had always felt there dissipate, leaving a feeling of lightness and peace. She sighed and allowed it to move through her then noticed Eleanora and Charles looking at her.

"It is done," Eleanora said and swept her gaze around the building. "It is done." Turning to look at Claire, she continued, "Thank you, my dearest one, for none of this would have been possible without you."

"No, it is I who should thank you," Claire replied. "You have shown me so much."

"All I did was help you to remember what you have always known deep down inside but now it is time to go forward, to make this place what it should always have been, a place of healing and love."

"Is William all right now? Will he have to suffer as the result of his actions?"

"He has reconnected with his true self now and it has given him the courage to face what he has done. When he returned to the Light he had to experience for himself all the suffering he caused to others. This was done, not for punishment, but with love and forgiveness so that he might learn. It was not an easy process for him but from it has blossomed empathy. In the future he will consider the effects of his actions and allow compassion to guide him. The fact that, in the end, he could not kill Robert as he intended and that some of what he created as William has turned to great good will assist him on his path.

"From all the suffering he created has flowered great spiritual growth for all of us. I was able to give many healings, both when alive and in the churchyard, and Robert, as he sought to describe what happened to him at Mossman Gorge, has helped countless people reconnect with the Truth within them, their own Divinity.

"There are many such places as the Gorge. They have a special energy. They are areas of great natural beauty or buildings, such as monasteries or churches built in honour of God where many have sought sanctuary and reached for the truth. Sometimes, though, they can be a tiny hidden corner of beauty in the middle of a city, but they all touch people and lift them for a moment from their preoccupation with self to realise the greater dimension that exists inside them

And now there will be another such place, the hospice. Many miracles will happen here."

"What about Barrett?" Claire asked.

"He turned his back on Love when he sought revenge for the death of his family. His bitterness isolated him from Love's healing power and he lost sight of his soul. He will tread a difficult path until he fully embraces his true nature but, in time, even he will do so. Everyone will be redeemed in the end for we are all Divine and, as such, are all one. No one is excluded. The evil done by us is a product of our ignorance as we advance on the path of knowledge. It falls away when we realise this and learn to love ourselves no matter what and come to understand we *are* love, a love that can never be lost."

With these words, Eleanora lifted her hand in farewell, as did Charles, then they both disappeared.

Claire looked around at Arthur and Jared who still stood on the outside of the building. "Everything will be fine now," she declared and came to join them. Arthur looked dazed. "I saw the lady," he whispered, "the one who spoke to me in the rose garden."

"I don't think we've seen the last of her," Claire said and smiled. "I have a feeling that she'll be around here still, especially when we build the hospice." Arthur looked at her in surprise so she explained what she and Jared had decided to do. The old man nodded and smiled. "Yes, yes, that's a wonderful idea, as long as I can still work in the garden."

"Of course," Claire replied, "we wouldn't have it any other way."

Chapter 32

MARTHA LAY IN THE BED, her breathing faint. It would not be long now, Claire thought. She stared out of the large window with its view of the beautiful garden surrounding the hospice. Martha had so loved looking out at it these last few months. The medical staff had withdrawn now and only Claire and Martha's husband, Andrew, who held his wife's hand, remained. The stillness in the room grew deeper then Claire knew it was over. Andrew realised it too for he lay his head on his wife's chest and sobbed.

Claire saw Martha's spirit standing behind her husband. She laid her hand on his shoulder. He sensed it for he raised his head and looked at Claire.

"Yes, she is behind you. Martha says she will always be with you in spirit even though not in body. She wants you to still be happy."

Martha raised her hand in farewell then walked away through an area of brightness that appeared by the window.

"She has now returned to the Light," Claire said in a quiet voice. She withdrew and allowed Andrew time alone with the body of his wife. She phoned the counsellor who had been with the family during the whole of Martha's time at the centre. The counsellor would come and stay with Andrew and help him with everything that needed to be done. She would also continue to support him when he returned home. The centre had been hard to get going but now ran well, providing a peaceful and caring environment for the terminally ill and ongoing support for their families.

Claire left the building. The original Waterford Hall had been demolished and an all-new purpose-built building had been constructed in its stead. She walked across the lawn. She smiled at the violets growing everywhere. It had been five years since she and Jared had bought Waterford Hall but each spring, without fail, the tiny purple flowers bloomed.

Feeling tired, Claire made her way to the rose garden and sat on a wooden bench. This place made her feel good. Whenever she felt the need to reconnect within, she found peace in this spot, as Arthur had and William and Eleanora long before him. Arthur still tended the garden. Many came to walk there and, all who did so, felt the wonderful uplifting energy of the place. Claire and Jared had added fountains and more trees and a rich diversity of plants. They made secluded areas with seats for people to sit in privacy. Many of the dying loved to be wheeled outside to the garden, finding great solace in the presence of nature. Some had even passed away there. And the more people came searching for calm, the more peaceful the area became, the more the vibration rose, but also thanks to Eleanora, who Claire still saw from time to time.

She reached up and touched the amethyst necklace, which she still wore most days, and shut her eyes, relaxing as the familiar blanket of purple enfolded her. She sat for some moments, allowing the peaceful atmosphere of the garden to permeate her body but it wasn't long before she felt someone come up beside her. "Excuse me, Claire, I'm sorry for disturbing you, but I thought you would like to see this." She opened her eyes and saw Arthur standing in front of her. He held a large wooden box.

"Where did you get that?"

"I found it in the pavilion, at the back of the storage cupboard, behind all the gardening tools. I was having a clear out." Claire sat up, her senses alert. Arthur handed her the box. It was coated with thick dust and dead insects. She tried the lid. Locked. She rubbed the surface with her hand and saw dark wood carved with patterns like those on the box which went with the amethyst necklace. Claire grew excited.

"Wait, I reckon I can open it." Arthur took out his Swiss army knife and selected a thin pointed blade. He fiddled with the metal catch. "I don't think it's locked, just a bit corroded." He managed to release the lock and prised the box open. He placed it on the seat and they both stared inside. It contained a parcel wrapped in brown paper. Claire pulled it out and, with great care, undid it. Underneath was yet another layer of thick paper then some very heavy cloth. It smelt musty and old. Beneath was tissue paper.

"It's like pass the parcel, you know, the child's party game," Claire said, laughing. "There'll only be something very small inside."

"I think whoever did it wanted to protect it well," Arthur commented.

"Yes." Claire opened the tissue paper and found more fabric but this time soft mauve silk, still with its original sheen." She unfolded the material and it fell open into a beautiful flowing evening gown, miraculously well preserved. "Oh, how lovely," she said, standing up and laying it against herself.

"It suits you."

"It must have belonged to Eleanora but why would she leave it in the pavilion?"

"There's something else in here." Arthur reached in and pulled out a small cardboard box. As he opened it, a number of dried flowers fell out. "Oh, my goodness, violets, dried violets," Claire exclaimed.

"There's also this," Arthur said, handing her a piece of paper. He gathered up all the violets and placed them back in the box. Claire sat down with the dress on her lap and unfolded what looked to be a letter and began to read.

24th June, 1910.

To my dearest, darling one,

I long to hold you, touch you. I cannot stop thinking of you. Being apart from you is torture.

I had a dream in which you walked through a sunlit wood and everywhere you placed your feet violets sprang from the earth in honour of your beauty and the greatness of your spirit. The flowers now always remind me of you, so tiny and fragile, yet so exquisite in their beauty, their colour like your eyes.

And so, I had the necklace made for you, purple like the flowers. The crystal is an amethyst. The jeweller told me it is the stone of inner peace, of connection to Spirit, and that is what I wish for you. He said the jewel had been taken from a cluster of crystals that held great spiritual power.

I know you cannot wear it when you are with William but keep it safe where he cannot find it. Look into it when you feel the need and it will give you the strength to endure your trials until I can arrange for us to be together and I will see it adorn your graceful neck. Until then, I will think of you constantly, my beloved Lady of the Violets.

Yours Forever,

Robert.

As Claire fell silent, both she and Arthur became aware of a presence behind them. Eleanora.

"The box arrived one day, a few weeks after Robert and I met," the spirit said. "A man brought it to the door. As luck would have it, William had left for the factory. The dress was inside and so was the amethyst necklace. Robert never did see me wear it, but I kept it safe and looked into the jewel whenever I could. And he was right, I always did find peace gazing into the heart of the amethyst, in fact, it strengthened my connection to the Source of Love itself. And because of that, and because Robert gave it to me, I treasured it. While I lived with William, I hid the necklace in the pavilion so William would never find it. When I left Waterford Hall, I did not have time to get it and so it was left there for many, many years."

"That's so sad," Claire said.

"No, my dear. Don't be so quick to judge, for it was our salvation. Because the necklace remained in the pavilion, it survived the fire and because it did not stay with me at Bluebell Cottage, it was not stolen. Many times over the period I lived there people who disagreed with my healing practices broke in and destroyed my things.

"But I never forgot the necklace and it remained linked to me. And so, when William, drawn to the séances run by Elizabeth at Philip's house, began to possess him as a child, I told her where to find the necklace so it could help us.

"As you know, I could not stop William possessing Philip but I could help and influence Laura. Later, I made her put the necklace in her shop window for I always felt help would come through the power of the amethyst. It took a long time, for those who are ready to open up spiritually are as yet still rare, but, in time, it came to pass."

Claire touched the necklace at her throat, in awe at its power, at the forces of destiny flowing through the events that bound her and Jared to Laura and Philip and through them to Eleanora, William and Robert. Claire had a sudden vision of all of their lives woven together like the silver strands of the amethyst necklace. Such a tangled path and yet out of it so much love and beauty had been created, all of it arising out of the challenges of their lives. They had all been part of something so much greater than they ever could have known.

"It's all about faith," Eleanora said, "about connecting to the Light of Love, the true power in life, that which resides within us as our true reality, as even William finally realised. We need to keep trying to do this even when events seem so hard to endure and beyond our ability to comprehend. That is the sacred purpose of life here on earth."

Eleanora fell silent for a moment but then continued, "I never wore the mauve dress but I think *you* should." With these words, the presence of

Eleanora faded. Claire smiled at Arthur. He smiled back. They hugged, then both turned and walked away. Arthur went back to digging in the rose garden. Claire put the dress and letter into the wooden box and took them to her car. She closed the door and, with a backward glance at the house, drove away.

A few days later, Jared arrived back at Bluebell Cottage as night began to fall. He had been away in London for a week. Pulling into the driveway, he saw Claire had already left for the fundraising ball planned for that evening. Jared sighed. He just wanted to spend a quiet evening with her. However, the costs of running the hospice were enormous and so Jared knew how important it was. Events such as the ball also helped to raise public awareness around the issues of dying, how to make it as positive an experience as possible for all concerned.

He arrived late. The dinner over, couples danced to classical music played by a quartet out on the lawn by the lake. A tent had been erected in case of rain but the evening had turned out dry and warm. He saw Claire standing near the entrance. She looked breathtaking in an elegant mauve dress, which clung to her upper body then flowed in graceful folds to the ground. Coming up behind her, he grasped her around the waist. She turned into his embrace and they held each other close.

"It's so good to see you," Claire whispered.

"You look amazing," Jared said, when they pulled apart.

"You won't believe this," Claire told him, "but Arthur found this dress in a box hidden in the pavilion a couple of days ago. It belonged to Eleanora. There was a letter inside. It was Robert who gave Eleanora the amethyst necklace." Claire filled Jared in with the details. "I had the dress dry-cleaned and it's come up almost as good as new."

"Let's dance," Jared murmured and pulled his wife to him. Claire melded to his body as they moved to the soft classical music played by the musicians. As they turned, she noticed Bella sitting with Arthur off to one side. The two had formed a firm friendship, drawn together by their mutual love of gardening. Claire also saw Eve and Gerry who she had come to know well since moving to Bluebell Cottage.

All too soon, the music faded and Claire had to leave the dance area to focus on the business side of the evening. After that, time passed in a whirl: so many conversations to be had, raffles to be run, speeches to be made. She was grateful when, much later, well past midnight, the last guest and then the event staff left. Claire wandered away from the house and across the lawn towards the lake while she waited for Jared. She had no idea where he had disappeared to.

The mauve dress felt soft and cool against her skin and flowed around her as she walked. She felt like the heroine in one of the romance stories she no longer had time to read. Laughing with joy, she began to dance, spinning and whirling across the grass in the night, moving to a silent music that only she could hear. She came to the water's edge and stopped, looking up at the full moon shining above. Mist rolled across the water and, in that moment, became aware of Jared watching her. She started to move again, with slow graceful movements, sensuously undulating her body, allowing the spirit of life she felt so strongly within her and loved so much, full expression in her movements. Jared came to her then and they kissed for a long time, lost in the joy of being with each other, until Claire pulled away. "Let's go home," she whispered.

They drove to Bluebell Cottage in Jared's car. Claire went straight upstairs while Jared let in Magic, their smoky grey and white cat, and locked the front door. It was a while before he pushed open the bedroom door but when he did so, he gasped at the sight of Claire standing in front of the full-length mirror, lit by the glow of a single candle burning on the bedside table. Her hair curled around her shoulders, a perfect frame for the amethyst necklace gleaming with a life of its own at her throat.

Jared's gaze moved over her body. The smooth silk of her dress, gleaming in the golden candlelight, clung to her and her beauty took his breath away. "The dress matches your necklace perfectly," he said.

Claire gasped, her mind travelling back to the time she first wore the necklace. She had stood in front of the mirror in Laura's antique shop and seen herself wearing the mauve dress. A man had spoken. Now she knew who he was.

"The necklace becomes you," Jared whispered, the softness of his voice caressing her with its intimate tone. "You have never looked more beautiful."

Claire stared at herself now, at the love and purpose in her eyes and knew what she had dreamed of then, to be worthy of the necklace, to be more than a quiet girl yearning for something other than her humdrum life, had come to pass. Her life had changed beyond recognition. She now had Jared, who she loved with an intensity she had always dreamed of, and, with the wealth he had inherited from Philip, they had decided to travel to all those interesting places which had fascinated Claire for so long. She also, of course, had the profound fulfilment of her work at the hospice.

But, more important than any of these, she had become aware of the Source of Love inside her, the truth of her Being, one with all of life, and, in this, Claire now knew, she was worthy of wearing the necklace and always had been.

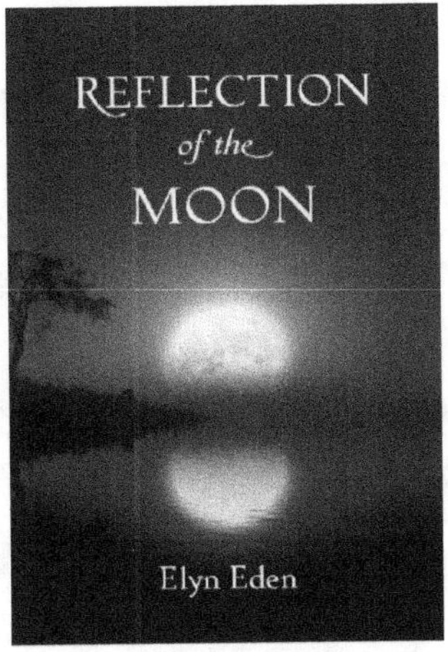

Sometimes a love comes into being so powerful it transcends time.

Ellie, an Australian woman, finds herself inexplicably grieving for a man who exists only in her dreams and is haunted by visions of a place she has never seen. Her life is thrown into turmoil and her whole view of existence is challenged. In search of answers, she is drawn to travel half way around the world to a small English village where she discovers a secret that changes her life and relationships with others forever.

Allowed to run wild through the English countryside as a child, Elyn Eden developed a great love for nature and expressed this through creative writing.

After moving to Australia, she visited a rainforest whilst on holiday in Victoria. Looking up, she noticed a leaf drifting down in slow motion and became captivated, watching as it fell into a stream to be carried away. Uplifted by the beauty and simplicity of this moment, it left her with a sense of the sacredness of life. As a result, she became inspired to write a novel, discovering the power of story to find meaning in the human experience and to tap into intuitive wisdom.

Like many, Elyn found herself faced with challenges. Seeking to find answers, she came to realise that, even in tragedy, miracles can occur, people are drawn together and profound healing and transformation can take place. These are the themes of the novels she went on to write, *Reflection of the Moon* and *Blanket of Violets*.

Elyn's aim is to create enjoyable, exciting stories encouraging readers to cultivate love and compassion for themselves and others, respect the natural world and to realise they are more than they think.